The
Ice
Sings
Back

M Jackson

The Ice Sings Back

A NOVEL

GREEN WRITERS PRESS | *Brattleboro, Vermont*

The Ice Sings Back is a work of fiction. Names, characters, places and incidents either are the product of the author's imagination or are used fictitiously. Any resemblance to actual persons, living or dead, events, businesses, companies, or locales is entirely coincidental.

The Ice Sings Back contains depictions of verbal and physical abuse; death of parents; death of a child; misogyny and sexist language.

First printing in hardcover February 2023. Paperback issued May 2023. Printed in the United States.

10 9 8 7 6 5 4 3 2 1

Green Writers Press is a Vermont-based publisher whose mission is to spread a message of hope and renewal through the words and images we publish. Throughout we will adhere to our commitment to preserving and protecting the natural resources of the earth. To that end, a percentage of our proceeds will be donated to environmental and social-activist groups. Green Writers Press gratefully acknowledges support from individual donors, friends, and readers to help support the environment and our publishing initiative.

Giving Voice to Writers & Artists Who Will Make the World a Better Place
Green Writers Press | Brattleboro, Vermont
www.greenwriterspress.com

ISBN: 979-8-9876631-2-7

Cover art & design & interior artwork bv Laura Marshall
Lemographie Art & Design

Author's website: www.drmjackson.com

PRINTED AT SHERIDAN PRINTERS, DEDICATED TO SOUND ENVIRONMENTAL PRACTICES AND MAKING ONGOING EFFORTS TO REDUCE OUR CARBON FOOTPRINT. AS A PRINTER, WITH PAPER AS A CORE PART OF OUR BUSINESS, WE ARE COMMITTED TO IMPLEMENTING POLICIES THAT FACILITATE CONSERVATION AND SUSTAINABLE PRACTICES. SHERIDAN SOURCES PRINTING PAPERS FROM RESPONSIBLE MILLS AND DISTRIBUTORS THAT ARE CERTIFIED WITH AT LEAST ONE CERTIFICATION FROM AN INDEPENDENT THIRD PARTY VERIFICATION, SOURCED DIRECTLY FROM RESPONSIBLY MANAGED FORESTS. WE ALSO MAKE ONGOING EFFORTS TO REDUCE OUR CARBON FOOTPRINT, REUSE ENERGY AND RESOURCES, MINIMIZE WASTE DURING THE MANUFACTURING PROCESS, AND RECYCLE 100% OF SCRAPS, TRASH, CARTRIDGES, EQUIPMENT, AND SOLVENTS WHENEVER POSSIBLE. DOING OUR PART TO IMPROVE THE WORLD WE LIVE IN. BEING GREEN IS AN EVERYDAY THING.

To Christine, the Tove in all of us.

How the difference between an igloo and a block
of ice is only the body sheltered beneath it.

~Sandra Beasley, *Japanese Water Bomb*

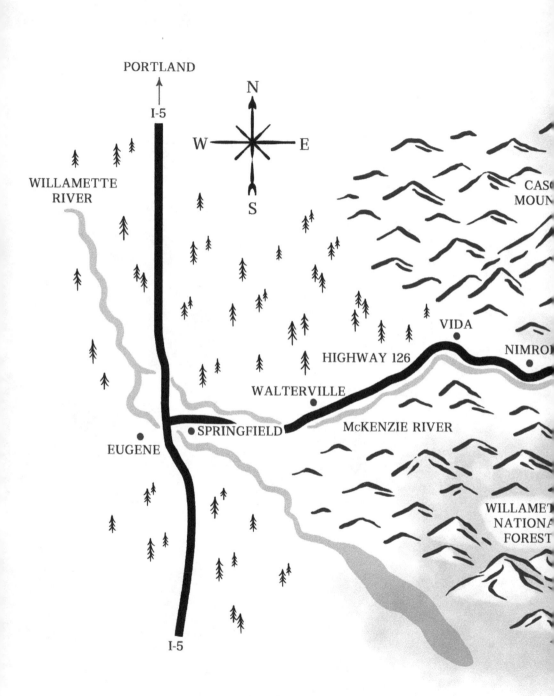

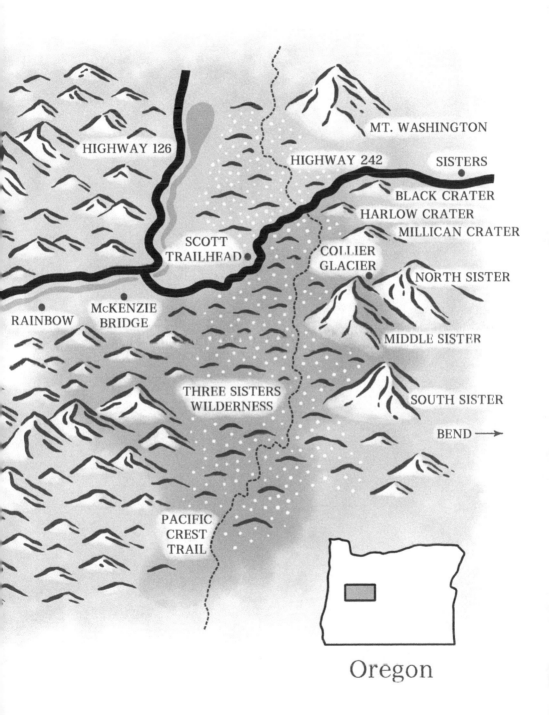

HIGHWAY 126

MT. WASHINGTON

HIGHWAY 242

SISTERS

BLACK CRATER

HARLOW CRATER

MILLICAN CRATER

SCOTT
TRAILHEAD

COLLIER
GLACIER

NORTH SISTER

RAINBOW

McKENZIE
BRIDGE

MIDDLE SISTER

THREE SISTERS
WILDERNESS

SOUTH SISTER

BEND →

PACIFIC
CREST
TRAIL

Oregon

1
THE
MOTHER

Mom. Wake up. Wake up."

Leonie Kane splintered an eye, peered at the small child standing beside the bed, ached for hours more of sleep. Cracked the second eye. "What?" she groaned, sleep linty in her throat. Rolled away, wished her daughter would disappear.

"Today is Hike Day, Mom. Collier Cone." Tone even, explanatory.

She heaved back over, squinted at the nine-year-old. Registered the point of the chin, the determined hitch of the shoulders.

"Hike Day!" Louder.

Leonie closed her dry eyes, willed her brain blank so she could return to sleep. She blinked again, focused. Still there. Warmth flushed through her; the girl was standing ramrod straight. She loved her beyond words.

"Yes, Amelia," she intoned solemnly. "Hike Day."

"We need to leave in twenty minutes. It is one hour and thirty-four minutes to the trailhead, and we need to be on the trail at eight. We agreed." Amelia's face scrunched as she stared down at her plastic wristwatch. She was a stickler about time.

She considered bargaining, but then glanced thoughtfully at her daughter.

Amelia was dressed in meticulously laced hiking boots, green corduroy pants, and a carefully tucked-in long sleeved purple shirt. Most days it was a battle for Leonie to get her daughter dressed and ready to leave the house. But here Amelia was now, dressed and booted. For nine years, Leonie had instructed Amelia never to refuse miracles.

She sighed, wished for something more expansive than a sigh, turned to Amelia.

She'd known from the moment she'd first held her daughter that she was unusual.

Even in the hospital, Amelia had not responded to cuddling. And though Arturo had insisted everything was fine, she knew. There was a certain stillness to Amelia that made Leonie hold her tighter. In Amelia's first year, she'd been a quiet, undemanding baby. Only later, when she was nearly three years old and still wouldn't make eye contact, did Arturo agree they should get the child assessed.

"It's Hike Day," she capitulated, threw back the blankets. No bargaining.

Thirty-five minutes later—exactly fifteen minutes late by Amelia's calculations—they were in Leonie's small gold Toyota Camry, driving through sleepy Eugene onto Highway 126, speeding east in the crisp fall air past signs for Nimrod, Rainbow, McKenzie Bridge.

Amelia had counted each minute aloud while Leonie pulled herself out of bed, dressed, made jam and cheese sandwiches, filled the thermos with coffee, packed soda, and gathered Amelia's guidebooks.

Just before Belknap Springs, an hour into the drive, she turned the little car right onto Highway 242—a narrow state highway that cut northeast through the Oregon Cascades. They drove in silence through the towering stands of Doug fir and red cedar and hemlock that crowded close to the sides of the road. Vine maples wove sparks of red and yellow through the lower canopy, and the ground was strewn with bright green ferns. Amelia stared out the window rapturously, and Leonie restrained herself from engaging her daughter in conversation.

Once Amelia was school-aged, Leonie sat through innumerable parent–teacher conferences where her daughter was described interchangeably as "sensitive" and "disruptive." In class, her teachers reported, Amelia tended to vacillate between complete silence and unrelenting lectures—blurting out specific, detailed facts about a range of environmental topics from moss reproduction to the frequency of silicate in the Galilean moons to the discharge rates of each of Oregon's 869 hydroelectric dams. She could fall into catastrophic fits of frustration when things did not go her way. There were long periods when neither Leonie nor her teachers could get her to eat anything other than cheerios, and even though Amelia had started eating more lately, she still carried the look of a malnourished child. She had a sharp chin and thin, bird-like bones, dark shadows under green eyes that in certain lights looked like bruises, blonde-brown hair that fell brittle down her back.

"Turn here, Mom," Amelia commanded.

She slowed the car and turned into a narrow dirt road marked with a sign for Scott Trailhead. Ten minutes later—Amelia continuing to count minutes helpfully out loud—Leonie had stowed everything into her backpack and locked the car. They were on their way.

Leonie had instigated Hike Day over a year ago, giving Amelia on her eighth birthday the responsibility of picking out a hike on their weekends together. She had split from Arturo several years previous, and they amicably traded off every other week with their daughter.

Typically, Amelia picked hikes in Eugene's local parks, but sometimes they went further afield. After Amelia had learned about volcanoes in school, she'd come home and demanded they go to the Collier Cone on the very next Hike Day. Leonie had been apprehensive about the length of the hike—they'd never done fourteen miles before—but Amelia was ecstatic and her excitement was infectious.

Amelia made them stop at the informational sign just past the trailhead. Leonie watched her daughter scrunch her brows and scan the colorful map. She turned and read the brief area description. The Scott Trail led out towards the Collier Cone within the greater Three Sisters Wilderness. Pictures on the sign showed a red and black cinder cone surrounded by enormous snowcapped mountains, glaciers and jagged rivers, old growth forest and sparkling alpine lakes. She was enchanted—the area appeared brochure-quality stunning and she'd never hiked there before.

"Let's go, Mom," Amelia commanded.

She turned obligingly, and together they followed the trail through the trees, heading for the promised fifteen-hundred-year-old-lava formations and the Collier Cone. They passed only a few other people on the trail: a young sunburnt couple, a man with a substantial dusty backpack, and an elderly woman with chin-length white hair. Amelia greeted each as she'd been taught, politely stepping off the trail to let each pass in turn. The older woman had chuckled and smiled, and Leonie was surprised when she saw Amelia smile back.

When they arrived at the first massive lava flow, even Leonie was suitably impressed. Her calves were burning, volcanic rock constantly chattered underfoot, and each step was like rolling on marbles. But, the twisted gray lava was sculpted into incredible formations and the views of the surrounding mountains and forests and lava flows were something else.

She paused, steadied herself at the base of the steep slope they were about to climb, squinted in the glare, scanned the dark red lava. While beautiful, it looked to her also desolate, like how she imagined Mars. Hard to believe this was Planet Earth. This was Oregon.

"Can you believe all those Oregon Trail people pulled their wagons through here?" she called to Amelia, who was further ahead. She hoped to slow the girl with conversation. She was out of shape, Amelia was not.

No answer.

Leonie tamped down a flash of irritation. She knew Amelia heard her but getting her to respond was a continual challenge. Sometimes Amelia would, but more often she did not.

The books she'd read and the various therapists she'd consulted had stressed that she should continue to verbally engage her daughter even if Amelia didn't consistently respond. It was frustrating, but Leonie kept at it. Lately it seemed to her as if Amelia responded more frequently, especially if they were hiking.

She tried again. "Have you played Oregon Trail yet in class?" she called to Amelia.

Amelia stopped, turned, looked down at Leonie from the switchback above. "No, Mom," she said dismissively. "That's racist."

Leonie felt both victorious Amelia had responded and startled by her response. "What?"

"It's racist towards Native Americans, Mom."

She swallowed, considered. She had fond memories of playing the computer game when she was younger. She'd even seen it recently in stores in the children's aisle. She had thought the game was making a comeback.

"When you start playing, you have to be white. The default is white." Scorn wove through Amelia's words. "If I want to be a Native American in the game, I can't. Even though I'm not white, right?"

She felt immobilized by her daughter's directness.

"Also, most of the attacks on the wagon trains heading west were not orchestrated by the tribes they were trespassing through but by other people who were…" Amelia paused, closed her eyes.

Leonie had seen her do this countless times before. It looked like her daughter was processing data, searching for the correct page. She knew Amelia was about to quote something verbatim. She often wondered if Amelia had a photographic memory.

"…white, male, and mercurial." Amelia went rigid, shoulders scrunched up by her ears. "No," she said. "That's incorrect. Wait."

She watched Amelia's eyes blink rapidly. She'd learned from therapy not to interrupt and not to feed a suggestion, even if the word seemed apparent. If Leonie did, Amelia could erupt in rage.

But Amelia unexpectedly smiled, a huge summer smile that warmed Leonie to her abdomen. "White, male, and mercenary," she said. "Mercenary. They preyed on the vulnerable, on the innocent—those in the wagon trains *and* on Native Americans."

Amelia paused, then looked in Leonie's direction with a still face. "Mercenary. Like Creighton Sears in my class. He steals Audry's lunch and says he can do it because she's Black."

Leonie felt her face go limp as her daughter's words registered. Pulse pounding, she moved quickly up the slope, lava rocks scattering, to stand closer to Amelia. She resisted with every ounce of her remaining energy her urge to reach, to sweep her daughter into her arms. Amelia disliked all physical contact.

Instead, she took a deep breath, clasped her hands together tightly, then asked, voice forced neutral, "Does Creighton Sears do anything to you?"

She watched Amelia link her fingers, draw her small shoulders tight, shrink into herself. Waited, recognized all the physical echoes of Amelia's distress. "Amelia?" she pressed, knowing she shouldn't, but also knowing she had to because she was her daughter's mother.

The girl looked up, directed her eyes half an inch away from Leonie's, gazed somewhere between her mother's hairline and ear. It was a learned gesture, one that Leonie had been working on for years—getting her Amelia to look people in the eyes.

"Yes," Amelia said firmly. "He says I have to give him my Friday hot lunch allowance because I don't belong here and will be deported to Mexico when I grow up."

She had to turn her face away, press her jaw so tightly together that she could feel her teeth pop. Tried to focus on a murmur, light and insistent, that thrummed from somewhere in the rocky background. Tried to breathe.

Leonie had instigated the divorce with Amelia's father. He was a good man, but she hadn't been in love with him for years. And while most of the time she was happy she'd left, moments like these she longed for the three of them to be together and wrapped fiercely around one another as family. Leonie felt her own whiteness left her woefully unprepared to talk about race with her daughter, wished that Arturo was there and could talk about what being white and Hispanic meant for Amelia.

Five deep breaths, then, she forced a calm voice.

"You know that's not true, right?" She knelt, her knee pressing into tiny sharp rocks. "You belong here with me, and you belong at your dad's house, and when you visit your *abuela's* in Pátzcuaro, you belong there! You're so lucky, Amelia, you belong to all of us in all these places."

Amelia bobbed her head while inside Leonie raged, pictured shaking little Creighton Sears until he screamed.

"I know what Creighton says is inaccurate, Mom, but I dislike that he speaks to me in that manner." Amelia's voice was small.

"Can I speak to Mrs. Flores about this, and about Audry?" she forced more calm into her voice.

Amelia shrugged a single shoulder, turned, and moved further upslope. Leonie knew the conversation was over.

Leonie took a breath, noticed small bits of volcanic rock inside her low-slung sneakers. Welcomed the opportunity to gather herself, to dump rocks out of her shoe and still her shaking hands. How dare he?

"Mom. Come on." Frustration lined Amelia's voice, the girl all limbs and speed. She was several switchbacks up the trail.

"Mom," Amelia called again, and she slipped her left shoe back on and got going. Increased her pace—thighs, knees, and calves screaming—but then she was there: on the edge, standing next to her wisp of a daughter looking down into the dark volcano.

"We made it!" she exhaled heavily, forced cheer into her voice thick with breath. The wind whipped up, sang a strange whistling sound, blew her long hair into a tangle. She was still distracted. *Creighton Sears.*

"Can we go all the way around the rim?"

The trail rose steeply in front of them as it led the way to the far side of the volcanic cone. At the top, the rim was shaped like a horseshoe. The side they were on was lower, and as the trail curved, the sharp bend was the highest point, and then it dipped and descended around to the other side. Leonie had never seen anything like it. She breathed deep the fresh air, took in the enormous landscape, the strong wind, the faint humming background. It *was* incredible. She tried to shake off her anger.

"We'll be able to see North Sister from up there."

"That mountain right in front of us?" Leonie asked suggestively. "The one we can see from here?"

"Mom. We'll be able to see all of the mountain from over there. It's a volcano too, just like what we're on, but larger." Amelia turned away without waiting, thin green-clad legs working as she moved up the trail away from Leonie.

Leonie closed her eyes, exhaled slowly. Every muscle in her body called attention to itself, and she eyed the higher slope with trepidation. The rim of the cone was a monotone of cinder and scree, all flat grays. Inside some stones were red, and the way the wind tossed the smaller scree around made her think of a cauldron bubbling.

Unease trickled down her throat. A cold sweat sponged between her skin and shirt. She shook her head, tried to dispel her agitation. It was probably little Creighton Sears haunting her thoughts.

Leonie tried to shake him off, summon compassion. He was just a child. And likely somewhere in his life someone was bullying someone in front of him. She knew children learned their behaviors by watching others.

Maybe she should reach out to his parents.

She shook her head again. Maybe. But only after she spoke to Mrs. Flores. Amelia came first, and Leonie would not let her daughter be harmed.

She looked up the trail, squinted. Amelia flickered in and out of sight. The cold sweat on Leonie's skin became a flood. "Wait up!" Leonie sped up the ridge after her, scree striking sharply on her heels.

All thoughts of Creighton Sears flew from her mind. Something didn't seem right. It felt like there was a danger that Leonie couldn't name. Her mouth flooded with adrenaline. Pure iron. The ground seemed to shiver.

Leonie shoved herself upslope. The air felt raw. She broke into a run.

She lost sight of Amelia.

Once, on one of their first Hike Days, she had lost her daughter in Eugene's Westmoreland City Park.

They'd walked down the bike path to the park, laid a blanket out in the sun near two large linden trees, and Amelia had run around the grassy slopes while Leonie had lazed in the bright heat. Drowsy, she'd fallen asleep for only a moment. When she'd opened her eyes, Amelia was gone.

At first, Leonie had just scanned the area, waited for Amelia to reappear. But then, heart clenching and cold sweat running down her back, she'd frantically searched the whole park, begged people to help. When Amelia didn't turn up, she rushed back to her blanket to call 911 in tears. As she dug her phone from her purse with shaking hands, she'd heard a voice and looked up. There was Amelia, perched high up in the linden tree.

Leonie had shouted, had ordered the girl down. When she finally held her daughter in her shaking arms and demanded an explanation, Amelia had said without emotion that she'd wanted to see what her mother would do if she vanished. She had choked, had felt her sinuses flood with iron. She'd resisted violently shaking Amelia. Instead, feeling the tears coating her face, she'd fiercely explained that if Amelia disappeared, her mother would absolutely die. Amelia had listened, then calmly patted her mother on the shoulder, disengaged herself from Leonie's arms, and moved away to examine the grass. Leonie was left collapsed on the picnic blanket, trying to slow her heart and swallow the burning bile in her throat.

Leonie ran fast along the Collier Cone summit, chest tight, after Amelia. The wind grew in strength and she pictured Amelia being blown off the volcano, her tiny body chucked down the sharp slope a thousand feet below.

As soon as she reached the top and could see down the rim, she stopped, both hands on her knees, bent over and sweaty, squinted her eyes and scanned for Amelia.

The volcanic grays and reds seemed uniform and grim, with no hint of her daughter.

Leonie looked all the way to the rim's far end, to the very edge of the trail at its steepest. Took a ragged breath.

Amelia was there, in motion, a tiny speck that looked to Leonie like a little girl-kite about to launch into the unknown.

"Stop!" she yelled, heart hammering, and Amelia for once heard, halted, turned and watched her mother lunge down the trail.

"That's the Linn Glacier," Amelia said informatively as Leonie caught up in a haze of blurred vision and uneven breaths. Amelia pointed to the white rectangle clinging to the north slope of North Sister.

"That's a glacier?" she wheezed, not even looking, fighting to keep her voice casual, holding her arms still against her need to squeeze the child to her. "Looks like a snow patch to me." She settled for reaching out a hand, touching Amelia's shoulder.

Amelia shrugged her off. "We'll see the entire Collier Glacier in a minute. Mrs. Flores said the view was blocked by the mountain until we get right above it."

"Mrs. Flores has done this hike?" She bowed her head, felt the panic-induced iron taste in her mouth slowly drain away. Took three extra breaths.

"Yes," Amelia replied. "But some of her directions have been inaccurate."

"Well, let's take note of those, and then you can report back." She eyed the rest of the trail wending along the narrow ridge, her chest still heaving. "Can we stick together hiking the rest of this ridge? It feels a little dangerous to me."

The child shrugged her pointy shoulder again, turned away.

"Do you want another layer?" Leonie asked, feeling the chill of the wind and realizing just how thin her daughter's purple shirt looked.

Amelia shook her head, walked a few steps, then a few more, and Leonie followed reluctantly. She could hear Amelia's breathing and a high reedy humming noise her daughter was making every few steps.

North Sister rose before them as an enormous squat block of mountain, and along its western slope was a deep trough lined with what looked like fine gray sand. Leonie stopped, stared down at the turquoise pools of water in the trough. The landscape looked surreal, like a painter had dumped grays and reds and blues in a hallucinating swirl. She didn't feel like she was in green, forested Oregon anymore. Instead, somehow, she'd ended up on this sharp ridgeline above the unimaginable.

"That's the Collier Glacier." Amelia pointed at the rumpled patch of snow and ice sweltering in the dark gray valley below. She seemed impervious to heights. "She used to be where we are in 1906, but she started to thaw and hasn't stopped."

"But that's like over a mile, maybe two. You sure? Did you read that somewhere?" She looked down at Amelia, admired her mind that could hold so many facts and figures. Perhaps her daughter would be a scientist when she grew up.

Amelia shook her head negatively, eyes trained onto the ice. "The glacier told me."

Leonie felt her eyebrows shoot to her hairline. "Really?"

"She used to flow all the way out there to those mountains," Amelia said, pointing towards where they'd parked the car, "but then this cinder cone popped up and blocked where she could go."

"Wow. That doesn't seem nice." She looked hard at her daughter. Amelia rarely anthropomorphized things. "She?"

Amelia giggled, a pure bubbling sound that set Leonie's heart afire. "She's still upset about it!" The girl laughed, delighted.

The wind grabbed at Leonie's sweatshirt, yanked her sleeves, made her legs wobble. She glanced up, saw clouds billowing across the sky, felt chilled standing on the exposed ridge. She wanted to enjoy the moment with her daughter at the top of their hard-earned hike, but where they stood seemed unsafe, dangerous.

"I think we should hike back down, maybe eat the last sandwiches at the base, then head back? It's a full seven miles, and it's getting late." Leonie glanced at her watch. It was already noon.

Amelia stared at the glacier. "We should stay. She likes me."

"How about five minutes, then we go?" She bargained. "Maybe we could walk a little ways back, get off this steep section?"

Amelia ignored her.

Leonie looked closely at her daughter. Amelia's hair was flying about in the wind, her cheeks were flushed, and her pale green eyes were trained like a lighthouse onto the ice. Leonie's stomach clenched. She'd seen Amelia fixated on things before, and she'd had more than one instance of physically having to haul her screaming, kicking, flailing away from whatever it was that she wanted.

"Amelia?" Leonie asked, soft. "Amelia? We have to go." She reached, gently jostled the little girl's shoulder. "Hello?"

Amelia planted her feet, shook her head. "No, Mom. I have to stay here." Said flat, monotone.

Frustration flared in Leonie's stomach. This could not be happening. They had a long way to go, and she couldn't carry her daughter down such a narrow slope without endangering both of them. Especially if Amelia was fighting her.

"Yes, Amelia. We're leaving, now. No argument." Leonie kept her own tone even, but stern. She shook Amelia's shoulder once more. "Now."

Amelia cocked her head, as if she was listening to something, then looked right up at her mother.

Leonie was shocked. Amelia never made eye contact. Ever. Her daughter's eyes were bright, slightly glazed.

"You'll regret it." Amelia emphasized each word.

"What?" She couldn't keep the astonishment out of her voice. "That's it, we're going now." She took an uncompromising step towards her daughter.

Amelia stepped back.

Leonie froze. One more step and her daughter would go over the edge.

Amelia stared directly at Leonie. Her face was still, her chin cocked.

Leonie did not move a muscle. She felt like a clenched nerve. She drew in a single breath, silently calculated how she could leap at her daughter and grab her before she slipped past gone forever.

But then Amelia broke eye contact, grinned, raised her hands up. "Okay."

She let out a deep breath, felt bewildered at the sea change. "What? Okay?"

Amelia nodded once. "Yes, we can go. She said I could come back and keep her company later."

Leonie did not question, did not respond, did not wonder. Instead, she breathed out the scene they'd just avoided, stepped forward and nudged her daughter in front of her to get her moving, and the two hiked down the narrow cone rim, the wind pushing shark sand into their faces. The temperature rose and fell as dark clouds moved in across the blue skies and the landscape tremored.

At the base of the volcano, they paused at a small, vegetated boulder and split Leonie's last sandwich. Amelia didn't speak, and Leonie didn't make conversation. She just sat in the patchy sun and enjoyed the feel of jam in her mouth. The sun baked her skin, and relief and enjoyment washed around inside of her. Gradually, she could hear

Amelia humming again, a tune Leonie had never heard her hum before, and the sound blended into a blur of pleasantness that chased Leonie's sense of unease away.

Once they finished eating, she wrapped up the lunch bags. Casually, hoping it would work, she set up her phone on a rock. Turning, she asked Amelia to stand next to her for a photo.

Amelia looked at her with narrowed eyes, and Leonie instantly recalled every other time she'd tried to take Amelia's picture. It was always a battle. Leonie sucked in her breath, ready to retreat. But then Amelia tilted her head, as if she was again listening to something, and nodded at her mother. Consent.

Leonie did not question her luck. She stood beside Amelia, smiled, and the camera clicked. Then she was reaching past her daughter in an instant, sticking her phone back into her pocket, hustling them down the trail. Small victories.

Leonie led the way, serenaded by the pitter-patter of her daughter's footsteps, and they walked through lava flows and meadow flats and marsh lakes and stands of dead trees and living trees and even though they'd already hiked the out and back trail that morning, everything felt different. Fresh. The sun dropped lower in the sky and the light changed and the wind eased even as the clouds started to pile up in the sky and she could feel the temperature drop on her skin. Miles fell away as she hiked, the steady pace even and careful.

"Do you think we should hike the whole Pacific Crest Trail one day, Amelia?" Leonie asked eventually, pensive, walking through a wide flat meadow full of spent wildflowers and sedge grasses. Amelia didn't answer.

Leonie stopped, turned. The trail, the meadow, as far as she could see, was empty. Her daughter had vanished.

2
THE
DAUGHTER

Donna Watts dangled her ice-white legs off the rotting porch, felt rusted nails dig into the flesh of her thighs, shifted. Stretched into the brief sunlight, warmed herself. She angled her head back, craned up at the Doug firs towering hundreds of feet over the cabin. The trees blocked most of the sunlight and Donna marveled that one sunbeam could fight through all that growth and somehow still manage to touch down onto the cabin porch and heat her legs.

She reached a hand, stuck it into the discernible light beam, felt the searing hot heat of the sun. It was like fire in her palm.

Sun flames.

Donna stared at the light, admired how it made her fingers almost translucent. Sighed, wished it was that easy, summoning fire to her fingertips.

If she could, she would.

And she'd burn it all down.

But she couldn't. Nothing was that easy. Risk assessment.

She wiggled her fingers in and out of the light, marveled again that somehow the sun had reached her, thawed her, given her one moment of sincere happiness and heat and power and flames. The green beads wrapped around her wrist rattled reassuringly. But then, the clouds flickered, the trees shifted, and the light was gone. Donna tried not to make too much of the synchronism, the sunbeam, the flames.

Forced herself to remember why she was there, frowned.

A piece of red plastic in the grass snagged her eye. Donna squinted but didn't rouse herself to investigate further, just stared, waited to see if more would be revealed. Enjoyed the waiting, the wondering, simultaneously fighting back against an urge to look around and see if her therapist was there in the corner to witness Donna waiting, enjoying an experience, pausing.

Donna's newest therapist liked to repeat refrains like 'be calm,' 'find safety,' and 'hold patience within.' Say the words, her therapist told her. Embody the words, and they'll be realized within. Donna released a long-held breath.

The sunbeam flicked back on, glared stronger on the grass in front of her, and gradually she made out the red head of a small plastic dinosaur, half an inch in size.

Donna closed her eyes and began sifting through thirty years of carefully organized memories. She visualized a tall metal filing cabinet with eight stacked drawers. Her current therapist had helped her build out this coping mechanism. Each drawer pulled out five sections and displayed rows and rows of neatly labeled folders. Donna avoided the drawers near the bottom of the cabinet—those drawers were locked and she had no interest in ever opening them.

Instead, she mentally reached for the second drawer, pulled it open, ran her fingers across the marked plastic tabs clipped atop each folder. The order pleased her, soothed her. She flipped through individually labeled childhood memories until one clicked and she selected the folder and opened it and scanned through the memory of the breakfast cereal she used to eat when she was young—sugary grains that had always revealed a plastic toy lurking at the bottom of the cardboard box.

Her parents sometimes let her play with various disinterred breakfast treasures on the cabin porch until eventually they went feral. Then the toys made their way in the world on their own. And, while Donna had no memories of this particular dinosaur, she felt satisfied she'd placed it, categorized it.

Quietly, she returned the folder to the file, mentally closed the cabinet drawer.

No harm done, she told herself. Everything was okay. But for fuck's sake, that was close. Donna squeezed her wrist tight. Stay safe.

Donna looked down, saw her fingers turning white as they dug into her left wrist. "Stop," she said. Forced her hand to unclench, open, release herself. "No cognitive distortions," she hissed. No blaming. No punishments. The place was full of memory anchors. Accidents were expected. She was not at fault.

"Be nice to you," she murmured, rubbed her wrist.

Donna looked out at the small clearing surrounding the cabin, the flat of cool grass and moss that likely carpeted over countless plastic toys of her youth. The sun vanished again, and the temperature dropped several degrees. Donna looked up, saw tree tips dissolve into clouds. She stood, stretched, looked around once more with veiled eyes.

She looked at a small patch of ground near where she'd parked her car. Donna remembered once being eighteen and vomiting blood in that spot and instantly slammed shut that memory, hadn't meant to open it. Tested again the drawer locks, made sure they were secure. No more slipping.

Redirected herself.

Considered which map layers she'd use if she was going to map the clearing. A good Oregon base map, likely provided by USGS. They had quality publicly available data. She'd maybe add topography, some land cover layers to help a user understand the interaction of forest, river, mountains, and lava in the area. Demographics, if only to show that barely anyone lived out in this lonely stretch of Lane County. A parcels layer to confirm just how miserable Ray's little slice of owned heaven actually was.

Donna snickered to herself. She imagined drawing the map, then the pleasure she'd get from deleting the whole damned project from the database. Delete the cabin, the clearing, the land. If only. Donna loved being a cartographer.

She looked out around the open area, carefully allowed herself to access memories from the first drawer, the benign background folders. Stayed general.

Remembered how she'd grown up in the cabin, a small gangly child hemmed in place by the steep surrounding forest. A childhood fenced by chores and winters and Ray's fundamentalist beliefs. Very little back then broke the monotony of her days.

The wood rounds to be split, stacked, carried in.

The game to clean, portion.

The hand-hewn floors to scrub, rinse, dry.

The meals made, eaten, washed, repeated.

The too-few trips to town.

Remembered how when she got older, she was infrequently allowed to walk the forested trail along the McKenzie River from the cabin to McKenzie Bridge, the closest community. One way took an hour on foot. On those rare trips she'd linger slow in the aisles of the McKenzie Bridge gas station and think about the sweet candies laid out in neat rows on the wooden shelving and how surely the Devil was tempting her through such bright displays.

Whenever she returned from a trip to McKenzie Bridge, Ray would tip her head back, fingers stinking of chainsaw oil, dig his nails into her jaw, hold her face. He'd lean close and inspect her teeth and smell deep into her mouth to determine if she'd given in to the Devil or if she'd leaned into the supportive arms of sweet Jesus Christ and resisted all such temptation.

Giving in to the Devil was always followed by a belting to cleanse her. Donna had long associated the two and learned to avoid both.

Ray never seemed to realize the draw to the gas station for her wasn't the candy itself. Rather, it was the order, the rows and rows of different candies, each categorized into specific cardboard boxes, each small, sweet item located in a specific place. The order had pleased Donna as a child, had given her a calm that she carried tightly in her chest as she slow-walked the path back home through the dim forest. Inevitably, that pleasing peace would drain away the closer she got to the cabin and an unpredictable Ray, waiting.

Donna had gone the other day to the gas station, had wandered in and bought a newspaper and a kombucha and eyed the row of candies and sweets. She could have bought the entire lot, boxes and boxes of candy she'd never had an appetite for. She resisted the urge, instead left, drove her car back to the cabin, sat on the porch and read the newspaper and listened for Ray.

A chill crawled down Donna's spine and she shivered, shook away the specifications she hadn't meant to review. Her therapist had suggested allowing herself to review only one or two full memories in depth each day she was at the cabin. So far Donna had barely managed to do one.

Instead, as soon as she felt a memory, an association coming on, she tried to push it away, slam the filing cabinet shut. But the longer she stayed at the cabin, the harder it got to control, the harder it got to stay away from the cabinet.

"Daughter!" a faint voice murmured through the poorly chinked cedar logs.

Donna instinctually blanched, caught herself cringing, unfolded herself. Stood up straight. All those years and that voice still regressed her more than anything else. Steeling herself, she turned, called, "Coming."

Donna's therapist had worked session after session to prepare her, to ensure she stayed calm and quiet and patient. When Donna drove up from Eugene, maneuvered the hazy and winding state Highway 126, she'd dipped into her toolbox of solutions and recited calming chants aloud in the empty car: "I am calm." She said it again. Then: "I am not angry; I am in control." But pulling off the highway onto the cabin's rutted driveway had inevitably triggered her gag reflex and she'd barely managed to open the car door before she vomited down the side of the running board.

Donna knew then she was not prepared. She knew she was not in control.

Now, hand to the cabin door's latch, she drew a deep breath, opened the screen door, let it slam into the back of her.

She'd chosen to return, on her own terms. Mucking around in memories was not something she was interested in doing.

Donna knew she had one task. She hoped to complete it and then close the file forever. It was time.

She fortified the spiky psychic walls around herself, stacked bricks and logs and hate high overhead, moved forward.

She entered the dark two-room cabin.

Donna paused, let her eyes adjust in the dim, skimmed the room without settling onto a single thing in the midst of the chaos. She tried not to register the stacks of broken, grubby furniture, books swollen with mold and stuffed in rotting cardboard boxes, tools caked with rust and grime piled haphazardly, splits of wood and crusted dishes, heaps of clothing and decaying costume jewelry and moldering shoes. Filth.

Her first day she'd wondered about the piles of stuff, had even poked around in the boxes and pulled out bizarre items like deteriorating handbags and high heels with pantyhose jammed into them. But her mind had trembled at the possibilities of what she was touching. She vowed to ignore the mess, had recognized that anything outside her task was not relevant, had labeled it a data layer she would not explore at this time.

Donna instead walked through the larger room into the smaller, nostrils flaring in the stale, yeasty air. Motes of dust, unclean floors, sour cigarette smoke, wet mold, and something rancid caught in her nostrils as she moved into the overheated dark. A wooden pole bed was placed squat in the center of the room below a shuttered window. The only light that entered the room filtered through the wads of newspaper stuffed into the gaps in the cedar log walls.

Donna approached the bed, looked down at Ray.

She swallowed, fought to neutralize her face. Swallowed again. Felt grossly dehydrated, as if her tongue was suddenly too large for her mouth.

Ray Pencovitch lay flat, his once-large frame shrunk, his muscled logger arms now loose and weak, his mottled skin drooped in folds. Gray-black hairs sprung isolated from a head checker-boarded with age spots larger than Donna's fist. Above the disintegrating cotton blanket, his hands were claws, crossed immobile, knuckles swollen and joints twisted, elongated fingers warped in such jumbled clumps they could no longer command a chainsaw.

Ray's mouth was open, his pink tongue visibly muddling between rotted gums. A clear plastic oxygen tube ran down either side of the man's face, the prongs of the nasal cannula clamped around a septum flattened long ago in one of the McKenzie Highway's roadside bars.

Donna visualized a white beach. Tahiti. Or Hawaii. The precise geolocation didn't matter. Her third, maybe fourth, therapist had taught her to focus on the atmosphere, the ambience, not the physical place. Donna thought about the sound waves made when they gently nuzzled a soft sandy beach. Added some data layers of precipitation, wind speed, cloud cover. All, minimal. Paradise.

"What do you need?" she asked, tone dry and empty.

"Water," Ray mouthed, tongue darting across dried lips.

The only things still piercing about Ray were his eyes, bright beams of blue that stabbed at Donna from under brows jungled with age. She avoided his eye contact, stared at the age spot shaped like Texas above his left eye, thought about stepping into soft warm waves. Wading. Swimming.

Donna picked up the plastic hospital-grade cup with a thin white straw, brought it to Ray's mouth. He sucked greedily; she skimmed her eyes over the junk in the far side of the room, the stacked cardboard boxes brimming with more clothes and shoes, a three-legged stool with a cheap tin sitting on top, a rotting leather boot, two rolls of wrapped fishing line.

Donna looked to the far side of the room, saw the mix of mud and newspaper Ray had used to patch the clefts between the logs. The grain pattern on the peeled logs was beautiful, looked like the first topographic maps she'd seen when she learned GIS in university. The professor had brought in a hand carved wooden relief map of the Oregon Cascades and Donna had stared at it for the entire class. The detail, the precision. Even though the majority of her work was now done on a computer, Donna was still—maybe even more so—appreciative of any cartography done by hand.

"Finished?" she asked, voice loud, echoing.

Ray closed his lips, mouth momentarily shielded from view. Donna returned the cup to the nightstand, turned to leave the room.

Ray jerked in the bed, shot an arm out across the blanket, clamped onto her wrist as if his hand was a turtle beak. Donna started in surprise, looked down at the gnarled hand clutching her wrist, then dispassionately yanked her wrist free.

"Is there something you want to tell me?" she asked, rubbing her wrist where their flesh had touched. The spot seared, and she wiped it on her shirt.

Donna had told herself before she arrived that it would be possible to refrain from direct physical contact. That hadn't been realistic, of course, but after each incident she'd taken up with a bar of soap at the spigot outside scrubbing until her skin was raw and her thoughts returned to numb.

"Stay," Ray rasped, but Donna turned, wrist burning, left the room, left the cabin.

Walked across the clearing with strides stretching further than her narrow gait. Wrenched open the passenger door of her car, pulled the soap off the dash, hurried to the back side of the cabin, twisted on the water, washed.

The cabin had never had running water. But when Donna was little Ray had stretched plastic tubing from Horse Creek to the two large barrels he'd ferreted from somewhere. One barrel was black, the hot barrel they'd called it, and the other blue and full of cold water. Donna had taken her weekly bath in cloudy, lukewarm water drained from the solar-heated hot barrel. The washtub was a small pit in the ground lined with a patched blue tarp. Donna would wash tornado quick, and then her mother Julene would take her turn, long brown hair wrapped up onto her head. Ray would watch from the porch, reciting aloud holy scripture, eyes never straying from Donna's mother, washing, wet.

Chilled but cleansed by the handwashing, Donna walked back around the cabin and sat down again on the porch edge, stared briefly at the red plastic dinosaur, then watched the light drowsily move across the ridge. Nearly three o'clock in the afternoon. Perhaps she should drive to the gas station, get another newspaper. But it would be time soon to start dinner, heat the thin gruel Ray gummed. How the last year had shrunk and weakened him.

Scrabbling sounds from inside the cabin roused her to the realization that something was wrong, and she stood up, took a breath, pictured white sand and blue water. Added a population data layer to her visualization—people happy, singing. Waited until her heartbeat slowed, then walked calmly through the screen door, through the main room and back into Ray's bedroom.

Ray was not in his bed.

She looked, found him on the floor, tangled in the blankets. Livid eyes lasered her. He moaned.

Flames flared hot and bright inside of Donna, nearly overtook her in the moment and she wrapped her arms quick around herself, rocked. Took a deep breath. Her second therapist, the one she'd seen when she was much younger, had underscored that she had to learn to control her anger.

"Dammit, Ray." Donna forced down her irritation. "What the fuck?"

This wasn't the first time he'd done this. And she knew each time it was a ploy, that he wanted her to pick him up, to touch him, to connect her body to his. Ray had, until the end of last year, been an enormous man, towering near six and a half feet tall, several hundred pounds of muscle and religious certainty. When Donna was small he'd convinced her he was sired from the last mountain giants that inhabited the Cascades. He'd told her over and over that his size and strength were gifts from God, bestowed on him personally, that few men could break a stone with just their fists like he could.

Even though he'd shrunk over the last year—the likely outcome of several strokes and cancers—Ray was still a heavy man. And Donna knew picking him up would involve her cradling him.

Donna knelt before his floored body and breathed the fire that still surged through her. "You do this on purpose," she accused him. She struggled to keep her voice calm, patient. "You do this to goad me."

She rocked back onto her heels, looked at his twisted bulk wrapped in the blanket. One white foot stuck out, sock half on. Blue veins bulged.

"Okay," she bargained. "Is there something you want to tell me?"

Ray moaned, spittle dribbling, closed his eyes, looked away from her. His thin chest rose and fell, and Donna closed her own eyes, visualized swimming in the ocean with fins on her feet, smiled at the picture. Breathed through her nose.

"Can't all be bad, can it?" Donna asked, pressed her heels into the floor. "Remember that time when you and I were driving somewhere on the highway, up near the top of the pass, and you stopped for hitchhikers? You told me you always stopped for hitchhikers, it was how you built karma. And then you all smoked the whole way to town? I realize now it was probably pot, but I didn't know then."

Donna stared at Ray, looked at his closed eyes. "I remember then you drove us home, and before I got out of the truck you told me you loved me."

She waited, but he didn't open his eyes, just held his pointed face away from her.

"Oh well." She rose back up onto her feet, tapped her shoe on the floor by his head. "You were probably high." Tapped harder.

Waited until he opened his eyes, looked up at her. "Wouldn't want to have an accident, do we, Ray? That wouldn't be very good."

"Daughter," he groaned, stuck a hand towards her foot.

Donna neatly sidestepped his hand. "Fine. It is, after all, important to establish a pattern," she said.

She left the room, walked to the solitary table, picked up her phone, and went outside to the edge of the clearing near Ray's long-parked truck, searched for cell service. Three more steps east and a single bar lit up on the phone. She dialed 911.

"My father is sick," Donna said to the operator when the call went through, "and he's fallen out of bed. I need help lifting him back."

She gave her name and address, directions to the cabin, hung up the line.

Last time it had taken the firefighters near an hour. She hoped she'd only have to do this production one or two more times. Donna whistled, waited in the dimming light, kept her mind calm. Filing cabinet locked. Thought about vector and raster data, the pleasure of using points, lines, and polygon data. Sorted discrete and continuous raster data. Population density was discrete. Temperature or elevation measurements were continuous. Donna loved the order of cartographic data.

She heard the engines before she saw headlights. Glanced at her phone. Thirty minutes. Quick.

A red SUV with the unit's numbers marked on the door came up the pitted dirt road, followed by an ambulance swaying in the potholes. She didn't recognize the vehicle. A new team, different from last time. Donna's heart sank, her jaw tightened.

The drivers left their headlights on in both vehicles, illuminated the clearing that had darkened into the evening. Two large men in blue pants and tucked polos got out of the SUV.

"Donna Watts?" the man on the left called. Two more people got out of the ambulance. A crowd.

"Yes." Donna stepped forward, towards the man who'd called her name. "That was quick. You all didn't come up from Eugene, did you?"

"No," the other man said. "We responded from Thurston Hills, Camp Creek area. I'm Chief Thomas Addington, this is my colleague, Jonas."

"Thanks for coming, Chief Addington."

Donna eyed the firemen carefully, made note of their physical features. They looked rather similar, blurring into one another. She wasn't sure she'd be able to individually pick them out of a line-up. Risk assessment. She looked harder, took in more detail.

The chief was over six foot, clearly hadn't met a dentist he liked, and had the appearance of a lot of once-physically fit men going soft in the belly as they aged. He didn't concern her. But the other one looked ex-military, white, had an upper body that shouted gym time, a hooded expression that raised Donna's hackles. She knew that look.

Both men gazed around with eyes cocked, assessing, and the two medics hung close to the ambulance.

Paranoia flared in Donna's stomach. Did they think she was going to ambush them?

"What's the issue?" Chief Addington asked, obviously in charge.

He turned, squared his shoulders at her. Donna did not move, held ground in the center of the clearing. She was not a big person, but she wasn't going to be intimidated by a rural firefighter jumped up on big engines and minuscule authority.

"My father's inside the cabin, on the floor." Donna spoke calmly, willed her voice quiet, controlled. "Like I told the operator, I can't manage his weight myself."

"Huh." The chief worked his jaw, stared at her. He was clearly still evaluating her. "When we go in there, what will we find?"

She stared right back at him. He had teeth like barnacles. She planted her feet deeper into the dirt, centered herself. Hands on her hips. They didn't know anything.

"Ray Pencovitch," Donna licked her lips, worked to keep the spite from her tone. Centered on waves on a sandy beach before her eyes, breathed. "On the floor. I think he was trying to find his smokes."

The man held up his hands defensively. "This is tweaker territory, everyone knows that. Nothing like baiting the services for a fix."

"I don't want anything but two seconds of your help."

He nodded. "Okay. But let's take this slow."

The two firefighters split, stepped around her, moved onto the porch. Careful, like geese flying in formation. Donna smiled internally at the image. Kept her face blank, pleasant.

The two medics stepped forward from where they were still tucked in near the side of their rig. Donna saw one was white, male, rather lean and tall. She couldn't place his age, but he didn't seem like a threat. The other looked Asian, was a woman, and by the look of her no more than a teenager. She was about the same height as Donna.

"Mind if we check in on him?"

Donna narrowed her eyes. The medic who spoke was the woman.

"I'm May Young. This is Baker Baynestone." The man beside her nodded in greeting. He appeared bland, nonmemorable.

Donna shook her head at both of them. "You can if you'd like, but I'd advise not. He gets worked up when he sees you folks. He thinks you're going to take him to hospital."

She turned when she heard the two men on the porch open the screen door, calling, "Mr. Pencovitch?"

The woman medic walked stiffly to the back of the ambulance. When she returned, Donna saw she'd pulled a medical bag out. She brought it to the front of the vehicle where the medic named Baker had not moved.

Donna wasn't sure if she was supposed to talk to the medics— they hadn't come last time—so she maintained her silence, tried to project calm.

The two firefighters returned in under five minutes while Donna and the medics waited outside.

"We put him back in the bed," Chief Addington explained, stepping down from the porch. "He's pretty groggy."

Donna nodded.

"Are you going to take him in?" the fire chief stopped two strides away from her. He was clean shaven. Was somewhere between his mid-forties and mid-fifties. "He's not doing great."

"I know," Donna said. "But he's refused everything. I've got all the paperwork he signed if you want to see it. He intends to die out here."

"Do you mind? We have elder care protocols."

Donna nodded, and moved for the first time from the clearing, around the chief, up the steps, into the cabin, opened the cardboard box at the base of the kitchen table, retrieved the manila envelope on top. Had a flash of pleasure at the sight of a well-organized box. Glanced at the papers.

She'd paid good money for the forgeries.

Carried the envelope back outside, handed it over, stepped out of arm's reach. "Everything you need to see is in there."

They all moved back to the ambulance where the interior light shone brightest, laid out the paperwork on the bench seat.

Donna maintained her position in the clearing. She knew if any of them made a move towards her she could disappear into the woods in any direction and remain unfound. She heard the chief talk through the paperwork to the other two.

The second firefighter called Jonas stepped nearish to her. Too close. He had breath like a burnt clutch. She considered, moved back a step. She would cede ground this once, but if he tried to get closer she'd hold fast, potentially instigate a minor aggressive move.

"How long you been out here?" He looked around, clearly taking in the small cabin, single shed, dingy outhouse, Ray's white truck and Donna's Subaru. Everything else was tall trees and ridgelines.

"A bit." Donna shrugged.

"Much longer?"

"Hard to say." Donna made a show of staring up at the sky, not wanting to make small talk.

"Have we met?" He peered at her face.

Donna scanned him, brief. A single glance out of the corner of her eyes. He looked like he was in his twenties or thirties, so maybe they'd passed each other somewhere in these hills, but if so, she wasn't going to admit it and allow him to lay some line of connection between them.

They had one task—putting Ray again back into bed—and now Donna wanted them to leave. She shrugged vaguely at Jonas.

The chief walked back around the front of the ambulance, his body causing the headlights to flicker. "Thanks, Donna," he said, his tone now friendly. "All this is in order."

"Of course it is, Chief," she snarled, the rubber bands holding her real thoughts contained snapping in the tension. "What did you think?" The last sentence escaped before she could stop herself.

He raised two hands up in front of his blue chest. Clearly his go-to gesture. "Whoa," he said. "You called us."

A beach. Small grains of sand. A baby seal, slowly swimming along the water line, towards adulthood and freedom and the world's oceans healthy and blue. A setting sun. Calm. In control. Donna sighed at the vision, was happy with her data layers. Breathed in, out.

"I needed the help," she said, voice calibrated bright. "Thank you, all of you." She gestured with a soft open hand at the four of them individually.

"We could take him in, you know. Get him more comfortable, pain medication, then you could bring him back out." This, from the woman. Girl, really.

"Great idea," Donna lied, covered the panic in her stomach with a pleased voice. She felt her hands shake, stuck them in her pockets. "But not necessary. That will only disrupt him."

"Okay," the chief said. "Since he's on oxygen, try not to let him smoke. He might set the whole place on fire."

Donna nodded. "Noted."

"Is there anything else we can do for you?"

The anger in her stomach lurched up onto its hooves, and she feared the crew sensed it. She watched the chief carefully, tried to read his impassive face. "I'm fine," she finally said, allowed a weak smile to stretch across her face. "This is all just a lot."

She waved as they backed out of the driveway, headlights blinding her. She knew what she looked like; a lonely figure lit up against a dark cabin. She relaxed her shoulders, slumped a little, stood still until the sounds of their vehicles completely died away.

Donna straightened, regained her ramrod posture. Walked back up to the cabin. Lit the kerosene lamp on the kitchen table, carried it into Ray's room, looked down at him tucked ever-so-gently into bed.

"Do you have something to tell me?"

In the light, his eyes glinted as he glared at her. A wet smirk appeared at the corner of his mouth. "Whore," he muttered.

Donna felt her stomach clench, her eyes twitch. She lowered the lamp to her side, leaned down over him. Whispered, "Die already."

3
THE
MEDIC

May Young stared out the windshield at the thick rain pouring over the ambulance's headlights, thought about how it hadn't rained like that all summer. But now. Torrential. A Pacific Northwest hurricane of rain.

Closely packed trees taller than anything she remembered reared up on either side of the narrow mountain highway, and the wet road slapped the small ambulance with irregular shudders, sending shivers through May's abdomen.

May looked over at Baker, saw his hands gripped old school at ten and two, face aglow in the dial lights. He stared straight ahead, prominent chin pointing at the windshield. May thought he looked a little like Derek Shepherd from *Grey's Anatomy*. She'd binged all sixteen seasons during her medic training, was absolutely devastated when Derek was declared brain dead in season eleven. May wished the surgeons hadn't been so arrogant. They could have detected Derek's head injury sooner and his character would still be on the show.

May turned away from Baker before she started filling the silence with a nervous ramble. But then her not talking greenlit her brain, and she started to worry. Maybe Baker was on pills, about to lose control of the ambulance. She should have looked more carefully in his bag when she was loading the gear, checked to see if he had phenobarbitals, Seconal, Nembutal. The Seconal pills were oblong, bright red, easy to spot in the hand or pocket. May wasn't as good at differentiating all the white pills, the pressed powder rounds, but her medic training was giving her a crash course. Thank god most Valium had a v-donut hole, and Xanax had the brand name inscribed on the pill along with the dosage.

Watching Baker again, May sighed, then glanced out the window. His breathing seemed normal, eyes tracking. But May knew it was hard to tell. Amelia Shepherd had struggled with her addiction to prescription pills throughout *Grey's Anatomy*, and often the other characters had no idea. May studied Baker again from the corner of her eye. The sweat at his temples might just be because it was warm in the ambulance. She looked firmly away.

It was open along this stretch of highway. A burn had swept through the previous summer, incinerating trees and underbrush and melting chunks of asphalt. Baker had told her the first time they'd driven up this highway that the forest fire had been so intense, so hot, that it had sterilized the land, killed off vegetation, wildlife, and any organisms living below ground.

May was glad she hadn't been working at the department then to see that. A year ago. Finally twenty-one and legal to go out and drink, and yet she'd been drowning that summer in smoke and medic training.

The quiet in the ambulance grew, and May tried to redirect her thoughts and not obsess on Baker's potential addiction to prescription pills that if she was being honest with herself she had zero evidence for, just nagging worry. She also tried to keep her mouth glued shut, to not open it and fill in his silence with long meandering stories that did nothing but coil around her unease and squeeze.

Too late.

"Donna seemed off her rocker this time, didn't she?" May said, finally. "Maybe pills, you think?"

Baker shrugged noncommittally.

May was unsure how to interpret the shoulder movement. It wasn't combative, but neither was it encouraging. Was it an indication that he wanted her to continue? Or stop talking? She could never tell. That was one of the things her mother picked at her about. She needed to learn to pay more attention to subtle cues.

She pitched on instead. "I mean, that first time we went out there, Donna just seemed defensive, like, a step removed from reality. I remember she stood in front of that cabin as if we were going to attack her. Then, the second time, she did the same thing, as if we hadn't just been out there two days previous. But today, she just sat there on that porch zoned out while her father's facedown one room away. That seems odd, doesn't it?"

Baker released the wheel, reached along the console, turned up the speed of the windshield wipers. They whooshed back and forth, back and forth. He swallowed. Didn't look at her. None of them in the department looked at her. Not really. Perhaps because she was taller than some of them.

"It's not any of our business," Baker responded, slow.

"She's neglecting him," May retorted quickly, relieved he'd responded. She wasn't actually sure if Donna was neglecting her father. But at least now Baker was talking.

"Do you really think so?" he asked, looking at her out of the side of his face.

"Keep your eyes on the road," May said automatically. "No. Maybe. I don't know. But the whole situation seems off. Donna seems off. Her dad seems off."

Baker gave a second noncommittal shrug. "Look close enough at anyone's situation, and you'll find things that are off."

"Thank you, Oh Jedi Master," May mumbled sarcastically. She tilted her shoulder away from him to stare out the window. Retreated into herself. If her parents were sick, she'd sure as hell not let them rot in some cabin in the dark woods. She'd haul them kicking and screaming to McKenzie-Willamette or Riverbend, sit in the hospital's plastic chairs and wait.

May could imagine the whole scene. She'd hold a paper cup of coffee she wouldn't drink and she'd exchange sympathetic looks with the other people waiting and every time a doctor who looked like Derek Shepherd came through the double swinging doors she'd look up hopefully to hear the news of what could be done to save her parents. She'd even adopt an understanding smile when the doctors gazed down on her imaginary five-foot frame and perfect slim figure and shiny long black hair. She'd watch as the doctors felt themselves drowning in her perfect, large eyes. They'd stammer, startled by her classic Korean beauty. May would then smile mysteriously at them as they asked if English was her first language, or if she'd prefer a translator for Chinese or Japanese or something because they wouldn't recognize that she was a perfect Korean. She'd not tell the doctors in her fantasy that likely she spoke English better than they because she'd been an English major at college, or would have been if she'd finished, but she hadn't finished university yet and wasn't sure if she'd go back because she wasn't really sure what she should major in even though her mother said it was quite clear she should be a doctor or a real estate agent. No, in her fantasy May would smile quietly and wait for the doctors to deliver the news that her parents were gravely ill and each needed one kidney and would she donate both of hers?

May's eyes blurred briefly at the flight her fantasy had taken—the image of both her parents ill making her throat thicken. She wished she was their perfect daughter instead of who she really was: herself. May leaned her head against the passenger window, tried to collect her thoughts and not see her squished face reflecting in the glass. Her parents were fine, in good health, both swearing by a health tea they drank each morning, imported every few months from several of May's cousins who still lived in Busan.

May had talked to them the day before yesterday before her shift began. They'd sounded worried for her, asked her how long she planned to work as a medic before going back to college. Reminded her she could always come work for the family real estate company or go visit cousins back in South Korea and they'd find her a real job. May had immediately switched topics, described a show she'd started watching on Netflix called *Third Watch*. Her parents had picked up the hint, fallen silent.

She genuinely didn't know how to answer their questions about having a career. May could barely figure out what she was doing each day, let alone the next week, the next month. Selling properties seemed mind numbing. But trying to be a doctor seemed too hard, too unattainable.

She'd decided to try being a medic mainly because she wanted to be helpful, to have a job where she could save people and be important. Most of the shows she watched were medical dramas, and the medics were always extraordinary, saving lives left and right. May wanted to do that.

Plus, a year ago, an ambulance team had come storming down her apartment building's second floor hallway and pushed through her neighbor's door and hauled him away. Another neighbor had said it was a clearly an overdose. May had had no idea her neighbor was on drugs. He'd seemed just like her, a young college kid who ordered a lot of takeout, but then, clearly he was on pills or something and took too many of whatever it was and the medics had to come and May had been so impressed. They'd been cool, efficient, professional. They knew exactly what to do, when to do it, and how. And, as May's mother never failed to point out, May sometimes struggled with the simplest decisions.

It was after that incident, and after she'd failed her chemistry final, and after she was considering taking a break from college because nothing seemed to be working, and after she'd been simultaneously binge-watching *Scrubs* and cruising the internet looking for work, that she'd seen the job advertisement for the medic-training position at the small, mostly volunteer run fire department just east of Eugene.

The job posting made May jump, instantly imagining herself in a position to help people.

Once Chief Thomas Addington had reviewed her scanty qualifications and stressed three times the low pay, she'd been assigned a six-month probation, handed a pile of books and the passcode to endless online training videos. And to her surprise, and her mother's, May had worked quickly through her EMT-Basic. She was now plowing determinedly through the trainings and hours to get her EMT-Intermediate license. She enjoyed reading about medical procedures and seeing how they were used in real life situations, like on *Grey's Anatomy*, *House*, or *Scrubs*.

The shift work she did with the department had started officially after she passed her first licensure. The range of calls she'd been on since had been staggering. So many drug overdoses over a geographic range that felt endless. The west side of the Cascades in Lane County was vast, and it seemed like each call she responded to involved a forty-minute drive in a rickety ambulance, downed trees, and a bunch of guys asking her if she knew how to insert an IV. It was both thrilling and not what she'd imagined. May had hoped she'd get to see the same people every day, and wear bright medical scrubs.

Baker swerved to avoid a tree branch on the road. The light outside the ambulance was tidal, heaving strong, then weak, through the windshield wipers. It made May nauseous.

She looked away. She knew she'd get a headache before they got back. She glanced at her soaked shoes, tried to get the smell of Donna's dad's cabin out of her nose. It had been rancid in there. She didn't honestly know how the woman stood it. Maybe pills were the trick.

"These Cascade Mountains go on forever," she said absently as the ambulance swished around another dark ridge.

"Cascade Range," Baker corrected. "Will you radio in that we're ten minutes out?"

She nodded. Forty-minute drive to put a dying man back in his bed. Third time in two weeks.

At least they hadn't gone with the department's brush truck. Turning it around in Donna's yard the first time had left ruts even a kangaroo wouldn't have cleared. Chief said the second time Donna had called in that they could respond with just the ambulance.

"How common is it to respond to cats-in-trees types of calls?" she asked Baker. On *Third Watch*, the show depicted call volumes that were constant and overwhelming, challenging the various characters who had to juggle life and death while looking good in crisp blue uniforms. Especially Kim Zambrano. May wished she had long silky hair and a long neck that she could casually drape a stethoscope around. Instead, she had dull hair, a short neck, and worst of all, May was tall, over five foot ten. Her mother called her a giant, was continually buying her flat shoes and clothes with horizontal stripes, and bemoaning that height was one thing plastic surgery couldn't fix. May sighed.

Baker glanced at her, smiled. "You've been on the job, what, a hot second?"

"I've been doing shifts for quite a bit," May clarified. But then felt guilty. It wasn't Baker's job to track her employment. "That's not what I meant, though. It just seems like a waste of resources to keep putting Donna's dad back in bed."

Silence in the ambulance.

May eyed Baker, waited, words crowding her lips like wasp stings. She assessed him, realized she'd been so focused on herself lately that she didn't have a clear picture of this almost-perfect stranger who rode alone with her in ambulances. If he was a future patient, she wouldn't be able to describe him succinctly to all the proper channels. Her tongue felt dry, like she'd eaten sawdust. A total lapse. If she didn't pay better attention to those around her, how would she do her job?

May tried to be nonchalant as she stared at Baker, noted his frayed work pants, heavy boots, tucked in button-up shirt. He was lean, taller than her. He always had a ball cap on, one of those big trucker-style hats that outdoor companies smeared their logos all over. He had brown, short curls streaked with gray that stuck out from around the cap and reminded her of McDreamy's hair if he'd ever worn a hat. Baker's face was sun-bronzed, which May interpreted as evidence that he must spend a great deal of time outside. She always wanted to be more active outdoors, but it was hard to go outside when she also wanted sit and re-watch a television show.

"We don't have other calls to prioritize over Donna," Baker said softly.

Rotating, May tracked her thoughts back. "Why doesn't she just take him to the hospital?"

Baker wriggled his upper body. May presumed that was a response.

"Is this really a good use of resources? Our time?" May pressed. She wasn't sure why she was pushing the issue, but it felt momentarily good to pretend to be pissed off about something.

Baker shrugged again—a nonchalant gesture that seemed so natural she wondered if it was practiced. Maybe he watched the same shows she did. She should ask. But didn't. She didn't want him to think she spent all her time off in bed, eating crackers and binge-watching shows. May waited, stared at his jawline, wished hers was a defined line instead of rounded like an ambulance tire.

He must have felt her scrutiny. He looked over at her, cracked a half smile. "I'm an ol' medic who volunteers at a fish hatchery, May. I've got the time to help the likes of Donna Watts."

Embarrassment flooded her and she felt the bite of her inexperience. She shouldn't have said anything.

May looked out the window, pressed her lips shut. She wished she could shrink away completely into the seat, fold her too-long limbs in half, tuck her enormous feet into thirds. They finished the rest of the drive in sodden silence, rain pouring down.

Pulling into the short, paved driveway towards the department's parking bay, Baker slowed the ambulance and turned to look at her. "May," he said gently. "You're new, and that's okay. But trust yourself. You're doing great."

She flushed, unsure where to look. No one in the department had ever given her a compliment. She studied the fire department building before them, the huge bay doors, the light pouring from the first and second floor windows. Movement caught her eye near the corner of the east bay.

May pointed. "It's back."

Baker clicked his tongue. "Well, don't encourage it. Chief will blow a gasket if we feed it."

May nodded, and Baker coasted the ambulance into the parking spot, killed the engine.

As she slid out of the vehicle, she told Baker that she'd fill out the post trip report, do the mileage, and inventory the ambulance supplies. He raised an eyebrow. She rambled that it would help her to get more familiar with the equipment and procedures.

Really, she wanted to be by herself.

Baker nodded, closed the ambulance door, walked away.

"Idiot," May whispered to herself once she was alone. Why had she whined about Donna? She hoped Baker wouldn't think she was insensitive or didn't want to go out on unexciting calls.

The shows May watched portrayed medics and firefighters as rowdy pranksters and companionable workout buddies. They were almost always men—many of whom weren't above the occasional sexist dig like *Third Watch's* Bobby Caffey, but, in a pinch, were there to rise above their biases and help out victims. May had felt companionship and solidarity with the characters on the shows, and she'd hoped her first department would be like those.

May hung up her damp jacket in her locker at the edge of the bay, looked at the image she'd pinned at eye level. It was a photograph of the original cast of *Grey's Anatomy*, showing her favorite three doctors, Meredith, Izzy, and Cristina. They felt like her friends.

May knew that everyone expected her to pick Cristina as her favorite character on the show. Cristina was played by Sandra Oh who was, like her, Korean. But that ship had sailed the first time she watched *Grey's Anatomy*. May's mother had spent the entire episode picking on her for not being as smart, as pretty, as accomplished as Sandra Oh's character.

May walked to the edge of the parking bay, looked out into the night. It was still raining.

She heard a *thump, thump, thump* and glanced at the perimeter of the building. The dog she'd seen earlier from the ambulance was sitting just under the eave, against the mossy metal siding, tail wagging, looking up at her.

"Hello, Foxface," she murmured quietly, Baker's words of admonishment echoing in her ears.

The dog was small, with ears semi-pricked, matted gray and white fur that was quite wet, and a filthy fluffy tail. She thought it might be a mix of a border collie, shepherd, or retriever. It had a long muzzle and a black button nose and eyes that stared hopefully into May's.

May never had a pet as a child. Her mother said she wasn't responsible enough.

May looked around, but didn't see anyone else, so she shoved her hand quickly into her pocket and pulled out the half-eaten granola bar she'd been hiding there. She pulled off the remaining wrapper, handed the bar to the dog. "Go on," she said sternly.

"Young, conference room!" The Chief's voice echoed through the gear-choked cement bay. May jumped, jerked away from the garage entryway, hit the red button to lower the bay door. The dog melted into the darkness and May scrambled down the row of lockers.

The door to the break room-slash-conference room was open. May smelled the burnt coffee fumes from the hall. She walked in and around the large table where Baker and a few others were already seated, went to the counter by the sink. Leaning against the fridge, she subtly flipped the coffee pot off. The smell made May sick. She reached, poured herself a glass of water, rested against the refrigerator door, listened to the chief. He was standing in the open doorframe to his office, clutching a wad of paper.

"There's been a SAR call for a missing child, Amelia Kane, nine years old, at 20:35 this evening," the fire chief debriefed. "Call made by the mother, a Leonie Kane, who was hiking with her child on the Scott Trail off the 242. Child disappeared sometime in the late afternoon on the return from the Collier Cone, mother searched for several hours, hiked back to the Scott Trail parking lot, drove east to access phone service, and placed the call to dispatch at 20:35."

He shuffled through the paperwork in his hands. "At this time, we are not responding to the call, but likely will be requested to assist at 05:00 tomorrow morning if the child has not been located by then. Call went to dispatch in Deschutes, so Sisters-Camp Sherman and Deschutes County were first on. They reported that they're going to engage in a night mission, mostly a verbal road and trail call-out, but because of the inclement weather, they notified us, Lane County, Linn and Douglas dispatch. They're hopeful they locate the child tonight, but if they do not, that's big territory up there. They're asking for ground pounders, trailing dogs, all hands. Questions?"

"Do you want to page out?" the guy sitting next to Baker asked. May glanced at him. Jonas. Wondered if the question was more per-formance than anything else. Chief would make the decision whether to notify all the department's associated volunteers, and that decision required no action from anyone in the room. May smirked, then realized other people could see it, melted the smile back to a blank face again. She knew Jonas asking meant he wanted Chief to know he was thinking about it. Jonas wanted to jump to a larger station and move up the career ladder, but in order to do that he needed Chief's recommendation, or, at the very least, a promotion.

The chief looked at the papers in his hand again, then gazed out at the people gathered in the small room. "This is going to be a hard one, guys, if it doesn't get solved tonight. No one likes looking for lost little girls in the mountains again so soon, and after tonight's rain, it will be exceptionally hard to find traces of her. Let's hope it works out tonight." He cleared his throat.

"But, if they request help, we need to be ready to leave at 05:05. We'll take the bush truck and ambulance and POVs. Leave the rest."

"Longmyer, Ramírez, and Bishop. You'll be in the bush truck with me tomorrow. Likely I'll tuck into IC, and you three will be solo pounders. I have no idea where you'll be sent, so prep up radios and forty-eight-hour packs. It'd be a good idea to also take some of the new ropes."

He looked at his papers again. May noticed his hands were twitching. She scanned his face. Adderall and Dexedrine in amounts greater than ten milligrams could cause twitching. Being chief of the department, overseeing fire and medical, May knew that was a lot of responsibility. But those medications didn't cause gum decay and dental rot. And the chief definitely had bad teeth. Maybe the chief compensated by taking stimulants? Dr. Webber had started drinking again in the sixth season of *Grey's Anatomy* due to stress. It was understandable.

"Baker, you go solo, you know those mountains like you know your mother." Everyone laughed, and May strained a smile onto her face. Forced herself to look like she thought the comment was hilarious.

"Jonas, you'll pair with Young. She's doing her SAR training but doesn't know a wink about this area. Right Young?"

May bobbed her head, acknowledged the many eyes staring at her against the backdrop of the hulking refrigerator. She was the only one standing, besides Chief. Were they all wondering why she was so tall? Or perhaps the etiquette in the department was that only the chief stood? May slouched, bent her knees, could feel sweat trailing down her spine.

"We all need to do a better job helping Young settle in. She's really good and I give her my vote of confidence, but let's all give her the help she needs, okay?"

Blood rushed to May's face as the chief's words sank in. She hadn't realized that she needed so much help. The chief moved on, covering the logistics of the next day. May concentrated and tried to follow the rundown, but she was distracted, thinking of ways she could be a better medic. She'd been acing all the exams. Even Chief had said he was surprised how quickly she'd finished her EMT-Basic. She'd been going out on all the calls that came in during her shift. Maybe she'd prove herself by finding Amelia Kane tomorrow if they were called up. She pictured the child wandering around in the mountains, lost, in the pouring dark rain, long white dress damp and trailing.

A twinge of sympathy panged May's gut. Thank god it wasn't her. She'd never survive alone out there.

"Everyone, go home or bunk up. Get some sleep, we're at it early," Chief concluded, and the meeting broke up. People left to prepare gear and equipment for the next day.

May sorted her SAR pack, made sure her radio was charging, then slipped into her bunk in the sleeper room. She was asleep before the lights clicked out, and then instantly awake at 4:29 a.m., a minute before her alarm clicked on.

She'd always been able to control when she fell asleep and woke up, secretly considered it a superpower. She'd never told her mother about it. She knew instantly what her mother would say: *Men don't marry women for their wake-up skills. Men marry women for their looks. May should put in more effort. And try a new face cream.*

Baker was pouring coffee in the break room when she entered. He wordlessly handed her a cup. She gulped it noisily—sounds to fill the silence. Chief arrived right behind her through the doorway, took a cup and nodded morning to both of them.

May watched Baker take in the chief, then to her surprise, watched Baker turn to her. "Do you want me to help you go over your

SAR pack, see what you forgot?" He laughed gently to take the clear suggestion of incompetency out of his words.

May was momentarily at a loss for words. "Thanks," she stammered. "But I used the department list to check out the equipment."

"No time anyway," Chief interrupted. "You got what you got. We're on. I just paged out, so we're rolling out in two blinks."

Over the next fifteen minutes, trucks and cars scrambled into the station, and people May had never met piled into the bays to grab gear from their lockers and pack supplies.

At precisely two minutes past the hour, the bush truck, three private vehicles full of volunteers, and the old ambulance were idling ready, headlights pouring a damp glow into the darkness.

"All vehicles, all vehicles, radio check."

May sat shotgun with Jonas, and she responded on the ambulance's handheld, then Jonas nosed in behind the lead truck. The first fifteen minutes up Highway 126, they sipped their coffees in quiet.

"We'll probably arrive at daybreak," Jonas said eventually. "Sunrise is around 7:00, but we'll have enough dawn light to get organized."

May nodded, mildly surprised at the unsolicited information. In the months or so she'd been around the department, Jonas had been mostly taciturn, looking over her head in the breakroom or stepping into the chief's office. When she'd started her shift work, he'd pointedly told her to ask him if she had questions, but so far hadn't seemed available to answer any. She didn't know much about him other than what she'd picked up here and there, that he wanted to be chief at a big station one day. He was in his late twenties or early thirties, she guessed, and he likely lived somewhere near the station because she'd seen him show up in under ten minutes when they had a call, dark hair wet from a shower. He'd been at the department for three years, had a dog. She only guessed that last part because often his blues were covered with animal hair. May had meant to ask him, but so far hadn't found the moment.

"This is an exceptionally difficult area," he continued, and she must have made a startled face, because then he was looking at her sardonically out the sides of his eyes, a smile lingering somewhere around his lips. They were thick and fleshy. "Thomas told me to 'fam' you on the ride up. Hence."

"Ah." May said, straight face intact. More helping.

Jonas continued, "The topography of the Three Sisters is rugged. The area runs pretty much from the 242 south and east, from about 2,000 feet to 10,300 in elevation. 1.6-million-year-old stratovolcanoes, the most dominant of which are the Three Sisters—North, Middle, and South Sister. Fourteen glaciers—the biggest of which is the Collier Glacier. Cinder cones and lava flows and hundreds and hundreds of lava tubes, a lot of which are covered in forests of enormous evergreens with branches, especially pines, firs, and hemlocks, that come down to the ground and create curtains that would hide a body, well, forever. Oh, and rivers, which are horrors to cross, terrain that is super steep, and communications that are spotty at best. All over roughly 281,000 square acres."

"Jesus," May said. "You have a lot of facts about this area you can just rattle off." She was impressed. She couldn't have listed so many numbers about her own life.

"Fine. It's big."

May eyed him, tried to assess his mood. He seemed cheerful, so she snorted, rolled her eyes. Tried to charm him. "Come on, you know what I meant."

Jonas didn't look at her, and May kicked herself for saying anything at all. Maybe she'd misread him. She looked out the window, counting fifty trees in less than thirty seconds, tried again, made her voice soft, subservient. "Are there a lot of trails?"

He nodded once. May felt rewarded, encouraged enough to continue on.

"Will we use them?" she asked, opening her eyes wide and deliberate as she faced him. Did her best impression of a helpless Korean girl.

"The trails are great," he said, clearly thawing a little. "There's some 260 miles of trail, most of it running off or around the Pacific Crest Trail, which runs 40 miles through the area north to south." He added, somewhat quietly, "I've hiked all 260 miles of trail up there."

"Wow, Jonas," May said, pointedly whistling. "That's a lot of trail time!" Went for the compliment versus the shitty aside about the numbers.

He shrugged a shoulder modestly. "It's how I decompress when I don't want to go to the gym."

May caught the proud smile, noted it. He responded to praise and compliments, not to sarcasm. Just like Dr. Burke, her least favorite *Grey's Anatomy* character.

"Since you're an expert, can you tell me more about it?" she asked, hoping she wasn't too obvious. But for the rest of the ride Jonas did exactly that, described different trails and landscapes in the Cascades. He drove steadily, both hands on the wheel, and May for once wasn't worried. She listened to his nasal voice, stared out the window, and by the time they pulled in at the Scott Trailhead, she had absorbed the vastness of the area they were about to search.

"The whole of Sisters and Bend is up here," Jonas murmured as he followed the lead truck into the end of the parking area. "Wow."

May saw nothing but a sea of trucks, vans, and ambulances all with their headlights on. Even so, the morning darkness made it too hard to assess the landscape.

Over the radio, Chief told the crew to stand by as he went to check in with Incident Command. He returned fifteen minutes later with instructions, and everyone got out of their vehicles and huddled around him near the back end of the ambulance. May leaned against the brake lights.

Chief issued a perfunctory overview. "Amelia Kane was last seen in a long-sleeved purple shirt and green denim pants. Here's a school picture taken two months ago." He distributed paper printouts of the missing girl's portrait.

"A few points so we're all on the same page. First. The mother, Leonie Kane, is here onsite, refuses to go down. Sisters-Camp Sherman interviewed her last night in more detail. She appears understandably distraught and unstable, so steer clear. Police from Eugene are coming up, due in an hour, to interview her. Until we get more information on how to proceed, we're treating this as a normal SAR. No questions."

May nodded and looked around at the crowd of people, wondered what they thought of the chief's comments. Was it possible the mother killed the kid? That would certainly match the few Netflix Scandinavian noir shows she'd watched. She shivered. The idea of finding a murdered child seemed horrific.

"Second. It appears that the child, Amelia Kane, might be on the autism spectrum, and may not respond to verbal calls. We're still going to operate a full call-out for the ground search, whistles, everything, but be aware you could be right next to her and she might not respond. Visual assessments are key."

May wondered how last night went for the volunteers as they spread out in the dark and rain across jagged terrain, calling for an unresponsive child.

"Third. The mother noted the child's fascination with the Collier Glacier, and the possibility that the child might have returned to that area. We're not searching it yet, as Command wants to focus on either side of the trail from mile four to the roadside areas. They're thinking a lost child would more likely hunker down in the rain than continue another six miles into increasingly rough territory. But Command will make search adjustments as necessary in the hours and days to come and I'll pass that information on to you."

Chief looked up, made eye contact with each person on the team. His eyes lingered inquisitively on May, and she felt a cold flash run up her spine. She wondered what was going on in his head.

He took a deep breath, continued. "Fourth. The media is no doubt, no doubt, going to be up here in a few hours. If this SAR goes on, and given the recurrence of these incidents, likely more media will continue to arrive. As usual, direct all media to the Incident Command spokesperson who," he looked at his notes, "has not been assigned yet. Check back with me, then, and we'll go from there. Last. As always, be careful. Radio check-ins on the hour here, channel eight."

Chief closed the notebook, nodded firmly, looked at Jonas, then May, with eyebrows up. She responded to the summons, walked towards him. He unfolded a large map onto the hood of the bush truck.

"Do a hasty search," he directed May and Jonas, pointing to the map. "Head down Scott's Trail to the PCT to Harlow Crater. There's an OHEWS cabin on the east side, with a narrow spur trail easy to miss off the PCT here," he tapped the map. "If you get to here, you missed it, so flip around."

They both marked the points on their own maps.

"OHEWS is manned, but radio comms aren't picking up last night or this morning. A woman runs the station, but she might be out doing field work, or her makeup or something. According to Corvallis, if she's not at the station, she's likely out on Millican or Black Crater. With the rain yesterday and last night, that seems unlikely, but because the cabin isn't responding, speculation is pointless. Get to OHEWS ASAP, get the radio working, see if she's got any information on the child, then radio in for a report and a new mission."

May nodded in confirmation, heart pounding, and he turned away from them to issue directions to other team members. She collected her gear from the back of the ambulance, shouldered her pack, radio checked the communications center, and then followed Jonas out of the buzzing parking lot, across the highway, and onto the trail. At least twenty people were hubbed up around Command, and the immediate quiet that descended upon them as they moved into the forest was a relief.

The light was grainy in the moments before sunrise, the first birds of the morning stirred with halfhearted chirps. Everything was wet, and May was glad she'd waterproofed her boots the week before. The sound of dripping was the soundtrack to the fast pace Jonas set.

A mile in, May was vibrating, couldn't handle the silence. She stopped, kneeled, pretended she had to tie her boot. Wished there was some type of narration that went with this search to fill her in on all the subtext.

"Hold up," she called, flapping her shoelace about. Jonas turned, saw her crouching over her shoe, stopped.

She fussed for three seconds, then, as she rose, voiced the questions buzzsawing in her brain. "What did Chief mean?" she asked. "About the other incidents?"

Jonas rotated, hiked away from her, water pants whispering. He gave no indication that he'd heard her. May tamped down the annoyance that surged in her, hurried to catch up, for once grateful for her long legs and wide stride.

"Wait, Jonas!"

He slowed, turned, looked back at her.

"You seem to know everything that goes on," she said, making sure her voice came out admiring. She gave him her best appreciative gaze. Worried she was piling it on too thick.

His eyes cut a gray-blue and the lines around his mouth tugged low. He looked handsome in the pale morning light.

May wondered briefly if he was going to ignore her. But then he drew a breath, opened his mouth. "Amelia Kane is not the first person to disappear in the Three Sisters," he said. "In fact, it seems like women and girls go missing out here all the time."

4

THE
SCIENTIST

"Goddammit!" Ros Fisher spat viciously, ducking the muck and gravel flying at her. "Fuck you! Intrusive igneous dirtbag!"

The black truck spun, hurling waves of mud as the driver screeched the tires and yanked the vehicle out of the pullout.

Ros flipped her middle finger at the disappearing taillights and wiped angrily at the coarse particulate mud coating her face, jacket, pants. She should report that vehicle to ODOT. Would report it, she decided.

She spat silt out of her mouth. Whatever. Kids in jacked-up trucks doing donuts in pullouts. Not the first time, not the last time. It just reinforced why Ros chose to live at a remote Oregon Cascades field station. She turned away from the road, assessed the supplies stacked at her feet, now also coated with fines and grime.

She leaned down and wiped the wooden boxes into reasonable-ness before jamming everything into the pack she'd brought. Taking a deep breath, she heaved it up onto her back, adjusted the wide canvas straps that dug immediately into her shoulders. Ros had been using the station's original 1950s era government-issued external frame pack to haul supplies back to camp since she started the job. Each time, she cursed at how uncomfortable it was. She'd tried a few times to use her modern hiking backpack, but the items at drop-off were unpredict-able and often unwieldy. Ros found it easier to take the external frame and suck it up for the eight-mile return.

The re-supply was a coarse smear on the map, a narrow dirt pull-out near the McKenzie summit of Highway 242 that had a sizable wooden padlocked box set discreetly into a mound of lava. Because Ros could rarely predict her daily schedule at the station and the drop-off wasn't made at a consistent time, she almost never saw the Forest Service delivery guy who drove the re-supply for all the research stations in Oregon.

Ros surveyed the pullout, noted the large puddles. It had rained the night before and the usual mix of vibrant ash, pumice, and rhyolite in the pullout had transformed into a gray-vomit slog. That was what likely had attracted the kids in the black truck, the chance to do a little volcanic mudding. She hoped uncharitably that the sharp fines would erode the alternator wirings and leave the kids stranded somewhere far from coffee.

She smiled briefly at the thought, then chided herself for being such an old curmudgeon.

The kids probably hadn't even seen her.

Ros sighed, felt her wet toes squish around in her boots. The wet socks were what she was most pissed about. She'd gambled that her hiking boots would last one more season, but both boots were already worn flat. The right sole had completely separated from the leather at the flex point of the toe, and the left heel lugs had been sanded down to nubs. The mini tsunami from the truck had washed over her boots and soaked through their cracks. Everything felt gritty, wet.

Typically, Ros looked forward to re-supply day.

Just about every second Tuesday Ros hiked or skied the eight miles to the pullout, heart beating in anticipation at what she'd find. Sometimes the Forest Service staff sent extras, like chocolate, or beer, or books. But even the regular stuff like food or equipment was exciting. Ros recognized that other people probably didn't get so excited at the sight of a new voltage meter or channel locks. But she did.

It reminded her of when she was a kid squirming to be allowed to walk down the driveway to the mailbox where she'd hope to see her name splashed across an envelope. That had never happened, but Ros still carried the optimism forward to re-supply day.

This re-supply, despite the rampaging truck, was a good haul. Along with the standard two weeks-worth of food, four novels she'd requested, and new ten-gallon water drum to replace the one that had finally cracked, the re-supply also included four three-inch diameter PVC pipes.

The pipes were five feet long each and stuck up from the top of her pack like a set of antennae even a spruce sawyer beetle would stop and admire. Ros had some winterization scheduled for the meteorological equipment she monitored, and she'd been waiting for over a month to get the last of the piping to finish the work. She was excited.

Ros scanned the pullout one last time before clicking the chest strap on her pack in place and turning for home. Her boots scrabbled on the loose regolith as she walked briskly away through the medial space between the old lava flow and the forest, and then along the inconspicuous trail south.

Five steps across the basaltic andesite lava, rain started to drip from low clouds. A quick glance told her they were cumulonimbus. Ros stopped as soon as the first drops splattered on her shoulders, maneuvered out from under a tree, turned her face up to the sky. Squinted.

Were the clouds vertically developed or uplifted?

Dark and ragged base, but uniform gray interior extending thousands of feet up into the atmosphere. She smiled at herself; she was wrong. They were nimbostratus clouds. Ros could make out just a few shreds of pannus clouds just below the primary base. She liked nimbostratus clouds—to her they were ponderous, slow clouds that released precipitation over a steady, hours-long duration. They were predictable.

Fat drops washed down her face, cleared away some of the muck. Ros felt her sour mood splash away, her internal isostasy settle into balance. Her thoughts meandered at will, unsorted, unstratified, and Ros was content.

The area needed rain, and it would lessen the sharp volcanic fines that got everywhere during the hot, windy summer season. Rain would collect in the tanks and save her several water collection trips. Rain meant fire season might be over. Rain also meant fewer hikers.

Ros's field station was tucked up in a small gorge on the east side of Harlow Crater, with a view through the trees of Millican Crater and Black Crater and all the forest burns in between. Both peaks hosted extensive monitoring equipment as part of the Oregon High Elevation Weather Station—OHEWS—network. The acronym served as a single name for both the cabin where she lived and worked and all the surrounding data-gathering centers she controlled.

The trail to her cabin was a lightly trafficked spur that ran east off the Pacific Crest Trail. Sometimes hikers came up the trail if they saw her porch light or heard the generator, but generally people steered clear.

When she did have random visitors, they were usually curious day hikers or people down from Lava Camp. Ros tried to be friendly and open to them, but to her it seemed obvious that if a person decided to take a job staffing one of the most remote field stations in the Pacific Northwest, they wanted to be left alone. Ros preferred living without unannounced guests.

Or, she had.

Of late, Ros had been feeling hostile pricks of loneliness, the type that came upon her suddenly and stabbed so hard sometimes she felt like doubling over in pain. It was as if the solitude she'd coveted for so long was no longer enough, as if the life she'd carefully shaped was weathering at the edges. She worried her loneliness could only be cured by further, more immersive loneliness. Or by quitting her job.

She wondered if the work was getting to her. The week before, she'd talked up a Doug fir like it was a colleague.

Perhaps soon she'd go down, get some face-to-face interactions with people who could talk back. She'd skipped her last three cycles out, had preferred to stay in the cabin and read. But now, Ros felt like she needed people.

She hiked on, hummed along with the raindrops careening into the lava. Tried to remain good humored even as the plastic pipes caught on every tree branch she ducked and she lurched back and forth beneath their snags like a drunk train. Tried not to focus on the fact that the water drum had decided to take on an inch of rain for every foot she hiked. Or that it was pouring hard enough now to strangle frogs. Instead, she focused on the lava and forest and clouds and rain, and by the time she'd scrambled up the last lip of trail to her cabin, she'd almost managed to right her little ship.

The loneliness lingered, murmured and flowed downstream quietly in the background.

Ros dropped her pack onto the porch with a satisfying thunk, unlatched the door, and stepped into the cabin. Propping the door open with a loose brick, she simultaneously stripped off her wet, filthy clothes and stirred up the coals in the wood stove. Shirtless, in panties and wet wool socks, she shuttled back and forth out to the porch to bring in splits of wood to feed into the stove. Within moments, Ros had a roaring fire.

She stood in front of the hot flames, removed the rest of her clothing, and poured water from the counter jug onto a rag and started wiping down her puckered skin. Ros appreciated her body in the fading light, how it gleamed every shade of brown imaginable, from her bronzed copper face to the skin below her elbows and above her collarbone that looked just like sun-soaked umber. Her torso and legs were shaded what a fellow graduate student in chemistry and casual lover had once described as "near-perfect siderite."

After her bath, Ros pulled on warm dry cotton sweatpants, a soft t-shirt, and zipped up a fluffy down jacket. She dried her short curly hair with two passes of the towel. Each stroke brought her mood to keel, and by the time she was bathed, dried, and clothed, she was back to even.

Glancing at the clock, she saw it was nearly three in the afternoon. There wouldn't be enough daylight to carry the pipes and other winterization gear up Black Crater. Besides, it was pouring glacier rain. Ros decided she'd start the project tomorrow. She reached, flicked on the gas stove to heat water. Now was time for coffee.

Moments later, ceramic cup of coffee in hand, Ros wandered out through the open cabin door and leaned on the porch banister. She took in the cool air and the rain glazing the surrounding trees, outhouse, generator, equipment, radio tower, and sizable lava stacks. As she scanned the clearing around the station, her eyes caught on movement and her breath stalled.

Two people were at the forest's edge. One was sitting, the other, standing.

"Fuck," Ros mumbled, gripped the ceramic cup harder. Scrutinized them.

Why hadn't they come straight up to the cabin? Why were they skulking? She took a forced breath, drew up her scant social reserves. It had been a long, physically demanding day and she was tired. But it might be good to have some human interaction. She knew she was lonely; she'd been admitting at least that truth to herself for weeks.

Or months, if she was for once actually honest with herself.

"Hi there," she called out, feigning a brightness she did not feel. She stepped to the edge of the porch. The two figures shifted immediately. The seated person stood.

"Hello!" one called back, a man's voice, deep, resonant. They moved away from the trees into the open area around the cabin. As they got closer Ros saw the second person was a woman. An exceptionally tall woman with thick dark hair who looked utterly bedraggled, sodden from head to boots.

"You PCT hikers?" Ros asked, staying just under the roof edge and dry from the rain. "Isn't it a little late in the season?"

"Nah," the man called back. "We're just doing the Oregon section. I'm Trick."

"Ah. I'm Ros, nice to meet you." She surveyed them over the rim of her steaming mug as they moved farther into the clearing.

Trick looked like he'd just stepped out of an REI catalogue. Had a mat of dark beard that covered his face like tree moss, a sunburnt face, and brown eyes that locked immediately with Ros's.

The woman was kitted out in solid black rainproofs that clearly sluiced all water directly into her boots. She stepped around the man, looked at him, then at Ros. "I'm Ash," she said, a smile tinged with weariness lighting up her face.

"You both look awfully soaked. Want some coffee? I just made a pot and have enough to fill an underground tank." Ros gestured up onto her porch. "If you want to dry off a bit."

The man stepped in front of the woman as if the two were playing checkers. "Thanks Ross," he said.

"Not Ross. Ros, like Rose," Ros corrected automatically.

The man smiled. "Sorry. Ros." He gestured back to the forest edge. "We got here a little bit ago but decided not to bother you."

"Trick," the woman said, tone sharp.

"You were, uh, less than dressed," he explained, looking at Ros with a mix of appreciation and something else she couldn't quite put her finger on.

"For fuck's sake," the woman whispered.

"Okay." Ros kept her face blank, tone neutral. She considered for a moment telling the hiker to get the fuck off her property, but then looked again at Ash and saw the exhaustion carpeted over the other woman's face.

"I'll get some coffee," she responded finally, flatly. She turned, went inside, poured two more cups. Took her sweet, plodding, glacier time.

When she went back out, the two hikers had taken shelter on her porch, their packs chucked into a haphazard pile by the steps. Ros handed them each a coffee in silence, noted their non-reactions to her gift, then stepped back. This was her cabin, and she didn't have to force conversation.

When no one said anything, she picked up a few splits from the wood rack by the door, went inside without a word, fed the stove. Set a pot of water onto the burner to boil. Reached for vegetables out of cold storage, began chopping. Stir fry for dinner? Or steamed veggies and pasta? She mulled the merits of each dish as she hacked at a carrot. Her ears were tuned for voices outside, but she focused on the mundane tasks before her.

"Thank you for the coffee," the woman's voice rang from the doorway.

Ros looked up and turned, took in the wet black hair knotted into a bun, the rips in the waterproofs. The woman's eyes were skirted with huge dark circles. Her cheekbones were like pedestals supporting folds of corrugated skin, reminiscent to Ros of solidified pahoehoe. Ros hadn't seen someone look so tired since she was in graduate school.

"Sorry about Trick."

Ros raised an eyebrow, pressed her lips together. So what if she was in her panties earlier? It was her cabin.

"He's using your outhouse. Without asking. I'm sorry." The woman coughed. "He can feel like a bit of a..." Her voice faltered for a moment. She seemed at a loss for words. "A transgression," she finished weakly.

Ros glanced at her, watched her lips shape words, noted the slight smear and dribble of the pronunciation. Wondered if the woman had a speech impediment. There seemed to be a tremor in her neck, shoulders.

"The sea has not advanced," Ros responded.

"What?"

"A geology term," Ros explained. "Transgression."

The woman looked at her blankly, then leaned heavy against the door. Ros felt compassion flair inside her mouth.

"Ash?" Ros verified, and the woman nodded. "Come, sit. You look like you've been in a bear fight; just wrung out."

Ash smiled gratefully. "I am."

Ros had seen that the woman was tall, but watching her stride through the cabin, Ros was struck by her sheer dimension, the width of her gait. But despite the space she commanded, Ash had a calm presence, a grace to her movements as if she might have been a dancer. Ros watched—almost mesmerized—as Ash moved towards and sank down into the wooden chair nearest the open door.

"Thank you."

She nodded her head in acknowledgement, then turned back to the counter. Cabin sounds filled the air. Ros's carrot chopping, the snap of the wood stove, the hiss of the gas cooktop, rain falling on the tin roof. It felt warm to Ros, cozy, exactly what she'd always wanted.

"How do you run all this?" Ash waved a hand full of long brown fingers at the computers and radio and stoves and lights.

Ros glanced at her, read genuine curiosity, smiled. "Mainly solar panels," she said. "In winter a snow machine comes when there's enough of a passable snow layer, brings a couple drums of fuel for the generator, propane canisters, logs for firewood, all the big heavy stuff.

But the solar panels do the primary lifting, and the generator acts as back up."

"What do you do out here?" Ash sipped her coffee, leaned back in the chair. It creaked. The woman looked like she was going to melt into the cushion.

Ros took a deep breath, adopted an official voice. "I'm a year-round researcher and technician for OHEWS." Ros turned away from the cutting board, popped a hip against the chinked wooden edge of the counter.

"What does that mean?"

Tilting her head, Ros again searched Ash's face for signs of actual interest, gauged her response on how much she assessed Ash to care. Most people didn't want to hear about science research and asked just to be polite. But Ash looked attentive, her eyes open, listening. Ros noticed her darker skin, thought it looked an almost similar shade to her own, wondered what Ash's race was. The woman had a shape to her eyes that made Ros suspect southeast Asian, but she kept herself from asking. Ros hated it when people asked her who she was, or where she was from. She couldn't truthfully answer those questions.

Ros cleared her throat. "Well, broadly, I oversee this little one-horse field station. I take care of all the equipment. The craters around here are literally bristling with instrumentation, sensors and such pulling in all sorts of data, if you know where to look. We disguise most of them pretty well or fence the hell out of them. Keeps the vandalism down."

"Vandalism?"

"Well, it's a state-wide pastime to shoot at anything that looks useful, government-run, or scientific."

Ros had repaired vast amounts of instrumentation over the years that had been choked full of lead of all varieties. She knew firsthand that Oregonians were extraordinarily well-armed.

"I also host visiting scholars. Writers, artists, scientists, all sorts. They apply and come up and stay in the tiny cabin you might have seen right behind this one? Actually, a new fellow is coming the day after tomorrow, an acoustic ecologist."

"Huh," Ash said, voice like river gurgle. "And you also do research?"

Ros nodded, slow. "Yep. I study the effects of a loose polar vortex on Cascade geology, which is a fancy way of saying I'm a geologist and an amateur meteorologist. I watch what the clouds are doing, take the occasional rock sample, keep an eye out for fire. That sort of thing. Year round." Ros drew a breath, heard the words rambling about inside her mouth, flushed slightly.

"Sounds like heaven," Ash sighed.

Ros beamed, surprised. Usually people said it seemed lonely, pointless. But it wasn't to her. Ros treasured her work, the quiet, the orderliness of a world atop the Cascades counting clouds and rocks.

Ash must have saw her surprise. The woman lifted her long fingers into the air. "I'm a women's doctor," she responded. "Mainly an OBGYN, in Eugene, at Sacred Heart. It's full-on one thousand percent at the hospital all the time, and then, in my abundant spare time, there's fancy dinners and fundraisers and women's health initiatives and state banquets—all the necessary side parts of being a career doctor."

Ash burble-laughed for a moment, and Ros smiled back automatically. She wasn't used to other people in her cabin, and the sounds of Ash's voice and laughter felt both new and somehow right.

"Honestly, the idea of being up here away from people sounds perfect. But my bar is low: I'm excited when they let me out long enough to go buy a latte at Farmers Union."

Both women laughed again.

"Whenever I go down the mountain, I indulge in way too many lattes," Ros admitted. "It would be a serious problem if they ever let me have an espresso maker up here. I'm a complete coffee addict."

Ros watched Ash tighten her grip on the mug in her hands. "I miss real espresso. Trick and I took four weeks off to hike Oregon border to border along the PCT. I've never done a long-haul hike like this, so I thought it would be fun. Get out of the hospital, recharge, have a chance to reconnect with each other. We're both so busy with our work."

"Is it fun?" Ros watched as Ash drew in a deep breath, closed her eyes. A smear of water dripped down from her bun, left streaks on her dusty face.

Sympathy defrosted in Ros's stomach as she watched the other woman shake her head. Ros would hate to camp in this rain. She opened her mouth, surprised herself. "If you'd like, you're welcome to spend the night in the Fellows Cabin. No one is staying there tonight, tomorrow night. Use the amenities, few that they are."

Ash lifted her chin, looked directly into Ros's eyes, nodded. "Thank you."

Ros smiled again. "Wait to thank me. That cabin's a hundred and thirty square feet. You might have more room in your tent."

"That sounds great," a voice said from the open door, and Trick walked into the cabin. He wasn't a big man, but it seemed to Ros as if all at once the furniture in the cabin re-oriented to face him. She picked up her sharp knife, made paper thin carrot slices.

"Cool radio set up," Trick said. "Do you have Wi-Fi?" He pointed at the computer monitor and stacked laptops.

Ros nodded, waited two beats before responding. Carrots first, then him, payment for the undressed comment. Sighed. Told herself to stop being inhospitable. She turned, looked at Trick. Softened her face.

"Trick," Ash interjected, her voice pitched so soothing Ros felt she could float in it. "Since Ros has invited us to stay, why don't we?" The woman turned to Ros. "We could share dinner together? We have more than enough instant food if you're interested." She laughed softly.

"Don't we want to get in a few more miles tonight? It's like, only four o'clock?"

Ash shook her head silently, pointed a single finger at the open doorway and the rain sheeting down outside. Ros didn't blame her. It felt to her like the cabin was a polynya, the rain as inviting as converging pack ice.

Trick swiveled, looked down at Ash. "Well, if you want us to stop, I guess…"

"Great," Ash said immediately, voice so bright Ros winced. "Want to set us up in that back cabin? I'm going to finish my coffee."

"Whatever you want, babe." Trick set his own cup on the table in front of her, dropped a kiss on her head, turned to Ros.

"We're grateful," he said, almost formally. "My thanks. You need any help in return? I could chop some wood, I'm handy with an axe."

Ros shook her head, felt her jaw twitch. "Nope. I'm fine."

"You sure?" He gazed around, then back at Ros. She watched his eyebrows climb up his forehead. "No offense, but the place looks like it needs some muscle."

Compressing her hands, Ros mutely shook her head. Stared at the carrots lined up like perfect kindling splits. Admired them. Considered how leopard spots could be visible from space, from tree line, from five feet. She stiffened her neck, tried not to cluck her tongue.

"Okay," he shrugged, then Ros heard him shift, head back outside towards the back cabin.

The rain picked up force, collided into the roof in sputters and splats. Ros flashed on a memory; her mother used to say during similar storms that the rain had put her high heels on. She smiled to herself, glanced around the little kitchen. Was content with what she'd created. She saw more coffee in the pot.

"Want a top-off?" she asked, rotating towards Ash. The woman nodded slowly. Ros poured the last of the coffee in Ash's cup, then her own. Hot steam rolled up into the air like a hazy altostratus cloud.

"Sorry, again," Ash said, hands tucking in to one side of her face.

Ros acknowledged the comment but didn't respond.

She longed for a distraction. Not for the first time she wished she had wireless speakers. She would have enjoyed turning on a little music, a little Valerie June, swimming her brain along currents other than those of her own thoughts. Perhaps in the next re-supply order she could request some? Along with new boots. Her toes flicked at the misery of walking all the way back to the cabin today soaked.

"He can be thoughtless," Ash offered. "About how he moves in the world. He thinks he already knows everything about everybody."

Ros had no response. Clearly the woman wanted to talk about Trick. But Ros did not. He wasn't interesting to her. He was a nonentity, and the quicker she forgot him, the likelier her equilibrium from earlier would return. She replaced the coffee pot, contemplated starting another. Reached for the beans and hand grinder.

"Completely changing the subject..." Ash's voice cracked hesitantly, "This is going to sound totally bananas, but you ever hear any weird sounds out here?"

Ros twisted in mild surprise. She set the grinder back on the counter, then opened a cabinet, grabbed a box of shortbread cookies, rambled over and sat down at the table, turned towards Ash. This she would talk about.

Opening the box carefully, Ros extracted two cookies, then pushed the packet at Ash. Cocked her head. Contemplated Ash's question. "Weird?" she asked. "Like, tree-falling weird? Or, Bigfoot-weird? Pacific-Northwest-tree-octopus-weird? Or, aliens?"

Ash laughed, a light crackling sound that lit up the room, made Ros smile again. Ros felt something inside her buckle and slush, as if her stomach had liquefied from the sheer pleasure of listening to another woman laugh. She relaxed back into her chair, noticed how a lank of dark hair had loosened from Ash's bun, slid down on her face. Ash had noticed too, brushed the strand back, tucked it behind an ear. Ros looked away, felt like she'd seen something intimate, private.

"I mean weird like, well, like children-of-the-forest-weird." Ash reached for a cookie, nibbled it distractedly. "The last few days, since we hit the Le Conte Crater, I've been hearing what sounds like children laughing. Day and night."

"Serious?"

Ash lifted her chin, looked somehow embarrassed and stubborn in the same moment. "Yes. And I don't think they're auditory hallucinations. They're too real. Sounds distinctly like two to four girls, just off the trail, having a great time."

"Weird," Ros said. "And, sorry, obviously, there aren't any children around? Hikers with kids?"

Ash shook her head. "No, you're fine. I wondered the same thing too. But I haven't seen anyone else. And I've looked and looked. Like, wandering around the woods on either side of the trail, looking. Frankly, it's both creeping me out and making me want to *join*, like, laugh *with them*. I mean, at times they sound like they're right there." She pointed at the radio station sitting two feet away from her.

"I've never heard anything similar to the laughter you're describing. I've also never heard about it from other people or in area reports." Ros leaned back in her chair, considered. The woods were full of things that transformed everyday sounds into something more. She'd heard what sounded like singing a few times that always seem to stop as soon as she crested whatever she was climbing. But never laughter.

"Trick says he didn't hear it," Ash continued, "but he's actually quite deaf from his job, refuses to wear ear protection."

Ros flipped her hands open on the table. "Well, I can ask the acoustic scientist when she gets here the day after tomorrow."

"It's weird." Ash stared down into her coffee. "There's also this other sound, seems just out of range, like a melody I remember once hearing at a—"

"—Ash!"

The woman stopped speaking, looked through the open door.

"Ash!" Trick called again.

"What were you saying?" Ros prodded.

Ash shook her head. "Never mind," she muttered. Rose from the chair, thanked Ros for the coffee and cookies, and then headed outside into the soaking rain.

Ros looked blankly at the woman's disappearing back, felt bewildered. She glanced up at the clock, was surprised at the time, slid over into her habitual slump in front of the radio parked in the charging port. She heard faint sounds of conversation coming from outside the cabin but couldn't see through the rain-covered windows. She picked up the radio, called in.

"Hey O-Hews Harlow Crater, this is Parker," a voice responded statically.

Ros rolled her eyes. Parker was one of the newer staff at the Corvallis office, and she often had Ros repeat everything two to three times. This was turning into a day. Ros gritted her teeth, started the nightly check in, running though the series of authorizations, meteorological reports, instrumentation statuses. Fifteen minutes later, in a conversation that should have been five minutes, she confirmed receipt of the re-supply. After a second of waffling, she also put in an order for new boots.

"Two boots, O-Hews?" the young woman's voice echoed.

Patience, she told herself. "Yes, Parker, confirming, two boots, sized nine and half, right and left." Repeated it twice. Before signing off, she reported the presence of two overnight hikers in the Fellows Cabin.

Ros heard a slow chuckle behind her.

"You have mighty persistence." Ash leaned in the open door and nodded toward the radio. Her head just brushed the door jam. "Sorry about earlier, just running off. May I come in?"

Ros waved her in, and Ash entered wearing dry pants and a thick sweater. She'd clearly towel dried her hair and it was now caught in a bun at the base of her neck. All the little hairs stood out like a frizzy halo against her scalp. She looked slightly revived.

Ash headed for the rocking chair in the corner between the two big windows facing east to Black Crater. "And I thought new med students were bad."

Ros just shook her head, leaned back in the radio chair, sighed.

"Trick's got dinner going outside," Ash sank into the rocking chair, a slight sigh escaped her lips as she made contact with the cushioned seat. "That's nice," she breathed.

"It's my favorite chair," Ros confided. "It's been here for years. I haven't the slightest idea how it ended up here. But now, it feels like mine. If I ever leave here, I'll prolly take it with me."

"We never really know the complete history of what we love, do we?" Ash smiled, ran her hands down the rocking chair's arms. "Were you doing a check-in of some sort?"

Ros clicked her tongue, turned in her chair to face away from the radio set up. "I'm supposed to radio in each day, and I try to be regular on the time. If I missed one or two, they'd likely send the cavalry up for me."

"Ros?" Trick's voice called through the doorway. "May I come in and put these hot packs on your table?"

"Sure." She eyebrowed Ash, who shrugged nonchalantly.

Trick walked into the cabin balancing three foil packets, each cut open at the top and steaming out small altostratus clouds. He smiled blazingly at Ros. "We thought we'd treat you because you're letting us dry off here. So, you can choose between beef stroganoff, three-cheese mac and cheese, or…" he lifted the last packet and squinted at it, "adobe chicken and rice."

Ros released a quick groan. "Good god. I haven't had a dehydrated meal in forever. Those smell delicious." The aromas of the strongly seasoned meals swirled in the warm cabin, vortexes of garlic, paprika, chilies, limes, and oregano competing for dominance. "What happens if we eat family style? I have bowls."

She rose before he could object, shuffled down three different bowls, forks, spoons from the shelf above the counter, set them on the table. Trick placed the packets at the center of the table, and Ash slid from the rocker into the third wooden chair. Ros ruffled into her fridge, handed round three IPAs to cheers from both Trick and Ash.

Dinner turned out to be fun. Trick dominated the conversation, entertaining them with sidesplitting stories of his work as a heavy equipment operator assigned to Eugene's Downtown Riverfront restoration project, which mostly consisted of Trick and his colleagues running away from attacking nutria and their voracious, orange teeth.

Ros savored the company, the different food, and Ash's sly wit. She laughed through stories and ate two helpings of the adobe chicken. She nearly went in for a third. The rain continued to fall heavy outside and a cool breeze wafted in through the open cabin door. Apart from occasional bleeps from the radio, the only sounds were their voices and the rain.

It was genuinely nice to have guests, to offset the other three hundred days or so when the nights were quiet and she was alone. Ros wouldn't trade that quiet, but sitting with Ash and Trick, she briefly felt what she might have missed had she chosen a different career. Ros recognized the moment for what it was, then, let it go.

When they had finished dinner, Ros made the other two remain seated and whisked away the nearly-licked foil packets. Bowls and silverware, she threw into the sink. Hunting for something that would pass as dessert, Ros was down on her knees in the kitchen looking through bins in the pantry for another box of cookies when she heard Trick get up from the table, move toward the doorway.

"It's getting cold out," he said casually as he toed away the engineering brick propping the cabin door wide open.

Ros caught his movement out of the corner of her eye. She pulled herself upright and onto her knees. Sweat instantaneously flowed from her pores, serrated down her back, face, and stomach. Her mouth went desert dry.

"Stop," she said thickly, but it came out as an indistinct gurgle.

Ros watched the door slide shut and remembered clouds, smelled piss, saw red spots in the corners of her eyes.

She heaved to her feet, flung herself toward the door, but black took over the red spots and her vision hazed and sudden dizziness made her unsteady and she collided with a table chair and heard Ash cry out in surprise.

"Stop!" This, a panic-stricken yelp.

Trick twisted awkwardly and dropped his hands to his sides. His face was an ocean of incomprehension as Ros rushed him.

All Ros could see was the closed door and she focused on where she knew the door handle would be. Black spots impaired her vision, and iron flooded her mouth. With two hands she pushed Trick hard on the chest to get him out of the way, didn't look as he pitched backwards to the floor. Her pulse hammered uneven as her fingers caught on the door handle and she yanked. The door ripped open and she shoved the brick back in front of it. She rested one hand against the smooth wood of the doorway, hung her head and took gulping breaths—in, out, in—saw nothing but shadowy spots.

"What the fuck?" Trick shouted from the floor.

Ros ignored him, leaned weakly against the cool damp door, felt her dizziness ebb away. She waited for her sight to return, pointed her face at the rain and the dark skies.

Cool air caressed her eyes, neck, hands. She lifted her head, eyed the clock. Couldn't focus on the hands, couldn't tell how long it had been. However much time had passed, it felt like a full tidal shift in the Bay of Fundy. She was worn to her core, a solitary horst abandoned on all sides.

She pushed off the open door, walked past Trick where he was still sprawled frozen on the floor, past the kitchen table and Ash wide-eyed and unmoving, sank down into the rocking chair, folded into herself, covered her face with her sweaty hands, and breathed again—in, out, in.

"What the fuck?" Trick repeated, getting to his knees. His tone had regained control, had deepened.

Ros felt the man's anger wrap around her intentional breaths. But she said nothing, couldn't open her mouth, could not explain.

"We're getting the fuck out of here," Trick climbed to his feet, his movements loud and jarring, clanging in the cabin. "Ash."

Ros didn't hear her response, instead heard Trick scrape his beer off the table, surge from the cabin, steps thunder cracks on the porch.

Darkness settled in around Ros and a tingling sensation crept into her legs. Eyes closed, she focused her breath, tried to bring her heart rate down. She listened to the rain, to the sounds of water hitting the roof and streaming off the gutters, the splashing of the rain chain onto the moss-covered lava rocks. Puddles of water echoed. She focused deliberately, tried to calm herself.

Wood creaked.

Ros's eyes twitched open. She saw Ash across from her in the kitchen chair, steady, watching. Ros could hear the other woman's breathing, a sturdy in and out that rang meditative, deliberate. Without much thought, she matched her breathing to Ash's, their chests rising and falling synchronously.

"Good," the woman said, soft, voice velvet.

Ros lifted her chin, locked eyes with her. Ash nodded. She looked different somehow, more alert, professional.

The stillness in the cabin pressed in on Ros and she leaned back, breathed, opened and closed her eyes. Her stomach loosened. She felt almost relaxed when the cabin's atmosphere was split apart by the tonal beeping of the radio, then several seconds of high-pitched hissing. Ros reached shakily from the chair, switched the radio's power off.

"What was that?"

"The radio call?"

"No."

"What?"

"You know what I mean."

Ros fenced her words. "It's a long story."

"I have all night." Ash settled, lifted her feet and tucked them into the chair that sat across from her. She gazed benignly at Ros. The sides of Ash's face, Ros noticed, softened in the cabin light.

"You want to therapist me?" Bile rose in Ros's throat. She couldn't help it. Ros loathed therapy. Talking about her family was never going to bring them back.

Ash shook her head, frizzy hair swaying. Her voice was unruffled. "Nope. I have a policy of no doctoring outside the hospital. This is just me, asking. One woman to another. It's up to you to tell me what you want."

Ros's face hurt. She could feel the oxidation of her skin, the sensation of rust forming, her armor flaking. Weariness wove through her bone marrow.

She considered. Recognized within herself the desire to remain quiet and thus remain exactly how she appeared when Ash first met her—a fully competent scientist running a field station.

Words rolled around her tongue and Ros could taste them, identify individual sediments and crystal structures. She summoned a polite sentence in her mind. She knew Ash was the type too nice to pry further.

Ros formed the final sentence in her mind.

A strong end-the-topic-sentence.

But as Ros curated words in her mouth, she noted that Ash didn't interrupt. Instead, the woman loosened her shoulders, waited, kept her eyes anchored. Ros fought a distracting urge to stretch out a finger and stroke the loose skin folded up like puff pastry atop Ash's cheekbones. She'd seen lunate fractures with the same silhouette in rock denuded of ice.

Her thoughts must have been visible.

Ash reached up, touched her own face. Patted the swollen pleats of skin under her eyes. Smiled lopsidedly. "Technically, I get these from my father. Bad genetics," she explained, rueful. "But they really started in earnest on this hike." She swallowed, "I'm not sure why."

"What causes it?"

Ash shook her head, sent her dark hair swaying, shrugged. "Medically, we aren't sure. A lot of things. Inflammation? Stress?" She blinked her eyes. The droopy skin barely moved. "Various medical conditions?"

Ros crossed her legs, uncrossed them, stared at her hands. Her nails were crescents of dirt. More lunate fractures. "I'm sorry."

"Me too. I look like a stuffed pumpkin."

They laughed together, a soft melody winding through the palpable strain in the dark cabin.

Ros took a deep breath, recognized that Ash was giving her an out, a line of humor she could follow to the exit. Or she could stay, choose to talk. A flare of gratitude towards Ash grew in Ros's throat. It felt like Ash was exerting zero pressure on her. That the lineaments that had locked Ros into the ways she'd handled such moments in the past had melted as the two women laughed together. She felt an urge to speak, to be heard, to release the words swirling in her mouth.

"I don't do closed doors," Ros offered. "Ever."

"Sure," the woman said, shifted, folding up deeper into the chair.

Ros flushed.

"It's okay." Ash obviously recognized the panic on Ros's face. "You can talk or not, but please know, it's okay."

Ros summoned a brush-off sentence. She could feel it framed in her mouth. But then she opened her mouth and different words emerged. Different sentences, flowing like hot ice.

"I'm from around here. Mostly. It used to be me, my mom, and Herring. My mom was named Flower, so she named me Rosmarinus, an Oregon native rose. I couldn't stomach the name when I got older, so I shortened it. Mom had this long black hair that went all the way to her bottom. My sister Herring had the same hair. You ever seen obsidian?"

Ash rocked her head forward, back, listened.

"Their hair was like obsidian, long liquid black. A little like your hair. Mine, by comparison, is stumpy, curly. I used to be so jealous of them. They were a pair, and then there was me."

Ros wiped her hands on her sweatpants, cupped her knees. It felt like a hummingbird was caught in her throat. She felt undone with no real cause besides her mouth was moving and it was all coming out.

"I was seven, Herring was twelve. We were going somewhere, I think we might have been driving over to Warm Springs. Driving the 242. I know we were past Scott Lake because there were bathrooms there. But we'd passed them, and Herring needed to pee. Like bad. So she's whining to my mom, both of them sitting up front, me in the backseat. I remember Herring actually reaching and yanking on these long strands of jade beads Mom used to wear around her neck. At some point, Mom must have had enough, because then she was pulling the car over next to a lava formation and telling me to stay in the car, that she was going to take Herring to pee. And they got out of the car, and, I just remember, so clearly even today, the sound the car made when she hit the lock button."

Ros threaded her fingers together. When she was younger, the sound would keep her up at night, the *beep-beep* sounding so loud she couldn't sleep.

"I couldn't get out." Ros paused. How does one describe the sensation of being trapped forever? "The car was faulty and I was locked in for three days until some hikers came by, saw me, and broke the passenger window with a rock."

Ash inhaled deeply, nostrils flaring while she sat ice-still in the chair.

Be done with this, Ros told herself. "So I've always had this excessive claustrophobia. If I'm in control of the way in or out, I'm usually okay. I'll leave a door open…"

Ros looked at Ash, didn't know what to say next.

"That's horrific, Ros," Ash murmured.

"It's a lot of rocks to lug around." Ros tried for humor.

"I'd say."

Ros wasn't sure how to read the expression on the woman's face. Waited.

"I like that you use science to explain yourself."

Ros lifted a shoulder, defensive. "Don't we all?"

A computer fan hummed, and the rain continued to fall. Ros couldn't hear individual impacts on the roof anymore, instead all the drops sounded as if they landed at once, pounding down as if the sky was fighting to get in. She looked through her downturned lashes at Ash. "Thanks for listening. Sorry I'm depositing all this on you."

Ash's eyes flashed in the cabin light. "You're not dumping. I asked. We all carry things."

"You?"

"Of course." Ash flicked a resigned smile. "There's this." She touched her face, gentle, just below the pahoehoe skin. "And there's Trick. He thinks we're out here hiking. But in reality, I'm just trying to decide if I should stay or not."

"Oh?" Ros restricted her response to a small lift of her chin.

"He says he loves me." Ash pulled in her bottom lip. "But he also says I'm not very loveable."

"Jesus."

"There are moments when I'm certain I'm leaving." Ash rubbed her forehead, closed her eyes briefly.

Ros weighed diplomatic words.

"But he can be great. Astronomically great. For months on end." Ash dropped her hands into her lap. "Sometimes not-great-all-the-time is better than being alone?"

Ros crooked her head. "Really?" Heard the implication of the word on her lips, the observation from a woman who chose to live alone in the clouds.

Ash slumped her shoulders. "Yep, I just heard that come out of my mouth." She paused, cleared her throat. "I worry sometimes that I might be a little too much, you know, the doctor lady with the career, money, house in Laurel Hill. Add the height, being brown in the white wilds of Oregon, and, well, from my view the dating pool is rather shallow."

"Being alone isn't so bad," Ros said gently.

"Ha!" Ash said glibly, looking away from Ros. "You know, if I'm honest, it isn't even about that. That's just an excuse I tell myself."

Ros waited, felt soothed by the continual patter of rain.

"The problem is that I do love him." Ash glanced back, and Ros was startled to see a wet glaze in her eyes. "Actually, Ros, you two have more in common than you'd guess."

"Really?" Ros tried to keep the skepticism from her tone.

Ash trained her eyes on the cabin ceiling, took a deep breath. "Yes. You both have unresolved childhood trauma. You, being stuck in a car and claustrophobia." Her tone was clinical, professional. "Trick, well, he lost his sister."

"What happened?" Ros asked, her tone carefully neutral.

"I don't know the all of it. Trick's sister was older, a teenager, he was quite young. She was driving back from a daytrip to Cougar Hot Springs. Police found her car on the side of the 126 below McKenzie Bridge. They think she might have had car trouble. A few motorists said they saw her get into a white truck."

Ros exhaled, cradled her hands, felt herself go cold, numb.

Ash sighed. "As a medical professional, I see this every day at work. Unresolved trauma and how it impacts adult lives. I look at Trick and I can see the anger simmering just below the surface. I know it's not the best thing to diagnose your partner, but it's pretty obvious, and it helps me understand why he behaves the way he does."

Ash looked out the window. "The few times he's ever talked about Hannah, it sounds like he's twisted up emotionally, struggling with anger and abandonment, a lack of closure. It's complex and confusing, but he's literally deaf to the idea of getting help."

Ros took in the woman's profile. Coughed, tried to get her numb throat to make noise, tried to summon words that would help but could think of nothing.

"How much can you understand someone, want desperately to help them, but also know you can't?" Ash's voice came out as a whisper. "At what point do you leave and never look back?"

"Well," Ros paused. "I know we don't know each other, Ash, but I'm here if you ever need a long walk and talk."

Ash looked up, met Ros's gaze. "Thank you."

Rain came down in a symphony of wet notes, and cool air moved through the open door. It was going to be a wet, dark night. Ros pulled the blanket draped over the chair around her. Realized she could see her own breath. She wished she knew where to take them now, how to move herself and Ash through the pall of bleakness that pressed down around them.

"Ros," Ash said, disrupting the quiet. "May I ask you a different question, changing the subject away from my dismal love life?"

"Go ahead." Ros's pulse increased; she could feel nerves tingling in her legs.

Ash glanced around the cabin, was visibly trying to pick her words. Ros waited, heart suspended in her throat.

"What happened after?"

Relief sluiced wetly over Ros. The question sat vibrating before her. Finally, in the open. She took a breath, held it for a long moment. She looked out the open door, the dark night and the falling rain.

"No family showed up if that's what you mean. The police checked in with the tribes after, but no one was missing anyone like me, so I was sent to state foster care with a set of questions I have to accept I'll never fully understand, nor answer."

Ros paused, looked at Ash. The woman nodded for her to continue.

"In a way, I think, science saved me."

"How?"

Ros squeezed her eyes shut, blinked, then opened them, looked again at Ash.

"My mother didn't give me an everyday name. She gave me a Latin name. Rosmarinus. I took it as a sign. When you don't have anything, the littlest things seem to matter. Latin is the language of science, so I went in that direction. Science is reliable, predictable, answerable."

"Medicine helped me," Ash concurred. "I thrive knowing that X and Y result in a predictable outcome. It's comforting to know what to do."

Ros watched Ash. Waited. She knew exactly what Ash was going to ask next even before the woman had fully articulated the question. But Ros didn't dread the question. She'd asked herself the same question her entire life.

Ash leaned forward.

"What happened to your mother, your sister?"

Ros sucked in her cheeks, exhaled hard.

"I don't know," she whispered. Ran her finger down the arm of the rocking chair, traced the wood grain. Looked back up.

"I watched them walk into the lava. I never saw them again."

5

THE
DAUGHTER

The morning air was warm but laced with a winter-is-coming bite. Donna pulled an old, long-patched, puffy jacket from the duffle bag in her trunk, shrugged it on. Sleeping in the car was getting colder and colder. She looked around the clearing.

She considered driving round, getting a newspaper at the gas station. Reconsidered. Might be good to take a walk. In her mind, Donna heard her therapist agree, so she smiled. A reward is always constructive, especially in stressful circumstances.

It had rained steadily the past few days, a clingy Oregon drizzle that coated everything as it came down. Donna shuffled between the cabin porch and the front seat of her car, back and forth, back and forth. At least she'd brought a few new map design books to whittle away the time. It shouldn't be too much longer.

She followed Horse Creek away from the clearing, fall leaves crunching underfoot. The creek babbled furiously beside her, but she concentrated on the path that used to be there. When she was younger, she and her mother regularly walked along the creek, Julene humming and foraging for edibles while Donna bounced between vine maple trunks and sang and—stop, she commanded herself.

Donna focused. She wasn't ready to enter that memory. She closed the drawer with a clang. Instead, stayed in the present, looked for the trail amidst the wet overgrown undergrowth. Couldn't see it. Decided to simply follow the creek.

She heard the McKenzie River before she saw it, sensed the rumble of water beneath her feet, the noticeable thickening of the vegetation, the congealing air around her face.

She stepped out onto the nondescript confluence where Horse Creek flowed into the larger river. The area was larger than she remembered, but then, it was fall and the creek flow was slow. The river was sluggish too. Even the recent rains hadn't given them too much of a boost. It had been a long, dry summer. Donna was surprised a fire hadn't swept through, saved her the work of burning the cabin to the ground.

The confluence exposed round, gray river rocks of varying sizes, and Donna slid onto one moss-covered rock a foot or so from the water's edge. The whoosh and splash of the river soothed her, and she allowed herself to loosen, unwind, let her thoughts drift. Imagined mapping the geological changes of the McKenzie River.

Her fourth or fifth therapist had once told her water was restorative, and Donna wanted to be renewed, wanted to let go, to start over. She closed her eyes.

She used to come to this spot when she was little. She'd wander back from McKenzie Bridge, gallon of milk or loaf of bread clutched tight, change tucked into her pocket until she pulled it out and counted it again and again to make sure it was all there before she got back to the cabin and presented herself for inspection to Ray.

Donna's younger self used to sit on the rocks of the bank, stare at the McKenzie. She knew that the river ran another sixty miles west toward Eugene, that it flowed right along the highway in some spots, right along the backyards of people with much bigger houses and fields of filberts and berries and nuts.

Her mother had told her once that the McKenzie actually disappeared for three miles under the ground, hiding in the lava, and re-appeared at a place upriver called the Blue Pool. As if nothing was amiss. Donna had never seen the Blue Pool, but she thought a lot about how a river could just appear and disappear. She wished then that she could too, that she could build a raft and put her mother on it and they could disappear.

Ray had sneered once when she told him her plan, how she wanted to raft to Eugene. He told her she had no skills to build a watercraft, that anything she built would fall apart in the current and she'd disappear for real in the voracious river.

Donna ignored those words. She'd had faith in herself, knew she could tie logs tightly.

Then he said that even if she managed to build something that could float, she'd just run into dam after dam after dam on the river, and then what would she do?

Her heart shriveled then.

It was the first she'd heard of dams, water walls, and she realized that she'd never escape by way of the river. So instead, as she grew older, she'd just walk the river trail back to the cabin and stop at the confluence and sit and admire the water, how it would whoosh, and she'd mentally allow herself to drift away until she felt runny and liquid enough inside to go home.

A whistle interrupted Donna's peace. She cracked an eyelid, looked up. A predator bird flew over the river. Brown wings, white head, white body. She squinted against the glare, spotted the bright yellow eye and the question mark of a beak. An osprey. Donna smiled, watched the bird scan the river. She hesitated, faltering, but then allowed herself to open a file from the third drawer, review a treacherous memory.

Sitting at that spot when Donna had been about ten, she'd heard that same osprey whistle. But she hadn't seen the bird. It was early summer, and the water was running high. She alternately picked at the scabs on her knees and stared into the sky between the crowded trees. She started when a voice called out, "He's right above you."

Donna had froze when she heard the voice, sunk her head down into her shoulders and remained still. But when she heard a laugh, she bobbed up and looked around; saw two boys in a drift boat floating in the middle of the river. They waved when she looked at them.

"Look up!" one of them had called.

Donna had instead studied them, took them in from where they were sitting in a wide, flat-bottomed, wooden boat with two long oars poking out from either side. The boat had been painted red but was now peeling. It had a pointed stern where one of the boys sat holding a fishing rod. The other, the one that called out, hunched in the middle of the craft holding the oars. They both had floppy brown hair, wore faded t-shirts and cutoffs. Maybe teenagers? Donna had reached low, subtly, fingered a rock into her hand, clutched it.

"It's an osprey! It might fly off with you!" The boy at the oars twirled the boat around quickly, laughed again.

She'd finally looked up then, and there, high in a Doug fir leaning out over the water, she saw the bird strangling a branch and staring at the boat. She felt kinship with the bird. She, also, didn't know what the boys in the boat wanted.

"You live around here?" the boy asked, chatty. "We do! We're down near Nimrod."

Donna had lifted a shoulder, shrugged at the question, clutched her knees, hunched. She wasn't supposed to talk to strangers.

"You should come fish with us sometime, we're getting rainbows. Jonas got one longer than his whole body last time!" the rower pointed at the smaller boy in the stern. He'd shrugged sheepishly.

"Okay, then! We'll see you later!" The boy lifted his hand from the oar, gave her a friendly wave, nosed his boat back into the current where it caught, and then they were speeding away down river. Donna had watched until the drift boat disappeared and then sighed quietly, wishing and wondering.

She would have stood there longer, but then she smelled cigarette smoke.

Her pulse accelerated; all the hairs on her arms stood to attention. "Drop the rock, daughter."

She swiveled. Slow. Just her head, eyes wide, neck barely moving.

Ray walked out of the undergrowth and into view.

She'd seen the cigarette dangling from his lips, the heavy leather boots and canvas pants and work shirt rolled up at the sleeves. The shotgun in his hands.

Quickly, using just the edge of her eye, she'd taken in his face, assessed how this was going to go.

He'd been home over the summer more than ever before, chainsaws lying quiet on the front porch. There had been fewer and fewer logging jobs. Donna spent more time folding sheets from the laundry her mother took in from the tourist inns on the highway.

When Donna had been really little, Ray had worked steadily. He once bragged he knew every inch of board feet still growing in the Oregon Cascades, that he knew the hollows and high points of the region better than anyone. Often, he'd be gone logging all week except Sunday. He always came home on the Lord's Day, and the family would pray together from morning until midafternoon.

But over that past year, he'd been working less, and growing more unpredictable. He'd disappear for a while and come back with eyes that glittered, face polished to a sheen, a smile that breathed sour malt. Her mother's mouth would tighten, and Donna would watch him from a distance, see if he was jovial or sullen. When he wasn't happy, Donna knew to stay clear.

"Drop the rock," Ray had ordered again, louder this time, stepping fully in front of her on the riverbank. Donna saw the glaze in his eyes and the looseness about his joints and the strange turn of his mouth. This was not going to end well.

She'd scanned the area without ever moving her head. There was nowhere for her to run that he wouldn't catch her in an instant. And running from Ray was a sin. Fear pulsed through her. She was a fool. She needed to learn to always have an exit. No one to blame but herself. Her fingers had cramped immobile around the small stone, and her forearm shook with the strength of her grip. Not obeying Ray was another sin, and sometimes it took weeks to recover from his cleansings.

She'd prayed, resisted vomiting. Focused on her hand, forced her fingers finally open, and let the sweaty small rock tumble to the ground. Ray had smiled then, a stretch of his lips.

"Good girl," he'd said soft-like, moving slow, closer across the rocks. Donna watched the point of the gun, felt an urge to piss. She didn't know how long he'd been standing in the woods, watching her and the boys on the boat. Talking to strangers was a sin. She held her breath.

Ray stepped down the bank to the waterline, stood between Donna and the river. He paused, lingered while Donna's heart pounded, studied her with a blank expression and hooded eyes.

"Snuck up on you, didn't I, daughter?" he'd said, almost a whisper. "I can sneak up on anyone."

Donna had nodded, unsure if she should smile or laugh along with him. Instead, she waited, watched. With her knees clutched tightly to her chest, she felt sweat pooling in her groin, held herself tight inside.

Ray's eyes swung upward, and before Donna could cry out, he'd lifted the shotgun and the muzzle aloft with the butt against his shoulder. The sound was deafening, echoing and echoing. Donna's ears rang but she was okay, okay, okay, and for a minute that stretched long she kept her eyes tightly closed and checked her body and found herself blessedly unharmed.

She opened her right eye.

Ray was still, standing, nearly lounging, gun snaked around his right arm. Brown and white feathers drifted in the water. "Saved you, didn't I?" he'd said when he saw her looking. "Stupid fucking spotted owl."

Donna didn't know where to look, couldn't let herself see the bird, stared at her knees and willed herself not to cry.

And then casual as day, Ray walked right up to her, across the round river rocks, and kneeled in front of her. He lifted her face, held her chin gentle, squeezed lightly with his fingers until she looked directly into his eyes.

"Your ears ringing?" he'd asked, all calm and mild like a supplicant on his knees.

She'd nodded and tried not to look for the gun, tried to stay still and tell him she was his little girl, but then felt a chunk of snot roll from her left nostril. His face tightened and revulsion washed over it.

But then he'd said, "Oh sweet daughter, it's okay."

Something inside her had loosened and tears rolled sodden down her face.

"Sweet, pure innocence, my little daughter," he'd breathed.

She waited.

Ray's eyes darkened and narrowed, his grip on her throat tightened, his thumb pushed into her mouth as his pointer and ring finger dug into her jaw.

Donna tried to stay still, but the pain grew until she strained to pull her head away. Ray had sighed as she struggled. He brought the cigarette to his lips, tucked it into the corner of his mouth, and, so quick she didn't see it coming, he'd backhanded her. Donna's vision swam. Her lip and nose ran hot with blood.

"Listen to me, daughter," he'd said in a low voice. "I know what happens to girls like you."

He'd blown a cloud of cigarette smoke at her face. Donna had felt the gust of his lungs cool the hot blood on her nose and lips.

"I saw you talking to those boys," he'd continued. "You're too far gone, there is nothing I can do to save you."

Donna had shaken her head frantically, whispered as best she could around the vise grip of his fingers, "No, no, no…"

Ray drew deep on his cigarette. "Don't you know what happens when you lose your purity?" He exhaled.

She'd nodded, her face up and down and up and down as he loosened his grip.

"What?" He let go of her jaw.

"The end of me, the death of me," she recited, wet, terrified, nose, mouth, chin throbbing.

"Did you lose your purity, daughter? Do you want me to end you now?" he'd asked tenderly, rocking back onto his heels.

Ray had picked up a round river rock, bigger than Donna's head, had hefted it in a single hand. "Do you?"

Shaking her head, she'd kept her eyes trained to the ground, unfocused and hitched out, "No, no, no."

"You know I can help, daughter? I've helped others. God will reward me, daughter."

There was a pause, a quiet where Donna hadn't been sure what he was going to do. The uncertainty felt sharp as a knife on skin, but then she'd heard a crack and flinched and the rock fell at her feet. She'd gone cold, numb, empty. Urine leaked down her leg.

Ray had laughed. "I'm watching you, daughter."

He stood to his full height, towering above her. He turned, stepped up around the rocks. Donna heard him whistling and rustling through the woods and she'd held her breath. Waited and counted and waited and didn't dare look at the rock or the bloody bird bits or the river.

The river.

Donna exhaled.

Water had witnessed so much suffering.

She closed her eyes, considered leaving the memory, stopping there, but she knew what her latest therapist would say. Follow the whole thread, read the whole file, don't hide from the pages, take power from the past. If she was reviewing the memories on her terms, she could minimize the chances of re-traumatizing herself when the memory popped up unbidden.

It helped, the file folder analogy. Over the years, other therapists had told her that she'd eventually heal and forget, that one day she'd be able to let it all go.

But that wasn't true, and she knew that they knew that. Donna knew she would never heal. She would never really forget. All she could do was risk assessment, gauge the level of harm.

Unless. Perhaps. If she could finally close the files for good. And then burn the entire cabinet down. That's how she'd let it all go.

"Finish the memory," Donna told herself, and settled back onto the river rock, closed her eyes.

And there she was, child legs moving quick as she walked the path along Horse Creek back to the cabin. She'd allowed herself a few minutes to cry, washed her face in the McKenzie, and then turned homeward because she knew being late for dinner was a sin and her pants were soaked with piss.

Walking into the cabin's clearing, she'd seen straightaway that Ray's truck was gone and that her mother was kneeling in front of the large gray tub at the side of the house washing sheets. Donna bee-lined for her, quick-walked through the long grass until she reached her mother's side.

Julene Pencovitch looked up. Her eyes narrowed, face softened. She wiped a sudsy hand on her faded skirt. She reached out and gently stroked Donna's swollen nose, bruised mouth, and bloodied chin.

"He said he smacked you for talking to boys," she'd said. "I didn't realize…"

Donna hadn't winced at her mother's touch, just looked fixedly into her soft brown eyes until something tightened inside of her and she knew she wouldn't cry.

Julene had eyes that were brown on the outside and gold on the inside, framed by short, soft lashes that Donna sometimes wished she could stroke. Her mother was a small woman with a narrow frame and long black-brown hair swept with gray that she kept wrapped into a bun at the base of her neck.

Donna dropped her eyes, stared at her mother's knees digging into the wet dirt beside the wash tub. Her mother's hand lingered on her shoulder, warm and damp with the wash. Donna felt the beads of her mother's bracelet roll along her arm.

"I didn't do anything," Donna had whispered, the words slipping around her sore lips.

"Shhh… shhhh…" Her mother glanced around the clearing.

Julene had turned Donna toward her, placed both hands on her shoulders and held her steady. "Don't ever say that, Donna," she'd said. "When you get angry and fight him, it only makes it worse."

Donna stared at her mother, noticed that the bruise at Julene's throat had faded, that she looked exhausted, worn down.

"Your father has lost all his work, Donna. Those environmentalists, you know. He doesn't like me doing this…" Julene pointed with her chin at the washing. "He feels God has abandoned him, that he has to work harder to cleanse the world to gain back God's love." The permanent furrows striping across her forehead tightened and the two lines running from her nose down to the sides of her mouth deepened.

Julene squeezed her shoulders tight, shook her a little. "Try to understand him, Donna. Find your compassion. Remember that you can't give him an excuse for anything right now, daughter. You are responsible for your behavior, don't provoke him…"

"Mama," Donna had argued, "can't we go away?"

Her mother sat back on her heels, detached her hands from Donna's shoulders, crossed them over her small chest. She looked straight into Donna's eyes. In a flash, she raised her right hand and slapped her across her already swollen nose and mouth. "Don't ever say that," she'd hissed. "Ever."

Donna had put her hands out, stared at her mother, unbelieving.

"Women never speak in anger, and you are a woman."

Julene had never hit her before. She'd been angry, hurt, lost, but had stood before her mother still as a tree.

"Your father is my husband and I made vows before God," Julene had whispered fiercely. She wiped a hand down her own face.

Julene had pressed her lips together, brought both trembling hands over her daughter's chin, her mouth, her nose. Had shook her own head, covered her face with her long fingers, the nails rimmed with dirt. The green beads had rattled together. Donna watched her mother's shoulders begin to heave, stared inured at the bowed neck before her. If her mother was crying, she made no sound.

If Donna could have done that moment over, she would have reached out a hand, would have stroked her mother's face, given her compassion and love. But those were all things Donna wouldn't learn about until later, until after all that time in the hospital and then laying on the old sofa bed listening to Blazey Watts read to her.

She was ten years old back then and hadn't known anything. Her therapist reminded her regularly that what people do when they're ten years old is often because they're ten years old. That all that compassion and love Donna wished she could have given to her mother in that moment—it was also important to extend that to her ten-year-old self.

If Donna had known, she would have said, "I love you."

But she hadn't said that.

Instead, with her twice-beaten face she'd turned away from the woman kneeling before her. Instead, she'd looked at the trees growing up around the clearing, swallowed down all the anger and hurt and vomit and words, stood numb in the late afternoon light.

"I'm sorry," Julene had whispered through hands still clenched over her face.

She'd just stood there, a statue of betrayal in piss-soaked pants, tried not to listen as her mother offered her explanation.

"There's nowhere to go, Donna. I have no money, no job, no family. Where would we go? And how? Your father never taught me how to drive." Julene dropped her hands from her face. "He wasn't always like this."

Donna let the words sink in before she glanced back at her mother. For as long as she could remember, Ray had been rough, righteous, violent. Jolene registered the disbelief smearing Donna's face. Her eyes had tightened, and Donna had watched her hands clump together.

"I've asked for help," Julene had whispered. "They said they'll try."

Donna felt nothing, but her anger disappeared. "Are you going to hit me again?" she'd asked tonelessly.

Donna's mother slowly shook her head no, and then Donna had walked away from her, a slow halting trudge that carried her to the porch steps. As she moved up each step, she heard the low thrum of the truck's engine, Ray returning.

The memory stopped there, and Donna opened her eyes and took in the McKenzie washing by from her seat on the round gray river rock. She checked in with herself, noted her stomach muscles tightening, clenching. There was bile rising in her throat, the high whine of mosquitos circling, the tears on her face.

Donna glanced at her watch, noticed it was almost time for Ray's supper. Stood. Took a deep breath, pictured tropical waters—blue, let the data layers wash over her. Thought about choropleth maps, proportional maps, symbol maps. Breathed deeply again. Filed the memory, knocked the drawer shut, locked the cabinet.

She was almost done. There weren't too many more left to review.

Worry wrapped unexpectedly around her spine.

Donna shoved her boot into the ground. No, she told herself. No cognitive distortions. That's catastrophizing, and she wouldn't do it now after she'd made it so far.

Ray would tell her, or he wouldn't. Either way, Donna knew what she had to do to move forward with her life.

6
THE
MEDIC

Smoke rose from the cylindrical chimney jutting from the small cabin's roof. The contrast of burnished metal against the green moss varnishing the roof was somewhat pleasing to May. It reminded her of the episode when all the male characters from *Grey's Anatomy* went camping in season three. .

Behind the cabin, May could see the dead, scorched trees that bordered the living ones along the steep slope of the crater. The vision counteracted May's momentary pleasure. The trees looked like sentinels supervising the morning gloom. May shivered as she scanned the area around the camp, decided to focus on the prettier aspects of the landscape. She didn't see Amelia Kane.

"Is there protocol for waking a research station?" she whispered to Jonas.

He shook his head wordlessly, then stepped confidently from the spur trail into the meadow area in front of the cabin. "Hello," he called out. "Anyone here?" His voice rattled through the clearing, echoed off trees, came back sounding wet to May's ears. Her boots, pantlegs, and sleeves were damp from the hike, and she shivered in the early morning air.

"Half a minute!" a low voice shouted back, and then a head popped up in the window next to the cabin's half-open front door. A minute later, a woman with an unraveled head of curls stepped onto the porch, a mug steaming in her hand. She wore sweatpants and a down jacket, but May noticed her feet were bare.

"Welcome to OHEWS," the woman said, resting a hand on a porch pole. She bounced on her toes. A quizzical smile split her face as she took the two of them in. May could see her dark eyes, the swathe of freckles blanketing over her nose and cheeks. In May's mind, she looked like a heron right before taking flight. "I'm Dr. Ros Fisher. What can I do for you this early morning?"

Jonas stepped forward and May followed behind, unclipping the chest strap on her pack as she went. "Hi Ros," Jonas said, voice authoritative. He introduced himself and May. "Sorry for the early hour. We've got a missing child in this area, wanted to check in with you. Your comms are down, so we're making a personal visit."

May stepped around Jonas's expansive shoulders to stand beside him. She was always doing that on department calls. Most of the guys were actually the same size as her, but they all ended up blocking her when they took an official stance.

May looked away from Jonas, watched the woman's face cycle through a series of emotions so rapidly, May almost laughed. As Jonas's words sunk in, Ros had gone from a welcoming face to a concerned one, then mugged sorrow and incredulity. May's mother would have scorned her for allowing so many emotions to be legible on her face.

May shook her head, pushed thoughts of her mother away. She didn't belong here, and May had a job to do.

May glanced at Jonas, saw him looking carefully at Ros. May followed his line of sight.

Ros took a step backwards and was squinting at something inside the cabin. Then she turned, disappeared. May and Jonas waited.

May's hackles tingled, and, in her mind, she rehearsed scene-safety protocols. She wondered if Ros was going to come back out on the porch with a weapon of some sort. She tensed her shoulders, eyed a stump nearby that maybe she could dive behind for safety.

In less than a minute, Ros was back, walking along the cabin porch, feet still bare, no weapons visible. May twanged in sympathy for the woman's toes which, if they'd been her feet, would have been freezing and threatening to fall off. She hated the cold.

"Wow," Ros said. "The station's radio was flipped off. I just turned it back on. Odd. Probably why you couldn't get me."

Jonas tipped his head. "No problem."

May didn't buy it. She suspected Ros was lying, could tell by the way the woman averted her face, twisted her hands. May narrowed her eyes at Ros, looked closer at her bare feet, rumpled clothes, frazzled curls. To May, Ros looked possibly hung over. And something else, she appeared almost fearful. Who turned an entire comms system off when that was their sole job? May shifted her eyes from the woman to the cabin, then to the meteorological equipment laying haphazardly around the open area.

May considered the sizable fuel drum tucked in by several piles of split wood. Maybe the woman was trafficking drugs. PCT hikers could ferry the drugs up the trail from California, drop them off at the station, and the woman could distribute them throughout her network. On the third season of *Shetland*, Detective Inspector Jimmy Pérez was amazed to discover drugs were being trafficked all the way out to the remote archipelago. May knew drugs could show up anywhere, even field stations in the Cascades.

"Have you seen a child around here, Ros?" Jonas asked. "We're looking for Amelia Kane, nine years old, went missing somewhere around Scott Trail yesterday afternoon."

"I haven't." Ros shook her head. "But I do have two trail hikers staying here in the Fellows Cabin, and they came from that direction yesterday. Why don't you two get comfortable, have some coffee, and I'll roust them for a chat?"

May stepped forward, said, "Okay." She didn't want to cede all the talking to Jonas. She eyed him as the word left her mouth, assessed how he took her tepid power play. But he wasn't looking at her, and May couldn't be certain he even heard her. Stomach deflating, May stepped back to her earlier spot, just behind his left shoulder.

Ten minutes later, Ros had handed them both coffees, and May sat on the edge of the cabin's low steps while Jonas had disappeared into the forest. He'd taken his coffee and said he was going to radio in the status of OHEWS. Ros had disappeared, but May could hear her somewhere inside the cabin. She leaned, glanced surreptitiously under the cabin porch, saw nothing but black plastic tubing and rotting pieces of firewood.

Water dripped from the moss roof and wind roved noisily through the trees. May realized the past night's heavy rain had dampened the area's sounds. It reminded her somehow of people underwater shouting about their lives. Or, maybe trees underwater. If trees ever shouted about their lives. She wasn't sure.

May was sipping her coffee when a man careened around the corner of the cabin. May choked a little as she scrambled to her feet in surprise. He stopped directly in front of her, looked her up and down.

"Who are you?" he said.

May was unsure of his tone, and instinctively drew back, shrank into herself. Then caught herself cowering, tried to push through it. Thrust her chest out, narrowed her eyes into what she thought might be an authoritative face. She tried to channel Meredith Grey standing up for her right to do surgery, tried to stretch to her full height, look tough. She wasn't sure if she succeeded. The man just stared at her, frowning through his dark beard.

Perhaps she could defuse him with kindness. "Good morning," she said, cautious.

"Maybe," he said, "It's still wet, too cold, and the lady that runs this place is literally nuts." He twirled a finger around his ear. "Cuckoo."

May was unsure how to respond, tried to keep her face neutral, her weight on her toes.

"Anyway, she just told me to get up and get out of here."

"No, I didn't," a brittle voice said behind May, "That's ridiculous." Ros stepped from the cabin, leaned into the open doorframe. "I just asked you to come speak to the officers."

"Oh, we're not officers," May corrected, flashing placating smiles at both Ros and the man standing less than a foot from her. Waited to see if her smile eased whatever was wrong, but neither responded, and May felt momentarily lost.

She remembered the protocols she'd read, memorized, practiced. "Sir, are you by yourself?" May asked.

"I might as well be," the man said, his voice spiked.

May didn't understand what the man meant and was taken aback by his barely veiled hostility. It felt like it was directed at her. But she'd never met him before. She swallowed, felt her throat dry up.

May remembered that risk assessment in her job was paramount, that the first thing a responder did in any situation was assess the scene for safety. If Meredith had done that in season three of *Grey's Anatomy*, she wouldn't have been knocked into the water and almost drowned. May registered that she did not feel safe on the steps with the man and his unexplained aggression. She decided to move up a step, up onto the porch, take the higher ground. Be just above eye-level with him. She regarded him carefully.

Cleared her throat.

Started over.

"I'm May Young. I'm out here on a SAR call for Amelia Kane, nine years old, who is missing. She was last reported sighted along the Scott Trail, and Dr. Fisher here says you were in that area yesterday?"

"We were!" another voice interrupted.

May swiveled, watched as a third person came swiftly around the corner. As she got closer, May could see the person was a tall woman with a red knit hat jammed over thick black hair.

"Sorry, I was getting dressed."

The man didn't acknowledge the late arrival, didn't even shift his eyes. May noted Ros smiling at the woman, a greeting.

"Yes," the woman continued, somewhat breathlessly, when she popped up onto the porch. "We were hiking northbound yesterday on the PCT, coming from near Lane Plateau, got here yesterday late afternoonish after it started to really rain, stayed here the rest of the night."

"Well, I stayed in that tiny cabin back there," the man interjected, scowling again. "Where did you stay?"

This, directed at the tall woman. May looked at the three faces again. Maybe the two women were in a love triangle and that was what was making the man angry? May loosened her shoulders in relief. He wasn't mad at her.

May shook her head and tried to focus. She observed the new woman closely. She had the thick dark hair May's mother dreamed of. But her face appeared drawn with dark fleshy circles under her eyes. Were those bruises? May considered abuse. She wondered if the man had beaten her. Or maybe not. May mentally kicked herself for her gendered assumptions. Perhaps Ros had beaten the other woman. Hadn't her EMT training taught her that men and women could be perpetrators, and it was her job to see the world through genderless eyes?

"Are you okay, ma'am?" May ventured. "I'm a medic." She loved that sentence, the way the words felt in her mouth, the solid career implications. She loved the respect it commanded, the knowledge it implied, the ability other people assumed she had to fix them. May stood straighter, tried to project confidence.

The woman looked at May, surprised. She didn't respond.

"Answer the question, Ash," the man said. "Are you okay?"

"What are your names?" May jumped in, feeling somewhat like she'd embarrassed the woman.

"I'm Ash Moonieida. And this is Patrick Froyn, Trick Froyn." The woman smiled warmly at May. "And yes, I'm okay."

May unzipped the hip pocket on her pack, pulled out a brand-new waterproof notebook. She'd never used one like it before. Typically, in the ambulance, she used the department's formulaic run reports. But during her SAR training, she'd bought herself the notebook, loved the purple cover and the silky feel of the pages' waterproof polypropylene resin, how each slipped coolly through her fingers. Turning to the very first page, May wrote down their names. Worried over spelling, and looked up to see if she could clarify, but no one was looking at her.

"Moonieida?" she asked, hoping the question was clear.

"Oh perfect one—," Trick said.

"Stop." Ash cut him off, voice hard. She turned to May, spelled the letters of her name out.

"Where are you two from?"

"Eugene," they answered almost simultaneously.

"And you, Ash?" May pressed, looked up from her notebook.

"Eugene," the woman repeated, face no longer warm.

May realized her mistake instantly, flushed. She, of all people, should know better. She'd lost count of how many times people had asked her where she was from. And now she'd done it to someone else. May waffled on whether to apologize, but then chose to just recover, move on. "Did either of you see a child on your hike?" May asked, using her professional I'm-a-medic voice.

They exchanged a glance she couldn't discern, and May saw Ros cross her arms over her chest. Trick snorted. Ash's eyebrows went up as if she was asking a question.

Trick shook his head. "No," he replied firmly. "We didn't *see* a child."

May waited. Her gut tingled—she hated the feeling that she was missing something. During her EMT-Basic, the video instructor had said that when you were soliciting incident information from witnesses, the more you waited, the more people said. People tended to babble. May could relate. But she was learning. She could maintain just as much of a stoic professional silence as Jonas or Baker could. Sometimes.

She took two breaths, waited, wondered if it was enough, then asked, "Did you see anyone else?"

"Yes," Ash answered almost reluctantly, but firmly, as if she'd been holding her breath. "Several people, in fact. Surprising, given the weather and that we really haven't seen all that many people during the entirety of our trip. We were hiking north from our camp near Elk Lake Resort."

"You saw people at the resort?"

Ash shook her head, sent her dark hair tumbling and hat waving. "No, no. Sorry. On the PCT. From morning through about early afternoon, north of the Le Conte Crater. We saw a pair of hikers, then a man all by himself with a dog, an older woman who I only saw from a distance, and then a group of three, that I think were day hikers from the resort? We chatted a bit, then they headed south and I went north."

"I didn't see that group," Trick cut in. "And, really, I don't know—"

May was intrigued. Could any of the hikers have somehow gotten up to the Scott Trail and kidnapped Amelia Kane? But where would they have hidden her when Ash and Trick hiked by? She interrupted Trick.

"—Could you give me a description of any of the hikers you passed?"

Ash licked her lips, tipped her head up, trying to remember. "Um, I mean, not really. Not the first hikers. The man and the dog… well, he was older, brown hair. The dog was maybe a lab? The older woman, she had on green pants, a sweater I think. And the group of three— well, they were in their twenties, perhaps."

May wrote down the descriptions as Ash talked. Looked up when Ash trailed off, saw she had wrapped her hands around opposite elbows and was hugging her arms into her body. "Anything else?"

Ash coughed, and May watched her make eye contact with Ros while Trick scowled, crossed his own arms over his chest. No one said anything.

May's hackles rose again and she felt her pulse pound up her neck. She wished she had a physical manifestation of her hackles, something like Captain Saru's spiky threat ganglia that stuck out of the character's neck on *Star Trek Discovery*. May wasn't that into sci-fi, but she'd enjoyed watching the first season of *Discovery* one evening when she wasn't working. The medical advancements on the show were really cool, and it made her reconsider whether she wanted to move her burgeoning medic career into actual medical school.

May looked again from Ros to Trick to Ash. Something else had happened, she was sure of it. Maybe this was why all three were clearly riled up. She considered how to phrase her next questions, was just about to ask when Jonas called her name as he strode back up the trail.

"You get everything here?" he asked, looking from her to the group and back. "We need to roll. Command wants us to head up Black Crater, do a hasty, then join the pounders out by the Collier Cone."

"I could help. I'm heading up Black Crater this morning," Ros offered, stepping away from the cabin door she'd been leaning on. "I need to go up and pipe some equipment," she explained, pointing at a stack of white PVC pipes on the far end of the porch. "It's over seven thousand feet up. I can glass from up there if you like. If the child went up a lava crop or mountain-goated the Sisters, I'll see her."

Jonas jerked his head in gruff acknowledgement. "That'd be great. We're actually short searched today. We were supposed to have another twenty volunteers up from Eugene, but no one wants to leave their Ducks game to look for a lost girl."

"Well, I'm happy to help. I know what this is like." Ros looked away, and May saw Ash glance at her, face creased in concern, then send that same look at Trick.

"Can I go now?" Trick interrupted, sharp. "I have things to do."

May shrugged, dismissing him, but then Jonas was there, stepping up closer to the man. May recognized his technique, what the textbooks had outlined as "standing ground." To leave your hands at your sides, ready, but not acting; to have both feet placed firmly; to stand like a solid, mildly threatening person. It could be quite effective. But you weren't supposed to get there at all. You were supposed to defuse before you had to stand your ground.

"You seem angry," Jonas said to Trick, tone cool, controlled. "Why?"

It was as if everyone standing around the cabin all at once held in their breath. May felt as if she could physically reach out and touch the tension crackling in the air. Jonas and Trick stood with eyes locked, Trick working his jaw. She could not fathom why Jonas would provoke Trick, why he didn't do what their trainings stated over and over: defuse situations, deescalate.

"I am," Trick stated. He raised his hands jerkily, but Jonas didn't move, just seemed somehow to swell larger.

May watched Trick calculate Jonas. She was surprised when after ten seconds she saw a smile slink across his tanned face.

"Women," Trick finally said. His delivery was flat.

May was bewildered. Women?

Jonas barked out a quick laugh, reached, swatted Trick on the upper arm. He stepped back, all tension evaporated between them. "Fine, man," he said. "I get it."

May purposefully stilled her face, glued her eyebrows into place, stole a quick glance at Ash, then Ros, but the women's faces were equally expressionless.

"Let me radio in for Black Crater confirmation, Ros," Jonas commanded. "Young, pack up and roll."

May didn't know where to look, or how to interpret what had just occurred. "Jonas," she sputtered, following him as he walked rapidly to the forest edge where they'd left their packs.

He didn't acknowledge her.

"Jonas," she repeated, stomach swirling.

"What?" He looked up from the pack he was kneeling on.

"I think there's something else going on here. We're missing something?" May clamped down on her lips, suppressed the urge to keep talking, explain everything she'd seen. She twisted her fingers into fists, wished her hands were small and delicate.

"Good instincts, Young," Jonas praised without looking at her. He stood up, then held eye contact. "But we're out here looking for a little girl. Do you see her here?"

May shook her head, stomach dropping. Her ponytail scratched her neck.

"Do you think any of these people took Amelia?"

She shook her head a second time, felt her tongue freeze to the roof of her mouth.

"Okay then. Nothing else is our business. You're not wrong, Young, just distracted. That's okay," Jonas assured her. "You're new." He turned back to his pack, knelt again, zipped closed the compartments. He heaved it up over his shoulders as he stood.

May mirrored his movements, clipped on her own heavy pack. She willed her face to stay calm, to drain the red she knew was there flashing for all to see like a lit-up stop sign. She knew she watched too many dramas. Before, she'd blissfully walked through the world never thinking twice about people's inner lives, their private habits, their secrets. But now that she was a medic, it was all she saw. She even thought she'd caught her own mother popping pills a few weeks ago. It turned out to be a Tylenol. May had been mortified; her mother, hysterical. If May was a real doctor, she'd screamed, she'd know the difference. May jostled her pack, settled it on her shoulders. She needed to focus, stop imagining things.

"Sorry," she mumbled to Jonas, but he was finishing a radio call and didn't seem to hear her. She listened as Jonas relayed Ros's request and Command confirmed it, issued more directions. Sounded like they were going to go straight to Collier Cone. "I'll return the coffee cups," she whispered to him. He nodded.

May walked back through the clearing to the porch, set the mugs on the steps, turned to go.

"May?"

May twisted, saw Ash standing on the edge of the porch, an uncomfortable look on her face.

"Can I talk to you for a second?" The woman tugged her knitted hat off, ran her hand through her dark hair. May felt a momentary surge of envy.

May nodded for her to continue. Ash gave a nervous laugh. "I'm not sure this is helpful, but—hmmm. How to say this? We camped the night before last near the Lane Plateau, coming up from the Le Conte Crater…"

"Are you telling her?" Trick's voice cut in, and May momentarily closed her eyes, wished she had a superpower that could make other people disappear. Heard her own thought, what it meant on a day she was searching for a missing girl, blushed to her hairline, mortified at herself.

Trick stepped closer to May than was comfortable. "Not helpful, Ash," he hissed. May blanched at his tone, glanced sharply at both of them.

"They have a child to find," Ash insisted. Trick shook his head. "You heard it too!"

"Heard what?" Jonas asked calmly, moving into the conversation, placing himself between the two hikers and May. "What are you talking about?"

"We heard some type of humming, really weird, and then laughter," Ash explained. "I heard it, Trick heard it."

Laughter? May tried not to groan. They'd heard laughter, and that was why they were all acting weirdly?

"We've heard it all along the PCT, starting, like, two days ago. But it was really strong when we camped two nights ago. Then coming on the trail here. It sounds like a bunch of children laughing just out of view. I swear I'm not crazy," Ash said, her voice sounding desperate. "I know what this sounds like. But I honestly kept hearing it, and Trick heard it too."

Jonas turned to Trick for confirmation, and the man shrugged his shoulder. "I didn't hear it."

"Huh," Jonas said. "Well, we can report it, and Command will take it from there. We've got your contact information?"

"Your assistant has it," Trick said.

Jonas bobbed his head in confirmation, climbed the porch into the cabin, and made his way toward Ros.

May froze, tried to swallow the information Ash had just given her alongside Jonas's tacit confirmation that she was, indeed, an assistant. When Alex Karev called Meredith a nurse in the first season of *Grey's Anatomy*, other doctors had defended her and punished Karev. But up here, no one was defending May. May fumed.

By now, Jonas was strolling back down the steps, standing next to her. "Alright?" he asked.

The next thing she knew, they were headed down the faint spur trail toward the PCT. For May, leaving the station and hurrying to the Collier Cone was all a blur.

They stopped every four minutes when Jonas's watch alarm beeped. They both yelled Amelia's name, whistled, then hiked on. The repetition lulled May as she moved—the sound of her feet hitting the damp trail, the gentle chime from the clipped bells on the back of their packs, the sun exposure on her neck and shoulders. It was peaceful, and soon, the embarrassment she felt at being called Jonas's assistant dulled marginally. She lost the sound of footsteps, just held calm the tinkling of the bells, the calls of birds overhead.

Suddenly, a squelched bark came from a lava-rock jumble to May's left. She jerked her head around, but then a bark came from the right. May stopped in the middle of the trail, pivoted her head, scanned.

"Pika," Jonas said without turning to look back at her.

May searched for the furry creatures, but didn't see a single one. "Let's break," she retorted, not waiting, reaching up, unclipping her pack, letting it drop to the trailside. "I need water."

As May drank, she inspected the landscape around her. Trees bent like old shepherds and clustered along rock outcroppings. Squatting to look beneath them, May heard Jonas explain, "Whitebark pine. Lots of them out here are over three, over five hundred years old. Incredible plants."

May's radio squawked, and she heard the chief's voice calling her. She responded. Resisted identifying herself as Jonas's assistant.

"ETA to Collier Cone base?"

She looked at Jonas questioningly, and he raised his shoulders and guessed forty minutes.

"Okay," Chief's voice tinned through. "You'll miss the main line-up. They're going to do a visual line search of the whole crater with a couple of dogs. Command wants you two to do a hasty of Little Brother and then work the western edge of the Collier Glacier. Copy?"

Jonas pressed his radio before May had a chance to respond. "Command, copy. Do you want us to access Little Brother via Opie Dilldock Pass or go to the southern access point?"

Silence for a moment, then the voice rattled through once more. "Southern access on Little Brother."

Jonas confirmed. They gathered their gear. "They're tracking us quite closely," May murmured, somewhat comforted that someone knew where they were. She had no idea, and she'd been studying the map closely.

"They can't lose us," Jonas explained. "But they are tracking. They have to. They need to know exactly where we've searched and haven't searched."

They made swift time on the trail and May lost herself in the rhythm again. Ascending Opie Dilldock Pass, the blue ridges of Oregon's western Cascades unfolded around her, punctuated by sharp volcanoes and outcroppings of lava. The horizon line was hazy bright, and the sky was brilliant blue. The weather improved as they hiked, with few clouds in the sky even as the wind blew fierce.

At the top of the pass, they sat down side by side on their packs, took a brief break, stared out at the enormous hulk of North Sister. "You want to know something cool?" Jonas asked, looking at her almost shyly.

May nodded.

"That's a shield volcano," Jonas said, pointing at North Sister. "Last erupted in the late Pleistocene. Just a huge hunk of solid basalt that used to be inside the core of our planet."

"Wow," May breathed, unsure what response Jonas wanted.

"Wow is right." He bumped her shoulder with his. "Thanks for humoring me."

May glowed inside, pleased she'd gotten her response right. She looked around at the rocks surrounding them, tried to further the conversation. "Is all this lava from that mountain?"

"Most," Jonas said. "But so much of this has eroded away from weather, glaciers, rain. All of it. It's pretty amazing, heh?"

May wasn't sure 'amazing' was the term she'd use, but she chose to keep that opinion to herself. Instead, she twisted on her pack a little, considered how to ask Jonas about what had happened at the field station.

"Thanks," she eventually said, "for helping back there."

"With the angry guy?" Jonas asked.

She nodded, wondered how he viewed what had happened. If she could directly ask him about the assistant thing.

"May, you were doing great. And I was always there, prepared to back you up. Chief gave strict orders." He laughed, then stood up, stretched.

May watched him swoop down, throw his pack up onto his back. He turned towards her, and she was surprised when he reached a hand down, pulled her up. "You've got this," he said.

May clipped her own pack on. Sighed quietly. The moment to ask had passed, she knew it. But at least they were on good terms. Maybe if she was lucky she would spot Amelia and that would impress Jonas and he'd see her as an equal. She followed Jonas down the other side of the Pass, skirted far west around Little Brother, moved towards the Collier Glacier. The wind picked up, blowing small pieces of sand into May's face. She could taste dirt in her mouth.

At a point on the trail that looked entirely random, Jonas stopped, pointed east at the Collier Glacier. "We're going to head into the glacier base here," he said. "It will be tricky and fine picking, but I know you're up for it. Just don't put your hands down anywhere, this lava can be sharp."

May looked at her hands, envisioning them ripped to bloody ribbons. Not what she wanted. She wished she'd brought gloves. She folded her hands into protective fists. "Jonas, if we're struggling to get through this, how likely is it that a child can?"

Jonas shrugged. "Command commanded," he said.

He stepped off the trail. May looked around one more time, then followed.

They moved upslope through a thick stand of dead trees, then came out onto a ridge lined with huge blocks of craggy, dark rock. Following the ridge upwards, they climbed what felt like to May several times higher than the football stadium in Eugene where she'd once gone with her parents to watch a game, only this climb had mountain debris tumbling away on either side of the knife ridge. The wind buffeted them, and May walked carefully, her shoulders forward, head tucked. The higher they got, the harder the wind became. It was almost as if the mountains were trying to stop them from getting to the top.

The last few steps up the ridge were precarious. May could feel the rocks scrabbling under her feet. Jonas stuck his hand out and pulled her up onto the edge. His body was a steadying force between her and the wind.

"Jesus," was all May could muster once she got her feet under her. She could barely see across to the other side. She squinted directly below them, saw a steeper ridge, a deep channel, and then the glacier at the bottom.

"This is all volcanic material," Jonas said, pointing in front of them, his tone smooth and unconcerned in the high wind. "But see how this entire mountain flank is cut in half? That glacier gouged out this huge valley, this trough, ground through the volcanic dirt like it was butter. So to get to the other side, we have to walk this ridge, then dip down into the valley onto that scree slope, cross the glacier edge, and go back up the other side. We might run into the—"

"Look!" interrupted May, and she pointed northeast. Brightly dressed figures fanned out in a line on the rim of the volcano.

"Nice eyes," Jonas praised her.

May glowed, watched as he keyed his radio and reported his visual confirmation of the Collier Cone search team.

The wind began to slam them at irregular intervals, making it hard to brace and remain upright. Sand blew, and they made quick work of moving across and down the scree slope. May focused on how the sounds of their footsteps along the ridge echoed weird chiming sounds as they displaced rocks that collided with one another below them. She thought she could smell currents of sulfur dioxide as she hiked.

May worried the volcano might erupt while they were hunkered down near it. That would be just her luck. She shook herself, told her brain to stop being irrational, to focus on her foot placement so as not to get blown off the slope and down into the glacier trough. Told herself to be careful.

And then, halfway down the scree slope, she stepped on a larger loose rock that bucked her off her feet and suddenly she was sliding, falling back on her bottom and pack as she skidded down slope. She twisted, dug her heels in. Thought about screaming. She'd seen the gutter far below between the scree slope and the glacier that was packed full of rocks and snow. She was going to fall into that, die.

But then, only fifteen feet down, she suddenly stopped, her pack wedged onto a rock.

May lay on her back on her pack, tasted gritty dust in her mouth. She waited a moment, heart pounding, until she realized she was fine and filthy and somewhat exhilarated. The worst had happened, and she had survived. She watched Jonas move quickly towards her, yelling to see if she was okay.

She smiled. Maybe she was going to be able to do this after all.

She waved one hand almost languidly at Jonas, then, slowly, stood and brushed the rocks out of her pockets, pants, boots. She even felt a few rocks along her back, under her shirt. Unzipping her down jacket, she untucked her shirt and shook it out. Red rocks fell like rain.

The wind screeched by, touching her exposed skin and making her shiver. She zipped up her jacket, then paused. She'd caught the sound of a child's laugh somewhere behind her.

May went rigid. Closed her eyes, stood frozen, listened with precision. The wind whistled again, shrieking around her ears.

Nothing.

Then, more laughing. The sound of delight.

Forcing her eyes open, May scanned the area. She waved frantically at Jonas, unclipped and dropped her pack, pulled out her field glasses. She traced the ridgelines around her, looked and looked but didn't see anything.

"Did you hear that?" she shouted at Jonas when he'd maneuvered carefully to her position on the slope.

He looked at her, his eyes narrowed, face blank.

Excitement pounded in her throat. "Laughter! Like, a child's, but hushed?"

Jonas shook his head slow. "No, didn't hear anything besides you avalanching down this slope."

His tone momentarily deflated May. But she resisted, scanned the area around them. She'd heard laughter.

"But it's hard to hear anything with all this wind. Let's get down to the moraine, try to get a clearer view."

May shook her head, heart pounding. "No, I heard it here. We stay," she said firmly. "It's SAR 101, Jonas."

She caught the tightening look on his face, but she suddenly didn't care. Amelia Kane could be near them right that moment. She braced herself for an argument, but he didn't open his mouth. Instead, he pulled his own binoculars up to his face, scanned the area. Minutes ticked by.

"You sure?" he asked eventually, looking east.

May nodded. "Yes." Firm. Confident. She'd heard it. "Do you think it's Amelia?"

He dropped his binoculars. "It might have just been the Collier search team, Young. With this wind, sounds can carry."

May kept looking, heart hammering in her chest. Her throat felt tight. Could it have been the search team?

"I don't hear anything, nor do I see anything." He didn't look at May. "Are you one hundred percent sure?"

May swallowed. Was her brain playing tricks on her? The hikers at the station had said they'd heard laughter. Had her subconscious tried to recreate it?

"I don't doubt you, Young. But I know you're new, and you just took a big spill. Do you want me to radio this in to Command? Or should we get going and search where they've directed us to?" Jonas's voice was calm, reasonable.

Indecision cascaded over May. She didn't know what to do. She thought she'd heard laughter, but now, she wasn't so sure. They hadn't seen anything. She waffled. Looking at Jonas as he looked steadily at her, she conceded grudgingly. He had more experience, and there was the possibility her brain was being dramatic.

"Let's just go," she murmured.

Side by side, they slid to the bottom of the slope. May felt uneven, her feet not sliding as gracefully as Jonas's. She broke her awkwardness by stopping every few feet on the slope to turn, listen, but she heard nothing. The only thing she could detect was a faint humming, a thrum that sounded like a heartbeat. But she refrained from telling Jonas. Not that she could, anyway. He didn't stop when she did, and he had started walking so much faster than her that he was already on the steep ridge just above the Collier Glacier.

May jogged down the rest of the way to catch up with him, her pack bouncing erratically. Breathing heavily, she didn't say anything when she reached his side, instead just looked at the glacier below them.

The ice flowed along the mountain and looked like thick cake frosting. May was surprised how gray it was. The side of North Sister opposite them slanted steeply, as if someone had just shaved off an entire side of the mountain. The valley the glacier was in was full of grayed scree. It sat both on top of and all around the glacier. Small patches of dirty blue poked through, and down towards the Collier Cone large gray and brown lakes bloomed at the edge of the ice.

"We're going to go all the way down to the ice edge, then follow the slope up and around to the other side," Jonas said. "This is the most dangerous part. We'll need to be careful going over those two big snow patches bridging out to the ice, but I think it'll be fine."

May nodded in agreement, sweating from the exertion. She'd never seen a glacier up close, and heaving her heavy pack up and down the loose slopes was starting to exhaust her. She'd give anything to sit down, eat a sandwich.

Jonas led. They traversed the tricky slope, keeping the glacier parallel by about a hundred feet below. The slope was loose, but had a surprising amount of plant life. Moss, May guessed. All moss, everywhere.

They hiked for ten minutes before the wind picked up again. It had been calm, but now it came roaring down off North and Middle Sister and freight-trained them, causing May to stop and crouch. May had only paused twice before to listen for laughter, but after she'd seen the irritated look on Jonas's face, she stopped. Instead, she worked hard to keep up with him. But now, the gusts felt like the wind was trying to rip her off the slope. Billowing up from the ice, it was freezing, and May's exposed cheeks were simultaneously sandblasted and icy. She hunkered down, shouted at Jonas.

"I thought it was summer!"

Jonas turned, acknowledged her comment with a brisk head bob, shouted back, voice friendly. "You've got this. Let's get across this snow patch, hunker down over there together to wait for the wind to pass."

Jonas prodded the snow with his toe, stepped onto it, then quickly across the patch. He gestured for May to cross too.

She walked out onto the slushy snow, watched her boots sink a few inches. She worried for a moment that the snow wouldn't hold, that it would give way and toss her under the glacier's edge.

She eyed the patch, tried to estimate how thick the snow was stacked up in the gutter between the slope and the glacier.

"Let's go!" Jonas shouted.

May committed.

Her first few steps, and the snow held. Then she was almost across.

Just as May reached the snow's far edge, the wind slammed into her back and knocked her forward onto her knees. She stuck her hands out to catch her fall, sank elbows deep into the snow. She tried to push herself up but felt her legs flounder in the loose snow.

May windmilled her arms, then froze all motion. She heard high-pitched laughter coming from behind her. She jerked her head around, looked down at the glacier, saw nothing.

The laughter was all around her now. May tried again to stand, pushed into the snow, pushed against something hard, something like a long, cold stone.

Whole seconds dragged by, entire heartbeats where May could feel each knock of her pulse, each molecular exchange between oxygen and carbon dioxide in her alveoli. She heard laughter, she heard humming, and she knew what she was touching before the words came screaming from her mouth.

She looked down into the snow, into the hole her flailing arms had created. She knew that the stone she was pushing against was not a stone.

She squinted, registered with her eyes what her fingers already knew.

She was touching a foot. A foot connected to a human leg.

7

THE
SCIENTIST

Ros dragged her feet, dodged grasping Doug fir branches that seemed to claw for the plastic pipes every few steps. Her mood was bitter.

She yanked the pipes through the last few trees, cleared the forest line, looked back down the dark trail. "I could burn you down," she hissed. Turned her back on the trees.

She glanced up at the hundred feet or so remaining to the summit of Black Crater. There, she could drop the absurd load of winterization gear. But the loose crumble of rock underfoot slowed her, slid her back every third, fourth step.

"Hard to hear my own thoughts with all this damned noise!" she growled, eyes flicking up at the helicopter that thumped overhead.

She tried to focus, looked at her feet and the lava beneath, tried to identify the individual scoria and basalt and rhyolite and obsidian and brittle dacite. Scuffed some of the smaller rounded bits with her boots. Rocks were so much more respectful than trees. She remembered how along South Sister, near Rock Mesa, miners had come for the dacite. They sold it as kitty litter. She smirked at the thought, imagined all the world's cats shitting in materials sourced from her mountain. Her mood lightened and she kept moving up, calves aching.

The hike up the shield volcano from her cabin wasn't really that far, her pack wasn't that heavy, and the fourteen-hundred-foot climb to the summit where all the monitoring equipment sat wasn't really that steep. But Ros's mind was heavy, full of lead lined with osmium, and she felt like she was walking underwater on a planet where someone had turned up the gravity by an order or two of magnitude. Pushing through the forest earlier—stomping over the thick ground cover drying into winter, the huckleberries with their faded leaves and the low-slung mosses dangling from trunks and branches—she'd been impervious to the beauty.

She knew why she was off kilter, knew exactly when it had started. Her conversations with Ash had stirred something inside of her that she habitually avoided.

Ros sighed, turned, dropped her pack and heaved herself down onto a crumbling log. She looked at the white bark pine trunks sticking up out of the side of the slope, bleached and sandblasted, fatalities of one of the innumerable local volcanic eruptions. Wondered if it was Black Crater itself that had vented the trees into pale white ghosts, or if it had been from neighboring Belknap. Didn't matter where you turned in this landscape—seemed like everything was trying to kill you. Or maim.

Ros's spine tingled, her teeth hollowed. She tilted her head, noticed a humming that was reedy, high pitched. When she swiveled her head, though, she couldn't locate the source. It was as if it was all around her and coming from inside her skull. She twisted, scanned the rough terrain below her through the Milli Fire scar and all the way down into the valley bottom.

She stared into the trees, tried to make out human figures amongst the trunks.

Her skin crawled.

The humming was jarring, like someone had taken an axe to a singing bowl. She blinked. At that moment, she wouldn't have been surprised if her long-lost mother and sister stepped from the tree line shepherding Amelia Kane.

Ros sighed again, felt foolish.

She was a scientist, she reminded herself. She investigated

geology. Tangible. Rooted in the ground. Not ghosts. She squinted up at the clouds, took in the weather, saw no recurrence of the nimbo-stratus that had dumped so much precipitation the night before. The only evidence of the clouds was the damp ground soaking through her pantlegs.

Ros took control of her thoughts. Reassured herself by identify-ing three cloud genera and what conditions they required to appear and grow. She peeked at her forearms to confirm it wasn't insects making the crawly sensation on her skin. Leaned back, allowed her-self to consider ghosts scientifically.

There were ghosts that haunted this landscape, real ones that she could still see signs of if she looked. Like, wolverines.

She knew that wolverines used to claw about the mountain-ous rocks, roam the lava and snow and solitary paths right where she sat. State officials claimed they'd extirpated the creature back in the 1930s, but isolated sightings, tracks, and skeletons kept popping up. A colleague of Ros's who worked in the Wallowas, a mountain range out east on the Idaho border, had told her of two breeding pairs of wolverines who'd been sighted recently on wild-life cameras. Ros had asked if the wolverines would return to the Oregon Cascades, but her colleague had snorted and said that the animals would have to cross a great deal of territory full of armed Oregonians. If they shot at the Rajneeshees, they'd sure as hell shoot at the wolverines.

Ros groaned aloud at her thoughts, couldn't quite get her head around the idea of how anyone would find value in pleasure killing, in extirpating an entire species.

She looked back down the trail into the woods she'd just hiked through. Perfect for wolverines, corporeal or not. Maybe they'd return one day?

She tried to hold the train of her thoughts, pull the brakes, but it was too late. Her mind flowed to the next obvious set of questions: If wolverines could return, perhaps Flower and Herring could too? Amelia Kane?

Ros blew a stream of air through her pursed lips. "Stop it," she told herself.

She knew she was being purposefully morose. Hell, if she was going to fixate on ghosts, why didn't she look at the landscape itself, the high volcanic peaks that were so eroded by eruptions and glaciers and fire and weather that today they stood barely a fraction of their former selves? Or the plant life, the bananas and figs and grapes that had once covered Eocene Oregon? Why not think of the Miocene-era shovel-tusked mastodons, or the tiny single-toed Pliocene horses, or the Pleistocene dire wolves that had all wandered Oregon for eons before fading away into haunted stone? What about all the ghosts she didn't know about, the unimaginable creatures erased by flood after flood throughout the Ice Age that had scoured down from Lake Missoula, burnishing away the footprints of incalculable lives before? What about the generations of First Peoples from time anon who had been slaughtered during colonization?

"Stop," she said, out loud. Her voice echoed and thrummed.

She looked around. The side of the crater she was on was an old cirque, a once perfectly respectable shield volcano with an enormous chunk gouged gone by a long-disappeared glacier. Another ghost. She paused, scanned the half-open valley full of burnt forest, imagined the glacier. Everything in her field of vision—from the flank of Black Crater to the most remote mountain peaks—screamed glacier ghosts.

Ros thought about the geomorphology of the area, pushed her thoughts into the well-worn grooves of science felt her pulse calm. The tiny hairs on her arms that had been standing like defensive spikes relaxed against her skin. She breathed in, out, leaned back against the warm earth, tried to tune out the humming, thought about ice.

During the Pleistocene, the most recent epoch that lasted some two and half million years, the Oregon Cascades had been covered with two separate ice caps. One ice cap had been parked up on Mount Hood, and a second had centered around Mount Jefferson and extended south to the Three Sisters. The glaciers coming off the Sisters today were mere remnants of those much larger ice systems, liminal afterthoughts hacked off by Ice Age glacier ghosts.

Ros remembered her first year at OHEWS, when she'd spent most of her time roaming the Three Sisters Wilderness, learning the intimate contours of the land as she scanned the clouds and rocks and kicked up forest fire ash and searched for optimum research sites.

Back then, as she'd searched, she'd stumbled repeatedly across monstrous scratches in the bedrock, deep claw marks vivid in exposed igneous. And while she knew that glaciers had moved across the bedrock and ripped such marks into the land, her heart and brain had caught each time she saw them. What if it had been something else?

The air vibrated around Ros and she shivered, felt a flash of anger. She looked up, saw another helicopter. And a third. Wondered what the hell was going on that there were suddenly so many of them. It had been as quiet as mouse hiccups when she'd left the field station earlier.

Maybe the search had located Amelia Kane?

Hope flashed through Ros. The last thing this place needed was another ghost. She stood, picked up her gear, and march-hiked the remaining distance to the summit of Black Crater.

At the top, she did not pause, did not take in the view. Instead, she blazed past the remnants of the old Forest Service fire lookout tower, past two large iron-striped extrusive outcroppings she usually rested on, and didn't slow until she arrived at the tucked-away field tower. She tossed her pack down, careful not to crack the plastic pipes, and stretched her back. She looked up at the tower. A tripod of shiny metal supports was bolted into the ground. They met at about Ros's shoulder height where they reinforced a single unit antennae that extended into the sky, an absolute invitation for lightning in Ros's opinion. She gazed at the tower and thought, not for the first time, how much it looked like an enormous metal mosquito sucking blood lava from the land.

Heavy wire guy lines stretched from the top of the tower to smaller anchor points in the rock. Instrumentation and sensors bristled on almost every surface—precipitation collectors and air samplers, prongs measuring wind speed and direction and force, various devices Ros put up and took down as researchers cycled through funded projects at the universities in the valley. The environmental data was linked to a battery powered radio transmitter that bounced off several relays as it connected to the sensitive ground tracking antenna set up at Ros's cabin.

Below the tower was a solar array that powered the sets of twelve-volt rechargeable batteries stashed in a sizable metal lockbox. When Ros opened the box, she was always blasted with the smell of mouse shit. The box held the brain for the tower—he small conduit and computer that physically transmitted the data. Ros slipped in a key, held her breath, and popped the box, checked the backup batteries, then plugged into the data port to start a manual data download.

Stepping away from the tower, she sat against the iron-striped rock she often used as a bench, scanned the area with her field glasses. She rattled off the geography she knew by heart. To the north, Mount Washington, Three Fingered Jack, Jefferson, Hood. To the east, Black Butte and the Oregon scablands. To the south, the Three Sisters and Broken Top, Bachelor, Diamond Peak, Thielsen, Bailey. To the west, the blue rumpled ridges of the Coast Range.

Focusing on the more immediate forelands of mixed conifer and forest fire scars before her, she ran her glasses over the 242, her own cabin on Harlow Crater, southward to the Collier Cone. No helicopters in sight. They'd all disappeared.

Wind blew through her hair, the sun warmed her core, and Ros felt better sitting up high, a part of the sky, scanning the topography. If that little girl was near Black Crater, Ros would see her.

She weather-vaned, assessed the conditions. Sun on her face: temperature in the high sixties. Small hairs on her arms gently lifted: east winds ten to fifteen miles per hour. Humidity, barometric pressure, dewpoint, visibility. She couldn't detect any more humming.

Looking up into the sky, she assessed low, mid, and high-level cloud layers. She counted nine full-sized Cumulus parked directly over Belknap Crater, two fluffy Cumulus floating nearby, and one stalled on Mt. Washington's pointy horn.

She suppressed a sigh, looked away from the Cumulus dotting the sky over the Three Sisters, tried to resist the tug of memory. But her conversations with Ash had aroused everything raw within herself and she couldn't stop.

Ros slid back into her childhood, back into the car. She saw herself laying there, watching the clouds drift by, hoping her mother and sister would come back.

She remembered them walking away, straight into the lava, but she never saw them disappear. They were just there one moment and then gone the next. She'd sat there, waited in the backseat with a thick wool blanket wrapped around her. She'd been patient at first, stared at the highway, the lava, the sky, but then it seemed a lot of time had passed and they hadn't returned. She'd crawled up into the front passenger seat and screamed their names. She'd honked the horn, slammed her fists into the wheel, but it didn't make any noise. She tried each of the doors, but they did not open. So, Ros had gone back into the back seat, laid down, and stared crying at the sky. Crying turned to sobs turned to hitching and heaving, and she'd screamed and shouted and called and pleaded and no one heard her and night fell and she saw stars—the Big Dipper and Little Dipper and Cepheus and Leo and Virgo and streaks of clouds that came and went—and eventually she slept until she woke again cold and terrified.

They still had not returned.

Ros had sat desolate and terrified. She'd pissed herself in the night and the car smelled thick with ammonia. She was ashamed and afraid. When cars or trucks drove by, Ros would scream and scream and scream until she was hoarse, saliva and phlegm and tears coating her swollen face and glazing the inside of the car and windows. She beat on the glass with her small hands, flaying her knuckles raw, but she could not break out.

Ros learned later that the locks were faulty and that if she'd pulled down the back seats, she could have slid into the trunk and pulled the switch to open the trunk hatch and escape, but she hadn't known that then. And so she had passed from panic to hysteria to fatigue to terror to indifference. Cars and trucks had rocketed by and had not stopped, and she knew she was alone.

Eventually, she'd laid down in the back seat and blurred in and out of consciousness. She remembered watching clouds shaped like animals talking to her and caressing the sides of the car and the door handles and then coming in through the glass. The clouds had wrapped themselves around her and she'd no longer felt alone.

She did not remember anything detailed after that, just that she'd stared with dry, open eyes at the sky and hummed a song with no ending, no beginning. She had no memory of later, when two Linton Lake hikers passed by the car on the third day and saw her and broke the driver side window and pulled her out and carried her to the hospital in Eugene. She awoke three days later to doctors, nurses, state patrol, and detectives leaning over her bed, and the only thing she knew then was that something had forever changed inside her.

Movement caught Ros's eye, and she rotated her field glasses toward the Collier Cone and a speck of blue moving along the crater rim. Ros watched the speck carefully, her pulse quickening. But then another speck joined the first, and another, and another. She swallowed. She knew Amelia Kane was alone, so those specks could not be a tiny, lost girl.

She thought. Then, raised her glasses again to the Collier Cone. Realized she was probably seeing the search and rescue team.

Ros pulled the bulky HT radio from where it was clipped on the outside of her pack, flipped it on and to the channel Jonas had indicated. She radioed the search base to confirm with the dispatch that searchers were on the volcano's rim. She waited for a response.

Nothing but radio static.

She checked her radio settings. The green battery light was lit.

She called in again.

No response.

She set the HT at her feet, shivered in the silence. She picked up her binoculars again, watched the specks of people, wondered if it was the searchers why they were looking around the crater and the Collier Glacier. She estimated there were at least ten or fifteen people scattered around the area. It was out of the way for a girl whose last known position was several miles north.

Ros ran her glasses over the Collier Glacier itself, scrutinized the white surface shimmering faintly with atmospheric distortion, blinked slow. Not a thing moved on the ice.

In her abdomen, Ros felt a small snick, a clipped pull tugging her forward, towards the glacier. The ice called to her, Ros could feel it. It was the closest thing to clouds on land. It drew her intensely. As if they were kin, her and the ice.

Ros ran her glasses up the length of the Collier. She wondered what that ice had seen over the millennia, how it had survived. What it had done.

Glaciers, she mused, were continuously dissolving and resolving. They smothered. They sustained. They survived. They destroyed.

The Collier was no different.

She set the binoculars back in her lap, squinted at the faint ice she could just see with her naked eye. The glacier seemed to wave at her. Ros knew it was atmospheric distortion that caused the movement, but unbidden she still reached up a hand, waved back.

She'd learned about the Collier in graduate school when she was studying Pacific Northwest geology. It was the largest remaining glacier in Oregon, named after a man who'd climbed the Sisters in the late 1880s. Ros always thought that honor should have gone to Ruth Hopsen Keen, a public school teacher in 1930s Eugene. Keen had created the first and only photographic decadal record of the Collier, photos that were of incalculable value to modern scientists—Ros herself had used Keen's images in her dissertation.

"OHEWS Black Crater, OHEWS Black Crater." Ros's radio crackled.

She was jerked from her thoughts. She scrambled to pick up her radio. It was working again.

"OHEWS, we're reminding you of a 12:00 noon, 12:00 noon pick up of Tove Andersen at the 242 re-supply. Tomorrow. Confirm?"

"Confirmed, Corvallis, confirmed." While Ros had been looking forward to meeting the new fellow, she'd entirely forgot about her pending arrival.

"Confirmed, OHEWS. Also be notified of an early delivery arriving with Andersen."

A smile curled up one side of her face. "Would that be boots, Base?"

"Perhaps, OHEWS."

Ros grinned. That was quick.

Signing off, Ros felt a wave of inertia come over her, and she picked the field glasses up again. She knew she should stand up, start installing the new plastic pipes, then hustle back and get the Fellows Cabin and Main Cabin sorted, but instead she sat rooted on the summit rock, allowing her curls to tangle with the wind. She scanned with her binoculars. Twelve Cumulus now. Patches of high-altitude Cirrus, mare's tails. Ros stared through the clouds, then back down to the glacier.

It pulled at her somehow. Again.

Her field glasses dropped down into her lap, and her feet drifted out in front of her. They were warming in the sun and faintly tingling from the wet of the just-damp ground. Ros could hear a hazy humming, much more pleasant than earlier. It lulled.

She closed her eyes, felt herself leaning forward.

But, then, a discordant thumping grew in volume. Ros squinted into the bright sky.

A helicopter. And a second one. And a third.

She watched the helicopters, how they clustered around the Collier Glacier. She shook her head. They must have found something to risk going so low and blowing all that volcanic particulate to high hell with the rotor blades. One had a low basket hanging from it. Her heart panged for Amelia Kane. Maybe they had found the little girl.

Wind caressed Ros's face. She blinked, tried to slow her thoughts.

Whatever ghostly traces Flower and Herring once had left on the land unfolding in front of her eyes, Ros knew logically she wasn't ever going to find evidence of them. To her, that was clear, scientific fact. But some days, most days, she caught herself looking anyway, despite her scientific certainty, because she knew looking gave her some sense of control.

That was what she'd tried to explain to Ash that morning before she'd left, but the conversation had veered out of control.

After the search and rescue people had come and gone, Ros had made breakfast while Trick packed in the Fellows Cabin and Ash poured herself a coffee. She'd called it a "social coffee," and Ros had restrained herself from snarking too loudly about how this was precisely the reason she'd chosen to live alone. But after Ash had poured the coffee, she hadn't been social at all. Instead, she'd sat in her chair quietly, looking out through the open door. Ros had flipped tomatoes silently in the cast iron pan.

When Ash did start to feel social again and spoke up, she'd apparently had to repeat herself twice before Ros heard her.

"Does it make it harder when you hear about other missing people?" she'd asked when Ros had responded, her voice soft, just the two of them in the stillness of the cabin.

Ros had stiffened, surprised.

"Not anymore," she'd finally replied. "So many people have gone missing out here that I've stopped personalizing it. There are many variables."

"Variables?"

Ros had turned down the burner, looked at Ash sitting wrapped in a blanket by the table. The woman still appeared exhausted. "Yes. Factors, details, choices that I have not only no knowledge of, but also no control over. I don't know what happened to that little girl out there, but whatever it is, it can't be good."

Ash had nodded, had cupped her coffee mug with both hands. "I hope this is okay to ask, but did the police ever tell you what they thought happened to your mom and sister?"

"You're okay." Ros flipped the tomatoes a last time, reaching for the bowl of eggs on the counter. She picked up a fork, paused. "Not really. I mean, over the years, various police would come, ask questions, but it always seemed speculative. So many theories, potential outcomes. I was asked countless questions, but no one ever answered the questions I asked."

Ros pushed her curls back, tucked them behind her ears, swirled the eggs. "Maybe they'd gotten lost, been exposed to weather, gotten hurt somehow. Maybe it was a serial killer. Maybe they fell into a lava tube. Maybe they got disoriented. Maybe they hitchhiked into Sisters. Maybe they got separated." Ros lifted her spatula. "Maybe, maybe, maybe."

"Does Oregon have serial killers?" Ash had pleated into herself, had shifted her long legs and set her cup on the table. She looked out the window, then back at Ros. "I mean, I guess it does, right?"

"Like Butcher Baker killers? That sort of thing?" Ros had answered lightly, stared at the eggs without seeing, winced at the artifice in her tone.

"God, I've read about that guy. Jesus. To be in Anchorage back then. He actively hunted women for over a decade. A *decade*."

"Yep. He extirpated them. And when one of the women he'd attacked, Kitty Larsen, escaped, no one believed her." Ros had said it quietly, to the eggs.

"No one ever believes…"

Ros had twisted her shoulders, turned to look at the other woman sitting at the table. She'd considered Ash for a moment. Opened her mouth, closed it, opened it again. Might as well commit. Ash had started it.

"When those SAR folks came here about Amelia Kane, I was worried about the child," Ros had said. "But Ash, I immediately thought about that child's mom, Leonie. I've looked for my family for years. And now she will too. But with what support? I bet half this state will think she killed her daughter, and the other half will think she should be jailed for neglect."

The words had balled out of Ros's mouth, rolled frenziedly free.

"People barely believed *me*. That Flower and Herring just walked away into the lava. They all thought I knew more." The bitterness in her tone was unconcealable. "A kid."

"I'm so sorry, Ros." Ash had leaned forward, compassion outlining each syllable.

Ros had tried to change course, had run a hand through her curls again and felt damp sweat exploding on her scalp. She'd summoned a weak smile, shrugged a shoulder. Had both accepted and dismissed Ash's kindness. She'd turned back to the obviously overdone eggs. Had looked down at the white chunks in the pan, sighed. But still hadn't been able to stop herself from finishing it. So she'd turned back, faced Ash, opened her mouth once more. "And, yes. Oregon has serial killers."

She'd drawn a long breath, closed her eyes, listened to the ragged sound of her voice as she rattled off names she'd memorized years ago. "The NFL guy. The Highway 16 guy. The shoe guy. The Green River guy. The Molalla Forest guy. The list, the guys, just keeps going."

She'd opened her burning eyes, looked at Ash full on.

"Oregon has serial killers. But who's looking? Women have been going missing out here in horrific numbers since always. But people only pay attention when they're forced to, when it's right out in the open for everyone to see."

8
THE
DAUGHTER

Donna last set eyes on her living, breathing mother when she was halfway through her eleventh year. Ray'd been out drinking, and both Donna and her mother knew what would happen when he returned.

They sat in the quiet of the cabin, her mother staring out the window and Donna tucked into her side on the floor near the wood stove, warmed but wary. Tracing the floor grains with her finger, she'd been alert to her mother sitting stiff, waiting. Donna had thought, at the time, her mother's thoughts dwelled upon Ray.

Since Ray had shot the osprey out of the tree, he'd grown only more erratic, angry. He rarely left the cabin for paid work. He'd taken to driving the highways at all hours of the night, climbing into the truck after dinner and reversing full speed out the dirt lane. Donna was never sure if night had ended or if morning had started when he returned. He'd blare the truck horn to summon Julene. Donna would watch her mother help Ray from the cab, the small woman's arm muscles shaking as she half carried Ray to the porch. To Donna, her mother's face was a kaleidoscope of reactions, scowling when she scrubbed his boots, softening when she massaged her husband's shoulders, blank when he handed her presents of clothes or shoes or jewelry, wary when he accused her. When Donna saw her mother's face go taut, she knew to sneak out of the back of the cabin and hide in the woods. Risk assessment.

If Donna had thought hard that last night, it would have been about how her mother had been different, how she wasn't working, wasn't knitting or sewing or anything. But Donna wasn't thinking; she'd been hunkered down quiet. When she peeked beneath the bracelets of green beads, there had been purple smears on Julene's wrists, flames of purple-black gouged into the flesh. Her mother couldn't move her wrists very well. Donna couldn't either.

When the whisper of an engine murmured through the dark woods and between the cabin walls, Donna's mother stood quickly like a jack free of its box. Only later did Donna come to understand that her mother had been expecting the car.

Headlights washed over the porch. Julene had pulled Donna to her feet, pushed her away from the warm stove, and out the door. Donna stood there like a donkey before slaughter, head hanging, while Julene knelt behind the wood rack. She removed a small cloth bundle. Julene stood, hugged the bundle to her chest, then shoved it into Donna's hands. She'd whispered, "Books, change of clothes, something to remember me by."

That whisper never left Donna's mind, just looped over and over in the years since.

"Books, change of clothes, something to remember me by."

Donna had not understood, had not connected the bundle to her mother to the car to what was going to happen. She just stood there clutching the wad to her stomach, still expecting Ray to appear. Even as her mother had pushed her down the steps, two hands pressed hotly into her back, Donna did not understand. When the trunk opened, a small crack that Julene made larger by yanking, she just stared at her mother blankly.

Standing on the porch now, Donna strained to remember.

Had she said anything to her mother in that moment?

Donna opened the file, pulled out the stored images. Her, eleven years old, not comprehending what was happening, standing near the trunk of a car. Staring at her mother.

Had she said goodbye?

Donna closed her eyes, reviewed the memory. But just like the color of the car, or what they'd eaten together last, or the feel of her mother's dress—so many of the details of that night were lost to her.

"Daughter." Ray's voice wheezed faintly, pulling Donna back to the present.

Donna pivoted instinctually, shoulder low, pointed, on guard. She closed her eyes again, batted away the reassuring image of a white beach, meandering seals, the comfort of contemplating qualitative versus quantitative data sets. Didn't want to float away. Rubbed the beads on her wrist. Wanted instead to remember. There was something there, like a faint whisper.

"Daughter." Again, insistent.

The memory evaporated.

Wrenching her eyes open, fire raged inside. She'd almost remembered. She stormed through the screen door, seething, into the cabin and Ray's rotting stink.

Donna heard her therapist yelling, telling her to walk away, to never approach anyone in anger, to breathe and visualize and breathe more. But Donna ignored her therapist and instead exhaled hot irritation and anger and boiling fumes. Stood above Ray's bed, hissed, "What?"

Ray's eyes opened, eyelids detaching gummily. His eyes wouldn't focus.

"What?" Donna repeated, her anger still knifing just under her skin.

"Make her stop screaming," he breathed.

It took three blinks for Ray's words to land, register, process. Her heart leapt to her throat, and she softened her stance, dropped her hands to her sides, rearranged her face.

"Who is screaming?" She calibrated her tone soft, forgiving, leading.

Ray jerked his head, twisted the folds of skin around his neck, clawed the air.

Speaking sweetly like a well-mannered woman, she leaned closer. Considered addressing him as Father, but instead, waited. She knew she should save that, for later. Perhaps kindness would move him now.

"I can help, Ray," she said evenly. "Just tell me what happened."

She leaned away as Ray jerked again. Again. Something was after him in his mind. Good, she smiled. Hope it got him. Stabbed him in the teeth.

"Who is screaming, Ray?" She reached for the plastic water cup beside his bed. "Tell me, and I'll give you water." Bargaining with the devil, she knew. A woman's deal.

A pink tongue darted from Ray's mouth, searched for water. His blue eyes were half closed, rheumy, and she suppressed an urge to slap him. Barely.

"Fine," she said loudly, like Ray was not just dying but also deaf, "I'm taking the water. I'll come back in ten minutes. You tell me who is screaming, I'll give you water."

His mouth made a hissing noise, but Donna averted her eyes and left the room, fire flaring back in her stomach so fast she felt like she had diarrhea. She gulped the evening air when she arrived back to the porch, scanned the clearing like it could tell her something, breathed.

She didn't know how much longer she could do this. She sat heavily down on the steps, hung her head. She was exhausted. She closed her eyes. Remembered.

Julene had picked her up, lifted Donna off her dragging feet, laid her in the trunk like it was a coffin. She'd tucked Donna's dress around her legs, patted the bundle gingerly. Donna was sure her mother had said something then. And Donna was also sure she'd said something to her mother, but, again, there was nothing. When she strained her memory, the only thing she could recall was a faint rattle as Julene dragged the green beads off her wrist and pressed them into Donna's small hands.

The file was incomplete, was missing data. Her therapist said Donna might never remember.

Her memory jumped and the trunk suddenly closed, the car moving. It was ink-dark and she'd laid there in quiet horror and pissed herself more than once and time blurred and the car stopped and the trunk opened and all she saw was a yellow-lit garage. Then a woman with bright white hair was scooping her out and pressing her against her shoulder like a doll.

There must have been talking, the lady probably said things, but they were all muted, as if listening to a movie underwater. Donna saw this memory in third person, the reel unwinding as the woman in the floral tent dress carried her to a bathtub and set her in it and turned on hot water. The water had terrified Donna, and the woman had said something, then sat heavily on a closed toilet seat and plucked at Donna's clothes. But Donna had been too scared and too confused and too everything, so she'd soaked in the hot water stiff and rigid and fully dressed.

Later, the woman had handed her a sleeping gown three sizes too big and decorated with kittens. Donna had gotten the idea and slipped it over her head and then unzipped her dress and let it fall to the ground and the woman had beckoned her to a bedroom and she'd crawled into the biggest bed she'd ever seen and the woman had settled into a wide-based rocking chair and picked up a book and each time she'd woken up in the night, the woman was still there, reading a book and humming.

At some point, Donna had cried, asked over and over for Julene. The woman moved to the bed, picking her up and gently rocked her while making murmuring noises. Donna had wept for her mother, had asked where she was, and the woman had held her tightly and told her she'd never lose Julene. "Sometimes," Donna remembered her saying, "even though we can't seem them, they're still with us."

Donna had fallen asleep at some point that night clutching her mother's bracelet, and the days and months that came after glommed into a fragmented blur. While she could recall in vivid detail the weld beads along the inside of the trunk, she couldn't remember the older woman's face or voice or house or any other events relating to her, the details of how long she stayed with her, what happened immediately after. She was simply there in Donna's memory and then she wasn't.

Even today, thinking of her, all Donna could summon was that the woman had white hair, smelled slightly sour, made comforting humming noises.

At some point, Donna moved. She had a brief memory of two women she'd never seen before arriving in a car one morning and taking her to a house on the outskirts of Eugene. Later, when Donna was older and had gotten her first degree in cartography, she'd spent many hours driving around the Thurston neighborhoods after work, then Santa Clara and Danebo, then east Eugene. She'd never found that first house again, nor the second.

She lived in the second house for several months. She didn't remember much, only the sensation of looking up every time the door opened, jerking her chin and shoulders and eyes towards the person coming in.

One memory Donna did recall clearly was a day when the two women whom she'd seen earlier reappeared, this time introducing themselves as social workers named Maureen and Alai. They had sat her down in a kitchen and asked her to describe what she'd experienced living with Ray. Donna had stared at the linoleum and remained mute, just as she'd been taught by Julene. But the women had stacked so many questions upon her that she'd panicked and peed herself and the women had left.

After that, she was told she would need to be re-homed. Donna had a crystal-clear memory of that moment, of asking when Julene would join her. Both social workers had shook their heads, had said a nice lady had offered to open her home to her, and did Donna want to go there and start school in the fall?

"Julene might join you later," Maureen had said, eyes on Alai, and then Donna was in a car again being driven across Eugene.

Donna did remember her first meeting with Blazey Watts. Blazey was in her mid-fifties then. She wore her blonde-gray hair shoulder length and a pair of oversized brown glasses. She'd opened the door of her purple house as soon as the social workers pulled up, had invited Donna in, made a cup of hot chocolate for them both.

"And this," she said after introducing herself, "is Tuck Everlasting." She gestured to a huge black and white dog with fluffy fur sticking out of every possible surface. The dog had licked Donna and she'd cuddled into his immense side as Blazey chatted up a one-sided storm.

Blazey told her she was a professor at a university in Eugene, liked to garden bright flowers, did not know how long Donna would stay but hoped it would be for as long as she wanted. Blazey was impressed with Donna's physical strength and predilection for neatness. Suggested they later take a long walk up a thing she called a "butte." She said she did not know when Donna would see Julene again, but she sure hoped it would be soon, and until then, she was happy to help Donna in any way she could.

A snapping branch interrupted Donna's review. She was back, on the cabin porch, staring at the clearing. She glanced down at her watch, realized thirty minutes had passed, sighed. She wanted to go through those early years again and again. Comb through them. Find anything that might cut through the fog of missing words, memories, time. What had her mother said before putting her in the car? She must have said something.

Donna shifted her hips, looked out at the grass, the trees. There was something she knew she was missing, and it was just out of her reach. She rubbed the beads on her wrist, stood.

She walked back into the cabin, back to Ray's bedside, set the cup she still clutched back down on the tabletop with a clatter. Thought about the different approaches she could take to get Ray to talk. Thought about strangling him until he agreed, but then worried that he was so frail she'd accidentally snap his throat and then that would be a mess she'd have to deal with. She looked down at the man, considered her options.

Ray's eyes fluttered open. Still blue, but now faded, diluted with pending death. Donna turned away, revulsion and excitement colliding inside her.

"She's in my head," Ray whispered, words oddly clear from his buckled lips and rotted gums.

Donna stared down at him; aware she'd taken a threatening posture. Ray seemed slightly more coherent than earlier. She reached down beside his bed, saw his eyes tightening as he followed her movements. Her fingers brushed the oxygen tank regulator.

"Daughter," he whispered.

She considered flipping the valve for the regulator off and watching Ray suffer as he asphyxiated. Let herself linger in the fantasy.

One of Donna's earlier therapists had told her nothing was out of bounds in fantasies as long as they stayed in the mind. Fantasies might help her control her anger, might help her keep calm. Donna could visualize anything she wanted as long as she refrained from making the fantasy real.

Donna visualized setting Ray on fire, making him suffer horribly. She pictured stuffing his gray face with the body of the rotten, long-dead osprey, strangling his squelchy neck until he confessed.

All fine.

Donna tightened her fingers, pushed, flipped the knob on the oxygen regulator up one notch, increased Ray's continuous flow. Leaned over the old man.

"Is there something you want to tell me?" Sweet, peaceful.

Ray scrabbled at the air with his lobster hands, gummed his pink tongue. "Screaming."

"Who? Who is screaming?" Donna was all concern and daughterly affection.

"Laughter. They're all laughing at me."

"Ray." She repeated his name three times, loud.

"So cold," he murmured, eyes closing. Mouth loosened. "I made them so cold."

Something roared inside Donna, tore away her calculated approach and laid raw her fury. "Dammit Ray!" she shouted, slammed her hand hard against the bedside table. "Tell me where Julene is!"

Rage burned over Donna, hot and eruptive. She seized Ray's wrist, held it tight with one hand even as his skin burned her palm. She understood she could snap his frail bones. Was tempted. Jerked his arm hard instead. His eyes lurched open, panicked. Satisfaction blossomed in her stomach, made the monster inside her purr. She did nothing to tamp it down.

"Do not go to sleep," she ordered him. "Tell me what happened to my mother."

Ray tried to pull his arm free, feeble and impotent against Donna's anger, her strength.

"Don't like that, do you?" she said, squeezed harder.

His eyes met hers, wide and scared. "Screaming," he whimpered. "Laughing."

"You used to laugh at me, right Ray?" Donna rattled the beads on her arm loudly. Ray's eyes sparked, gawked at her fingers vised around his wrist.

"Remember that time you came home from wherever the hell you were and we'd been doing the laundry but it had rained and the ground was wet and you hit the brakes but then slid the truck oh so slowly into the drying rack? And Julene and I had laughed because it was funny, and god knows we lacked anything really funny in our lives."

Donna traced the inside of her mouth with her tongue, swallowed to clear her dry throat. "Remember how you got out of the truck, saw us laughing? You didn't like that."

Donna felt her face burning, could see all her different therapists lined up inside her mind, shaking their heads, holding up cue cards with the words "risk assessment" scrawled across them.

"Mother couldn't see out of her eye for weeks after that."

In one flash, Donna pictured the white beach, the peaceful water, the quiet landscape. But then she looked around and saw that she was alone in her tropical setting, alone and sweating and discarded.

Eyes straining, veins pumping hot, face sweating, Donna breathed her anger, reached her arm back and slapped Ray across the face. Hard.

"I loathe being hit."

The nasal cannula tucked into his nostrils flew off. The thin skin around his upper right cheekbone tore. Blood flowed from his nose and mouth.

Donna tasted iron, felt fire. Opened a memory.

The first time Donna slapped someone, she hadn't stopped after the first blow. She'd followed it with ten, twenty more, landed kick after punch after kick until the adults tore her away.

She'd been at Blazey's for over a year at that point. She'd started school and didn't say a word and went to class and ate lunch by herself in the cafeteria. Blazey once told her that treading water was okay, but couldn't last forever.

One day in art class, when Donna had been carefully filling in a dark tree outline with a 4B graphite pencil, the classroom door had flown open and a woman had rushed in. She'd stood with her back to the class, speaking to the teacher, but the glimpse Donna had caught of her face was just enough.

Donna had felt her blood run cold, had stood and asked, "Mother?"

The woman turned at the sound of her voice and it had not been Julene and Donna's heart had shattered.

The girls sitting behind her had laughed, had started singing. "Donna's mommy is a crack whore."

Donna hadn't just reacted, hadn't just lost her temper and exploded. Instead, she'd seethed herself into a white hot, emotionless void over the remaining forty minutes of class while the girls taunted her. Three minutes before the end of class she'd stood from her desk, walked to where the girls were laughing, had launched herself at the biggest one in a blur of kicks to the face and throat and head and then the teacher had lifted her from behind and dragged her down the hallway and threw her outside into the grass. Donna had vomited into the lawn as something inside her shattered and the numbness that gripped her vanished and she was gasping like a fish set free on the face of the sun.

Blazey hadn't been able to do anything except load her into the car and drive her home and carry her onto the couch and stroke her hair. It was much later when Donna's gasps became words, and then she was flood-talking, telling Blazey about the girls and their taunts and then the ride in the trunk and Julene and Ray and the cabin and how she feared she was turning into Ray and that she'd never find her mother, and Blazey had listened and listened and listened and when Donna was hoarse from talking Blazey had held her tight and wrapped her arms all the way around her shaking body.

Donna squeezed her hot eyes, remembered being held, her hair stroked while anger boiled her insides raw. She raked her still-clawed hand down her own face, opened her eyes, looked at Ray cringing below her. Took in her other arm, still raised, poised. The flames inside her flowed down her arm; she nearly struck him again.

But as she looked down at his collapsed, bloody face, she

snagged his eyes, malicious and blue and scared, and also somehow triumphant.

She lowered her hand slow to her side and forced a breath out, one long breath, and imagined Hawaii. Kauai. White sand coast. Black volcanic rock wrapped with pale sand darkened where the blue ocean licked it. Crackling foam. Made sure this time she wasn't alone in her imagination. Pictured someone running a dog. Blazey under an umbrella, stacks of books. Donna tasted real salt on her lips, felt her body relax, fingers unclench.

She came back to the small cabin room, the stench of a rotting, unclean body, the filth of a life piled up, molding.

"I'm sorry I acted on my anger," she said to Ray, staring down at him in a way that allowed her to not really see him.

He coughed, chest shaking, saliva bubbling. She addressed the age spot above his eye.

"I'm not sorry I struck you. The last time I was on this property looking for Mother, you beat me. So I am not sorry to return the favor." She sighed. "But I will endeavor to control myself better."

She waited, gave him time for a response. But he was mute, eyes now closed.

"This will be easier if you just tell me." She said it flat, felt the resignation in her tone. Her palm stung from where she'd touched him.

Silence.

She sighed; knew she wasn't going to get any further. He wasn't going to say anything more.

She reached for the plastic sippy cup, placed it under Ray's face so he could drink from the straw. She held it steady, let him drink as much as he liked, didn't look at him or his oozing nose, didn't focus on the smell coming from him or the room. Let her mind float elsewhere until he finished. She replaced the cup, turned to leave.

"Daughter," Ray whispered.

Donna paused in the doorway, looked back at him. His face was a swollen wreck.

"The laughter," he said, voice just above a faint mutter.

Her heart pounded. She held her breath. "What about it?"

He curved his neck, strained to look at where she was standing. "Can you hear the laughter?"

Disappointment sunk into her stomach. Donna lifted her hands to her face, ran her fingers under her eyes, thought of beaches. "No, Ray," she said, flat, emotionless, drained. "I don't hear laughter."

Ray shifted his whole body in the bed. "Daughter," he slurred. "It comes from the ice."

Donna turned away, left him and the room to rot.

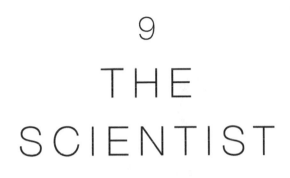

9
THE
SCIENTIST

At ten minutes past noon, Ros stepped down off the lava onto the cracked pumice ringing the Highway 242 re-supply lot. As soon as her foot hit flat ground, she slipped. Pumice scattered like ball bearings.

She swore, regained her footing, looked up. A rickety blue Ford Ranger with a needled tree decal was parked next to the wooden box, tailgate down. Two people were at the truck's nose, one leaning on the hood like a pinup with an enormous topknot of dark hair. Long legs. Hips. Ros took in the troubling curves, the contradictions of the tightly buttoned shirt. Red lipstick visible to the space station.

She stopped in her hurried tracks. Really?

She exhaled, felt her jaw loosen, realized the pinup was watching her, continued over. "Tove Andersen?" she called from five paces out. The figure nodded, straightened off the hood, leaned away from the young man in the green Forest Service outfit standing next to her like an electrified cactus.

"Sorry I'm late." Ros had spent most of the morning frantically cleaning the Fellows Cabin and the Main Cabin. She hadn't slept much the night before. Visions of glaciers and helicopters kept unspooling like a movie before her eyes.

The Forest Service driver lifted his head, trebled nervously at Ros. "Hi, I'm new, first day doing supply runs, got mail here for you."

Ros barely glanced at him. "New, did you unload all the supplies?"

He shrugged sheepishly, shot a glance at Tove, then back at Ros. Looked at his boots.

"Anytime," she barked, irritation pooling in her gut. Ros was aware of Tove standing quiet, watching.

This was not the Fellow Ros was expecting. Tove was decked out in bright blue tights, wore what looked like slippers on her feet, a full face of makeup, and enormous sapphire stud earrings. She looked as if she was dressed to go to a fancy party in Hollywood, not a research station in the Cascades.

The driver rapidly unloaded parcels from the back of the truck. Ros watched him silently. After the last bag, he raised the tailgate with a clank, turned to her. "I think everything's there for you," he said, uncertainty skimming across his face as he moved to the driver's side door.

"Wait, New," Ros commanded. "Let me look over this before you disappear." She could feel Tove staring silently at her. She scanned the boxes, hoped for boots, assessed the regular bags and boxes, then registered the eight oddly shaped cases piled next to the supplies.

"Is that all you?" she asked, turning, addressing Tove.

The woman brightened, stepped forward, clearly taking Ros's question as her cue. "Oh, everything! Two weeks of recording gear. Five microphones, including that really big one." She pointed a long arm at a case that looked like one of the long PVC pipes Ros had lugged up several days previous, her voice smooth and burbling. "My array, amps, recorders, batteries. So many batteries! Tripod, wind pro, parabolic dish. That's the thing in the round case. It's light even though it's big. In that stack are my computers, drives, and, in that case—"

"Okay, okay, I wasn't asking for an inventory." There was no way they were going to haul all the gear in a single trip. Ros slipped the external frame down off her shoulders, dropped it to the ground. "Did you bring a cart for all this?" She winced at her own caustic tone.

What was wrong with her? She went to great lengths to hide her snarking self that showed up when she was sleep deprived or stressed out. But she wasn't hiding it now. And this wasn't how she was supposed to greet a Fellow.

Tove coughed, raised her chin, planted her long legs into the pull-out's dust. "I'll carry it," she said, her smooth voice colder, flatter. "The cases are misleading. If I can jettison a few here in that supply box, I'll condense this to a single load."

"Fine." Ros turned to the driver. "Did you see boots from Corvallis?"

He shook his head, confused, and Ros released him with a curt nod. Disappointment curdled in her stomach.

She busied herself filling her pack with the food and supplies stacked on the ground. She watched out of the corner of her eye as Tove elegantly shuffled gear. The woman was true to her word and had it reduced by a third after she'd repacked the cases into the re-supply box. They were plastic, hard sided, and Ros was certain they'd be fine in the big box for two weeks.

In less than ten minutes, they were ready to go.

Ros was reluctantly impressed. Her pack groaned with weight, and Tove's gear was loaded up into a gigantic hump that dwarfed the woman. She'd also strapped on a smaller front pack over her chest and had two gear bags gripped tightly in her hands. Hands, Ros noted, painted with bright green nail polish.

"You've done this before," Ros said, begrudgingly, facing her.

"That's the first nice thing you've said to me." Tove grinned, a smile that dazzled and sent hot sparks down Ros's legs. "Of course I've done this before."

Ros eyed Tove, flats of lava fanning out in every direction. The woman had golden eyes, a richness that seemed melded from citrine and pine tree amber. She contemplated her responses. "I live alone," she said eventually.

Tove lifted her arms, shoulders, the gear. She shrugged. "I'm easy."

What did that mean? Ros felt irritation flare at the ambiguity. "It's eight miles in," she said, the only thing that came to mind.

"Where does the trail start?" Tone stubborn.

Ros gestured at the lava's edge away from the road, and Tove took the lead. As her legs settled into Tove's pace, Ros studied the other woman from behind. She guessed Tove was maybe in her late twenties, early thirties. She wasn't tall, maybe five foot five, but to Ros, she seemed all legs and arms and hair. She had black hair; the kind Ros knew would swell as soon as humidity touched it. The strands were thick; Ros's fingers tingled to touch them and see if they were soft.

"What is this lava?" Tove asked after a mile or so, her pace a consistent three steps ahead.

"Aa," Ros replied, slightly bemused. An obvious softball to get Ros talking. She accepted, continued explaining. "The type that flows really quick from the eruption site. This came from the Yapoah Crater off over there. I'll take you up in a few days if you like."

They maneuvered across more uneven lava, and Ros noted the burnt trees on the left that crowded up to the edge of the flow. Likely from the Milli Fire in 2017. That forest fire had burned over twenty-four thousand acres in the area, all from a single lightning strike. Lava flows acted as natural fire breaks, and many of the flows had helped contour where the fire could move. Ros considered pointing out the burned trees to Tove, but then thought better of it. She'd answer questions, but she wasn't a cruise director.

After a few moments, Tove called back again. "Is the other pahoehoe? The super smooth stuff with the ropes on top?"

Ros smiled, felt a small laugh brimming. Tamped it down. "You know your lavas. Pahoehoe is easier to walk on. Not as rough as this stuff."

"I read a bunch before I came up here," Tove said, guileless. "Pahoehoe gets this leather top that cools before the insides do. It makes a gurgling sound as the wrinkles form."

"I've never seen it in real life." Ros wished she would. One day.

"I'd love to see it too. I think Hawaii's the closest. Also, after reading, I'm hot to see an eruption with rhyolite or andesite. Did you know when they fall, it sounds like tinkling glass bells, as if rain turned to glass. Can you imagine?"

Ros could not imagine it, but it struck her as magnificent. She tried to picture a glass rain as the two hiked along the rough lava, stepping up blocks and down crumbles. The only thing she could hear were their footsteps, her soles sludging on the lava. If only she had those new boots.

Ros rolled her eyes at herself, took a breath. She tried to surmount her irritability. She cast around for a topic. "You're at UO?"

The back of Tove's head bobbed. "I'm a postdoc. In ecology." Her voice traveled low. "I'm an acoustic field ecologist. I've been at the university the last few years, working on this project trying to assess how climatic changes are changing certain sonic signatures of the Oregon landscape." She turned, flashed a bright red-lipsticked grin at Ros. "Lots of 'C' words."

Ros's mind lingered on the image of Tove glancing over her shoulder. Tove's eyes seemed too large for her face, with dark, heavy drooping lids that almost gave her a sleepy look. In fact, they would have, Ros thought, if not for the fine black eyebrows that moved like coordinated tsunamis across the ocean of her face.

The lipstick wasn't a true red, Ros suddenly realized. It was more plum-red. A plum that melded with violet quartz. Tove had coated her lips with a color Ros had never seen naturally in the field. Something inside her twitched, made her teeth ache. Maybe the lipstick was what was making her prickly. Ros hadn't worn lipstick in donkey's years.

"Ros? Did you hear my question?" Tove stopped, turned back towards her.

"Sorry, say again?" Jesus, she was distracted.

"I asked, how is it out here for you?"

Ros acknowledged the question but didn't stop. Instead, she stepped around Tove on the trail. "It's good," she said, walking ahead now. "I get to do my own research, and then help people like you carry out your work, so it's always interesting."

Tove chirp-laughed, a sound that sent a ripple transiting the entire length of Ros's spine. "Oh, it'll be great to have help. Two weeks is not enough time!"

Ros sought clarification. "What do you need from me? What does your work look like?"

"God, you are kind and getting nicer by the moment. I was worried at first. Poor Newby."

Ros snorted as Tove's comment registered. "He'll do," she replied waspishly.

Tove walked around Ros, hitched her pack up higher. Ros couldn't see her full face as she passed, but could make out the chin, the painted lips scrunching, smoothing. Whatever she was going to say she didn't.

"Usually my work is up at dawn and dusk, setting up the recording gear, sprawling on the ground for hours, repeat, download, repeat, review the recordings, etc." Tove laughed, a low tinkling that reminded Ros of spring streams. Or now, andesite eruptions. "I'd appreciate guidance from you on all the best places to get a taste of this landscape."

"Taste?" Ros echoed, feet gliding over lava rock as she bent her ears, focused on Tove's voice.

"Well," Tove released a self-conscious laugh. "Taste. Word choice. I'm here to record everything. Leaves rustling. Hikers talking. Thunder. Snow. Plants hurting. Lava. Flowing water. Glaciers. Sneezing marmots. That's the thing. In order to assess how the soundscape is changing, we need to first create a baseline for that soundscape. And we don't have that. So that's the bulk of what I'm doing, getting field recordings, trying to figure out the keynote sounds, the various soundmarks—what is there, what isn't."

Tove described work she'd done down along the Umpqua, around Coos Bay, out on the Warm Springs Reservation. Ros let her words flow over her as they walked, moving through lava drifts and warm forests and open grasslands and back out onto lava. Her back protested against the heavy load, but listening to Tove's low chatter about sounds calmed her, distracted her from her aches and pains, her thoughts about Ash and Amelia Kane.

More quickly than expected, they turned onto the cabin spur and then, were in the clearing, looking at the research station. "Welcome to OHEWS." Ros groaned as she lowered the pack onto the porch.

Ros showed Tove around, gave her explanations of the shower, latrine, radio protocol, cabin quirks, and then left her to settle into the Fellows Cabin. In the Main Cabin, she flipped on the radio and scanned for chatter.

On the police channel, there was a lot of back and forth up by the Collier Cone, and after a few minutes, Ros realized one of the voices must be a spotter in a helicopter. They'd had two to three helicopters in the air for the rest of the afternoon when Ros had hiked back down from Black Crater, and she'd heard rotors most of the morning when she went out to pick up Tove. Two days of expensive helicopter time. Something must be going on with the search. She hoped they'd found promising signs of Amelia.

She went out to her porch to listen but couldn't hear any. They must be out by the cone. Ros went back in, sat back down at the desk.

Tove reappeared with two stacked cases in her arms. "Whatcha listening to?" she asked, gesturing to the radio.

"There's a search going on out here for a missing child," Ros explained. Kept her face still, language simple. Refused to get drawn in.

Tove's golden eyes widened. "Really?"

Ros smiled. Noted that Tove had reapplied blue eyeshadow. "Yeah, it's a shame. But," she said, "I don't think it should impact your recordings too much. We can work around where the search is."

"Oh no," Tove countered, waving her full arms. "I record everything."

They spent the rest of the afternoon exploring. Ros made sure to pack the spare parts she'd meant to take up to Black Crater the previous day. She set out, first, to show Tove the area west of the Harlow Crater, full of mixed living and dead forests and waves of scabby lava. After that, they hiked around Millican Crater, Tove almost ecstatic at the gritty, red scoria blanketing the darker basalt. Bleached dead trees listed in every direction amidst the burnout, and live lodgepole pines with tippy bent tops accompanied their journey to the crater rim. Tove ran her hands up and down their trunks, and Ros had to prod her along.

Eventually, Ros guided them higher towards Black Crater, wending through the gnarl of trails on the flatlands before settling her feet on the familiar trail up to the summit. She wanted Tove to get a view of the area, to see the Three Sisters and all the Cascade peaks.

Conversation up the trail was spotty, especially on the steep sections when both women fell silent in exertion. But once over the more treacherous terrain, Ros ventured a question that had been floating in her mind.

"Tove," she asked, choosing her words as carefully as she selected a chisel from her bag to split a rock sample, "I don't know all that much about 'acoustic ecology.' However did you get into that field?"

"She asks, politely, but skeptically." Tove laughed behind her. More glass rain tinkling.

Ros flushed. "No, not that. I meant—"

"No, no, I shouldn't tease you, we've just met."

"I wasn't—" Ros stopped on the trail, turned, towered over Tove on the lower slope. "I didn't mean to…"

Tove smiled up at her, a brilliant flash of white teeth that momentarily blinded Ros, the type of smile only years in braces could produce. "You're fine, really. I've got a raspy tongue. I was joking. I know you're crusty, but I can tell you've got a core of melted delicious butter."

Ros blinked, startled, unsure what to say. The woman licked her lips, and Ros felt unmoored.

"Do you, by chance, know my adviser at Oregon, Dr. Enohor Anifowose?"

Ros shook her head, flustered at the turn of conversation.

"Ah, you should meet her, she's a kick. You remind me of her." Tove laughed. "Anyway, you're fine to ask. You study rocks, right? Well, I study sounds. But, that's not my full training. Wait for it." Tove licked her lips a second time, and Ros had to look away.

"I was a plant ecologist first. In grad school, I studied how specific plants communicate. I started to focus on sound only when I realized the field was wide open and I'd be first author on pubs and grants. Fame and glory. But the more I delved into it, the more I realized, sound is everywhere, so why wouldn't plants, or all life, take advantage of it? And down the academic rabbit hole I went, Ros."

Tove released her chirp-laugh again, completely unselfconscious.

Tove just kept talking. "I found that plants do make and respond to sounds, which we've known scientifically since like the sixties, but, for whatever reason, hadn't ever asked why. I suspected that plants made sounds to communicate, to each other, to the wider world around them. And that opened the door for me to start wondering about what else makes sounds. I mean, we know, theoretically, that everything signals with sounds, and have data that bacteria, insects, plants, the planet, do. But what else?"

Ros refocused, took a swing at a question. "But plants, planets, the sun, bacteria, they don't have the mechanisms, sensory organs, ears, vocal cords, right? How, then, do they perceive sounds? Mechanical vibrations? Cosmic waves?"

"Everyone asks this, Ros! Great question!" Tove paused for a minute, breathed heavily. "I'm out of shape, good god!" Her chest heaved, the shirt fabric around her neck fluttering.

Ros stopped too, turned, looked down trail at Tove, at the woman's wide, panting face. The lipstick on her top lip had faded. Ros tried not to stare.

Tove shook herself, started moving again. "Humans, terrestrial mammals, we've all got external auditory structures like ears. Frogs, birds? No external ears, but they have internal ear drums. Snakes detect vibrations through their jawbones. Caterpillars, through their sphincters. Plants? Their leaves, flowers, and roots have all been shown to emit, detect, and respond to sounds. And this is cross-species. We've got data showing that bark beetles can actually hear trees experiencing drought stress, that they know which trees are vulnerable to attack. How, what different things in the landscape use to make, respond to sound, that's the question!"

They were nearing the summit. Ros slipped in one more question. "But, soil? Rocks? Glaciers? Things not alive?"

"I know, I know," Tove laugh-panted. "But even our planet makes sounds. I think a space agency or two has called it 'Earth Song.' Certain rocks sing, emit low-frequency sounds. Lava roars, yawns. I just keep surprising myself with what I find emitting noises. If the sun can make sounds, and the planet, and the plants, and the animals, and us, why not everything else?"

"Ice?" Ros gestured at the Collier Glacier as they crested the crater's edge and the full view of the Cascade volcanoes rose dramatically in front of them.

"Good god!" Tove exclaimed at the newly visible horizon, and Ros felt a surge of pride that overrode her sore feet and aching shoulders.

"What are we, like five hundred thousand feet above the world?"

Ros glowed, shook her head, and led Tove off-trail towards the tower. Told her to grab a seat on the rock bench while she fiddled with the winterizing.

"Keep an eye on me, Ros? I suffer from congenital clumsiness." Tove shed her pack and stretched like a cat near the edge. Ros looked, then looked away. Focused on the popped battery box and inspected the seams, looked for weaknesses in the plastic siding. She'd brought up a specialized caulk to ensure no water could seep into the data storage box. Focus.

Fifteen minutes later, she joined Tove on the basalt. "It'll take about ten minutes or so to download the station data," she explained. "So we sit here."

"I'm coming back here tomorrow," Tove said happily. "I'm glad I didn't bring any equipment this trip; you'd never be able to tear me away. This place is gorgeous. And the sounds!"

Cumulus clouds floated by in long streets, and the blue skies were streaked with a white haze. Ros noted the wind speed and direction, the temperature and humidity. Mountains new and old stretched away in all directions, torn up and torn down, evidence of glaciation and volcanic activity and erosion and weather. She scanned for helicopters, didn't see a single one.

Tove let out a low whistle, gestured widely at the landscape falling away before them. "One of the biggest misconceptions people have," she said, looking at the Three Sisters, "is that the wilderness will swallow your scream. As in, no one will hear."

A flash of cold slid down Ros's spine. Her thoughts roiled. Did Feather scream? Was Amelia Kane screaming now? Ros shook her head, banished the thoughts, rebuilt her walls. Forced a joke. "A tree falls in the woods, no one hears, right?"

Tove sighed dramatically, tossed a hand into the air. "Yes. But no one accounts for the other trees, plants, insects, mammals, soil, everything else listening in. They hear it."

"Nothing is silent."

"Nope. Nothing should ever be silenced," Tove intoned solemnly, then leaned her shoulder into Ros's. "She said, primly, hoping to impart a great metaphor."

Tove giggled, but Ros sucked her lips in, tried to calm her pounding pulse. What did the landscape hear when women went missing? What did the plants record? She willed herself to not think again of her mother. Of her sister. Of that little girl. Shook herself, wrapped her hands around her shoulders, refused to go where her thoughts kept trying to take her. Looked out again, pointed in front of them. "See all the dead trees? They certainly made noise as they went."

"What happened?"

"Forest fire. Happens all the time out here now. But in front of us, just here? That's the 2017 Milli Fire. If you look way beyond that, you'll see the scars from the Nash Fire and the Horse Creek Complex Fire that same year. You can see older scars from the Pole Creek Fire over there," she said, pointing to her right.

"All the fires have names? Like hurricanes?"

"Yes. And personality. Management, history. It's a reference point for a lot of folks out here."

Ros watched Tove carefully, saw her consider this. Ros waited, curious where she'd take the conversation.

"I remember once," Tove said, "as an undergraduate, this professor sending us out to get recordings of all the different trees on campus. And I learned the sounds of like, thirty different trees, maples, oaks, cottonwoods. I learned how to distinguish these trees without equipment, unaided, and then hear individual tree sounds change over seasons. It was, hands down, one of the most enlightening classes I've ever taken."

Tove clapped her hands. Ros thought she heard a faint gurgle of excitement in the woman's throat.

"We know so little, Ros. About sound, fire, humanity. It's exciting to me." Tove bumped her shoulder lightly against Ros's. "Like, as climatic changes occur and air temperatures shift, the density of our very air changes, which impacts animal and plant behavior, the nature of the sounds they make. Sounds travel further in cold air, right? So what happens when the air is warmer all the time? Some of my research shows that warmer air is increasing forest foliage, which dampens some sounds, making it harder for some species to hear mating calls or detect prey."

Ros groaned, laughed. "Sex just got harder?"

Tove cackled, mouth wide. "Not with me!" She laughed harder, and Ros joined her, throat flushing.

Tove crossed her hands over her knees and looked out at the landscape. "What glacier is that?" she asked, gesturing with fluttering, tapered fingers as she spoke.

"The Collier," Ros replied automatically, staring at the faded green forest carpeting the lower hills.

"It looks broken."

Ros turned, focused her attention on the ice. From her vantage, it looked like a pale apron, a small white slip in a black and red and green smear. Lifting the field glasses she'd brought, she scanned the ice, noted the swarm of searchers still there. Maybe they'd set up an ancillary base camp for the search. That would explain the helicopters and crowds.

"What happened to it?" Tove stared like she was transfixed.

Ros didn't lower her glasses. "Who broke the glaciers?" she queried, distracted. "Not easy to say. Easier to say who hasn't done anything to fix them."

The air shivered around them, the hair on Ros's arms lifting, stiffening. Ros was aware of the quiet weaving around them, the sound of Tove's breath, the wind, her own pulse.

"Okay, I lied," Tove said suddenly, almost guiltily, reaching for her pack. "I did bring recording gear."

She flashed Ros a bright smile and pulled out a box with two microphones strapped to either side. "Do you mind?"

"Of course not." Why would she mind? She watched Tove set up the microphone on a pointy chunk of basalt next to their bench. Each movement seemed graceful, practiced.

The woman turned, looked at Ros critically, eyed her from head to toe. Ros felt herself flush again.

"Okay," Tove said. "But would you mind taking off your pants?"

Ros's throat hitched. "Excuse me?"

Tove laughed. "Oh yeah, you've never done this. Okay. We have to lay here and be quite quiet, quite still. Even with that, though, you'll move somewhat. I do too. Since the fabric on your pants is swishy, it'll be picked up in the recording."

Ros looked down. For the first time in her life, Ros contemplated her pants.

"It's why I never wear rain pants, rain jackets. They make so much noise, they drown out the trees. I'd rather get wet and listen to the symphony. These cotton tights are as quiet as death!"

Ros laughed out loud, the pure absurdity and newness of it all chasing away the melancholia that had threatened to overtake her mind. She reached down, unzipped, dropped her pants.

Tove stood. "I'll go no-pants too, in solidarity," she said, chuckling, and peeled down her blue tights. "Now if other hikers come up here, they'll think they've caught the two of us in the act."

Ros felt herself reddening to her hairline. She looked away from Tove's pale thighs, the place where she'd caught a glimpse of dark curls edging the yellow fabric of Tove's underwear. Of course Tove would wear a thong into the wilderness. Ros felt awkward, overheated.

"Just lay down there, and then settle in. I'll try for about thirty minutes of ambient recording if that's okay? See what we can pick up from up here?"

Ros settled onto her back below the rock bench, head atop her pack edge, back and thighs and feet pressed into the rubbly ground. For the first few moments, she was uncomfortable, but gradually, in the heat of the sun, steeped in the fatigue of her body and the heaviness of her thoughts, Ros started to sink into a stupor.

She noticed the small pieces of rock first, ball bearings scrabbling under her skin, but then became aware of the smell of the rock itself—the warm dense minerality, the traces of rotting deciduous leaves and pine needles. The wind rustled over her, and a vast sea of different scents from somewhere beyond the rock ledge wafted across her face.

She tried to identify each new scent as she vaguely heard Tove settle in beside her. Waves of contentment washed up from her feet, across her thighs and stomach, from her chest into her face. Laying there, she felt at ease, as if she could feel the vast spaciousness of the landscape. It was intoxicating.

"Ros?"

She cracked an eye, peered, saw Tove sitting upright, face tilting down at her.

"You drifted off there."

"Really? Sorry." Ros sat up quickly, flushing for what felt like the millionth time.

"No worries, you looked adorable. And happy."

Ros swallowed, pretended she didn't hear the comment, wished she had her pants on.

"I've been sitting here, looking out at this landscape. It looks primordial in a way. Every direction I look, you know?"

Ros nodded. "I know. I feel that too sometimes." She rolled her tongue around her teeth, gazed past Tove out onto the volcanoes dotting the horizon. "Some of my more declensionist colleagues come here and see only ruin. Only destruction. But I look at all these volcanoes, all these glaciers, all these scabs of lava and forest-burn and life, and I can't help but think the opposite—that I'm seeing the beginning, not the end."

Tove sighed, then rose onto her haunches, reached for the recording, flipped it off. "I'm glad I got that," she said, and Ros's pulse rang.

"What else did you record?"

"Want me to show you?"

Ros nodded, and was somewhat surprised when Tove slid over, bent down by Ros's shoulders, tucked her knees in on either side of Ros's head, cradling it between her thighs. She placed a cool hand on Ros's forehead. Trying not to flinch, Ros said, "If you hand me your headphones I'll listen?"

Tove applied gentle pressure above Ros's eyebrows, shook her head no. "Let me show you."

Ros was not comfortable. She didn't know where to look as Tove stared down at her. Finally, she simply looked back up at Tove, met her eyes. In the light, her irises carried a redder amber, a leonine tilt. Ros felt unmoored by them and wasn't prepared when Tove leaned even farther forward, placed her hands lightly over Ros's ears. "I know you can hear me," Tove whispered, her lips micrometers from Ros's ear, "but I want you to focus on what you see. Just look up. Use your eyes."

Tove leaned away, out of Ros's view, and all Ros could do was stare up at the sky. At the altostratus clouds, faint sheets, ice crystals and water droplets in long blankets—blue, gray, pink. She felt secure looking up into a sky she knew wouldn't betray her, wouldn't change the laws of physics, wouldn't ever allow her to fall off the planet into the unknown, the darkness.

"Okay, now I'm going to place my hands over your eyes," Tove whispered. "I want you to focus on just what you hear."

Tove's fingers slid across her temples to her eyelids, covered them. She swallowed, felt her throat thicken. She strained her ears, identified the scrabble of rocks sliding under her as she tried not to squirm, the slip and hiss of Tove's clothing, the scratchy rustle of the wind. But most of all she heard her own pulse, her heart pounding. She felt herself start to sweat at her scalp, in her armpits, between her legs. Her heart squeezed against her ribs.

Ros jerked, grabbed Tove's wrists, held them tight.

"Shhh…" Tove soothed. "You're all right."

Ros's heart pounded harder; her hands trembled.

Tove lifted her hands from Ros's eyes. "You're all right," she repeated, her voice lifting slightly.

Ros wasn't sure if it was a question or a statement. She was blinded temporarily by the abrupt light, but, once her vision stabilized, all she could see were Tove's eyes. She searched and found no hint of malice. Just golden eyes. Ros swallowed the cannonball in her throat, nodded slightly.

Tove smiled, brought her hands up, covered Ros's eyes again.

Opening her mouth wide, Ros pulled in a deep, hitching breath. A second. A third. She kept her hold on Tove's wrists, felt the other woman's slow, steady pulse under her sweaty fingers.

"We have all kinds of words for wind sounds," Tove murmured down to her. "Beautiful words. Listen: *eolian, psithurism, whoosh.*"

Ros slowed her breathing, listened to Tove whisper about the wind. Felt her body relax again. A heaviness rolled up her body, weighted her legs into the ground, pressed her shoulders back. She gave in to it, released her grip on Tove. Dropped her hands down to her chest.

Eyes closed, then covered, Ros heard her own pulse, Tove's pulse. The wind and trees, breathing. A deep thrumming from somewhere. An insect bustling. Rocks rasping. And then, faint at first, she heard it, a melody, the barest hint of a song that sounded as if it was sung underwater, carried by the wind from miles away. It wrapped itself inside Ros's ears, caressed her brain and throat and down her stomach and she felt a strong urge to move, to twist her body free and slide forward.

But then Tove pulled her hands away, and Ros blinked at the glaring light and sudden silence. The sun had dropped low, and Ros had no idea where the time had gone.

She pitched forward to sit, swallowed, felt as if she'd temporarily lost something, as if the contentment she'd just experienced was now out of reach. She turned to Tove.

The woman smiled a faded lipstick smile, her face so expressive Ros nearly gave in to the tears boiling behind her eyelids. She shook her head hard, then stood, rocks shedding off her skin. She bent and pulled her pants and boots on, then walked away to the tower to disconnect the download and gather herself and get ahold of the howl blistering in her throat. She felt simultaneously calm and bewildered, grief-stricken and relieved, throbbing.

She made a meal of finishing her work on the tower to give herself time to get collected. When she walked back to the basalt bench, Tove was packed, ready to go. The two hiked in quiet back down to

Ros's cabin. When they arrived, Tove began plugging all her gear to recharge. Ros started dinner.

The pasta water was roiling by the time Ros handed Tove a cup of black tea, unsweetened. Tove had set up shop on the kitchen table, her laptop flashing various programs as she uploaded data. She took the tea from Ros and waved thanks, then gestured at the enormous headphones propped over her bun. She was listening to a recording.

Ros cut vegetables, threw green spiral pasta into boiling water. Turned when she heard a long tone and beep on the comms system. Someone was radioing the station. She cut her eyes at the clock. It was a little past six, so she wasn't late for her check in.

"This is OHEWS," she answered, speaking into the handheld.

"OHEWS, this is Chief Thomas Addington at the mobile field base at Scott Lake. I'm part of the Incident Command for the ongoing search and rescue operation for Amelia Kane."

"Did you find her?" Ros felt cold to her core, like someone had just dumped an ice bucket down her back.

The radio was silent, then static came through thick. "Can you confirm your identity at OHEWS?"

Ros shivered, was puzzled. "This is Dr. Ros Fisher, chief scientist at the Oregon High Elevation Weather Station at Harlow Crater."

More static, and then the voice responded. "Will you be at the station tomorrow morning at nine o'clock?"

"Affirmative, I will be." She waited, tension roiling in her stomach and her shoulders tightening into violin bows. "What is this about?" Ros stood in front of the window gripping the handheld and looked east, out at the Millican Crater, staring blankly through the trees as she waited. A full forty seconds of complete staticky silence ticked by. Bewildered, Ros turned, saw Tove at the table with her headphones clamped over her ears, face scrunched inches from the screen, staring at the computer. She flipped back around to the window, nearly lost her grip on the radio as sweat pooled in her palm.

What was going on?

"Radio check?" she said, irritated.

"OHEWS," the voice replied almost instantly. "We've got you."

"What is this about?"

There was a pause again, but shorter. "The SAR team has located… something… of interest. We'd like to discuss it with you in person. Confirmed?"

"Confirmed," Ros echoed, slowly set the handheld back into its port.

Ros's mind churned, a whirl of questions and outcomes and variables. She felt chilled, reached for the down jacket hanging by the door, slipped it over her shoulders. Her stomach heaved. Like she was seasick, and yet she was standing on a sturdy wooden-planked floor hundreds of miles from the ocean. She moved back to the window, gripped the frame with both hands, gazed out into the night. Wondered what they'd found. Wondered how she was involved. Felt rancid fear trickle down her neck.

"Ros?" Tove's voice broke in. "Can you come here?"

Ros turned slightly, saw Tove still hunched at her computer, headphones dangling off one ear. She held out another pair to Ros.

"I'm reviewing the audio recording from today. Just making sure there aren't glitches. And you've got to hear this, tell me if I'm crazy." Tove shook the headphones at Ros.

Dark spots danced in Ros's vision, sweat glazed her forehead. She gripped the windowpane harder, nails digging into the soft wood. Squeezed her eyes shut, felt the nausea come lurching hot up her throat. Tried to swallow.

Heard Tove say, "I have no idea how, but damned if halfway through I hear laughter."

10
THE
MEDIC

May sat huddled under someone else's heavy down jacket, feet dangling off the lowered tailgate of the bush truck. It was late, cold, and the sheer volume of people's voices, whining generators, vehicle engines, and wind flapping the canopy covers numbed May, chipped away at her already-exhausted body.

She pulled the jacket tighter, smelled the cigarette-mixed-with-lemon-balm aroma of the person who owned the jacket, wondered when they'd come and reclaim it. May could not recall where her own was—she suspected she might have left it up there, by the glacier, by all those bodies.

"Good job today, Young," a voice called from the dark.

May jerked her head up, saw Baker emerging from the parking lot, headlamp glowing from his forehead like a cyclops. He strolled over, leaned against the tailgate.

"God, not easy," he continued, arms crossed.

May wasn't sure what response Baker might want. Right now, she didn't really feel like talking. Then again, Baker was there, he'd sought her out, so perhaps she should put more effort into interacting with him. She wished he was as easy to talk to as Jamal and Lou. Even though every muscle in her neck screeched, she tilted her head, looked up at Baker. "Yeah," she managed. Waited to see if he wanted more.

"Whatcha doing sitting out here?" Clearly, he wanted to talk.

She leaned further back against the side of the truck bed. "I'm waiting for Chief," May explained. "He told me he wanted a debrief, to wait here at the bush truck. So, I'm here." She kicked her legs a little, tried to get the blood moving in her feet.

"But didn't I hear you radio in over an hour ago? Have you eaten?" Baker pushed away from the bush truck where he'd been leaning, swung his face two inches from hers. Looked hard into her eyes. "Young, how long you been sitting here?"

She looked down, felt profoundly tired. Worried that the person who owned the jacket would come back and take it. Realized just how cold she was. She pulled an arm from the borrowed jacket, looked at her watch. Wow. She hadn't realized what time it was. "Just an hour or so," she murmured. "But Chief is busy."

"Ah, Young."

May leaned away from him. She had no idea why he was looking at her like that, but she was too tired to fence, to soothe, to defuse. Couldn't be bothered to wonder at all. Honestly, all she wanted to do was lay down, go to sleep. She felt just like the first-year interns on *Grey's Anatomy*, the ones who knocked out forty-eight-hour shifts and still looked good. She suspected she looked less than good. Tried to shake away her mother's voice in her head.

"I'll be right back." Baker shook his head, turned on his heel, strode away into the sea of vehicles and tents surrounding Command.

May sighed heavily, closed her eyes as she felt unexpected tears gather. Opened them again, looked into her lap. All she wanted to do was just sit right there, wait, keep her big hands warm in the jacket.

She'd realized she'd forgotten her gloves when Jonas ordered her to dig away the snow around the shoe and leg she'd discovered.

May had initially screamed when she realized what she'd found, when she realized she was holding onto a human leg in the snow.

She'd screamed and screamed, and Jonas had run straight at her, across the snow. She figured out later that he had thought she was hurt, but then, when he saw the leg, he'd screamed right back at her.

"Dig, Young! Dig!"

He'd frantically cleared away snow, clawing clear the leg, the torso.

Later, it had also occurred to her that Jonas must have thought the person was alive. But she couldn't fathom why he'd think that. There was so much snow, what looked to her like years and years of snow stacked up. And the body was prone, one leg sticking towards the sky. No way the person was living.

But she dug anyway, using her bare hands. Pushed and moved snow until she'd uncovered the leg to the thigh. It took immense effort. Jonas had been right there. He'd even said at some point, "Is it Amelia?"

She'd stopped digging then, shook her head. "Adult," she'd responded, gawked at the denim covering the leg. She'd tried not to touch it as she dug but ended up repeatedly brushing her hands against its hardness—stiff, unyielding.

Jonas at some point had stopped digging, had gotten up and walked away, had gotten his radio out. He'd ordered her to stop digging too, to back off the snow patch and sit down on a rock and stop contaminating evidence. He was holding the radio in his hand and it was screeching, voices cutting through static.

"We've been told to stay here," Jonas had said at some point. "They're going to hike in a few people to help, but since this is obviously not Amelia, Command doesn't want to pull too many from the search."

May had gratefully sank further down into the hard, cold boulder by the snow's edge, had wrapped her frozen hands into her lap, wished she'd thought to bring chocolate or something to eat. Rookie mistake. She was starving. She hadn't wanted to ask Jonas and reveal what an idiot she was, but it took all her self-restraint not to ask him for food when she saw him pull a chocolate bar from his pack and shove it into his mouth.

She'd had to look away, away from him and the leg and body sticking out of the torn-up snow. Had physically tilted her growling stomach away and pointed her wilting face over the edge of the snow patch towards the glacier. Had tried not to think about food, about the leg, and the body, and the person she'd uncovered.

She had no idea what had happened, who the person was, and she promised herself that she'd not let her imagination wander, not escape away from reality by imagining something that wasn't real. She did know that *Grey's Anatomy* had at least ten episodes that dealt with John and Jane Does, and always, eventually, they were claimed. Their families always found them. May had hoped whoever was buried in the snow would be claimed by a family that would finally be healed by knowing what had happened to their loved one. She'd felt a momentary flash of warmth that she'd be able to help a hurting family somewhere.

To distract herself from her stomach, the leg, everything, May stared at the glacier in front of her. Breathed, tried to calm herself, warmed her hands. She counted the boulders scattered across the snow patches, looked up to the ridgeline, assessed the slope edge eroding away into scree.

The wind swayed her gently, carried a sound of light humming. May looked around at all the boulders around her—huge, dark lumps—and realized that she was sitting in the fall line for rocks directly upslope. She'd shivered, hoped nothing else would roll down while she sat there. Waited for Jonas to tell her to do something. Waited. Stared at the snow patch closest to her.

Stared, narrowed her eyes.

Her brain must have understood before her eyes did, before her mouth did. Had made sense of the boulders scattered across the snow, the dark slumped boulders closest to her that weren't actually boulders. That were not rocks that had just hurtled down from the mountainside, were not loose volcanic chunks eroded by weather, ice, and fire.

No, what she was looking at was something else melting out of the snow, something else melting far away from the leg she'd found.

Directly in front of her were the rounded shoulders of two other bodies emerging from the snow.

She'd screamed then. Screamed again and again and again. And then Jonas was there kneeling before her, his hands on her shoulders, saying "what, what," but all she could do was point. Even then he didn't understand.

"Oh my god," her voice wavering and liquid and hitching, "more people," and she'd pointed to the shoulder directly in front of her in the snow, and then Jonas had gotten it and she'd watched his face drain of all color.

Everything had moved extraordinarily quick after that. May estimated it was less than five minutes before a helicopter was hovering over them, kicking up scree and snow as two spotters photographed and radioed Jonas. She'd hunched for cover in the windstorm. Later, searchers had landed above them on the ridge and sent a team down the slope. She and Jonas had stood waiting, then moved high above the snow patch so as not to make tracks. Jonas had briefed the new people while May had stood mute, frozen.

People May didn't recognize in bright red jackets had swarmed in. Over the radio, Chief had ordered her and Jonas to return to Command. May wished she'd been quicker when the helicopter pilot explained that he was leaving some gear at the site, so weight-wise could take one additional passenger back to Command. Jonas had turned to her and told her it was likely that the chief wanted a full debriefing, so he should fly back, and would she mind doing a return on foot and they'd catch up then?

May hadn't had time to think, so she'd just nodded, and then, abruptly, Jonas was gone. She was left sitting on a boulder with her hands tucked into her pockets. She wasn't sure which way to go to get back and her brain felt foggy. She'd felt bone weary, overwhelmed, like she was holding back a year's worth of tears.

"You okay?" a voice came from the swarm of people surrounding the snow patch.

May looked up slowly and saw two guys drawing closer to her, faces concerned. She'd nodded to them, unsure who'd asked the question, but then the taller one moved closer and crouched down, level with her face.

He was older, in his thirties, gray-eyed, red-headed, and pale. In that moment, he'd reminded May of Owen Hunt from *Grey's Anatomy*. Except, he didn't have Owen's military bearing, was instead more flowy, all limbs and height and willowiness.

"You discovered all of this." He had a slight southern accent lining his words. His gray eyes scrunched kindly. "This is a lot, what you've found today."

May felt her lower lip tremble.

The man placed a gloved hand on her shoe. "Jamal, grab some mangos and a granola bar from my pack, top compartment, would you?" he'd directed the guy next to him, then turned back to May. "I'm Lou, that's Jamal," he'd explained. "We're EMTs from Eugene."

May had stared wide-eyed at them, unused to the direct attention, the obvious concern emanating from both men. Jamal was shorter than Lou and had a visible pouch of belly pushing out over the waist strap of his backpack. May watched him sort through Lou's pack, wondered for a moment if the men were real or figments of her imagination.

"I'm May," she'd eventually said. She'd rattled off her department number in the Thurston Hills, then hesitantly took the food Jamal had handed over.

May stuffed the dried mangos into her mouth, waited, repeated, and then had felt the sugar hit. It blunted down her emotions and weariness.

The din around them continued to hum but Lou had just sat patiently, unperturbed, rocked back on his haunches. Jamal had perched on a boulder that May had double checked was a real boulder. Both stared at her curiously, but she hadn't known what to say. She did not look at the bodies, did not look at the snow patch behind her teaming with activity. She couldn't. She pushed everything from her mind.

Instead, she'd chewed, hoped all the food stayed in her mouth, let the words logjam up behind her teeth. How long she would have sat there like a mute clown she wasn't sure. But then, her radio squawked and May jolted back to the present, recalled the chief's orders to get back to Command and debrief him.

She'd stopped chewing then, rousted herself and stood, grateful to have a mission that took her as far from everything happening behind her as possible. She thanked Lou and Jamal gratefully, then explained that she needed to get going.

"No problem," Lou had responded, also standing, stretching up to his full, well-over six-foot height. It was refreshing to May, made her feel not so gargantuan.

"You want any more bars for the trip? It'll take you a couple of hours. We've got tons."

She'd shook her head, not sure why she was refusing. Jamal moved around Lou, reached and single-handedly picked up her pack, twisted it around so she could step in, and waited while she clipped her waist and shoulder straps.

"Thanks again." Gratefulness and embarrassment crowded her mouth.

Lou and Jamal waved at her and moved off, heading up the slope. She'd stood motionless, followed them with her eyes, indecision surging up and down her spine. She wanted so badly to show she was competent, reliable, that she was a good medic. But she also didn't know what to do.

The scene was crawling with people at the edge of the glacier. North Sister glared down ominously.

Words bubbled at her lips, and even though she strained to contain them, they broke through. May found herself calling after Jamal and Lou, running after them, backpack jostling.

"Can you point me to the trail to get to Command?" she'd blurted out when she caught up to them, unable to meet their eyes. "My search partner went back with the helicopter, and I'm not familiar…" She'd trailed off, whispering her last words.

"This is your first time out here?" Lou had asked, his accented tone landing somewhere in the neighborhood of incredulous and astonished. "And your partner left you?"

"Jesus," Jamal's tone had been fierce.

May didn't have the energy to defend Jonas, nor did she want to try to explain him or the situation. Instead, she'd just focused on her orders. "If you tell me which trail to take, I'm sure I'll be fine."

"Well, it's not a question of a single trail—it's a bit of a maze of trails out here," Jamal had explained hesitantly.

She'd watched Jamal and Lou exchange a loaded glance. She felt her hackles go up. Were they laughing at her? Weariness mixed with anger swirled in her gut. Why did every day have to be a fight?

But then Lou had stepped closer. "Tell you what," he'd said, mollifying. "Earlier they were asking for volunteers to pound around Yapoah Crater. That's also north. How about if we three head that way together? Get you situated onto the main trail back to the Scott Trailhead? Once you're on that, smooth sailing back."

Lou's words had taken a minute to sink in. Once May understood them, she paused, simultaneously confused and grateful. "Are you sure?"

Lou had gestured widely at the melee around them. "This whole area, even if it hasn't been officially declared yet, is clearly a crime scene. The police are going to take over, and that's usually our cue. All we medics do is package people, right? We don't investigate horrific stuff like this, thank god."

May felt her clenched muscles loosen. She felt her tongue thaw back to its normal babble. "Thank you, thank you, thank you."

They'd gathered their gear, radioed their own Unit Commands, and then the three of them headed upslope, back down the ridgeline, and cutting through the lava beds toward Opie Dilldock Pass.

They'd hiked in silence for the first mile or two, concentrating on moving safely through the sharp lava outcroppings. The wind had quieted somewhat, and clouds raced across the sky. May'd strained her ears, but she hadn't heard the laughter again, nor the weird thrumming she'd heard earlier.

Jamal was the first to break the quiet. "May," he'd said from several steps ahead, tone serious, "I don't mean to be rude, but that was a really dick move, your partner leaving you out here."

May had smiled, tried to diffuse his criticism. "He's not my run partner," she'd explained. "I'm so new to the department, I don't actually have a partner. I usually just ride along with whoever's responding to the call."

Jamal had made a clicking sound in his throat, shook his head. "That's not the best way to train a newbie, either."

She'd shrugged. She hadn't known.

"We need to look out for each other in this job," Jamal had continued. "And honestly, if someone in our department abandoned a newbie on a search, I'd run his ass out with a flame thrower. I can't stand people like that."

May had laughed, and Lou joined her. "Agreed. We're at a station in west Eugene famous for its number one policy: no douches allowed. Human decency is the first prerequisite for anyone who works with us. If you want to help people, you have to want to help all people."

May had swallowed a grin, her feet and shoulders and pack aching. Wished she worked there.

Jamal had reached back, bumped her lightly on the shoulder with his pointer finger. "If you ever get tired of working out in the sticks and fancy a change of scenery, we're always hiring medics. Any stage of training. Just get ahold of Lou or me."

May's eyes widened. She felt warmth suffusing through her body for the first time that day, had thought about when Meredith on *Grey's Anatomy* had fought having her coworkers as roommates for over half an episode, but then finally caved in and was happy to have friends living with her. May mused that maybe if she switched departments, she'd be better able to make friends.

The thought had sustained her all the way to the intersection of the main trail connecting to the Scott Trailhead. There, to her pleasure and parallel awkwardness, Lou and Jamal had given her a hug. Then, they stood there and repeated explicit instructions on how to get back to Command until she felt one hundred percent confident. Lou also filled her hands with granola bars and a bottle of red Gatorade. She'd been overwhelmed, had stood watching the two guys hike off north towards Yapoah long past the time they'd disappeared from her sight.

She'd finally turned, trudged on alone. May felt the weariness she'd been keeping at bay creep back. She hiked oblivious to the lava formations stacked on either side of the trail. Her thoughts tacked and deflected, ran punishingly through memories of the day. She wondered if Jonas had meant to leave her on purpose. Wondered what was so different between him and Lou and Jamal. How he seemed to emanate a sense of command that was both frail and volatile and made her constantly unsure while Lou and Jamal had clear authority but also had known to help her without making her ask.

She couldn't make sense of it and her thoughts ran on indiscriminately. Discovering the shoe in the snow, the feel of the leg entirely frozen, the slips of cloth flapping like sunburnt canvas. The digging with her bare hands. May glanced at her hands, wondered if she had the dead person's flesh under her nails. May knew from her medic training that snow, ice, and cold slowed or completely stopped the decay process. The cold and ice chapter in the medical book had a subsection on Otzi, the prehistoric man found in the Alps in the early nineties. He'd melted out of a glacier, and doctors at first thought he was a regular hiker who'd frozen to death. But tests revealed Otzi was actually over thirty-three hundred years old. May had been fascinated reading about Otzi, how a visual assessment of a frozen body could not differentiate between yesterday and yester-eons. She'd watched the episode in season fourteen of *Grey's Anatomy* when April Kepner froze almost to death *twice*, had watched the show's doctors pound the life back into the character's frozen body, and taken notes on hypothermia. May hoped she'd never get that cold.

She wondered if the bodies she found were hypothermic, if they'd died from the cold. Perhaps, they were prehistoric, maybe part of a large hunting party of native people tracking mammoths across the landscape. Perhaps they'd all perished when the ice collapsed, people and mammoths falling together into a gory hole of spears and shaggy prehistoric creatures. But the leg she'd found had a shoe, and that shoe looked modern. It had once been a high heel, black, or, at least, faded black—the heel had been snapped off. May thought about how long women had been wearing high heels. On television, women wore heels even in Jane Austen's stories. But the shoe felt more modern than Jane Austen to May. Like, more nineties or aughts. May herself might have worn a shoe like that.

She'd shivered, dragged her tired feet forward, redirected herself to think purposefully of something else. Anything. Something warm. May thought about Jamal and Lou, wondered if they were at the Yapoah Crater yet.

May slowed, stared at a wall of lava intersecting the trail. It was huge. Gray rock blocks of all sizes jammed together. She could see parts of the wall where it gave the impression that different layers had been stacked atop one another neatly until someone had just come along and broken everything up with a sledgehammer. Barely any vegetation grew on the wall. The air smelled of hot dust, and there was a faint humming sounding in the background.

Patches of grass mosaiced in the stone. The land looked crusty, and if May was taking a medic test, she'd have guessed the land was suffering from psoriasis or some drying dermatological disorder. She'd treat with a prescription moisturizer. Or rain. She smiled at the thought.

"Beautiful, isn't it?"

May gasped, twisted her head around to the creaky voice.

A woman had appeared next to her, close enough that May could have reached out and touched her. "I get carried off by this place too."

May swallowed, instinctively moved back two steps, increased the space between herself and the woman. She released a shaky laugh, told herself to calm down. It was an old woman, after all. With a voice like a thousand paperclips being dragged down a windowpane.

"I'm sorry," May said. "I didn't hear you come up."

She scrutinized the woman, was surprised to see how elderly she was. She had white hair parted at the top of her head and cut to a chin-length bob, icy blue eyes. May couldn't tell what color the woman's original hair once was. At her advanced age she was faded down to an almost translucent white. May could even see blue veins throbbing underneath her thin skin, several broken blood vessels on her nose and cheeks. She had extreme facial muscle degradation with wrinkles flowing in every direction.

May's medical eye was drawn to the woman's large vascular anomaly, a port-wine stain birthmark shaped like a bird in flight, blotchy red, nestled between the corner of the woman's right eye and the remnants of her wispy eyebrow. *Nevus flammeus*, May recognized. Wondered if she had ever tried to get the birthmark altered, removed.

The woman had waited out May's scrutiny, face impassive yet open, and May realized she was gaping at the woman. She shook herself. "I was staring, I'm sorry."

The old woman's eyes disappeared behind creases as she smiled. "Beautiful weather today, huh, after yesterday's rain?" She gestured up at the sky with a hand curled like a lobster claw. Huge white clouds clumped about and the sun shone level with the horizon. Night was coming. The wind had completely disappeared.

Concern mixed with fringe nausea flared in May's belly. She could see the woman wasn't wearing appropriate clothes, was dressed in a faded pink sweater and pale green sweatpants, had no backpack, no hiking poles, seemed to be carrying literally nothing. What was an elderly woman doing out in this wilderness miles and miles from the nearest road?

The woman tipped her head at May, then stepped around her. "Have a good day." She'd then moved on down the trail from where May had just come.

"Wait," May called, indecision racketing up and down her spine. "Are you part of the search? Did you come from Command? Have you seen a missing little girl? Amelia Kane?"

The woman stopped, turned back, looked at May inquisitively. Her white bob swished lightly. Her eyes radiated brightly before dimming.

In that moment, without understanding why, May had felt profoundly disturbed. "Are you okay?"

The woman tilted her head, narrowed her blue eyes. Then a smile had flushed up and across her face. "You know," she said, "No one has ever asked us that before."

May had colored to her hairline. Her unease remained.

But the old woman didn't seem to mind. "Are *you* okay?" she'd countered.

May nodded. "I think so."

The woman moved so quickly towards her that May didn't have time to flinch. She was suddenly just there, standing close enough that May could smell her fetid breath. She laid a swollen, arthritic finger just below May's left cheekbone.

"You will be," she'd said, pressing lightly. "You're stronger than you think."

May had pulled her face back from the woman's hand and held her breath. But then, felt energy flow through her body and enliven her legs. Adrenaline, she'd told herself.

Lifting both claws into the air, the woman had beckoned at the landscape around them. "So many look and see only destruction. Some think we did it, that we destroy everything."

May had never seen eyes such a bright blue. They reminded her of a time during her first year of college when she'd visited a friend in her art studio. Her friend had set out a new painting with a blue so vivid May had not been able to stop herself and she'd reached out, caressed her fingertips against the paint, realizing only then that she had ruined a still-wet oil painting. Embarrassed, she'd fled, pretended a headache, hid in the car.

The old woman's voice dropped to a dry whisper. "But we didn't. That's the secret truth. *They* did it."

May had strained then to keep her face neutral, nodding. She'd read during her EMT training that Oregon had the highest rate of adults with mental illness in the country. Also, that the state had the dubious reputation of being one of the worst in providing mental health treatment or care. One in four Oregonians experienced some type of mental illness, and many of those people appeared and disappeared in the state's emergency rooms with suicidal regularity. May hadn't yet responded to many mental health calls, but she knew she would as she gained call volume.

The woman then took an abrupt step forward, and May again shrank back, a response she recognized as both ludicrous and curious. Clearly, there was something in the situation that made May's nervous system click into high gear. Risk assessment. May ran her eyes all around, checked for scene safety, worried she'd missed something.

"We don't destroy. We resurrect." Brusquely, the woman whirled, short hair fanning like a windmill, stomped aggressively away down the trail. Her steps were small, stabbing, and the distance grew between them while May stood frozen.

She'd watched until the woman disappeared over a ridge. Then, uncertain, May hitched up her backpack, turned back to the trail.

She was exhausted. Too much in one day. Too much.

Head hanging, she felt deflated and shattered. She glanced down at her watch, saw there was only an hour left until she'd be at Incident Command. May closed her eyes, summoned the last energy reserves she had left in her body, sped up her pace. One step and then another and the landscape soothed and calmed her and she barely registered the return of the faint background humming sound. She let her mind drift blankly.

Her thoughts tangled as she hiked, and something pinged, dragged on her memory. May thought about the woman she'd just encountered, the port-wine stain on her face, realized she'd seen that birthmark somewhere else.

May stopped walking, stood still, tried to picture where she'd seen it before.

Her mind jumped to her medic training, narrowing in on the units when she learned best practice protocols for dealing with missing or deceased persons. When she'd been doing those sections, she'd been voracious, churning through chapter after chapter, acing the online tests. To accompany the training, May had also binged the first two seasons of the show *Without a Trace* to understand the complex psychological make up of missing persons. She'd felt like an expert after that. For the section's final exam, she was presented with a real-life case of a missing young person. She had to make an assessment from the given details if she should a) activate an Amber Alert, b) notify police of a High Risk Missing Person, c) classify the case as a Long Term Missing Person, d) diagnose Alzheimer's disease, or e) take a Family Reference Sample for DNA reference. Of course, she'd chosen to notify the police, and had passed the exam flawlessly. As a reward to herself, she'd binged seasons three and four of *Without a Trace* in a single evening-into-morning.

An alarm bell was rattling in her head, but May couldn't picture where she'd seen the birthmark. Wasn't sure if it was on a television show or an exam, but she knew it was somewhere around there.

She was also too tired. The day had been too long, and she knew she was going to be working for several more hours. May knew whatever her brain was trying to tell her was important, but she also couldn't summon the energy to remember properly.

The lights of Command soon glowed against the darkening sky, and May quickened her pace, moved eagerly towards the ambiguous roar of people and generators and vehicles. She easily located Chief in the largest tent surrounded by people and equipment, but he asked her to wait a minute or two for him at the bush truck. Someone had handed her a jacket, and she'd gone and pulled the tailgate down and sank quietly against the edge of the truck bed.

"Food, Young," a voice interrupted her thoughts.

May flicked opened her eyes, squinted in the glare of Command lights, saw Baker standing by the truck bed. His trucker cap was askew. He was holding a paper plate covered with steaming beans, mashed potatoes, bread rolls. She leaned into the warm down jacket wrapped over her shoulders.

"I didn't know if you were vegetarian," he added, his face scrunched in worry. He pushed the plate onto her lap, handed her a plastic fork. "Eat."

She could feel tears welling in her eyes, and she swallowed the lump in her throat twice before she could bring the beans to her mouth. She kept her eyes down, focused on the food while remaining conscious of Baker standing there watching her. It was the second time today someone had seen she needed help and offered it. She didn't know how to respond.

"Young, I was told you were looking for me," a voice boomed from the darkness.

May's jerked, saw the chief striding through the artificial light cast from the halogen work lights. Jonas and another man were beside him. The chief had a clipboard in hand, papers, a huge radio strapped to his shoulder. Hadn't he told her to wait for him?

"You look worn out," he said, stopping a few feet from the truck. "You up for giving a statement now?"

She nodded, still chewing, uncomfortably aware she was ringed by men all watching her eat.

"Fine. This is Bradford, from Eugene PD."

Bradford extended his hand to May, waited while she hurried to put her fork down to shake it. He was muscled, with brown hair and tanned white skin that flashed against a crisp police uniform. He looked like he'd already been through the military a couple of times. She sat up straighter, wished she had better posture, less hair stuck to her sweaty face.

"We're going to walk through your statement and the discovery," he explained. "Bradford is going to take notes, and he'll give you a statement to sign later."

May nodded. She'd filled out countless statements since she'd started the medic job. Most days, it was just a run report, but sometimes, if the call included the police, it was different.

"Given how late it is, you can debrief us later about the morning interaction at OHEWS. Jonas has given us the main thrust," Chief looked down at his paperwork.

May nodded, opened her mouth, shut it, opened it. She looked around at the men's faces, felt a flash of eagerness to please them. "I'd look into those people there, Chief. There's something off about the woman running the station."

Bradford leaned forward. "What? How?"

May looked at the police officer. His eyes gleamed in the flood lights. "I'm not sure, exactly," she said. "But there's something."

Bradford grinned so widely it almost took her breath away. She felt a surge of pleasure at saying something he liked.

But then Bradford turned away from her, spoke. "I told you, Chief. With that woman's background, surely it has to play in here."

"What?" May asked, glancing between the men.

"We don't have time for this, Officer. Let's focus on the discovery," Chief barked impatiently. "May, focus."

Bobbing her head, she wiped her face, coughed again. A bean had gotten stuck. The men waited.

"Get ahold of yourself, Young," Chief ordered.

Finally, coughing subsided, she looked up.

"Okay then?" he asked, his tone laced with something May couldn't fully read. "Take us through walking down the moraine towards the snow patch. Did you see anything unusual in the area?"

May thought, remembered back. All she could summon was how steep, gray, and windy it had been. She shook her head. "Nothing."

"And then, Jonas crossed the snow first, yes?"

Agreeing, she twisted her fingers around the fork. Moved the plate off her lap, set it next to the extra fuel jug.

"When Jonas first alerted you to the presence of the body, what did you do?"

May looked up quickly, caught Jonas's eye. "What?" she sputtered.

Chief repeated the question.

Jonas returned her eye contact, stared steadily, face impassive. Confusion swept over her. She'd discovered the body. She'd yelled for him. He'd already crossed the snow patch. She was the one who'd tripped, fallen to her knees, stuck her hands out. She specifically remembered discovering the shoe, the leg. Hadn't she? Or had her brain made all that up?

"So then Jonas had you dig the person free, correct? And he radioed in?"

That had happened. May nodded, looked down at her hands. Her nails were shredded to their quicks. She had sizable cuts on two of her left fingers. All from digging in the sharp snow. If only she'd remembered gloves.

"Can you describe if you saw anything else around the leg?" Bradford asked.

There had only been snow, rocks, snow. And the leg. "Nothing," she said. "I don't remember anything else."

The police officer frowned, spider lines radiating from his nose. Fear pinged in May's stomach. Had she said the wrong thing? She searched back, tried to remember, but nothing else had occurred.

"Wait," she said, holding up a hand. Bradford leaned, smiled encouragingly at her. May felt a flare inside her chest, a need to please him.

"Before that," she said. "There was laughter. I heard it. In the wind."

The chief's eyebrows shot up, and Bradford looked away, rubbed his forehead with his fingertips. May read the disappointment on both their faces. Reminded her of the same look she often saw on her mother's face. Foolishness surged through her. She looked down at her hands, endeavored to say nothing more.

"Let's move on," Chief said, curt. "I don't have much time for this. When you determined you wouldn't be able to dig the body fully out…" he turned, looked at Bradford. "Young is new here. She didn't have her pack properly set up, no shovel."

"I checked with her before we left the station," Baker interjected. "She had everything."

The chief raised a hand, placating. "It's fine, mistakes happen, things get mislaid."

May heaved hot with embarrassment, her face ablaze. She could feel tears pooling again behind her eyes, couldn't bring herself to look up at any of the men. So much of today, she had screwed up.

"Jonas, where was your shovel?" Baker asked querulously, looking hard at Jonas. "Why didn't you two use yours? Why is Young getting this shit sandwich?"

"Hey," Chief cut in. "No one did anything wrong here. We're just sorting statements. Both Jonas and May did good work today. Let's wind this up. Everyone is exhausted, it's been a long day, and we're nowhere closer on our original search."

May mumbled into her lap, "Is there any word on Amelia Kane?"

"No," Bradford responded. "The girl hasn't been located. But sure as hell we're going to press her mother. She's the type. This whole situation seems—"

"—Officer" The chief interjected. "Stop." He turned to May. "Young, you can fill out the full-length report later, but nuts and bolts now. Jonas shows you the other bodies, you two radio in, the Camp Sherman teams arrive, takes over?"

May's mouth went cotton and she dry-blinked twice. Stared through her lashes at her lap, then up at Jonas. He was watching her with a completely straight face. She didn't know how to interpret his expression. If he was lying, wouldn't he look shifty? Was something wrong with her, the way she remembered the events? She was bone tired, she recognized. Maybe she misremembered?

"Young did incredible work today. Especially given how new she is to this line of work," Jonas finally said, filling in her silence. "I hope at some point a commendation is given to her. Thomas, I wouldn't have been able to do this without her."

May looked up into his face as his words sank in. They were supposed to be kind, but she felt the barbed wire in them. He was smiling, nodding, but his eyes looked like velvet in the darkness. He didn't look capable of harming her, but, risk assessment.

"Young," Chief said. "Focus. I know you're tired. Just confirm these statements and we'll all shift out to get some sleep before starting again tomorrow."

May glanced around at the faces of the four men in the harsh artificial glare from the portable scene lights. They all stared at her, and the only thing that mattered to her in that moment was sleep, laying her head down and closing her eyes.

11
THE
SCIENTIST

Ros waited, sat unmoving on the station's porch, mind sluggish but churning. Her legs dangled off the wooden edge, barely grazed the ground and patchy grasses clumped in threes. The trees towered darkly, faintly backlit with the suggestion of a morning light not set to arrive for another hour.

She hadn't slept. She'd laid in her bunk, eyes wide until the waiting chased her out into the fresh night air. She'd settled into a statue on the porch, a blanket loose over her shoulders.

Waiting.

So much of her life hinged around moments of waiting.

They were going to come that morning, and they were going to tell her something, and within her cavernous subterranean self she knew the possibilities were limited only by her imagination.

If it was cold on the porch, she didn't feel it. Everything around her was glazed in the blue light of before-morning. The darkness blurred lines, made the woods thick and appear as one single, massive tree. Closing her eyes, opening them, she faded for long seconds before jerking back. Awake. Alert. Ros forcefully calmed herself, summoned the traces of Tove's hands on her face. Closed her eyes, and when she opened them again, light had snuck through, transformed trees from blue-black to gold-black. She heard the first stirrings of morning chatter.

Answers to yarned questions roiled up against impossible scenarios. Ros could taste the metallic rot, could feel herself on the edge of being seven years old again, lost. Could feel her adrenaline slow, dancing with fear. She spoke quietly to herself, said words she was afraid weren't true anymore. Mouthed what it would be like to know, to have answers.

Sitting on the porch, Ros wished she still smoked—wished lit rag fibers and Cherokee tobacco would both force time to hurry and calm her thoughts. She bleared back through the days before, heron-pecked memories of Ash and Tove. There was giggling and plum lipstick and Flower and Herring and the ghost of Amelia Kane stalking her up mountaintops. There was the humming, the laughter she'd heard so clearly atop Black Crater that she could have sworn it originated within herself.

Closing her eyes again, Ros concentrated on Tove, on yesterday. Nothing further back, nothing forward. She knew the woman was still asleep in the Fellows Cabin, but Ros didn't want to wake her. Didn't want to bother her. Instead, just wished to channel her, to know what Tove would say in this moment.

Ros smiled into the morning gold-black light.

She knew exactly what Tove would say. Tove would make her pay attention to the morning soundscape.

Ros tilted back, closed her eyes, listened.

At first, she heard little, just the background hum of a forest rolling awake and her own heartbeat. But then, individual sounds, threads of sounds, darted into her consciousness.

Following the listen lines, Ros lingered on the *wicka-wicka-wicka* call of a Three-toed Woodpecker. Waited, concentrated, then smiled when she heard the quiet return call, slightly more easterly than the first. Warmth ran through her. She hadn't heard that woodpecker in years. It had always been there, but she hadn't been listening.

She fixated on a deep drumming, one of the woodpeckers likely tapping a hollow log. She allowed herself to be mildly surprised as she followed the reverberations of the drumming sound off various trees. The birds usually drummed in the spring when they were setting up territories and nests, looking for mates. But it was late autumn now.

Ros waited, held a breath, tried to sharpen her focus. She knew what was coming even if most mornings she hadn't given it specific notice. Right after the woodpeckers sounded off... there it was. Ros turned her face, smiled.

A high chirrup broadcast through the woods. A single call pitched high, repeating so quickly she wasn't sure how many individual notes were in the entire breath. But as soon as it unspooled, chirrups piped back from almost all around the cabin, calls that Ros hoped signaled that everyone had made it through the night, that the morning check-ins were a roll call for all the White-winged Crossbills that had chosen not to migrate to the Carolinas and instead winter out in the Oregon Cascades. Plenty of seed cones here to munch away the long winter. Ros pictured a female Crossbill in her mind, admired the delicate light red head feathers, the darker red splashes under the wings and throat.

Other birds took up the invitation to the morning symphony: the surprisingly harsh cheeps from the Canada jays, the congested rattle of Clark's Nutcrackers. Ros breathed the auditory distraction, the focus each sound gave her, the strength to turn away from questions piling up unanswered in her brain.

Eyes still closed, Ros broadened her attention, listened beyond the bird calls. Tove had stirred something in her. Dry fall leaves scrabbled at the foot of the cabin. Trees rubbed branches, barked calluses grating. Mist drops shattered. Somewhere, a faint thrumming, an energetic low-grade rhythm that sounded like Ros was sitting under electrified power lines. Closer, a wet rustle of something moving through the underbrush. Ros turned her head immediately in the sound's direction, strained her eyes wide. No person, no footsteps.

She looked down at her watch, saw hours more to go. Didn't move, didn't stand. She sat smothered with waiting.

Ros closed her eyes again, tried to listen, tried to find clarity and calm and distraction. But the birds were quiet now, and it seemed the forest held a single volcanic breath. The only thing Ros could hear was the background thrumming, a core-clenching vibration that somehow woke a distant memory in her.

Flower had often worn green jade beads around her neck, thick ropes that twisted tight above her collarbone and down between her breasts. They clacked together, a dull hollow plastic swish and knock that, throughout her early childhood, Ros had associated with her mother.

Once, when they visited a dingy shop in downtown Portland to have Flower's fortune read, Ros had slid back and forth through a thick beaded curtain that hung between the main room and a storage closet. She'd run her small fingers along the dangling strings, comforted herself with how they felt cool and calming on her hands and arms and shoulders and face. It had felt like she was surrounded, how every movement she'd made had incited an equal movement from the beads. And even though, a few minutes later, face inflamed and eyes narrowed, Flower had snatched Ros's bare upper arm so tight her nails had broken skin and dragged her from the shop, Ros had held the comfort of those beads deep.

Much later, sitting in the car with Herring outside of a motel, Ros had tried to explain the feeling of that beaded curtain, how it was like she was in the center of the hurricane that was her mother.

Herring had ignored her, had chewed her lip silently and sat stone-still in the front seat, staring at the motel room's small, curtain-covered window. But later still, driving the 242, Herring had tugged on her mother's beads, had run her fingers up and down the necklace and made eye contact with Ros sitting in the back and Ros knew her sister understood.

Ros opened her eyes, realized another hour had drifted by unnoticed. She pulled the blanket closer, shifted, stretched her legs and kicked blood back into her toes. Stomach acid gurgled into her mouth as she moved. Emotional bile wrapped in slime. She spat it out onto the ground.

While she was afraid and excited, she was also repulsed by moments like this, of sitting, waiting for news. She'd done it so many times before.

The police never had to say why they called, why they'd ask to meet with her. At home. At the station. At school. Over the phone.

In the early months, when she was fostering with a family in

Waldport, a spinning door of uniforms had kept arriving at the house with badges and tissues and theories. Each time, Ros would pant with anticipation at the imminent meeting, the arrival of police, the potential of news and hope. She'd skyrocket before and then crash numb and inert afterward.

But when she got older, sometimes one or two years would go by before the police phoned again, gave her an update entirely unchanged from the one previous. Often, they'd just ask her to repeat what she'd already said, or ask her if she remembered anything new. As if it was all up to her.

She stopped meeting with the police altogether when she was sixteen. She made that decision herself, inflexibly, after the police had called a meeting and shown her pictures of a man with a brown mustache and deadened eyes and she'd gone to the library after and read all the articles and looked at all the pictures and was so horrified at the details of what he'd done and how he'd returned time and again to the bodies of his victims that she hadn't been able to sleep for days. She couldn't stop seeing him do those things to her mother and sister.

She'd stayed up for nights, imagination in full swing, armed with the clarity that her mother and her sister had died horrifically as they tried to walk back to her. The certainty grooved itself into Ros's brain and she found herself unable to function, to step out from under the immense burden. And when finally, after weeks of agonizing, she'd called the police station, she was told the case was closed due to lack of new material and Ros had exploded and decided then and there that she was done.

On her seventeenth birthday, with the help of the foster family she'd been living with in Roseburg, Ros had applied for early admission to the University of Washington. She'd been accepted, and later, driving the I-5 north to Seattle in a rattly, ancient Geo Metro she'd proudly bought with her waitressing money, Ros had made the decision to entirely re-make her life.

She'd decided to be a new person, a new self. She shortened her name and vowed on that lonely car ride north to close the door on a story that she knew, by that point, would likely never be resolved. She decided to leave Flower and Herring as much in the past as possible.

Ros earned a bachelor's degree in earth sciences in just three years, presenting herself to her peers as an ordinary rural Oregon girl who liked science and didn't talk much about home. And, after a one-year break when she worked as a marine field assistant at the Puget Sound Conservation Center, she returned to the University of Washington for a doctorate program.

She'd been drawn to the course load of chemistry, climatology, and geology. She found satisfying stability in science, in knowing that if you knew the rules, you could predict the outcomes. By the time she was twenty-six, she'd completed her dissertation and was on the job market.

That she'd ended up taking the Corvallis OHEWS job struck her later as mildly ironic, closing a circuit she had attempted to avoid. Driving south on I-5 after a decade of being away from Oregon, she'd briefly pondered checking in with the police. But too much time had passed, and she was certain that if something had changed, they would have found a way to locate her.

She hadn't realized at the time of her hire that of all the stations the Oregon program ran, from Klamath Falls to the Blue Mountains to the Wallowas, she'd be right back where she started—up on Highway 242 at OHEWS Harlow Crater.

But she'd gone anyway, ghosts be damned.

Or so she told herself. Even as she walked the Three Sisters area time and again, looking, radio in hand, just in case. She told herself she was at peace in her world atop the Cascades counting clouds and rocks.

But then incidents like Amelia Kane turned everything upside down, and Ros was just back where she started, a raw wound with empty memories.

Footsteps jarred Ros from sorting her thoughts and memories. Twitching her eyes open, she saw Tove wrapped in a long down duster jacket walking from the Fellows Cabin. Her hair was loose, huge and thick and cascading like a fresh lava flow. Ros's breath momentarily stuck.

"Morning," Tove murmured, stopping in front of Ros. "Want some coffee?"

Ros nodded. Her tongue was dried to the top of her mouth. Watched Tove take in her blanket, disheveled hair, bare feet.

"You been out here all night?"

Ros nodded again, thought about explaining the unsorted, unstratified accumulation of her thoughts over the last hours, but the sympathy she saw in Tove's eyes stopped her. Saw that Tove likely thought Ros had been sitting on the porch all night in fear and sadness. She didn't have the energy to correct her, didn't want to explain that it wasn't fear that kept her anchored to the porch; rather, it was a complex mix of hope and dread.

Tove clucked compassionately. "Poor thing. I'll make you something warm."

Tove stepped around Ros, trailed a light, but electric, hand on Ros's head as she moved into the main cabin. Ros heard her rattle proficiently around the kitchen as if she'd been at the field station for months instead of a single night.

A steaming mug soon appeared before her, and Ros whispered her thanks into the cup as she cradled the coffee. The numbness fled from her hands. She took a gulp, warm liquid passed down her throat without registering taste. There was just warmth, aliveness, and, for a moment, she was content. But even that sensation was fleeting. On her second sip, she heard what she'd been straining for all night— footsteps coming from the direction of the spur trail. Warmth fled, aliveness wilted, and she watched as three uniforms emptied, one by one, into the clearing.

Ros did not rise. Couldn't.

The figures didn't stop advancing until they stood about six feet from her, crowded in. They were fully back lit in the pale morning light. The officers stood shoulder to shoulder with outsized packs that made them seem even larger and for all the world like Ringwraiths from a *Lord of the Rings* movie Ros had seen years back.

"Rosmarinus Fisher?" the man in the middle asked by way of greeting.

Ros tilted her head. No niceties then. They were going to get straight to it.

Fine.

She nodded stiffly to the man who spoke, head still tilted back. She resisted the urge to shade her eyes from the morning glare. Ros was looking directly east into the rising sun shooting through the forest.

"I'm Chief Thomas Addington, fire chief from Thurston Hills. This is my colleague Jonas, whom I believe you've met, and Bradford here is from the Eugene Police Department."

"Hello," Ros said, soft.

"Could you confirm your identity, ma'am?" asked the man to the right, the young one introduced as Bradford.

"I already did." Paused, assessed. Why did they need her identification right off? How did that matter?

"Do you have any formalized identification? A driver's license?"

"You mean formal," she automatically corrected. Watched Bradford's face draw in, his lips shape into a scowl. She lifted her shoulder an inch, brushed off his annoyance. Didn't care enough to joust with a police officer with aggression issues. "No, not on me."

Bradford took a notebook from his front pocket, pulled out a pen, made a show of taking a note. The other men were silent, staring at her, at the cabin, at the area in turns. They were fidgety.

Something was clearly amiss, and she felt an unexpected pull of unease. Her mind still whirled, and Ros wondered if they wanted her to feel uneasy. She silently shook her head. She didn't want to feel uneasy. She wanted to feel informed.

She swallowed the wave of irritation that slid over her, straightened her spine. Whatever this was going to be, she would not lose her temper. Shrugging the blanket off her shoulders, Ros pulled herself upright, felt a maddening rush of blood descend into her feet. Lifted her chin, waited.

"You were involved in the disappearance of Flower and Herring Fisher back in the late nineties, yes?" Bradford asked, eyes down on his notebook as if reading from the paper. It would have worked if only Ros hadn't glimpsed the sheet when he pulled it out, saw it was blank.

It took a second, but Bradford's word choice eventually sank in. Involved? Ros suppressed a laugh, a bark that she knew might be read as hysterical by the three men surrounding her. "Involved?" she echoed, astonished. "Involved?"

Aware her voice rose with each word, she spit out her incredulousness. "You mean did I lose my family when my mother and sister disappeared, you insensitive fuck?"

Bradford closed his notebook, extended his chin, and looked at her with a flat, disconnected expression. He eyed her up and down, made no effort to hide it, then looked at his colleagues, raised an eyebrow, turned back at her. "You were the last person to see them alive, correct?"

Ros closed her eyes. Drew in a breath, a second, a third. This wasn't what she'd expected, was not what she'd prepared herself for. Hot lava flowed through her veins. Her hands clenched the wooden railing, nails digging in. She forced her eyes open.

"I was seven years old," she hissed hoarsely. "Get off this property."

The officer laughed.

Ros looked at him in complete bewilderment.

"This is state property, ma'am. You can't order us off these premises."

The man named Thomas cleared his throat, reached a hand to her. "Miss Fisher," he said, "Please calm down."

Ros swiveled her face, glared at him. The fire chief had sounded sympathetic on the radio last night, and she felt betrayed for some reason. His expression conveyed no support, so she turned away from him, clasped the porch pole, rested her forehead against its cool surface.

"Ma'am, what do you know about the search for Amelia Kane?" This, from Thomas. "Miss Fisher. Please sit down, calm down."

Ros turned away from them, straightened, willed herself to not fall. Walked through the open cabin door. Looked around in the cabin, saw Tove, remembered Tove, who sat quiet at the table, coffee in front of her, eyes wide and cemented to Ros.

Ros read the expression on Tove's face, lightly shook her head in response. She needed a lot of things, but help wasn't the highest on the list right now.

"Miss Fisher." Thomas stood in the cabin entryway, took in Ros and Tove, "I need you to come back outside. I'm afraid we've gotten off on the wrong foot."

Ros couldn't bring herself to acknowledge him. She lapped the cabin, adrenaline and agony and exhaustion pumping through her body. Stopped in front of her desk. Looked down, saw the stacks of notebooks and paperwork. Her paperwork. She was a goddamned scientist.

"Tensions are high right now, Miss Fisher. We've got something like ten different departments, jurisdictions, and organizations all out here trying to find a little girl. We discovered something in addition to the search. Could you calm down enough to come back outside and speak with us?"

Stacked neatly on her desk were eight or nine nondescript field notebooks with black covers. She'd been using them for over a decade. Fill one up, start a new one. All her science, all her data, all her developments from student to serious researcher—she could chart that entire progress in such notebooks. She could probably even flip fifteen notebooks back and find the one where she first started sketching out the big questions that puzzled scientists in her field. She could list many of the great geology questions in her sleep, the topics her colleagues argued over endlessly in polite, passive language-laden peer reviewed papers. How did the Earth get formed? What triggered plate tectonics? What occurred at the K-T boundary? Is the planet really in a new geological epoch called the Anthropocene? How do climatic changes translate quantitatively into sea level rise? How deep is Kraken Mare? All questions that required method and observation and time and stacks of data sets. Questions that Ros could muse over with colleagues, could download the latest papers on, could chip away at with her own work.

Answerable questions.

Staring at the notebooks, Ros knew that for her, in science, it wasn't answers that drove her. It was questions.

But Ros knew that some questions were unanswerable. And for over a decade, she'd chosen to not dwell in dark places of unknowing, wondering unanswerable questions about what happened to her mother and sister.

"Miss Fisher?"

"Dr. Fisher," she corrected, reaching, equalizing what little power she had left.

"Ah," Thomas responded, shifted in the doorway.

She swung her head at the chief, assessed his wide, brown eyes. Didn't know if he respected a doctorate degree more than a marriage certificate. She looked down at his hands, saw he held a folder of paper. He waved it slightly, gave her a somewhat pleading look. More questions.

Ros swallowed, dry throat pounding. Stepped firmly into her power. "Only if he never speaks again." Time to make demands.

"Bradford?"

"I don't know his name," Ros lied. Refused the satisfaction of answering his name.

"Okay."

Ros shrugged one shoulder and maneuvered around the center table, slid past Tove, then by the fire chief, back out to the porch edge. She watched the chief nod briefly at Tove, then step back, whisper to Bradford. The officer backed up a few paces, sighed. Ros didn't deign to look in his direction but did keep him in the crosshairs of her peripheral vision. Jonas also stood a few feet back, kept looking around the station like he'd never been there before, like it was a crime scene.

"Let's start over," Thomas said in a soothing voice. "We're looking for Amelia Kane, a nine-year-old little girl last seen in the Three Sisters Wilderness wearing a purple shirt, green jeans. We realize that two days ago, Jonas here, and another of our team, May Young, checked in with you and took a statement, is that correct?"

Ros nodded a single confirmation, stared upward. The morning sky showed a uniform gray, a low blanket of Stratus clouds that looked like an incomplete fog. She closed her eyes, registered the temperature, wind, humidity. Recognized that there was a fine day unfolding, that the Stratus clouds would likely lift in an hour or so, reveal a solid blue afternoon. She felt a surge of happiness for Tove. It would be a good recording day for her.

"In the statements May Young recorded, it appears two hikers were also interviewed here. And none of you knew anything about the child's disappearance, or had seen her at any point? Is that still true for you?"

"Yes," Ros said quietly, wrath flaring in her throat like acid. She kept her face still, refused to give them a show of her insides. "I've never seen Amelia Kane."

Bradford snorted. The fire chief jerked a hand at him, twisted his body so it angled towards Ros. "As you've been doing your work out here, have you ever been out to the Collier Glacier?"

"Of course." Clipped. She wasn't going to give anything if they didn't.

"You ever explored the edge of it? What they call the moraine area?"

Ros nodded, then paused. She hated the feeling that they were leading her to something. This was not what people did to each other, not in the face of trauma and tragedy and the unknown. There was something they were building to, something they thought they knew, or she knew, and if they were humane or kind or decent, they would have come right out and said it. Instead, there was this performance that justified these men's jobs and their assumed power over her.

Ros felt sick watching them. She sucked a breath in, released it quickly. Time again to make demands. Get her own questions going. She wasn't a terrified seven-year-old. She was a fucking adult, a scientist. "What's going on?" she demanded. "What is this about?"

Thomas fell silent for a moment, then made eye contact with the other two. "Well, Miss Fisher."

"Dr. Fisher," she repeated, refusing to concede anything.

"My apologies," the chief said, then moved on. "When our search crews were looking for Amelia, they found a shoe in the snow near the Collier Glacier."

Puzzlement swarmed up from Ros's belly. "A shoe?" Her abdomen spasmed. She met the chief's eyes. Realized he was staring at her. Watching her. Assessing.

"A shoe?" she prodded again.

"Do you remember what shoes your mother or Herring were wearing the day they disappeared?"

Ros closed her eyes, breathed in memory. Cigarette smoke in the car, Herring in something maybe red. She tried to summon a memory of her mother from that day she'd long tucked away, but all she got were flashes, Flower's eyes, the click of the lid coming off a tube of lipstick, beads clacking, her mother with all her long hair swished over one shoulder.

"No," she whispered.

"Do you know what shoe size your mother or Herring might have been?"

Amusement rose as bile in her throat. Ros didn't know the size of her mother's feet, had never thought to ask when she was a child, and such information, while perhaps written down somewhere—what would it tell them now? That Flower's feet might fit into a found shoe and prove her existence, like Cinderella? Her lips tightened at the thought. "Is it glass?" she murmured, too late, couldn't take it back.

"What?" Thomas asked, leaning forward.

Ros shook her head, dismissed herself, forced her hands to stay by her sides and not fly up to her mouth, to keep in the giggle that threatened to burst forth. She could imagine the headline: *Hysterical Woman Giggles to Death.*

"Is this familiar to you, Miss Fisher?" he asked, reaching into the folder, handing a photograph to her. "We think it's too big for what we estimate your sister's feet to have been at the time of her disappearance."

The image showed a single shoe resting on snow, a white piece of paper with the number eighteen written in black marker next to it. The shoe looked like a canvas slip-on, had no laces, and was once white. It had begun decaying and there were chunks of fabric missing around the toe. The sole was stained brown.

Ros felt no hint of recognition looking at the image, no hint that it had perhaps once belonged to Flower nor Herring. She shook her head. "I don't know."

"Take your time," he responded.

"I really don't know, Chief Thomas." Ros was firm. She handed the image back, looked up, eyed the Stratus clouds. On second thought, it might drizzle slightly before it cleared up.

"What about this one?" Thomas pulled another image from the folder in his hands, passed it to her. A photograph of a faded red running shoe with blue piping. It looked like the type of shoe Ros herself sometimes wore.

"Or this one?" He passed her a third image, this time of a black dress shoe missing a heel. "Do you recognize any of these?"

Ros stared at the images, closed down quickly the memory of looking at other photos, of trying so hard to see something, anything that would tell them what happened. She tried to summon memory of feet or shoes or Flower. Nothing. Again, she shook her head. "The only thing I remember about my mother in relation to shoes is the sound of heels clattering on sidewalks. She wore heels, that bit I at least remember. But I don't recognize any of these."

"Okay," the chief said, sighing. He took the images back and stepped back from the porch. "We're not going to take up any more of your time, Miss Fisher."

"That's it?" Ros was incredulous. They'd hiked all the way to the station for shoes? Came on so strong just to leave? She narrowed her eyes at the chief, nearly missed Bradford's second audible snort.

"Chief," the police officer muttered.

"That's it," Thomas said determinedly, final, squaring off not against Ros, but Bradford. She couldn't see the man's face, but she saw Bradford raise his arms, cross them over his chest, shake his head. She watched Jonas step toward the pair.

Ros didn't care what was happening between them, but she did care about how she was involved. She moved from the porch edge, toed the damp ground with her bare foot, gingerly stepped towards them, drew herself tall. Took in a deep breath, pulled her courage from a decade of working successfully on her own merit. "What's this about?" she demanded, inserted as much strength as she could into her question.

They ignored her.

"Let's go," the chief said to Bradford, who was glaring with an expression Ros recognized as disgust.

Bradford twisted then, scowled at Ros. She knew before he opened his mouth that something ugly was coming. She waited.

"You know what they teach us at the academy?" Bradford called, even as the chief reached and put a restraining hand on his shoulder. "Hurt people hurt people. Those who see violence, enact violence."

Bewilderment stung her. Whatever she expected, it wasn't this. She analyzed his words, puzzled them for a brief moment. "What kind of simplistic pseudo-science junk is that?"

Bradford stepped swiftly around the two other men and charged up to Ros. Stood so close she could feel his breath as he glared down at her. "Me, I think it's even more clear than that. When we're looking for a suspect, I don't think we should look at the normal people. Instead, we should look for people like you, Rosmarinus. Broken people."

"That's enough, officer. Stop." The chief was suddenly there, putting his hand on Bradford's shoulder.

Bradford kept talking. "What are you really doing out here, working where your family disappeared? Why do people keep disappearing around you? Isn't that sick?"

"Officer Bradford, I'm ordering you to step away from Miss Fisher." Thomas's voice boomed, full command.

"You strike me as a liar, Rosmarinus."

The cabin porch squeaked, and then Tove was moving across the deck, down the steps, sliding her body between Bradford and Ros, hands on her hips, immovable.

Bradford was forced to step back as Tove took up the space between them. "Who are you?" he exclaimed, eyes raking Tove.

"None of your business, you amped up shit. Fuck off, get away from us."

Bradford didn't move. He glared at Tove and Ros. "Who are you?" he repeated. "Answer now."

The anger in his eyes flashed cold like diamonds on royalty. Ros realized that the man might hit either of them. She was unsure what was happening but refused to bow. She took a breath, held her ground.

She felt Tove stretch her hand back, reach, and then her fingers entwined around Ros's. Ros wasn't sure which one of them was shaking, but she felt safer clutching Tove's hand. She couldn't see Tove's face, but she saw the knot of hair bob, lift, angle, and she knew Tove was glaring up at Bradford. Admiration waved over her.

"No," she said.

Bradford closed his mouth, shook his head, stepped back. He looked at both women, took in their held hands. He swung about, glowered at the fire chief. "Fine," he said, raising his hands. "I'm so tired of everyone shoveling all this shit on me when all I'm doing is my fucking job. Trying to protect people from scumbags."

Warmth radiated through Ros as Tove's back and thighs pressed against the front of her body. The woman clicked her throat, gripped Ros's hand tighter. Ros stood still, looked over Tove's shoulder, watched currents detonating between the three men, did not understand what was happening beyond the solidity of Tove.

"Officer, you need to step away." The chief's voice was steel.

"Haven't you read the case profile?" Bradford spat. "Her own mother and sister disappear. And she comes back here—for what? We've had reports of at least nine women missing in this area. And now, an hour from this very fucking station, what do we find? Come on, Chief, this is a no brainer. Copycat? Replicating her own tragedies?"

"And what have you ever done about all those missing women?" Ros hissed, Tove's fingers clenching hers.

"Jonas, escort Officer Bradford to the trailhead immediately. Immediately." The chief's command was forceful.

Ros watched Jonas step forward, reach to place a hand on Bradford's shoulder. But the officer shrugged away, turned, looked at Ros one more time, shook his head, then walked searingly back to the forest edge. Jonas glanced at Thomas, then trailed Bradford.

As the two moved away, Bradford's words sunk in slow to Ros. Her, a killer? She suppressed an inappropriate urge to laugh. Her fingers twisted tighter in Tove's. What did he mean, something found an hour from her? Ros turned, stared at the fire chief. His face was like grated stone.

"I apologize unreservedly for Officer Bradford's behavior. No excuses. I can provide you all the necessary information if you want to file a complaint."

"Thank you," Ros said softly. "But tell me what he meant. Now."

Tove squeezed her hand, three pulses.

Thomas cleared his throat. "You understand that this is an ongoing investigation. I can't disclose any details."

He drew a deep breath, shifted in his stance, looked down at his large hands. Sighed, looked back up and Ros caught his eye. She saw pity there alongside something else. "But. I'd be breaking protocol, but after Officer Bradford, I think you deserve to know a few details."

Ros nodded, mute.

Thomas waved the pictures in his hands. "Two days ago, near the side of Collier Glacier, we found these shoes in the snow."

He paused, seemed to be trying to collect his words. Ros waited.

"They were on or near the feet of at least three, but possibly more, individual bodies. We've not yet been able to identify the remains because, even though they've been preserved in the ice and snow, they are, well, incomplete. Some are quite far gone. We suspect there may be more."

Ros felt her legs weaken, but then Tove's arms were on either side of her, holding, keeping her upright.

The fire chief released his breath into the clear mountain air, finished it. "The bodies are all female."

12
THE
DAUGHTER

It rained hard for the third day in a row. Donna leaned on the porch banister and watched water slap the earth.

She was restless.

When she'd made her decision to come to the cabin, when she and her therapist had talked through what that would look like, what tools she'd need, it hadn't occurred to her that Ray would take so long dying. The hospital had been pretty clear about the expanding growths in his stomach, lungs, brain, and bowels. It was going to be quick, and it was going to be painful.

Donna's therapist had suggested Donna take this chance to forgive the man, to let go of her anger as she sat with dying Ray, to use this opportunity to get closure and work towards being a better person. Reconciliation, she'd said. Family reunification. Forgiveness.

Donna had agreed while her mind spun data layers, while she'd connected points and lines and polygons and visualized exactly what she could do. She most certainly could tend Ray through his last hours, but she could also use the moment to complete some of the files in her cabinet. She could understand the timeline of events.

But the weeks at the cabin had stretched into months and Donna was still no closer to finding the truth about had happened to Julene.

And she needed to know. It was the single most important question she had.

She worried that the answer was right in front of her, but that she had a cognitive filter permitting her to only see specific details and ignore everything else. It wouldn't surprise her—filtering, ignoring, denying were all survival mechanisms the mind activated in stressful circumstances. God knew she experienced stress every moment she waited at the cabin for Ray to die. Or talk.

She needed a reward. To release the stress. Plus, rewards were motivational. Kept a person going.

Donna mentally browsed her options. Would she prefer a tangible reward like new, warm socks? Or, a self-care reward, like a hot coffee and a walk? Maybe a guilty treat reward? Donna smiled at the thought, saw her therapists smiling too.

She walked to her car, opened the trunk. A plastic bin labeled "Rewards" was half buried under blankets and clothes. Donna opened the lid, pulled out the smaller bag labeled "Sweet Rewards." She took a milk chocolate bar from the box, put everything back, then wandered back up to the porch, munching.

Donna loved the organizational aspects of therapy, the safety and control she could attain through specific strategies and practices within her larger treatment plan.

Her new therapist was all about working towards Donna's goals by creating healthy distances and tools to safely navigate the immense trauma Donna carried. One of her earliest strategies had been to get Donna to produce distance between herself and her father so she could manage the thought of living in the same world as him. She suggested identifying the man as Ray. A term that did not force a connection Donna loathed. It had helped.

But time was ticking, and Donna wondered how long she could reasonably mind browse, stand on the porch, sit on the porch, transit from porch to car. Do any variance of those three acts over and over as she waited for Ray's last breath, waited for the inevitable moment he answered her questions. But the longer Donna waited, the more she worried she was making an enormous assumption based on her own wants. Perhaps Ray would not, in his final moments, confess.

The sugar from the chocolate started to vibrate through her. She needed to do something. Turning on the heel of her boredom, she walked the length of the porch, stopped at the entrance to the cabin. Lifted the latch on the screen door, drew a purposeful breath.

Donna visualized her cabinet—rows of files in folders tucked into drawers with locks, memories she would not open.

She nodded, made sure the locks were secure, then stepped inside the cabin.

Took in the topographic data layer:

One kitchen table.

Two chairs, one broken, missing a leg.

The old barrel wood-burning stove.

The counter and the sink with the hose for water that snaked out the window and around back to the black and blue barrels.

The piles of boxes stacked up against the log walls disintegrating into one another.

Stepping into the main room, keeping her hands tucked behind her back, Donna toed one of the boxes. A corner of rotting cardboard gave way, and without kneeling Donna could make out stacks of newspapers. She jounced another box open, saw cups and plates and mouse shit. Another box was full of what looked like women's shoes.

Donna shook her head, kept her imagination shuttered.

She stepped back, stomach stirring, retreated to the edge of the room by the kitchen table. She jostled another box under the table. The cardboard split down the side, the box spilled open.

Donna shuddered, swallowed the hot bile that catapulted into her throat. Couldn't stop herself. Her eyes locked on the box's contents—reams of oily, dirty chainsaw chains snaked into rust clumps.

Donna's memory cabinet tipped over, unlocked, and drawers clanged open and files flew like flocks of startled birds.

In an instant, she snapped back to her eighteen-year-old self, standing in front of the cabin, fists clenched, glaring at Ray. He held a chainsaw bar in his hand, chain dangling loosely. He was laughing.

Donna had gotten into the car that morning without telling anyone—Blazey, anyone—where she was going. Doctors later said what she did was unimaginable. Her therapist at the time labeled it "understandably misguided," the police said "impulsive," and Blazey had just said "fuck, fuck, fuck," and gripped Donna's good hand and rocked back and forth in the chair next to the hospital bed.

Her plan had been simple. She'd arrive, get Julene, leave.

She'd driven her little blue Ford Focus up east of the McKenzie Highway in a fogged blur, passed the cabin turnoff the first and second time, found it on the third try going five miles an hour. The trees had grown bigger and the vegetation was thicker, but then she was pulling into the familiar clearing. The cabin sat squatly in the middle, cedar shingles held together by moss and damp rot. And then she was getting out of the car, leaving the keys in the ignition. She took three steps and froze.

Ray had stepped out of the cabin to the edge of the porch.

For one long inhale, the two had stared at each other while birds chirped and trees cracked and clouds drifted. Then Ray descended the porch steps slowly, holding the bar chain he was cleaning, almost giggling in delight.

Until the laugher, she'd thought she'd be able to do exactly what she'd planned.

But then, Ray started laughing, deep stomach-shaking heaves. Donna went icy inside. She'd looked around at him, took in his greasy jeans and untucked hickory stripes. He looked unkempt, thin, and undernourished. Ray had never been able to cook, but he could eat. She widened her gaze, took in the porch bulging with saw blades, rusting guy lines, wire rope, severed peaveys, climbing spurs and choker hooks. The laundry line with no laundry dangling from it. The fenced, raised garden beds grown over by several seasons.

Donna realized then that she'd made a mistake.

Donna had just started her first year of college through a state program that allowed her to substitute her last year of high school for her first year of college. She'd decided to attend the university in Eugene where Blazey taught so she could get the exceptionally reduced tuition rate.

During Donna's second quarter, she'd enrolled in a course sequence focusing on spatial justice. The class centered on applying geospatial technologies. Hesitant at first, within days Donna was enthralled, learning to capture, analyze, and manage geographic information. She was hooked and electrified; she'd found something she was good at—bringing order to disparate cartographic data.

Soon she was crawling through various map-based services, files and extensions, data capture methods and map types and shape files, enormous sorts of information pulsing at her fingertips.

Things would have been fine if the course professor hadn't also emphasized the utilization of cartography to better identify environmental or situation factors in areas prone to gender violence. If the professor hadn't lectured each Wednesday on violence against women in the United States, how gender violence remained a top cause of death, how one in four women and one in seven men faced intimate relationship violence, how gender violence caused lasting physical, sexual, psychological, and economic harm. If the professor hadn't lectured relentlessly about how gender-based violence included an almost unlimited variation of physical and sexual and psychological attacks designed to violate the dignity of a person. If the professor hadn't required a final project for the class. If Donna hadn't selected to map the geography of domestic violence complaints and welfare checks in Lane County over the last ten years. If Donna hadn't sorted through all the publicly available police data. If Donna hadn't found a list of names.

Things would have been fine if she hadn't found her mother's name.

Julene Pencovitch.

A series of police welfare checks. When Donna looked to see who'd requested them, she'd whitened in anger and fury. And then she was at her social workers' office off Broadway in downtown Eugene refusing the coffee they kindly offered, questioning Maureen and Alai point blank, "What happened to my mother?"

And Maureen and Alai had looked at each other, two old women whose faces showed they'd seen more of life than most.

They'd spoken simultaneously.

"Did she contact you?" Alai had asked.

"We've been waiting to have this conversation with you," Maureen had said.

She'd just stared at them, mouth agape.

Alai had pulled an actual folder from an actual cabinet, opened it, and reviewed the file while Donna sat vibrating between disbelief and seething silence. Alai had looked at Donna several times, and when she'd assessed that Donna could control herself, she began to explain.

"Several years after Julene Pencovitch sent you to safety, we managed to finally get the police to start doing welfare checks on her."

"So what happened?" Donna had asked, tone serrated with calmness.

"Nothing, until a welfare visit paid by the police in August several years later reported that Julene no longer lived at that address. They discontinued welfare checks."

"What?" Donna had felt like the floor had fallen from under the chair she was sitting on. "What happened?"

Alai had closed the folder, crossed her legs. "I'm sorry, Donna, but we don't know. Our resources are extremely limited. There's over two hundred thousand women living in this county, and statistically a third of them have experienced some type of abuse. That's roughly sixty thousand women. Sixty thousand. How can we keep track of everyone? We do what we can and know it is never, ever, enough." Alai had almost spat her words out. "We rely on an informal whisper network. A few people said your mother was still living up there, others said that no one had seen Julene in years."

"The police only intervene in these cases if a victim reports a crime, or if there is a body," Maureen had added.

She'd shook her head at the two old social workers. "But people don't just disappear."

"Women disappear all the time, child."

Donna had no memory of leaving the office, of going home to her brightly painted room with two big windows overlooking Blazey's gardens, of feeding the cats and making dinner and leaving a plate in the fridge for Blazey because she taught late on Thursdays. She had no memory of trying to re-read her homework assignment, of typing up a report on different data, of emailing her professors. All she remembered really was lying in bed silent as a heron, castigating herself for never before having risked driving up the highway to the cabin to rescue her own mother. Why hadn't she?

Donna had decided in the early hours of that night that she'd drive herself up to the cabin and find Julene.

And then she was standing in front of the cabin porch and Ray was laughing and she'd realized that she hadn't planned carefully, hadn't considered all the data layers, hadn't done a proper risk assessment.

Ray had stopped laughing at some point, had paused at the bottom of the porch steps, scrutinized her.

Donna knew he could hear her heart pounding in her chest.

He'd hawked and spat and then said, "I thought you'd runned off. That's what she said, anyway."

"Where is she?"

"What's it to you?" he'd sneered.

"She's my mother."

The smirk on his face was vicious enough to force Donna back two steps, bumping her into her little car's driver side mirror. Heart pounding, Donna had lifted her chin, stood straight. Sought to wound him.

"She's not here, is she?" Cold ice had trickled down Donna's back. Triumph. "She left you, didn't she? Finally." She'd crooned the last words, sang them to him in spite.

But then his face collapsed in red-black veins and he was coming off the last steps of the porch, propelling towards her with the unstoppable force of a feller buncher.

Donna later couldn't recall if he carried the chain, but she remembered assessing if she should take a step forward, if she should swing at him first. Or, send a foot into his testicles. She understood in that moment that she had options. But there was another small part of her that also pointed out logically, calmly, that Julene had surely suffered while Donna had lived an easy life in Eugene. Did Donna owe atonement?

As those thoughts had churned, Donna had leaned back against the car, unsure. But, then, it didn't matter. He was on her and had her throat in his thick hand. The fist into her belly would have cleaved her in half if not for the force of his hand squeezing her neck. Two blows to her face, the first so hard Donna's cheekbone shattered, the second shooting molars out of her mouth in clumps of flesh and blood.

"Daughter, she never left," he had breathed into her ear, his body pressed tight upon hers. Donna saw only white. Bright spots that filmed her eyes from the first blow had fused into a single bright, white glaze. She stopped breathing, blood pounding so loud she couldn't hear anything but a single far off hum.

"I could snap you so easy," Ray had gloated. He'd pushed harder at her throat. White turned black, and Donna went blank and barely felt as his other hand pummeled her face, throat, breasts, then moved down her body punching her stomach and between her legs.

Ray had shoved his fists into Donna, holding her upright by the throat. The black lifted and Donna looked up. She made out the sky above the trees and the clearing and the cabin. She saw in the sky the bluest blue she'd ever seen, a blue that tasted of fresh cold water and revival, the blue of the room she'd sheltered in her first month in Eugene, the blue of the tile mosaic below a gurgling fountain at her school.

"Beg," he'd demanded. "Beg for your life."

"Mother," she'd whispered, barely able to shape the word.

Ray released her throat, hurled her to the ground next to the car's tire. The smell of sweet dirt, crushed moss, wet grass washed over her face, into Donna's broken nose, mingled with the burnt oil odor coming from the hot engine. Ray had kneeled into the dirt next to Donna's head, her one good eye just able to make out the rippled grain of loose canvas threads of his pants.

Nausea overwhelmed her and burned. Vomit flowed from her open mouth onto her face, throat, chest. Convulsions wracked her stomach, heaved her off the ground. Ray laughed.

"Can't take it like a man, can you, daughter?" He patted her head, gentle. "You're all alike."

Ray had wiped blood and dirt and vomit from her chin, smeared it into her hair. "You never stay clean, like God wanted."

Donna felt the heat from his body as he leaned in, nuzzled her exposed neck with his nose. "You smell like her," he'd whispered. Donna had tucked her knees up into her stomach, brought an arm up, wrapped it over her head. Heard thrumming from somewhere.

Ray's knees had creaked as he stood, and Donna had tucked deeper into herself. She tensed and tightened and gripped what breath she held tight in her chest.

Ray's feet stopped next to her head. All she could see were his boots, caked with mud. Left boot directly in front of her mouth.

"But you aren't her," Ray had said, words raining soft on her tucked shoulders. "She was clean. I protected her."

If Julene had left Ray, why hadn't she ever showed up at Blazey's door? Donna didn't understand why her mother had never come for her.

Donna's class at university had taught her how often women went missing, everywhere, and how rarely anyone really looked for them. The exception pivoted around specific variables: if the missing woman was white, urban, and well off. Women who registered within any other category sets were typically treated as expendable.

With her cheek resting in her own vomit and blood, Donna had closed her one good eye and visualized her drive up that morning beside the McKenzie River, visualized how the river had moved in and out of view along the highway, how the high mountain peaks and thick forests and scabbed lava flows had loomed overhead, how the endless landscape and ravaging weather had blanketed the entire region in blur.

Her mind had organized the data, had measured the possibilities as she lay in the dirt at the foot of her car, as her body had ached and screamed and broke and oozed and cried.

She'd learned in class that the variables of violence didn't center on how smart the attacker was. They could make as many mistakes as they wanted. Instead, what mattered was if Julene was deemed expendable, and if there were ways to hide what happened to her.

Ray was not smart, but he knew the landscape. The thick mountains, forests, rivers, lava tubs, glaciers, caves, landslides, everything she'd seen from the car.

"I protected her!" Ray shouted, an almost hysterical roar as he circled above Donna on the ground. "I protected her from taint like you! You'll never find her!"

The gentleness Ray had displayed earlier vanished. "Get out of here, filth, out of here!"

Donna had felt her kneecap snap, shoulder dislocate in blind searing agony, bowels loosen and empty into her pants in a mushy surge followed by a searing stream of urine. She had felt those things, but she did not feel them, really. Not yet. Instead, she had stepped away, outside of her body, tracked her wounds on a spreadsheet she'd pulled from somewhere, organized methodically the data layers of her wounds. Had taken comfort in ordering her injuries and memories.

Once, when she was eight or nine, she'd walked down the sweets aisle at the McKenzie River gas station and noticed how someone had come through and perturbed all the candy boxes. The Charleston Chews were mixed in with the Big Hunks and Heath Bars. Donna had waited for the attendant to help a customer and then quickly dropped to her knees. She brought order to the rows, neatly lining up each sweet in its proper box, making sure the Almond Joy dark chocolates did not mix with the Almond Joy milk chocolates. She was so involved in her task that she didn't hear the attendant until he came down the aisle clucking. Donna had risen guiltily, but the man smiled her fear away.

"Good job," he said, and to her delight he handed her a dollar.

"Can you tell your mother something for me?" he asked. "Just your mother?"

Donna nodded and the man had squatted closer, said quietly. "Tell her: friends are coming to help."

Later, walking back to the cabin, Donna had felt like she was on top of a cloud. Not because of the dollar, but because of the deep satisfaction she'd received from organizing, compartmentalizing, sorting out systems.

Donna laid on the ground beside her car and made a list:

Broken cheekbone, nose, thumb and three fingers, collarbone, kneecap.

Dislocated shoulder, wrist.

Three missing teeth.

Vision impairment.

Throat contusion in the shape of Ray's hand.

Pain throughout the body.

Bruising of face, throat, back, stomach, chest, arms, legs.

Donna had dispassionately reviewed the list, stepped outside of herself, knew what she looked like lying there on the ground. She appeared unconscious. Donna folded the paper list in her mind, shook her head, tucked it into a pocket. She would heal, she knew. She had before.

When Donna was little, she once watched Ray tease her mother, tickle her under the arms and chase her about the yard. This was after a long service, where Ray had read the Bible to Julene and Donna for several hours. He sat on the porch edge while they knelt on the grass. Julene's leg had fallen asleep. One second, she'd been beside Donna, the next she'd fallen over. Laying there, Donna had seen her frantic eyes look to Ray. But he'd just laughed, set the Bible down, stepped over, picked Julene up and rubbed life back into her leg. He'd tickled her.

Looking down at her own broken body beside the car, Donna had wished so hard that she could bring flames to her fingertips and smite down Ray. She'd whispered this promise to herself once, twice, and then once more before stepping back into her demolished body.

Donna went from black to white to unconscious to conscious. She registered a quiet, a cold quiet before the train of brutal pain arrived screaming. Time slipped and reversed and sped, and then she realized that her one good eye was still good. She cracked it open and saw the clearing around the cabin but could not see Ray. She lay still and time came and went. She tasted mud and blood and agony. And then he came into view, blurry feet moving on the porch and then not moving and then sitting. The familiar, intimate sigh of a beer can opening.

Donna had laid there until she couldn't, laid there until somewhere the sound of thrumming came through strong and purposeful. With one hand pressing into the ground—saturated with her vomit and blood and bits of glass—she pushed herself up onto her knees. She raged and screamed in silence as dizziness and pain and bolts of black, hot terror streaked through her. With her right hand she reached, touched the door handle near her head, pulled and pulled and then the door opened and she dragged herself into the driver's seat. When she looked through the windshield and saw the light had changed, she knew it must have taken over an hour to get from the ground into the car.

Time blurred again, and when she next came to consciousness, she was vomiting on herself, mostly hot mucus and blood. She wiped her face with a hand brought up to her mouth like an anvil. She looked around again when her good eye cleared. She saw Ray through the shattered windscreen of the car, registered then that all the car windows were broken. Didn't turn her head, though, just looked through the webbed glass at Ray sitting in a chair on the porch. He'd leaned back, was drinking a beer, watching her.

Donna had stared at him, and he'd held her gaze, fixed, a look on his face that Donna couldn't decipher with her blurry vision. He sat in the straight-backed wooden chair, the one she remembered him making when she was small. There was once a whole set of chairs he'd chiseled and carved through late afternoons while she'd made games out of the shavings and her mother had limped about the laundry.

Somehow, Donna flipped the car ignition on, had reversed back slowly.

She watched him take another sip of beer, and it had come to her then as the car rolled backward. She understood why he was sitting alone on the porch. She understood that there was only one answer to what had happened to Julene. And that she would make him say it.

13

THE SCIENTIST

"Y
ou're awake," Tove leaned on the open cabin door, fully backlit in the afternoon light.

Ros bobbed her head, melted deeper into the rocking chair. "I slept."

"You needed it. Yesterday was rough." Tove set her pack in the doorway, walked into the kitchen. "I'll make coffee? You want one?"

Ros nodded her head yes, stared blurrily at Tove. The woman looked like a hallucinating rainbow. She was wearing leggings again. These were a vivid yellow-green, reminiscent of carnotite. For a top Tove wore a tight purple silk shirt with pearl snaps buttoned neck to waist that strained over her chest. She'd wrapped a silver and red checked bandana around her topknot. A sheen of sweat glistened at her temples.

"Warm out there?" Ros asked, choosing to avoid the obvious scientist-in-the-field-outfit questions.

"It's hot. And humid. I think all the rain the last few days made for a sticky recipe."

Tove poured coffee beans into the old-fashioned hand grinder and sounds of cranking and crunching soon filled the small space. Ros looked out the open door. She'd gone straight to bed after the chief and his goons had left the day before and hadn't gotten up until now; it was late afternoon.

"I was nervous about leaving you, but wanted to get a recording of the lava in this humidity."

Ros closed her eyes, loosened her jaw, stretched. "You're fine. I'm glad you went." Tove didn't owe her anything. Ros knew it was really she who owed her. For being Tove. For coming and standing between her and that officer. Holding her hand. Letting her sleep safely. Feeding her. Ros sighed, reexamined the mystery of the woman standing in her kitchen.

Tove poured the grounds into the filter, lifted the kettle, concentrated. Ros tried not to linger on her legs, thighs, and rounded bottom. She crossed her own legs, compressed.

"I feel like I owe you an explanation." Ros watched Tove's forearm flex as she poured hot water over the grounds. The woman had muscle.

Tove sniffed. "Uh-uh. You don't owe me anything." She glanced at Ros steadily, then looked back at the coffee. "You're clearly a strong person who has been through a lot. I know we don't know each other that well, but, well, I'm here, and I'd like to help in any way I can. I like you."

Ros exhaled audibly out her nose. Was Tove shutting down the conversation? Ros eyed her, tried to measure what she knew about the woman versus how she was interpreting her words.

She decided to barrel on. It had been almost liberating, exhilarating, to talk with Ash. And yes, there might be consequences with Tove, but she'd face those if they came up. A pang unexpectedly surged through her as she imagined Tove packing her bags, hiking away.

She started light. "It's been donkey's years since I've talked about my past, yet somehow, in the last five days, it seems it's all I've talked about."

Tove bobbed her chin, then slid gracefully into a chair across the table from Ros, handed her a cup of coffee. "You want cream?"

Ros shook her head, took in Tove over the rim of the mug. Green eye shadow today.

Tove flicked a small smile, sent the creases at her mouth scattering like sunbeams. "I think, if anything, you might want to report that officer. He was a cranked-up douchebag."

Ros smiled. "He hated you."

Tove snorted, golden eyes crinkling. "He hated you too. What's that old gem? When in pain, women hurt themselves, men hurt others? Classic case."

"Fuck them," Ros breathed, looked out the door where the men had stood. Could see their watery outlines where they'd glared and leered and performed power. Stomach acid gurgled all the way up into Ros's throat. Forget them, she told herself.

She turned back to Tove. The woman's topknot was literally waving at her. She felt a tightness deep inside her thaw, the release of something she couldn't pin down. The sensation simultaneously aroused and terrified her. She tried to look away, but was held fast by Tove's mouth. Plum lipstick.

"I don't owe you, you're right," she stammered. "But I'd like to tell you."

Tove leaned back, relaxed her eyes, stretched her shoulders like a cat. Cupped her coffee. "Then I'd like to listen."

Ros took a deep breath, paused, and then systematically, as if she was reporting to her research funder, told Tove everything. She unspooled the entire sequence chronologically, described Flower and Herring, being locked in the car, everything that happened before and after—foster care and police department waiting rooms. She didn't censor herself, didn't stop. Just let every detail see the light of day. It was a dam bursting, words and truth flowed from her mouth out onto the table. Tove picked up certain threads and held her words and listened and inhaled and her hair bounced and hours ticked by and the radio hummed and then Ros realized her mouth tasted of baking powder and she was hoarse and she was done. First time she'd ever told anyone all of it, in one sitting, one truth. She felt light and a little woozy.

Tove's face was inscrutable.

Ros felt a panic rise in herself as silence settled around the table, wondered if she'd miscalculated. She stood abruptly, went to the sink, poured herself water, wiped a wet hand over her face. Brushed her curls back. Knew she was sweating like a beached ice floe. Closed her eyes, took a breath, then turned, faced Tove.

The woman was waiting for her.

"Thank you," she said softly, locking her eyes to Ros's. "Thank you for trusting me with your story."

Ros dipped her head, acknowledged Tove, but then looked away. She didn't know where to park her eyes. Cold liquid relief channelized in her veins, flowed exuberantly over her bones and arteries and organs like the glacier streams she'd seen in British Columbia. Those were the ones that in high summer busted up, out of the ice toward the sky in pure glacier magic. Her hands shook. She hadn't miscalculated. She looked out the open door, saw the afternoon light dimming. "Want a drink?"

"Oh yes!" Tove's eyes lit up. "This was a coffee conversation, but it needs real drinks to conclude."

Ros pulled two IPAs from the cool box. "They're pretty warm."

Tove took the bottle Ros handed her, their fingers lightly touching. "Bottoms up."

Sitting back down, Ros stared at her nail beds, noted the half-moons of dirt under her fingernails. Lunate fracture. Again. She wasn't sure what to say next, chose to wait.

Tove swallowed. "Can I ask you a question?"

Ash had asked the same thing. Ros picked up her bottle, then set it back down on the table. "Okay."

"Do you think the police have found them now?" Tove asked, direct, arms crossing tentatively over her chest.

Ros turned the question over in her mind. She understood that she had no evidence, that there was nothing she could do until she heard more, if she ever heard more. Knew the situation had the potential to make her crazy, or angry, or inconsolable. She didn't want to be any of those things. She wanted to focus instead on what was in front of her, like Tove and the pulse of her own heartbeat drumming through her thighs. "I don't know. But I'm not sure how much it matters."

Tove tilted her head.

Ros backpedaled slightly. "What I know is that the police have found tragedy up on that glacier, Tove. Whether it's my tragedy or another family's, I don't know. But it's real fucking horrible."

"Almost unbelievable."

Tove's words landed, and Ros squared herself up, defensive. "Unbelievable that someone has been preying on women?"

Tove hissed a breath in. "No, I meant unbelievable practically, not pejoratively. I know the world we live in."

Ros considered for a moment, rubbed her nails into her palms. "Sorry. Sometimes people ask if I'm ever afraid of being by myself up here. They never seem to realize that it's scarier down there."

The two drank in silence for a moment, and Ros heard the generator hum on, the faint pop and hiss of the radio. The creak of the roof. It felt safe, just the two of them.

"The police never found anything of my family—not a trace," Ros eventually said. "No clothing or purse or jewelry or anything. I used to obsess over what might have happened to them. Early on. The quest for answers, for anything."

"Naturally."

"But, it's been so long." Ros looked out the open door. "I've changed, and that took a lot of work. I'm quite aware that I…" she gestured around the cabin. "I did all this in spite of, not because of, what happened to them. Does that make sense?"

Tove glinted her eyes at Ros.

"So, I'm prepared for, and would genuinely like to know, the truth. But the truth isn't going to change all this, all that I am. The myths we tell ourselves can be more damaging than any truth."

"I hear that," Tove said. "What we tell ourselves, and the language we use, can be so much more… disabling."

Ros nodded, held Tove's eyes. "Yes, exactly. Truth doesn't give closure. Things never actually close. Or end."

"Our stories never finish, they transform each day. Hallmark, but true." Tove leaned back in her chair, looked contemplatively at Ros. Took a breath. Paused just long enough to shrug before saying, "Cheers to that."

"Cheers," Ros said, and took a drink, glad the mood had lightened.

She couldn't do any more darkness. She scrambled her thoughts, tried to move in a new direction. How did one follow a soul-baring? Ask about the weather? Ros ran her hands over the top of her head. "I should get a haircut."

"I like your hair," Tove replied instantly.

Ros ducked her head, ran fingers through the tight curls. Felt oddly shy. "Thanks. I always wanted it long, straight."

"Curls suit you. You look like a cumulus fractus."

Ros snorted, resisted rolling her eyes. "From you? Mares tails," she teased.

Tove smiled wide, bared her teeth, whinnied. An ache tugged low in Ros's stomach and she almost winced. Tried to push it away, was afraid if she acted on it, she'd ruin things. Realized she was staring, again, but then spotted something. Reached across the table slow, under the influence of a gravity she couldn't explain, lifted a small chunk of lichen from Tove's topknot.

"Epiphyte," she identified quietly.

They both looked at the gray, twisted foliage.

"Could be an endophyte."

"Do you think it was living on you or in you?" Ros asked, serious, smile locked down.

Tove considered. She looked to Ros as if she were giving the question the same weight she would her doctoral defense. But then smiled. "Well," she drawled, "I think any plant would seriously wish it could live in my pants."

They both laughed, sipped, laughed more, but the flush that overtook Ros didn't disappear as their laugher trailed off.

She stared at her beer, traced the rim with her middle finger. Recognized how different this was from all the other fellows who came to the station. "I'm glad you stayed," she whispered.

"I'm glad too," Tove said, her tone quieter than Ros had ever heard before. "Really glad."

"I'm sorry to dump all my life on you. But I think I needed to explain. To someone. All this."

Tove held up the bottle, gazed at the label, then drew it to her lips. Drank, throat heaving. Maintained eye contact with Ros as she swallowed, drew her tongue over her lips, set the beer back down on the table.

Silence grew intensely between them. Ros caught herself holding her breath, ignoring the stirring in her belly.

Tove didn't keep her waiting long. "First, Ros, you're, like, one of the most levelheaded people I've ever met, and I say that knowing I'm meeting you during some incredibly difficult circumstances. You give me hope—you've been through a life of loss but you're still moving forward, still hoping. That's amazing."

She flushed at Tove's compliment, then almost laughed.

"And second, you're not dumping. We all carry shit."

Ros let Tove's words sink in, then released the laugh she'd been holding. "Oddly, another woman sat there in that exact chair several nights ago and told me that same sentence. About carrying shit."

"Get a lot of women through here?" Tove tilted her head, eyes sparking.

Ros knew she was blushing again, shook her head. "No, no, not at all. Anyway. Her name was Ash—she and her partner were hiking the Oregon PCT—and the point is, she said the same thing you just said."

"And did you tell her about yourself?"

"Some," Ros responded. "First time in a long time. It felt strange, but liberating."

"Women have to tell each other their stories, Ros. It's how we rise together."

Ros agreed. She thought about Ash's strange face, wondered where she'd ended up after she hiked away. She ran her mind along the currents of their conversations, and then, like a lamppost clicking on, she remembered. She looked up, met Tove's eyes. "You know what else Ash said? The night they got here?"

Tove raised an eyebrow, sipped her beer.

"It slipped my mind with everything that's happened, but when they got here, it had been raining, and they came in to dry off. Ash asked me if I'd ever heard anything strange out here. Apparently, she'd been hiking the last two days or something and kept hearing... laughter."

Tove sat straight up, eyes wide. "Really?" she asked, then tilted her chair back, reached for the laptop by the desk. "Fascinating," she said. "Absolutely fascinating."

"I can't believe I forgot about it, especially since I heard it up on Black Crater," Ros felt foolish. Took a sip of her beer. But Tove wasn't paying attention. She had pulled her laptop onto the main table, cracked it, and blue light spilled out all over her face. Ros watched, hypnotized. It was like Tove had turned into petrified aquamarine.

"You know, there's something I found that I wanted to talk to you about." Tove's voice was pitched two octaves higher. "I've been meaning to, but, well, other things seemed more…"

Ros raised her eyebrows. "What did you find?" she pushed, slightly brusque.

"Just go with me for a second, okay?" Tove looked down at her screen, scanned her notes. "Have you ever heard of the Canadian scientist Julie Cruikshank? She's a real badass. I first came across her work as required reading for budding ecologists." Tove looked at Ros, a coy smile on her lips. "That was me. You know. Budding."

Ros had no idea what to say, tried not to see the deliberate glint in Tove's eyes. She nodded stiffly for her to continue.

Tove barely waited for the encouragement. She barreled forth. "What's relevant is her fieldwork on glaciers. She documented all these stories of glaciers as alive *and* capable of imbuing a livingness within the landscapes they exist inside of. She wrote about how some stories describe glaciers as knowable, as communicable, as singers of a landscape."

"This is all going to circle back?" Ros asked, perplexed.

"Hold your horses," Tove said, playful. "Listen. When I heard that laughter on the audio recording, it reminded me of Cruikshank's work. So, while you were snoozing last night, I jumped onto your incredibly painful Wi-Fi…" Tove rolled her eyes at Ros. "It's so, so slow!"

"Of course it is. You're at a *remote* field station."

Tove lifted her shoulders, brushed off Ros's comment. "Anyway. *Slowly*, I did a pilot sort through various databases. I found a lot of stories about, or adjacent to, glaciers. Attribution is hard for many of the stories—some are indigenous, some from early white settlers, and others I can't source their provenance. But with even a cursory glance, an interesting theme kept coming up."

"Like what?" Ros asked, gut sparking. She ordered herself to focus. On the data. On what Tove was saying. Not on Tove's mouth.

"Well, there are multiple versions of a story about how, before white colonization of coastal North America, a young woman called out carelessly to a glacier, speaking words that angered the ice and caused it to advance and demolish the woman's community. Or, in another version, the girl's grandmother sees the anger of the glacier and trades her life for her granddaughter's, taking responsibility for the girl's careless words. Other versions, the girl accepts her fate, apologizes to the ice and is consumed as the glacier flows over her."

Tove looked down at her computer screen again. "Sometimes the stories say the girl becomes the glacier, lives forever as ice. And that if people sing to the glacier, the ice sings back."

Ros leaned back in her chair. Waited.

Tove compressed her lips into a thin line as she scanned her screen. "There were a few stories from around the Oregon Trail era, where people were warned about staying overnight near glaciers. Some versions of those stories described how peculiar sounds were heard from them, and, as a footnote, how women and children sometimes followed those sounds and disappeared into the ice."

"One account, written by..." Tove leaned back, rolled her eyes up in her head as she remembered, "... god, what was that name? It was memorable. Yes!" She popped forward, eyes like saucers. "A Mr. Amos Alvin Alvord, written around 1850—and I'm unclear if he was transcribing someone else's story or his own experience—he wrote about how a glacier lured people by singing and humming, and then devoured their flesh."

Ros resisted with all her might, but the image of warm flesh swam before her eyes. Tove's flesh. The interior of Tove's wrist had a small patch of darker pigmentation that looked like drumlin, oval-shaped on the upper arm and tapering to a small point near where her wrist met her palm. Ros longed, in that moment, to explore Tove's wrist, to place her lips on her skin and inhale.

Tove took a pull from her beer. "Not, of course, the first time song has been used as a weapon—too many U.S. military examples to pull from. But, perhaps, the first time a glacier has been documented weaponizing its song."

Pretending she had something caught in her eye, Ros rubbed vigorously, gouged her fingernails into her skin to distract herself from Tove's wrist.

She peeked from under her eyelashes and was relieved to see that Tove appeared oblivious to the effect she was having on her. Ros ran her tongue along the corner of her mouth, leaned back, watched Tove.

"Another story I saw, and have no idea where it comes from, tells how a young girl loved her own blue eyes. One day that girl became a woman, and then, because all the village men started to follow her, she had to walk around with closed eyes. Well, that made her one day bump into the glacier, which pissed off the ice and it flowed over the girl and killed her. The men saved themselves by starting a huge fire. But that night, as they sat around their fire talking about the girl with the blue eyes, the glacier crept up and heard, realized she'd killed a girl fleeing a bunch of would-be rapists. She got so angry she flowed over the men and their fire and ground them to dust."

Ros shivered, shifted uncomfortably. "Jesus, that story is horrible on so many levels. You can't be a woman anywhere."

"Iceland?" Tove said hopefully, looking over her nose at Ros. "My people on my mother's side are Icelandic a few generations back. By all accounts, Iceland is a pretty good place to live lately if you're a lady."

"Live lately lady! That's a lot of 'L's."

"I have a strong tongue," Tove retorted, her face saucy. "I'd enjoy showing you."

Ros felt her face flame from throat to hairline. She looked anywhere in the cabin but at Tove who was sitting directly across from her grinning like a cat wearing plum lipstick. Ros tried to clear her mind, concentrate on Tove's words. "I'm not sure I understand..." she flushed, "these stories, Tove, how they tell us anything here."

"I'm not sure I do either," Tove continued, eyes glowing. "Some of these are oral stories that were transcribed, so they're not in their original format, language, or cultural context. It's like trying to put together a puzzle with barely any of the pieces, and no clue what the puzzle will look like in the end. Especially if these stories originate with any indigenous tribes. As a researcher, I can't just dive in and understand—I'm not equipped with context."

Ros watched Tove lean forward, her skin washed a faint blue glow from the computer screen.

"Are you a glacier spirit?" Ros asked lightly.

Tove paused, her face confused, but then caught sight of her arms in the blue light. She smiled wolfishly. "Not quite blue enough," she joked. "Actually, on my dad's side I'm a thousand generations Scandinavian, likely inbred, likely going all the way back to Erik the Red, Erik the Bloodaxe, Erik the I-Like-to-Rape-and-Pillage. You?"

Ros shrugged. "Not sure? Perhaps Coquille, Klamath, Siletz? I don't honestly know if I have people, or if it's just me. If my mother magically showed up, it's prolly one of the first things I'd ask."

Tove clicked her tongue sympathetically.

Ros crossed her legs, shuffled uncomfortably. "I read Thoreau as an undergraduate when I was starting my science studies, and it stuck, that old *Walden* gem: 'Why should I feel lonely? is not our planet in the Milky Way?'"

Tove pressed her plum lips together. "What did you take from that?"

Ros heaved her shoulders. "What everyone takes from that. That we're enough alone, that it doesn't matter if I don't have family, that I could spend a lifetime examining our world."

Tove set both of her hands on the table. "Bullshit," she said, flat. "Thoreau is either wrong or being misread. We are not enough alone, and while, hell yes, I love science, it's not what I snuggle with at night. Honestly, the idea of being alone for too long is suffocating, sounds like a tier of hell to me."

"I think, of late, I might agree more and more with you," Ros murmured.

"I hate it when the reality of ourselves collides with the idea of ourselves," Tove said snippily, grinning to take the barb out of the words. "Barf. Growing. I hate it."

Ros laughed, felt her skin tingle and her shoulders ease.

"I don't hate the snuggling part of growing, though."

Ros did not even mail a single look at Tove, did not acknowledge the comment. Rather, she stared with every bit of self-control she possessed at the table and waited for the moment to pass while she sat in a growing pool of her own sweat. She could feel the remnants of her former self wilting on the floor. She was flushed from head to toe.

Tove cleared her throat, looked back down at her computer screen. "Circling back bro-speak style, I think it's okay to not understand these glacier stories. Many of them are missing elements, are broken, are unfinished, or are translated imperfectly. And, critically, you and I are not a part of the societies that created the stories, so I don't think we're equipped with the context to fully interpret them."

Ros let Tove's words wash over her, tilted her head thoughtfully. Made the connection, leapt at it. "To be a bat," she murmured.

"Exactly!" Tove replied, tapping her forefinger on the tabletop. "Yes and double yes! Of course you'd know that. Nerd meets nerd."

Ros grinned at Tove's enthusiasm, replied, "I remember reading Thomas Nagel early on and feeling like my head was going to explode."

"I'm mangling his words, I'm sure, but…" Tove closed her eyes, "'I want to know what it is like for a bat to be a bat. Yet if I try to imagine this, I am restricted to the resources of my own mind.'"

"We can never really step into being a bat, being a glacier," Ros said. "Just step into ourselves."

"And yourself is a wonderful self," Tove said merrily. Face open.

Ros choked a little, foamed beer into her throat.

Tove moved on. "Now, I'm not saying, let's perfectly understand these stories and then understand what's happening out here with all these glaciers." She reverted to her more academic tones, tucked a strand of hair behind her ear, held Ros's eyes eagerly. "I don't think we could if we tried. What I'm saying is that we should pay attention to the themes that keep showing up."

Voice rising like a squeaky door, Tove kept talking, describing the different texts she'd read, but Ros had stopped paying attention. Instead, she concentrated on keeping her legs tightly crossed, willing the sweat gathering under her arms to vanish. Her groin ached, throbbed, and her throat was dry and caught when she swallowed. She was aware of every hair standing straight out on her body as she also sensed the waves of heat and femininity emanating from Tove. She was captivated by Tove's mouth, those thick lips turning and twisting as words tumbled out.

"Hello, Ros! You in there?" Tove snapped her fingers in front of Ros's face.

Ros jerked her head. Blushed again. "Sorry," she said. "I drifted off there."

"I should be offended." Tove smirked. "Where'd you go?"

Ros glanced out the open door, looked back at Tove, tried to dodge the question and the patch of skin on the woman's wrist. She'd never been more attracted to, physically lusted for, something like that damned wrist. She longed for it. "What were you saying?"

Tove cracked her knuckles, stretched. "Ros, we have these stories, all with different details, but they all describe basically one thing." She swallowed, then looked straight at Ros. "Too long, didn't read: glaciers are making sounds."

Ros steepled her hands, stared at Tove. "Go on."

Tove's hands flew in the air as she talked. "To my knowledge, no one has assessed the acoustics of ice. There is clearly something out here emitting sounds, perhaps low-frequency, and maybe some people can hear it—perhaps people in close proximity or who have sensory sensitivity?"

Ros leaned, set her elbows on the table. Tove was talking a mile a minute.

"And while the idea of glaciers emitting sounds is fascinating," Tove said, "there's more. Nothing really exists in a vacuum, right?"

Ros drew in a tight breath, guessed where Tove was going.

"Doesn't the glacier surging over those would-be rapists' fire and burning her flank sound a little like the Collier Glacier and that volcano popping up and burning her terminus?"

"Tove," Ros held her hands up. Her brain whirled like a blender. She wished she was firing on all her scientific cylinders and not so distracted. "Okay, okay. But bigger picture, just to be clear, are you saying that Amelia Kane heard a glacier singing and disappeared?"

"I don't know," Tove said, reddening slightly. "I also don't know if I *have to know*. Some of the data I'm referencing includes indigenous stories, and I know I don't possess the ontological perspective to fully *know*. But what I can say is that, as a western scientist, there appears to be an unexplained emitter of sound out here—and I know this not only because of stories, but also from the recordings I've made." Tove threw her hands in the air. "And I don't know if that emitter of sounds in any way intersects with Amelia Kane, or anything. But I think any good scientist considers all the possibilities…"

"The variables." The hairs on Ros's arm raised.

"Yes, especially in cases where disparate datasets overlap. Indigenous stories. Settler colonial stories. Local anecdotes. Audio recordings." Tove leaned forward. "Should we report this?"

Ros snickered almost instantly in response, then brought her hand up to her mouth, tried to tamp down a snort she knew was fighting to break free. "To who? That police officer?"

It was pleasurable to see Tove blush for once.

"No way. That guy needs to meet the working end of a crowbar."

"So, Mr. Fire Chief?" Ros narrowed her eyes. "Imagine if I said to him, 'I think the glacier is luring people and singing to them?' Oh yes. That will go far. I'm positive he'll believe me. Just about as likely as white people giving back Tomanowos to the Chinook."

Tove sipped from her beer, fingers lightly resting around the bottle's neck. "Women are hard to believe. If only you had an advanced graduate degree behind you to somewhat authenticate your scientific assessments. Oh, wait."

Ros stretched her hand across the table, held the neck of her beer out to Tove. "Dr. Andersen."

Tove clinked her beer bottle against Ros's. "Dr. Fisher."

They drained their bottles. Ros set her glass bottle on the edge of the table while simultaneously rising, then moved into the kitchen, squatted by the cold box. "Another?"

"Of course."

"Of interest, glacier ice does make this fascinating sizzling sound when you put a chunk of it in your whiskey. It's the sound of trapped air bubbles releasing as the ice melts. The scientific term is Ice Sizzle."

Tove chuckled, a sound that filled the entire cabin. "Sizzle," she echoed. "Glorious."

Ros's pulse pounded, and she shifted, searched around aimlessly in the shelves under the counter.

Tove's chair creaked, and her voice traveled quietly to Ros. "Well, if anything, it'd be an interesting paper we could write. Do an academic paper, pitch an accompanying general science piece?"

"I'd die reading the comments during peer review."

They both laughed. "Reviewer number three! 'What merit is there to researching the sound quality of a glacier? Surely these women can find something better to do with their time. May I suggest knitting?'"

Ros's chest tightened, and she imagined how much longer Tove would have to stay if they decided to do research together. Tove's voice wove around Ros as she remained hidden, kneeling on the floor in the kitchen. "I like the story of how a beautiful woman with blue-blue eyes was revenged by ice."

Ros located two IPAs from the box, glanced at the labels. Deschutes. Took a breath, then rocked back up on her heels, stood. Blood rushed to her feet, and she felt dizzy. Gripped the counter, glanced at the open door. Everything was okay.

She held the two beers up to Tove, who bobbed her head in agreement.

"You know, women and glaciers, we have a lot in common," Tove observed jocularly. "Everyone always talks about how glaciers are threatened. That they're vulnerable and weak. And now they need protection, right? Fuck that. Who hurt them in the first place?"

Ros sidled back to the table, handed Tove the beer. "Is it that simple?" she asked mildly.

"Thanks," Tove said, lifting the bottle into the air. "We know who created the problem, and now they want to own the solution. Bullshit."

"Huh," Ros murmured, walked back to her side of the table.

"It's the same, in a way, for us," Tove continued. "I applaud any block of ice that fights back."

Ros slid into the wooden chair at the table, felt it creak under her weight. Popped the cap off her beer. Glanced out the window.

Tove would be leaving in a few days, and then she would be up at the station, by herself again, a block of ice with no mountains to grind. She pushed back against the sudden melancholia, focused on Tove's face. Lingered on the green eye shadow.

"What?" Tove said, twisting her own bottle. "You're quiet."

Ros shrugged a shoulder.

"If we don't fight, we die," Tove escalated.

Ros tried to match her tone. "You know, even after Termination, the Siletz refused to disappear."

"Termination?"

"In the 50's. Congress passed the Western Oregon Termination Act, which essentially was a fucked-up way of ending the federal government's responsibility to tribes. Reservations, tribes were dissolved. But the Siletz fought back, stayed organized, kept alive." Ros licked her lips. "I like that the Siletz fought for themselves—but I know that they did it together, as a tribe. Some days, when it's just me out here, I don't know how much fighting I can do." She shook her head, chased away her thoughts, "It's too much, constantly being besieged on all fronts."

Tove took a noisy pull of beer, dropped her shoulders, then stood abruptly from her chair. Walked around the table. Stopped in front of Ros. Tove's feet were inches from Ros's bare toes.

Ros looked up, scrutinized her gold eyes. Watched as Tove reached, gently cupped her chin.

"Don't say that," the woman whispered. "You're a fighter. You've fought your whole life against big things, little things, the right to be in science, to be a woman, to exist hopefully in the face of ever-mounting loss. Even if you didn't know it, you were fighting. You wouldn't have survived here if you weren't."

The muscles in Ros's body froze, her skin felt thin enough to rupture and release her entire insides.

"If you don't fight, all this…" Tove gestured around them, "it'll bring you to your knees."

Ros felt fused to the wooden chair. Her feet stuck flat to the floor. Her eyes anchored to Tove's. She traced the interior of her own mouth with her tongue. Asked quietly, "What do you fight for?"

Tove raised her right eyebrow, nodded slightly, released Ros's chin. She turned, pushed Ros's beer away, then glided her bottom onto the table. Tove's knees hinged on the table edge, feet dangled lightly beside Ros's legs.

Ros watched, unmoving, as Tove reached and picked up her hand. Tove placed it gently on bright green thigh. Ros stretched her fingers and palm out slow, felt the warmth of Tove's leg. Lost her ability to breathe.

She heard Tove take an audible gasp. She looked up, then watched soundlessly as Tove took her hand again and pulled it away from her thigh, held it, then pressed it tight against Tove's left breast.

"I fight for me," Tove whispered, both eyes locked to Ros. "My future."

It took her a full blink to understand, to overlay the padding she felt with the breast she'd assumed. Her jaw loosened and she gawked at Tove.

"I had no idea," she whispered when her voice worked, hand sinking deep. "I think I've been entranced by your lipstick."

Tove warbled in her throat, a pleased smile flashing at the corner of her mouth. "I've learned a lot from Frida Kahlo," she murmured.

Ros blinked. Total unconformity of the landscape.

She'd been looking at the whole rock and hadn't taken into account layers, angles, division. What kind of observant scientist was she? She swallowed.

Tove was watching her, and when Ros met her eyes, Tove bowed her head forward and she, shaking, reached her free hand up and tugged at the knot, and then, all that hair was free, an unstoppable debris flow plummeting over Tove's shoulders.

The movement left Ros watery inside, and she gaped, felt transfixed, as evening light came in through the cabin's dusty windows and danced off Tove's loose hair. It looked like a curtain of satin, liquified obsidian. It took her minutes, hours, to re-focus, to remember, to come back to the real Tove sitting beside her on the table.

She raised her eyebrows, looked at Tove, hoped the woman read the question on her lips.

"CHEK2 mutation," Tove answered.

"When?"

Clearing her throat, Tove lifted her hand away from her breast, set it back on the table. Ros felt emptiness under her fingers, a flash of loneliness.

Tove brought both of her own hands to her neck, to her buttoned collar. "Two years ago." She tugged lightly, and the first pearl snap on the purple silk gave way. "When I was twenty-seven. Felt the first lumps when I was twenty-five, was told both tits had to go after the first round of chemo didn't work."

Tove pulled harder. Four more buttons gave way.

Ros sat motionless but could hear joyous, ecstatic singing emanating from her own core, could see the literal terror and desire she felt twisting together just out of the corner of her eye, could taste adrenaline and ice mixing in her mouth. She glimpsed the center white frame of Tove's bra like the flash of a geode.

Tove unbuttoned two more.

Ros couldn't look away, not from the golden eyes flashing, nor the long dark hair flowing, nor the purple shirt slowly splitting apart like two tectonic plates. Unbidden, Amelia Kane jumped into her thoughts, how the search for the missing became more about those looking than those lost. How, seemingly inevitably, women disappeared from their own stories.

Ros swallowed the chalk growing in her throat. She ached for more. She wanted to live.

"I don't want to disappear," she murmured to Tove, so soft she barely moved her lips.

"I see you," Tove whispered back, chin tucked down on her neck like a sleeping seabird. "You are not going to disappear."

Ros trembled as she breathed in her intense fear. She prayed the little girl was safe, prayed she'd get answers in the days to come about her own mother, her sister. But then, Ros pushed the whole crowd of ghosts away, out of her mind, far back with all the fear and uncertainty and other things that didn't belong in this moment, this breath between her and Tove. This living.

The shirt came completely unbuttoned and Tove slid her arms

free, dropped the silky fabric on the table. Her white bra had wide straps that glistened satin over her pale skin.

Tove reached for Ros's hand, but then pulled back, dropped her fingers twisting into her lap. Her chest rose and fell shakily. Ros saw for the first time a linear crack, inches to miles deep, in Tove's confidence. Compassion threaded with joy threatened to overwhelm Ros, and she felt hot tears boil in the corner of her eyes.

"Sorry," Tove said. "This is new for me."

Ros gurgled a shaky laugh, heart pounding, sweat blanketing her skin. Heat surged through her legs, stomach, chest. "Me too," she said. "May I?"

Tove nodded, pulled a deep breath.

Ros reached her fingers up between the fabric cups, unclipped the tiny plastic front closure, opened the sides, slid the straps back over Tove's shoulders. Let the thickly padded bra fall to the table.

"You okay?" she asked, almost choking on the mire of emotions surging up her throat. Here was now and this was happening and she could not have ever predicted this or dreamed this or hoped this, but she did not want to stop herself and she was damp and sweating and singing.

"I haven't shown anyone before."

Ros paused long enough to take in Tove shirtless on the table, still and backlit and unbelievable.

Currents of hot pulse-surged through Ros's entire body, hairline to toes, and she took a deep breath—one, two—and then she reached and ran her fingers like a khaki-clad explorer down Tove's shoulder to her bony clavicle, then down further, over the scar tissue half mooning from left sternum to armpit. The Earth's crust crumpled, the mantle imploded, and entire continents were displaced as the ice within Ros retreated completely and she was throbbing like lava. Her fingers shook as she ran them back along Tove's skin to the right side, tracing the line like a Braille map, tracking the small hummocks of scar welts telling stories that she wished with all her will that she'd one day learn the proper context to fully interpret.

Tove trembled, shook, as Ros's fingertips danced along her chest. Tove reached, then pressed Ros's fingers with her own hands, trapping them against her chest. "We've all lost things. But we've all also found things."

Ros could feel Tove's heartbeat pulsing through the scar's rumble strips.

"Look at me."

She looked up, met Tove's eyes.

"I see you. You see me."

Ros saw Tove's hard look, her eyes radiating an intensity that simultaneously terrified and exhilarated her. She paused, felt the flutters in her throat burn hot.

Then Tove grinned like a mad woman. "Sizzle," she breathed.

"Yes," Ros said, reached for the woman wearing plum lipstick on the table in front of her.

14
THE
DAUGHTER

Donna parked the car in her usual spot, stared at the dark cabin before her. She'd gone round to the gas station, had picked up bread and canned beans and other essentials—a newspaper and chocolate and a frozen coffee.

"It's not working," Donna said aloud, drumming her fingers on the steering wheel, looking about the cabin's clearing. Where she used to take baths as a child. Where she used to stoop and help her mother launder motel sheets. Where she'd kneeled and organized rocks and pebbles and twigs. Where Julene had grown winter greens. Where Ray had beaten her broken.

"I'm deluding myself," she said, talking to no one but herself and the humming trees looking expectantly at her.

She shook her head, reached for the newspaper, chocolate, and coffee. Tried not to think about having to extend her leave of absence from work a third time. The center needed her back, she knew. But Ray persevered.

Strategize, Donna heard Blazey say in her head. *Risk assessment,* Donna's therapists said.

Donna opened the car door and stood, clutching her purchases to her chest. Tried not to spill the open cold brew coffee. Slammed the door closed with a bump of her hip.

The thump of the door banging shut snagged her.

She stopped, waited.

Almost.

There.

The drawers in her cabinet jostled, the folders out of order slid into place, and then out of all the mixed-up data, Donna was finally able to make value.

She remembered.

Julene had lifted her into the trunk of the car parked right there where Donna was now parked. Julene had tucked Donna's dress in around her, handed in the cloth bundle, looked one last time at Donna, slipped off her green beads and placed them in Donna's hands. She'd stepped back, reached, banged the trunk closed. Donna had calcified with fear.

But then, in came a whisper through the cracks, the keyhole, the porous accommodating metal that graciously allowed soundwaves to pass through. Donna had heard her mother's voice. The car engine had revved, and Donna had felt the first jostle as the tires began to roll.

But her mother's voice was still discernible.

"Forgive me, daughter," her mother had whispered.

Donna straightened, stood immobile, let the memory replay in her ears once, twice.

She'd known to her core that her mother had said something. She'd known it.

And now.

She remembered. She'd had the audio file all along. It had just needed to be jogged, activated. She felt the hot burn in the corner of her eyes, the triumph.

"Nothing to forgive, Mother," she said aloud. "You tried to protect me. Forgive me for taking so long." Her pulse thrummed and sang and heat rose to her face. She felt a smile lift slightly, reached up her hands and held herself, her face, in stillness.

The trees around the clearing stood silent. The cabin leaned, and Donna could hear no sound other than the creek and a light wind rambling through the grass. She stood still and waited, felt peace swell in her belly and tension drain from her throat.

At least, amongst all the horrors and all the days, Donna knew definitively, she now had the data file to support what she'd always suspected but lacked tangible evidence for. She had irrefutable data. Her mother had loved her, her mother had tried to protect her, her mother had cared.

She stood still, the smile motionless on her lips, replayed the memory again, again. This was happiness.

Donna's fingers started to shake, her arms, shoulders, legs. She allowed the tremors to pulse through, the emotion to vent physically, the collision of desire and discovery. An urge to scream moved up her throat, but she didn't indulge herself. There was still the larger question.

Donna adjusted her posture, shoulders back, head lifted. This was it. She had hoped to learn everything, but if she didn't, at least she remembered this.

She walked back to the cabin, clenching her groceries. The thrumming grew stronger as she approached the porch. Three steps shy, she stopped, cocked her head, looked around. Donna was sure she was alone, but she heard something. A music almost, surrounding her. It was radiating, and she could feel the humming she heard now vibrating within her chest.

Donna threw her head back and laughed. Long and hard, booming resonant in the grim forest glade. The only thing she knew in that moment was that it felt good.

Her mother had loved her.

She cradled the heated feeling inside of herself as she moved up to the steps, stride sure and strong. Settled down on the edge of the porch, dangled her legs, set the milk chocolate bar and coffee down beside her thigh, opened the newspaper.

Donna went cold. Her joy evaporated. Her hands clenched.

The front page of *The Register-Guard:* "Women's bodies found piled in Three Sisters Wilderness."

Sweat iced down Donna's back, she tasted rage. Her skin was cotton, her eyes glass as she read, her brain stoic as data fed into her system and erupted bullet points.

- *A search and rescue team looking for Amelia Kane has discovered at least five bodies decaying in the wilderness near the Collier Cone off Highway 242.*
- *All women.*
- *Police expect to locate more bodies as they continue to search the area.*
- *Police suspect foul play but refuse to speculate.*
- *Police commissioner of Eugene acknowledges the horrific nature of the crime scene.*
- *Police detail body extraction difficult, delicate procedure.*
- *Police identify and release the names of two remains.*
- *Brie Anitala, aged 32, a white woman last seen nine years ago walking home from a night shift in Sisters.*
- *Dee Mercier, a 49-year-old Siletz woman with three children who disappeared twelve years ago outside of Bend.*
- *Public advise the public to stay away from the area.*
- *Police ask that anyone with any information regarding the case to call local police.*

She swallowed, swallowed again, again, again, her dry throat clicking as her eyes darted between the article's date from three days before and the actual text clumped in thick paragraphs below. Stared at the picture on the front of the newspaper, a low-angled image of the Three Sisters mountain peaks bathing in the glow of a setting sun. No pictures of the missing women.

Closing her eyes, she folded the newspaper calmly in half, set it gently to the side. Her ears pounded with blood, her stomach a single tight fist.

Risk assessment. Consequences. Calm.

Her brain twisted, data layers stacked, her therapists shouted and shook their heads while her inner cool self screamed through the calm, through the quiet, through the patience. Fury and anger boiled, simmered along the surface of her skin as she sat still, unmoving.

A terrible itching came over her and she stood, brain contorting. She tried to blink but her eyes were so tense her lids were locked open. Strategize. Put the data together. Map the next moves.

She moved to the screen door, traced a single finger along the latch. Considered. Her single critical question had focused for so long squarely on Julene. But now, she knew, it wasn't just about Julene. Donna's arm shook, her green beads rattled. Now, it was Julene. And all the others.

Donna tried to think clearly.

She could do it with a pillow. She'd planned for that outcome.

She almost opened the door.

But then cool calm settled over her and she turned, walked out across the clearing to her Subaru. She'd planned for so many outcomes, had mapped out so many ways her time with Ray could culminate. And no, she hadn't mentioned all the outcomes she'd envisioned to her current therapist. Or to Blazey. She just went about planning, layering data sets and gear and necessities, because there was no harm in planning for all contingencies. And planning was her favorite part of strategizing, of organizing options to stay in control.

She just hadn't thought it would actually go this way. Sometimes the data really was unpredictable. Donna would have smiled in that moment if her face wasn't still frozen.

Gently, she ruffled through the glovebox, moving papers and files and an ice scraper. There, slipped between tissues and tampons, were the cigarettes. Donna grabbed the soft blue pack, jostled it in her hand. American Spirits. She checked inside, counted six cigarettes. Probably stale. She hadn't smoked in years. Flipped the pack over, tapped the lighter out. Hesitated, was tempted to light up there on the spot. Needed it. But shook her head, knew she had to wait. Put the pack and lighter in her front pocket, then slammed the door closed.

Planning soothed her, focused her brain. She pushed aside her furious thoughts, gave them space to shout, but insisted they shout from the end of a tunnel where they couldn't break her calculations. Donna was numb, as cold as the bodies stacked up somewhere in the wilderness. She'd suspected that they were there, but for so long had only the bandwidth, the survival skills, to focus on one. Julene.

Not any more.

Donna propped open the screen door and main door with a rock, grabbed the one good wooden chair from the kitchen table, pulled it into Ray's stale room. Dragged the chair beside the bed. Slammed it down, loud.

Ray's eyes jerked open, followed her as she settled herself into the chair, stared at him. His face was still swollen.

"Where is Mother, Ray?" No preamble, no trying to coax him with water or kindness or hate. Just blunt—everything on the table now. "Where is Julene?"

He shifted, rolled his shoulders under the blanket, licked his lips.

"You're dying, Ray. You know that. Any day now." Her eyes roamed the room, landed on a decaying box on the floor by the end of the bed. Full of moldering books. She recognized a Bible.

"Confess before you stand before the seat of Christ and receive his judgment, Ray."

Donna sought to speak a language she hadn't heard since childhood. Tried to quote from memory. "Revelations? 'The dead were judged by what was written in the books, according to what they had done.'"

She leaned back in the wooden chair, heard it creak. "What's written in your book, Ray? What have you done?" Donna heard her voice, was surprised at the tone of strength and calm. "Where is Julene?"

Ray stared feverishly at Donna, pink tongue darting like a worm. She had to suppress an urge to pinch it off. He obviously didn't like her use of verse. But she was committed. Her stomach churned. "Revelations, Ray, yes. What else does it say?" She leaned back, pulled from patchy memory. "'But for the cowardly, the faithless, the detestable, as for murderers, the sexually immoral… something… they will be thrown into the lake that burns with fire and sulfur, which will be the second death.'"

He sputtered. She leaned forward, looked at him. "I'm not sure I got that last one perfectly right. No matter. Cowardly and faithless, confirmed. Detestable, confirmed. Murderer? Well, Ray, that's confirmed too."

Ray stopped moving, looked silently at her. She stared back, her face purposefully impassive, her shaking hands tucked imperceptibly between her knees. She tried to appear as stone. *Do not act on your anger*. Donna had heard that countless times from her first therapist.

"I'm positive I got the second part right, the part about being thrown into a lake of fire. You used to say that a lot when I was a child."

Ray coughed, gestured with a claw at the water cup. She handed it to him absently, made no comment as he drank. Set it back on the table when he was done. Waited. Heard her current therapist counsel calm, quiet, patience. Donna shushed her, turned back to Ray. "Fire would purify me, you said."

Ray's face twisted. "Tainted," he whispered, a dry rasp rattling in his throat.

A white beach floated before Donna's eyes, but she batted the image away almost instantly. The problem with that beach is that she'd never get a chance to go there with Julene. And that made her incandescent with fury when she truly thought about it. She needed to stay in this room, she needed to follow this through. For herself. For her mother.

"Cut the filth away," Ray rasped again.

Donna inclined back in the chair. Hoped his rasp was indicative of pending death.

"I know you did," she whispered, allowed one brief victorious smile to creep into the corner of her lips.

She reached into her pocket, slid out the pack of cigarettes. Languidly, she dragged one out, her fingers stroking the long smooth roll of paper. Looked at it for a long moment. Recognized that the angrier she was, the calmer she got. She felt poised on a knife's edge— deadly. Brittle. Like she could shatter apart into a thousand vicious obsidian pieces that would lodge themselves into Ray's organs.

Contemplated the cigarette again. It had been a long time. Tamped it against her knee. Dug for the lighter.

"Where did you hide her?" Donna asked, placing the cigarette between her lips, holding it as she leaned forward, tented habitually even though there was not a drop of wind in the room, lit up. Watched the flame glitter. "Up? In the Sisters Wilderness?"

Inhaled.

The tip of the cigarette crackled.

God, she adored smoking.

The first two inhales, the contemplative nature of breathing in hot smoke, the three-second pause before the nicotine train rolled in and over her and slowed everything down.

She'd given up smoking at Blazey's request. Blazey hated it, said it would kill her. But one occasionally, now and then, wouldn't hurt anyone.

Donna exhaled smoke at Ray. Repeated her question, weaving the words with smoke. "Where, Ray?"

Ray breathed in the cigarette smoke, coughed. Coughed again. Donna tilted her head as he glared at her.

"Want one?" Waved the lit cigarette at him. "Answer the question, Ray."

She waited, smoked. Waited, watched him. Sat back into her calm-edged-with-anger, felt both relaxed and ready to explode. Pushing into the chair slightly, she elevated her legs off the floor, pushed her feet up against the bed.

Ray coughed again, swallowed. Licked his lips. "I saw a great white throne..." Hacked dryly.

Donna held the water for him again, averted her eyes as he sucked eagerly on the straw. Set it back. Waited. Smoked.

"Great white throne," he whispered again.

"'And him who was seated on it,'" Donna quoted. "Revelations, Ray. I know it. Where did you put Julene?"

"White...," he muttered. "Ice."

She shifted her weight angrily, thumped the chair back down onto the floorboards.

"Did you see God, Ray?" Her voice boomed loud.

Ray moaned; his mouth puckered like a drawstring bag.

Donna was unmoved. "Hard to speak with no teeth, huh, Ray?" she said, voice concern laced with arsenic.

She pulled the cigarette away from her mouth, grinned widely, showed her implanted molars. "I lost three teeth here when you punched me in the face, Ray. For almost an entire year, I had to gum food and slur while my jaw was rebuilt."

Donna had no recollection of getting from Ray's cabin back to Blazey's in Eugene. She'd woken up in the hospital, Blazey asleep in a chair beside her. Unbelievable hot pain had electrified her body and monitors had started caterwauling and Blazey was leaning over her. The next time she woke up she was alone, in pain but less pain. And when she surfaced again the third time, Blazey was holding her hand.

There were weeks in the hospital that Donna could barely remember. The days had folded over into other days and months of physical therapy and only much later when at home Donna had remarked to Blazey about the new picket fence and Blazey had sighed and told her she'd crashed the Ford Focus into the old one.

That's what had alerted Blazey. She'd been in her office, working, wondering where Donna had gone, when she heard the car do a slow roll into the fence and stop. When she'd opened the car door and laid eyes on Donna, she'd called for help, gotten Donna to the hospital. The doctors were frantic and Blazey hadn't been able to say what happened, just agreed to the first and second surgeries, had sat in the hard-backed plastic chair for days waiting.

"I'm sorry I broke your fence," Donna had murmured through a jaw wired shut, sitting in the yellow high back chair by the bay window, looking at the bright white garden fence outside. Blazey was in her chair, the faded red comforter draped over her lap and dangling over Tuck, who was sprawled across half the living room floor. She'd put a bookmark on the page she was reading, turned, listened. "I went there to find Julene, but when he came after me, I couldn't defend myself." She'd seen the sentence float out of her mouth, unspool letter by letter. "I should have spoken up so long ago, told someone about Ray. I could have protected her."

Blazey had come over to the edge of Donna's chair, sank down onto the carpet before her, rested her head on Donna's knees.

"Why do you have to carry the burden of safety, dear girl?" Blazey had murmured. "We will only be safe when we choose to stop relying on violence."

Now, Donna dragged on her cigarette, inhaled smoke, held it. "I called the police on you." Her voice to Ray was conversational, as if she'd just asked him if he wanted a cup of coffee. Ray scrabbled the blanket away from his throat, pushed with his claws and elbows.

"No, no, not for the beating." Donna forced a laugh. "Everyone wanted me to do that, but I didn't want to go to jail too. And they made it clear I might, for harassing you."

That wasn't the whole truth. But Donna didn't think Ray would understand what her truth was, and she didn't feel compelled to explain. She had tried, though, that day confessing to Blazey.

"I feel like I should have done something to help Julene," she'd whispered as the woman had clung to her legs. "But I'm afraid all the time."

Blazey had leaned back onto her heels, hands still tight around Donna's knees. "Oh, my sweet daughter," she'd said, careful, voice measured but shaking. "Of course you are. We all are."

Donna's cigarette burned low. She dragged hard, luxuriated in the smoke. "I called the police on you a few months after I got out of the hospital," she told Ray, tilting back in her chair. "When I reported the disappearance of my mother."

Ray's eyes wandered. She put the cigarette in her lips, reached out, poked him hard in the side with her finger. "Pay attention," she ordered.

He jerked his chin towards her. "Julene."

"Yes, my mother," Donna answered. "I called the police; told them you did something to her."

Donna remembered gripping the phone so tightly her finger-nails gouged the plastic. She'd stood in the center of her bedroom in Blazey's house, her muscles twitching and aching from that morning's physical therapy. She'd wanted to stand unaided when she turned Ray in.

"But, do you know what the police said?"

Ray shook his head, blue eyes moving in and out of focus like a kaleidoscope.

"Not going to guess?" She sucked her teeth, hissing, then ashed her cigarette onto the floor by the excess oxygen tubing.

She took another drag, felt a whir in her stomach. "They asked me if I had any evidence."

Donna evaluated the cigarette. It was almost gone. Perhaps she would light a second.

"When I said no, the officer on the line laughed. Laughed. Said that *feelings* weren't evidence. That the law was based on evidence, on reason, on right and wrong. And that I could be charged with a felony and go to jail for wasting police time."

Last drag. Stubbed it out on the bedside table. "Second time I was threatened with jail for reporting a crime." Flicked the butt under Ray's bed. "Careful," she said. "Don't want to light anything on fire."

Blazey had encouraged her to call the police, report her suspicions about Ray.

"The anger you feel," she'd explained, "requires some form of calm, strategic action. This is what gives you power in this situation where you feel like you don't have any. Take your power by assessing the risks, formulating strategy. Call the police, report your father."

Donna had thought about it long and hard, laid on the couch as her body slowly healed, took fitful walks around the neighborhood, cane in hand, clipped off flowerheads, and read self-help books. Planned.

"Be strategic," Blazey had charged. "Assess risk."

"But there isn't any hard evidence, is there, Ray?" Donna asked, tilting her head to one side, hair swishing down her back.

Ray looked away, worked his mouth. Said nothing.

"There's barely any evidence that Mother existed. How could there be evidence that she no longer exists?" Donna mused. "The data doesn't support her. We live in a society where rules are made to purposefully render certain people invisible."

Donna looked down at her lap, considered the cigarette, her mother. A second cigarette might be too much for her lungs. But then, what the hell? What did any of it matter then, to her, to Ray, to what they'd found up in the Sisters?

She pulled the pack again from her pocket, eyed it. The cigarettes were slightly bent. She drew one out, brought it to her lips, lit it. Exhaled, blew out a long single stream of smoke. Twirled the lighter in her fingers. Glanced at Ray. He was watching her silently.

"So, you know what I started to realize?"

Donna stared at the glowing tip of her cigarette.

Thought about all the ways Ray had hurt her. Thought about all the ways Ray had likely hurt Julene. That tremendous diversity of hurts.

Took a deep drag, held the smoke taut in her mouth.

Thought about how when Ray acted upon his anger, there'd never been consequences. Thought about how when she acted upon on her anger, there'd always been consequences.

Thought about the sheer work of her anger, the lifetime of therapists, the hand wringing, and prescriptions, and Kleenex, and talking, and anger management treatments, and strategies, and visualization techniques. The mantras. The expectation that at all times she remain calm. The unshakable suspicion that something was wrong with her when she couldn't stay in control.

"I just realized," Donna said, leaning closer to Ray, emphasizing each word with an ashy jab of the cigarette in front of Ray's face, "that they all might have been wrong."

Women's anger always had consequences.

Brought her hand back to her lap, nodded at Ray. "Sorry, didn't mean to threaten you with this."

But consequences were not always uncontrollable.

She inhaled, expelled smoke in a long loud breath. "Being threatened, that's no good. I'd know. I've been threatened my whole life. Always in danger of losing something. Losing my purity. My life. Mother. My temper. My freedom. Now, losing the truth."

Ray waved his hands in the air.

Donna ignored him. "I've been afraid you wouldn't tell me about Julene, so I've been trying to be nice to you. Not put a pillow over your face."

She felt fury ring within her like a powerful glass bell. Stood up abruptly. Looked down at Ray. "Hold on a sec," she told him. Turned, left the room. Walked through the open doors, returned to his bedside with the folded newspaper. Set it gently on her lap. Steeled her face, waited.

Ray glanced at her.

"You know, for the last few years, I've been working at the Gender Justice Center in Eugene. I do data science, mainly cartography and data visualization. I love it."

She held Ray's eyes with her own.

"I love working with data science. People like you, they used to be able to hide in the noise, rely on no one matching the patterns. But that's what I do. I look through the noise."

Ray moved his knees up, stuck them akimbo to her. Defensive.

Donna closed her eyes, summoned her office and workspace and deep, comfortable rolling desk chair. She pictured her colleagues, tasted the exhilaration of sensory-precision she experienced when she ran analyses, when she took data sets that appeared, at best, incongruous or, at worst, incoherent, and made value. When she handed off analytics to her co-workers that ended arguments, influenced decisions, shaped policies and directions.

She thought about the years ahead, the keyboards under her fingers, the stacks and stacks of projects, the ways technology might continue to shift and where her work might go. Her mind thrummed.

Ray moaned, exhaled, and she glanced tightly at him. His face seemed paper thin.

Donna sighed. They were coming to an end now. She could feel it.

"Do you want a drag?" She held the cigarette in front of him.

He nodded his head. Ray had smoked all through her memory of him.

Gentle, she reached and held the cigarette for him. His lips creased around the paper filter, working to seal his mouth as he inhaled. Smoke blanketed his face, and Donna watched the little slipstreams created in the smoke by the forced oxygen by Ray's nasal cannula.

She settled back into the wooden chair, kept the newspaper pinned to her lap with an elbow. Looked around one last time at the cedar logs, wooden floorboards with beautiful grain, the boxes of books and clothes and a lifetime of junk. The rotting mattress. The nightstand with the oxygen tank resting below it. The cup of water.

"You're not going to tell me what happened to Mother." Donna looked down into her lap, saw the edge of the cigarette pack pushing out of her pocket. She pushed it back down.

He moaned, an incoherent gurgle, smoke trickling faintly out of the corner of his mouth. His hands curled, trembled into almost-fists.

She snaked the lighter between her fingers. "You're not going to tell me what you did to her, what you did to the others."

Ray's eyes jerked like startled rabbits.

Donna looked at him, eyes narrowed. "I know there've been others." She said it flatly, shook her head. "I see all the shit you've got stacked up in this house."

Ray's thin body pulled away from Donna even as his eyes narrowed hawk-like, a scowl pulled in under his collapsed mouth.

Donna unfolded the newspaper, held it up before him so he could read the headline. "I think this is you." She could feel her voice fracture; her anger shooting through like a solar flare.

"Daughter..." Ray whispered with some effort.

"Don't be afraid, Ray." Donna looked down at her hands, exhaled smoke heavily out both her nostrils. Calmed herself. Thought about her strategy, her plan forward. Breathed through her nose.

"They haven't connected this," she murmured. Donna remembered an academic paper she'd read during her university days. "The police have no real incentive to go after monsters like you. That's why they've got all these complicated rules, why they made a system designed to keep people from speaking up."

Ray glared at her. She wasn't sure if he was fully tracking what she was saying.

"As long as there are monsters, the police have a reason to exist. If they slay the dragon, their job is done. Following?" She looked at him briefly, took in his trembling lips. Continued, "Problematically, power is intoxicating."

Donna narrowed her eyes, inhaled. "Why eliminate a threat when it means losing power? Clearly there's a disincentive built into the system."

Inching, Ray moved a little higher on his pillow, slid his nasal cannula back into his nose with the back of his hand, eyes fastened to Donna's.

"I thought about bringing in all the boxes of stuff you've got in here, but I have trust problems. I know what happens when you report violence, and how little actually happens." Donna pushed back and looked up at the ceiling, the rotting logs black with mold. She waved at the ceiling with her right hand. "You should get that fixed, Ray. Those logs are a fire hazard."

Ray laid skeletal in his bed; the blanket gnarled up on his chest. Donna knew that he recognized his weakness, that he likely thought his best weapon was silence.

"I am tired of having to think around your crimes."

Donna studied him, watched to see if he understood. "It's time I look to the future, stop focusing on the past.

"I thought when your doctor called me trying to put you into hospice that there would be a chance to finally finish this." Donna pushed her hair back from her eyes. "Find out what happened to Julene."

Donna stubbed the cigarette out on the nightstand again, dropped the butt onto the floor. "I guess I could have just waited to find out in the newspaper." Kicked the butt under the bed. She sighed. "I should have done this a lot sooner."

Donna stood from the chair, held the newspaper in her cool grip, felt extraordinarily calm. Gazed once more down at Ray.

She turned, stepped away from his bed. Looked through the bedroom door to the open cabin door, out through the porch and lawn and darkness. Night had fallen. She looked back down at the lighter in her hand. Flicked her thumb, clicked the lighter awake. Stared at the little flame that sprouted up magically.

Ray grunted, clawed the air. "White throne," he moaned.

Donna didn't even look at him. She turned, leaned from the waist, a perfect hinge, held the flame glittering to the corner of Ray's bed. The spark caught almost instantly, biting into the fiber of the dry comforter, spreading. A cotton blend. It simultaneously ashed and melted.

The fire crackled over the man in seconds.

Donna tossed the newspaper onto Ray, stepped away into the room's doorway. Waited to ensure the flames were strong, moving across the mattress, the floor, the walls. She'd left the cabin door open to safeguard plenty of oxygen to drive the fire.

Flames engulfed the cedar logs, popping and sizzling and feasting, racing over moldering boxes of junk. A wall of heat forced Donna back from the room. She withdrew to the kitchen and out the cabin door, leapt down the porch steps, sprinted back across the clearing. Reached her car just as she heard the oxygen tank explode.

Panting, Donna leaned against the hood of her car, realized the heat and flames had singed her hair and eyebrows, felt her cheekbones ache from the stretch of her lips.

She inhaled deeply, smelled the linty, coppery scent of rot, of wood turning to ash, of plastic melting and fabric incinerating and her satisfaction incandescent and sharp.

She released a long breath. Pushed her green beads up her arm and thought briefly of Julene. Of the others.

Patted her hip and pulled the cigarette pack from her pocket. Drew the last smoke out.

Final one, she promised.

She lit the last cigarette, cupping her hand around the lighter's tiny flame. Inhaled deeply, watched the grass around the cabin scorch. Eyed the fire's progress. Watched as the roof caught, flames bulging around the edges, then up and through the tar-paper shingles. The porch was completely engulfed. The structure released a long-drawn-out cackle, then the walls fell inward, the cabin cremating itself.

Donna heard humming from somewhere, felt a deep calm contentment emanate in her core, noted the peace and power snapping up her spine.

She wiped tears from her face. Reached into her pocket, found her phone.

Consequences.

She was in control.

Dialed.

"Hello, 911?" she said. "I need to report a fire."

15
THE
MEDIC

May woke abruptly. Her legs ached.

Her hamstrings and quadriceps and adductors felt like they were on fire.

It was dark. She had no idea what time it was. She rolled, muscles throbbing, tried to feel for her phone, but then, right on cue, the alarm started wailing and May knew it was five in the morning in the bunk room. She'd set her phone the night before as she was crawling in around one a.m.

Chief had told them they'd need to be ready to go back up to the search at six, and May had wanted extra time to get her SAR pack properly sorted. Make sure she packed all the things off-list, the supplies she apparently was just supposed to magically know she'd need. And extra food.

The previous day flooded into her brain, flattened May into the bed. The bodies. The cold leg under her fingers. The hike back. Jonas. His lies.

She closed her eyes, felt her body sink into the bunk like an anvil. She couldn't do it. Couldn't get up.

But then remembered all the tragedies that Meredith Grey had faced. She'd been attacked by patients, lost her close friends, her father and mother had died, her husband had left her, then left her again, then died, she'd had a miscarriage, been shot, been in a plane crash, nearly drowned, had to hide from a guy shooting up the hospital. So many tragedies. Yet each day Meredith Grey got back up, saved people's lives.

May yanked her eyes open. She could do this.

The wool blankets scratched her bare legs, and May glanced around. She was alone in the four-bunk room. She swung down from the top, hit the floor, and stepped into yesterday's blue work pants with a practiced, easy motion.

Only after she was dressed did the smell hit her. Her pants stank like the floor of a cross-fit gym. She hadn't washed her clothes. She typically did three or four days in her work pants before washing them. Usually it didn't matter, but today, May shook her head. The stench was strong. She hoped it wasn't anything from the glacier.

She hesitated, but just for a second. She left the bunk room, went down the hall, peeked into the break room. Empty. Thank god. She didn't want to talk to anyone. She had yet to make any sense of what happened last night with Jonas, Chief, all of them. May slipped through the door, headed for the coffee pot.

"Pour me a cup?"

May jumped, spun, saw Jonas coming through the door behind her. He must walk on cat feet, she thought. She hadn't heard the slightest rustle. She closed her eyes, willed her mouth shut, reached down a second cup from the shelf.

"I take half and half. In the fridge." His tone was brisk. He settled himself at the table, opened a beige file folder packed with papers.

Listening to his file rustling, May kept her back turned. She concentrated on pouring coffee, mixing in the half and half. She waited until her hands stopped shaking before turning, handing him the cup wordlessly, trying to creep from the room.

"Sit, Young," Jonas commanded.

May honestly tried to resist. She faced the door, willed herself to take the knob, twist, exit, return to her bunk to sip coffee in peace and then repack. She realized she felt betrayed by Jonas, abandoned, manipulated. She'd thought they were friends but was now completely confused. She remembered finding the first body, and the second. Why had he lied?

She tried to leave the break room, but she couldn't. Instead, May found herself turning, slouching into the chair across from him. Obedient to her core, she knew, thanks to her mother. A good girl. Deferent to anyone in a position of authority. Even as loathing flooded up into May's mouth and seared the enamel off her teeth, she looked at Jonas with a neutral, slightly pleasant facial expression.

He was groomed neatly, hair glistening, likely fresh from a shower. His pale skin was faintly pink. She wondered if he'd slept. She could smell his shampoo. Fruity.

"Chief said he wants me to search with you again today, keep an eye on you." Jonas smiled, a quick flick.

May saw a snarl. Was distracted by his teeth. They were pale white, slightly yellow, and she thought she saw gray lining the gums above his incisors. Did Jonas have meth mouth? Meth was acidic, and it caused the teeth and gums of users to gradually decay away into gruesome black holes. But May knew not all meth users got meth mouth. In season four of *Grey's Anatomy*, when a man and his wife were cooking meth and triggered an explosion, they brought their baby into the hospital. No one suspected they were drug dealers because neither of them had meth mouth, but later, after Callie Torres did some quick thinking, the doctors were able to figure it out and save the baby.

Jonas coughed slightly. May jerked her eyes towards him.

"You know, I'm glad we have a moment before everyone comes in," Jonas continued, sipping coffee, waiting.

"May?" Jonas tapped the table. "May? Good morning?"

She blinked, realized he was still talking to her.

"May? Isn't this nice to have a moment together?" His voice was friendly, even.

May nodded as she wondered what she'd find if she emptied his pockets right then. His pupils looked a little dilated. Maybe that was why he'd lied. It had something to do with a drug habit. Compassion jumped in May's throat.

"I was thinking we should get a drink together later, or something, to talk, but this is nice, right?" Jonas gestured at his coffee, then hers, and gradually his words sank into May's churning brain.

Was he hitting on her? She sat up straighter, pushed a limp lank of hair out of her face. She hadn't even put face moisturizer on. No one had hit on her, well, ever. Her mother had told her that they were looking into paying someone to marry her so they could guarantee grandchildren. She shifted in the chair, caught a whiff of her metallic stale sweat, ammonia.

"Sorry," she murmured, felt the blush creeping up her collar.

Jonas tilted his chin, raised an eyebrow.

"I reek." The words fell like damning lodestones from May's lips.

"Those the same clothes as yesterday?"

May nodded, wished her other uniforms weren't in a pile on the floor of her bathroom at her apartment. She looked at the coffee in her cup, thought she could pretend she'd drank it all and stand, leave. She didn't want to be around Jonas, didn't want to think about him. She felt confused, on the verge of tears. Again. Why did she tell him she smelled? He looked like he'd just been professionally groomed. May hated that she ceded ground so easily. She knew next to him, she looked like a grease trap posing as a human.

"Huh," Jonas responded. "Don't your parents run a dry cleaners?"

"What?" May asked, confused. Her parents owned a real estate company.

"Oh, sorry," he said, flashed a big grin. "The people who run the dry cleaners by my place are Asian. For some reason I thought they were your parents."

May's mouth went dry, numb, her tongue flicked into a knot.

"Well, I can give you the address if you want to get your uniforms cleaned there, in the future." He leaned back, smiled at her.

May didn't know how respond, had no idea what to say. She thought she should point out the overtly racist nature of his comment, but even when she tried to come up with a sentence her mind just froze.

"I'm glad Chief is having me help you, May," Jonas continued, soft-like and quiet. "You're going to be an excellent medic."

May gaped at him.

"And I'll do anything to help you succeed," he said, his fingers tapping the tabletop. "That's why yesterday I stepped in and briefed

Chief for you. I didn't think you would want to be besieged by all that paperwork, especially being so new and going through everything you went through yesterday." Teeth out, yellow as Ritalin pills.

May tried not to get distracted again by his mouth. Maybe he just had gum disease, or light tooth decay. Didn't mean he had a meth addiction. May studied him, saw his hand twitch, his thumb drum against the ceramic mug. Focus, she told herself. Looked around the room, noted how the paint on the walls was watery, strained thin.

She churned Jonas's words over in her mind. Paperwork? Did he not think her smart enough to fill out paperwork explaining that she'd uncovered human remains under snow?

"But..." May muttered, then trailed off. She had no idea what to say. Again. Where had all her words gone? The image of a leg sticking out of the snow flashed in her mind. Tears welled in the corners of her eyes. The slightest thing since she'd joined this department, and she cried. She hated it. She squeezed her eyelids, forced her face under control.

When she opened her eyes again, she saw Jonas was watching her. His nostrils flared, eyes tightened, and both his hands gripped and ungripped the coffee mug.

She realized that Jonas had definitely not been hitting on her.

She took in a ragged breath, rubbed her lips together. Chapped. She could feel flakes of skin catching.

She opened her mouth.

Forced the words out.

"You lied."

She tried to sound firm, to pin Jonas to the chair with a hard tone. But all she could manage was a whisper and a brief flick of her eyes.

"No, I did not," he replied flatly. His aspect shifted. He sat stiff, crossed his arms. "I was there. I know what happened."

May's mouth fell open, and anything she might have said vanished. Sweat glowed rancid across her body. Was she not remembering accurately? Who had found the bodies?

Closing her eyes, she pictured the day before. Walked herself down the scree slope again. She was remembering correctly, she told herself. She found them.

"Young, let me give you some advice," Jonas enunciated carefully, leaned forward, set his fingertips on the table. "Keep your mouth shut. This is me helping you and has nothing to do with you being this department's diversity hire. I want you to succeed, really, and I will help you. But don't accuse people of lying." He pushed the chair back, stood abruptly, leaned over the table at her.

May shrank back, flattened by the competing veins of indifference and vehemence in his tone. Felt the room swing. Couldn't blink, tucked into herself, stared wide-eyed at him.

"Morning guys!" Baker called as the door swung open and he rushed into the break room. "Thomas says we're off like prom dresses in fifteen." He commandeered the coffee pot, tilting the remaining liquid into his travel mug.

Jonas looked once more at May, shook his head, then turned and left the break room. May's heart pounded, and she could feel blood rushing in her ears. She felt like she was going to vomit.

"Young? Hello? Did you hear me?" Baker waved a hand in front of her face.

She jerked her chin, met his eyes.

"You okay?"

Nodding, she coughed, cleared her throat. "Tired," she lied.

"Well, you're with me today. Thomas switched the roster up. You and me are going to man the medic tent, take care of any searchers that get cut up on the lava. That should be fun, eh?" He smiled, held out a fist for May to bump.

She gently pressed her knuckles into his, looked down at the murky reflection of her face on the plastic table. What the hell was wrong with her? Her whole arm was shaking.

"Sorry," Baker said. "Should have said we're going to man and woman the medic tent. Didn't mean to be an ass."

May shook her head, tried to focus.

"Coffee with Jonas, huh?" Baker continued, sipped his travel mug, leaned against the counter.

May squinted at him, took in the mug. It was plastic, had an 80's retro design of Crater Lake on its side.

"None of my business, Young, but well, careful there. Jonas is a bit of a snake pit." Baker shrugged his shoulders dismissively.

Fury erupted in May. Her humiliation compounded with the last two days, her lack of sleep, her profound disappointment with herself, and her exasperation with always being on the receiving end of unsolicited advice, the images flicking in her eyes of human remains carelessly piled on top of one another. She knew that she remembered exactly what had happened yesterday, the exact feel of the body she'd found. *She'd found.* Regardless of what Jonas claimed. Just because she was new didn't mean she was blind, confused, oblivious. Just because she doubted the hell out of herself, did not mean she was making up the day before. Just because she felt alone and withdrawn and unskilled, didn't mean she was imagining touching a dead leg. Just because she felt like her closest, most stable and safe relationships at present were with television characters, none of it meant she was a liar.

May stood up from the table, balled hands shaking, legs trembling.

Sparks pounded up and down her veins. She twisted her face at Baker, eyes wide.

"I liked you better when you talked less," she whispered.

Turning, she fled the room, down the bay and outside, leaned behind the building against the siding, drew huge wet breaths into her mouth.

Minutes ticked by as confusion and anger and sadness swirled inside of her. Why did she snap at Baker? What was wrong with her?

She leaned her head back, thought about leaving the department. Calling up Lou or Jamal. Ask them for a job. Tears eroded her cheeks. How could Jonas lie so openly?

A wet nose smeared across her hand, and May jerked, looked down at the stray dog. It had snuck up beside her, was sitting patiently, tail lightly thumping. She gazed into its friendly gray eyes and something shifted inside of her. She knelt, stroked the dog's thick ruff. It nosed her neck, tickling, and May laughed quietly.

"Ahh Foxface," she whispered. And then cried.

Throughout the rest of the day, into the next, and the next, May zombied through her shifts. She worked the medical tent, avoided Jonas, interacted minimally with Baker, and allowed her mind to churn in circles strong enough they emitted their own gravity. No one seemed to notice how withdrawn she was, and, for once, she was glad of her invisibility in the department.

The only highlights of her days were at their close. She drove back to the department and snuck out back behind the building to feed the stray dog. She'd give the creature bits of sandwiches she'd saved. The dog was simultaneously dirty and soft, and May felt distracted and soothed when examining the dog's markings as it ate. She lingered on the pale white patch on its front paw. She was comforted by its presence, by its apparent affection for her and happiness at the food she snuck it. It was sitting each day with the dog in the only place she felt safe at the department that she came up with a plan forward. While the dog wagged its tail and chomped down the food, May would pull out her phone and open her Notes app. She typed away each day, sentence by sentence. Inspired by Meredith and Cristina and Izzy and the courage those women had shown in the most terrible of circumstances, May decided to write her own report to the chief.

She didn't know when she would turn it in to him, and she sweated as she played out different scenarios of walking into his office and handing over her words. In one, she was vengeful, stomping in, slamming fifty pages of paper onto his desk, saying over her shoulder as she left that he'd be hearing from her lawyer. In another, she handed him the report and told him she would be on NPR that night, describing what *she'd* found and how Jonas had taken it away from her. Or, another, when, as she handed Chief the report, he waved it away, told he knew already that she'd been telling the truth all along.

However it went, May knew she needed to do it soon.

The opportunity came several days later. May was in the medical tent when the Chief appeared and ordered her to dismantle the gear and take everything back to the department. The search was being suspended, Eugene PD was taking over. He explained they'd regroup back at the station.

May had tried to summon some emotion within herself as she put the final crate into the back of the ambulance, some thought for the still-missing Amelia Kane. But her brain was completely frozen and could only focus on the report on her phone in her back pocket and how she knew she'd need to give it to the chief that day. During the two hour drive down the mountain with Baker she sat in blank silence, numb.

After Baker parked the ambulance in the bay and exited the vehicle, May sat in the passenger seat until the automatic lights clicked off. Indecision and doubt roiled in her stomach. She knew that she needed to give her report to the chief. She wanted to be heard. But she couldn't bring herself to act.

But then the bay doors opened back up, the lights flooded on. The chief pulled in beside her in the bush truck. He was alone in the vehicle and May felt suddenly certain. It was a sign, a way forward. She jumped down from the ambulance.

"Chief," she called. "Can I talk to you?"

He inelegantly rotated as he stepped out of the truck, heavy boots scrabbling on the concrete. "Young?" he asked. "Is that you?"

She stepped around the truck hood, SAR pack balanced on her shoulder, heart pounding. She was already flushed, she could feel it. "Yes," she wavered.

"I've got to take a piss," he said. "My office in three?"

May nodded but knew he couldn't see her. He'd disappeared into the single bathroom in the bay, the one she used to change into her uniform while all the rest of the crew stripped in front of their lockers.

She dropped her pack at her locker, walked out to see if Foxface was around for a little morale bump, but didn't see the dog. Walked to the medic desk in the back office, printed off her report. Then headed into the chief's office, a little room jammed with metal filing cabinets, firefighter posters, gear, a desk, and two chairs. She sank into the chair by the window, waited.

"Sorry," the Chief said fifteen minutes later, breezing through the open door and around the side of his desk. "That turned into a shit."

May flushed, tried to hide it. "What's going to happen with Amelia Kane?" she asked, ankles pressed together, feeling her heart rate already above one hundred and thirty.

He shrugged, looked at his desk piled with paper. "I don't know," he said. "I think some civilians are going to keep looking, but we're out of budget. Eugene PD is likely going to reclassify it a homicide investigation, especially given the graveyard in that randkluft at the Collier. They think four more bodies today. What a horrific mess. But for Amelia they might focus on the mother. More power to them. Let the police burn up their accounting."

"Four more?" May stopped, shocked. Maybe now was not the time to press her report on the chief.

But Chief kept talking. "They won't have to spend much on autopsies, I'll tell you between us. I talked to the forensics lead. The ice and snow preserved those women, froze their wounds. Each body so far appears to have been asphyxiated."

May swallowed thickly, gripped her chair. She'd read about strangulation in her training, primarily in the context of domestic abuse situations. Abusers who strangled often had superficial injuries caused by a victim fighting to live, while, conversely, the victim typically had far less visible wounds. Often, the only immediate sign of strangulation was the small bursting of blood vessels in the victim's eyes. Sometimes, when police or medics responded to a call, the victim could be arrested because the abuser had the more noticeable injuries. May had been trained to identify such situations, look for starry eyes.

"Their throats were literally crushed." He inhaled sharply, caught May's eyes. "But none of that is public knowledge, Young."

May nodded, shivers running down her arms. Tried not to visualize gruesome bodies thawing out of the ice, necks crushed. What a horrific way to die.

"But what about Amelia Kane?" she asked. "Any possibility she's up there?"

The fire chief looked at May across his desk. "We'll likely all find out at the same time, read about it in the *Register-Guard*. Seems like they're devoting their front page to the story each day. The police have released the names of two more today."

May tucked a loose chunk of hair behind her ear. Wished she'd showered, didn't, again, feel so dingy. "Do you think the mother did something?"

He angled back into his chair, eyed her. He was a long time responding. "Maybe?" he finally said. "But, I've been chief at this department for over twenty years. What do I know?"

May nodded. She didn't think a mother could murder her child in cold blood.

"In actuality, though, it's a bit of a statistical anomaly. From what I recall, usually it isn't the mother. Usually it's a known male."

"Eight times more likely. I read that in training," May said. "Ninety-two percent of female murder victims know the man who kills them."

He tapped his desk. "I'm more likely to kill a woman that Amelia Kane's mother is. But..." he trailed off, fidgeted, then ran a hand over his face. "I don't know any more." He sighed. "Lots of women have gone missing up there, but no one has paid much attention. Now the police on all sides of the Cascades are looking like complete fools. The Bend police didn't even devote a single day looking for Dee Mercier."

May eyed her lap, looked at the papers she'd carefully stapled together, recalled the feel of the stiff leg she'd handled in the snow. Raised her face back up. "Does it ever get easier?" she asked quietly.

Chief pushed the roller chair away from his desk, interlocked both his hands behind his head, leaned, flashed her a grin. "Yeah," he chortled.

Confusion twinged in May. What was funny?

He must have registered her confusion because he tapped the desk, leaned forward. "Did Baker not tell you? Remember Donna Watts? How many of those calls did you go on? Her dumbass dad tried to sneak a smoke, burned himself and the whole place to cinders. Springfield had to respond, three trucks. Nearly burnt the whole forest down. God, what a mess."

May pictured Donna, visualized the woman sitting alone on that cabin porch. Scenarios opened before her. But May shook them away. She told herself to focus. She eyed him with her firmest expression.

"Well, for what it's worth, I remembered something that might be helpful…" May trailed off, waited for some sign that he was listening. But he wasn't looking at her anymore. He was looking at the clock above her shoulder with such intensity that May turned in her chair, glanced at the wall. The clock was standard issue.

She twisted back, drew in a breath, hoped he wasn't already over this meeting. "When I hiked back from the Collier that first night, about forty minutes outside of Command I ran into an old woman with a birthmark shaped like a bird over her right eye."

"Huh?" He turned to her. "You didn't tell me that before. What's the significance?"

May tamped down a surge of triumph. She knew her television shows. This was the moment when she presented vital evidence and her superior recognized her worth. She shrugged a shoulder, tried to make it more casual and less scoliosis. Feigned demureness. "You haven't read my report," she said, tapped the papers in her lap. "You've only heard Jonas's account."

"Young," Chief barked, irritation crumpling his eyes into tank windows. "I don't have time for games."

"When I studied for my EMT-B," she inserted quickly, flustered that he was so quickly irritated. She didn't want to lose ground. "I had to learn missing person protocols. They were all local examples. One of the missing people was this girl." May took the top sheet off her lap, handed him the image she'd printed yesterday before turning into her bunk. She felt confident for the first time in weeks. This would do it; she could taste it.

"Amiah Benton. She went missing decades ago. Last seen hiking with her parents in the Three Sisters." Swallowing, May reached across his desk, tapped her finger on the girl's grainy face. "Note the birthmark. Like a bird, flying over the right eye."

He did not follow her finger, did not look at the printed page. He held his gaze trained squarely on May. His eyes were chalky, they looked like storm clouds. "I thought you wanted to be a medic?"

Electricity surged through May and sweat gathered under her thighs. She would have to fight for this one, she realized. "I think I'm smart," she replied, held the eye contact with him. "I work hard, I'm sharp. I think I can be an asset here, if you let me." Held her head up like her mother taught her, kept her face soft, non challenging to masculine authority. Best way to sell a property, her mother had drummed into her over and over. Be strong, but not challenging.

He brought his hands back down from around his head, sat up straight in the chair, rolled it forward to the edge of his desk. He looked at her thoughtfully, and May couldn't guess what he was about to say.

She held herself still, waited.

If it had been her in his seat, she would have praised the good work of her newest hire, asked how she'd learned to follow leads, recommended her for more training and a promotion. May's heart beat painfully as she waited for the chief to speak.

He coughed, rubbed his throat. "I'm intrigued that you're focusing on detective work, but I need to remind you that you're not a police officer. You're a medic, the newest member of our team—a strong member."

May allowed a brief smile to flicker on her mouth. So, he recognized how worthwhile she was, how much work she'd put in over the last few months.

"It's my job to assess new recruits, find out their strengths. Clearly, you have a lot of strengths. You've moved through some of the medic training faster than any of the guys here. Well done."

Feeling the heat on her face, May kept her face tilted as her heart pounded wildly.

"I've noticed especially your organizational capacities," Chief continued. "And we just got back from a multi-day search, and I know the gear is disorganized and a mess. What I'd like you to focus on is less the detective stuff, and more on getting the storeroom, gear room, and front bay ship-shape so we're ready for the next call."

He wiggled his mouse, woke up the computer screen on his desk, looked intently at it. Brows furrowed like crop rows. May waited, but he didn't look back at her. He was signaling that the conversation was done. He'd praised her, then sent her to organize and clean.

May sat motionless in the chair, tried to digest his words. What about Amiah Benton? Wasn't he at all curious why a woman who went missing decades ago was now strolling around the same trails where a child went missing? Wasn't that a curious event? And what was going on with all the laughter May had heard? That the hikers had also heard? Maybe he needed more of an explanation. May steadied herself, then stood, looked down at him. "Here's my written report, Chief."

She set the stapled report on top of his desk, next to his hand which did not move, did not reach for the papers. The hand was steady, long fingers wrapped comfortably around the black plastic mouse.

May turned to leave the office, slow-walked, willed him to say her name, draw her back in, tell her he was joking, that he found her an incredible asset to the department and a skilled medic. She moved through the doorframe.

"Young."

May's heart surged. She stopped, but didn't turn.

"Sit," he commanded.

He was a slow reader. He took an inordinate amount of time picking up his reading glasses, leaning back, settling in. May watched his bottom lip tuck, the way his eyes moved line by line, color on his face growing dimmer when the computer monitor fell asleep and went dark. She took in the chaos of his desk—the detritus of tools and paper and rope and mints and notebooks. No pictures. She wondered if he had a family. He'd never mentioned a wife, children. Maybe the department was his family. It usually was for the older men in the fire-fighting television dramas, especially the ones from the late nineties like *Third Watch*. She'd binge-watched all six seasons of that show, and totally understood why Sully never had a family except for the brief stint with the superhot Tatiana. But Tatiana had turned out to be a Ukrainian working for a Russian mob boss. She had a secret love child and was eventually murdered. If May had been on the show, she'd have told Sully to steer clear.

The chief stopped reading, released a barely perceptible groan. Set his feet on the ground with a loud thud. Narrowed his eyes at her. "That's quite a report," he said flatly.

May sat silent.

"Mystical laughter from the landscape? Seriously? Missing people making more missing people? Is any of this even provable?"

May kept her face blank. She hoped he'd agree, but then, he hadn't seemed even remotely interested in Amiah Benton.

"Instead of the likely scenario, where Amelia Kane tragically wandered off into a lava tube, you're claiming... what?"

May's mind went blank.

"And you're saying you discovered the bodies, and Jonas is lying? This is just..."

May swallowed, sat straight in the chair. She stared steady at him, pretended a confidence she didn't feel.

"This is all rather different from Jonas's report." His tone was dry, skeptical. "Rather different than the report you yourself gave me in person."

May brought her ankles together, hands folded, chin set at a ninety-degree angle from her neck. Told her brain to turn off. "It's the truth." She said it firmly.

"Young, I don't want strife in this department. I won't have it. Which one of your reports should I believe? Jonas only filed one, and as far as I understand, he certainly hasn't revised his."

Why did every conversation she have with the chief go in directions she couldn't predict? Why couldn't he believe her? She sucked air between her teeth, kept her eyes trained on his desk.

"This seems a little crazy, you know?" He set both elbows on his desk, leaned in. Voice low, intimate. His face suddenly seemed warm. "You doing okay? I'm not unaware you've been a little unwell since uncovering all of this. That can leave a mark."

May had seen Sully use this tactic on *Third Watch*. Be all intimate before he punched the lights out of a villain. But May knew she wasn't a villain, and she wasn't sure why the chief was treating her like one. May had a speech prepared. She'd run it over and over in her head over the course of the last day. And while she'd pulled liberally from a few of Meredith's scenes in *Grey's Anatomy*, she had inserted her own voice into it. She was trying hard to be a medic. She was smart, could make a career for herself. Hell, after a few years, she'd maybe even think about medical school.

"In all honesty, I don't think this matters very much. Right? You've already given me a verbal report, and, frankly, you weren't the lead on the search." His tone was almost cajoling. "I appreciate you bringing this to my attention, but I think the best way forward is—"

"It does matter, though," May interrupted quietly. "It matters to Jonas."

The fire chief pulled back, created distance between them. May noted his face was no longer warm.

"Well, he's a young, ambitious guy, May. He's trying to get his name out there, move up the ladder."

"Aren't I?" May whispered. Trying to get a career? Trying to get momentum forward? Trying to put one foot down on the ground, let alone a second foot?

"You've got time, May. You're just inexperienced." Chief gathered the individual sheets of paper together, tucked the printed image of Amiah Benton at the bottom.

May watched as he took the stack of paper, her words, carefully typed out on her phone in between days of patching up searchers' sliced feet. She'd read it, reread it, and palm-sweated all over it. But he just tapped the pages together, made it neat, then slid the whole stack into a cardboard box on the floor by his feet.

The room wobbled, and the corners of May's eyes felt hot, strained. This was not how it was supposed to go. This was not what happened on television. Blurrily, May saw her shifts, her training, her career accordion out before her, the days and months and years she would spend at this department with people like Jonas. She swallowed, summoned the speech she'd memorized, all the words she could say to the chief that articulated how she felt. Every character in all the shows she loved got a moment, a speech, a soliloquy, where they exposed their insides for everyone else to know them, love them.

But no words came to May's mouth and she sat mutely, her tongue made of ice.

"You're doing a really great job, Young. I've been quite surprised at what you've managed to accomplish so far. Great work." The chief jiggled the mouse, and his computer screen lit up again. "Don't forget about the gear sort," he said, turning his attention to the screen.

May understood she was dismissed.

She got to her feet, cleared her dry throat in affirmation, walked rigidly out of his office.

She stood in the middle of the bay, indecisive.

Then, she went to her locker, looked at the picture she'd taped up of Meredith, Cristina, and Izzy. May undressed, not in the small bathroom she always used, but right there, in full view if anyone had bothered to look. Folded her uniform. Set it deliberately on the second shelf. Slipped into her regular clothes. Peeled the picture off the locker, held it in her hand. May looked at the three women and saw clearly now that they were powerless to change their situations and tragedies. They were stuck forever in *Grey's Anatomy* world.

But May was not stuck in that world. She was in the real world.

May gently folded the picture in two, tucked it into her pocket.

She turned, walked out of the bay, across the gravel parking lot, unlocked her car. She felt aged. Her hands shook. She opened her car door.

May heard the sound of crunching gravel behind her and her heart jumped to her throat. She knew instantly that the chief was coming after her, that he'd realized his error and what incredible value she brought to the team.

He was going to apologize.

Perhaps life was like television.

May took a breath, fleetingly closed her eyes, then turned.

But it wasn't the chief standing behind her.

May looked down at the dog sitting quietly in the gravel.

The stray eyed her, tail thumping, ears partially raised.

"Okay," she said, opened her car door wider.

The dog pawed forward.

"Get in, Foxface," May said. "We're getting out of here."

16
THE
MOTHER

Leonie moved slowly up the trail, lava rocks and scree scrambling underfoot. She felt thin, like she was about to wash away. She ignored the wet gravel squishing, the damp foliage leaving elegant streaks across the tips of her boots. A spring shower had unloaded rain the day before, chased away the snow patches. But her only thought was Amelia.

She stopped, drank from her water bottle, looked around at the Three Sisters rising before her, the blue skies and racing clouds. It was a day a lot like the two hundred and eighty-four days previous.

Airborne spiders appeared in front of her, flapped, then vanished, blown by the steady wind.

The only thing she wanted was for her daughter to reappear.

Amelia.

She swallowed thickly, tried to push through her lightheadedness, forced her feet forward.

Every weekend since Amelia vanished, she'd driven up, twisting along the narrow McKenzie Highway, parked at Scott Trailhead, walked the trail to the Collier Cone and called for her daughter.

Thirty-six weekends.

Arturo accompanied her for the first few trips, but eventually he stopped, saying it was too hard to keep returning.

But still, Leonie went, every weekend. It both took every bit of strength she had and gave her strength to get out of bed each day.

When winter came and smothered the region with snow, she still drove up, go as far as the snowline allowed, park her car, and call for Amelia until her throat bled.

Leonie knew Amelia was gone. But it wasn't possible that her daughter was dead. Amelia, instead, was just away temporarily. She'd vanished. And that meant she could still be found.

No funeral, no memorial. She couldn't. Arturo had held a service, but Leonie would not attend, could not acknowledge what Arturo said was true.

She did not want to learn to live in a world where Amelia did not exist. To her, there was no firm evidence that Amelia had left the planet. Leonie knew Amelia could come back. Amelia could live.

In spring, the snow had lifted in the high elevations. The second weekend in May, she drove up and was surprised to find the snow gate just past Camp White Branch open. Driving further, she found all the gates on the 242 open. Leonie wound up the tortuous road, clutched the wheel through hairpin turns that stacked, one-two-three, right on top of one another. She was impervious to the majestic views, the long sight lines of rippling mountain ridges still swathed in snow. Her body crawled with a single desire.

Pulling into the Scott Trailhead lot, she parked her car where she and Amelia had parked nine months earlier. She saw the place as it was last fall. How Amelia was impatient, eager to go, but she'd wanted to make sure they'd grabbed everything. How when they had hit the trail, the girl was going so fast that she'd struggled to keep up. How Amelia made that strange humming noise, how they climbed up the Collier Cone, how Amelia talked about the glacier wanting a companion. Then, the picture they'd taken at the bottom of the cone.

That picture of the two of them. She cherished it, looked at it relentlessly on her phone. She examined her daughter's face for evidence of distress, painstakingly poured over the background to see if someone was lurking, waiting. She looked for what she'd missed.

At the trailhead, Leonie got out of her car, stretched her legs.

No other cars in the lot. It was still early spring. Not a lot of hikers wanted to argue with a snow- and lava-covered trail. But Leonie had snowshoes.

Leonie stepped into them, clipped the straps into place, and took off. She walked through the snow-covered meadow, sloshed through the stands of lodgepole pines and hemlocks. Knew the remote ache in her calves as the trail started to ascend, gradually, and then, there she was, out onto the first lava flow. The trail was bare for a while and she stowed the snowshoes and hiked along, looking to either side of the trail, willing Amelia to appear.

Every few minutes she stopped. Called to her daughter.

No response. Not even a bird call. It was silent.

Leonie let her mind wander down the worn grooves of what had happened after Amelia disappeared. How it had taken a full hour for her to realize the situation was real. How Amelia wasn't hiding. How, eventually, she'd decided to hike back to the carpark, had expected to find her there. How cold she'd been that night, sitting in the car as the first round of search and rescuers hit the trail, yelling, blasting emergency whistles. How, the next morning, so many vehicles poured into the trailhead parking lot and she'd felt a surge of confidence. So many people. She'd known they would find her.

But they hadn't, and in the days and weeks that followed, nothing made sense. The compassionate faces of searchers had transformed, into the hard faces of police, men in crisp blue polyester shirts, belts of hard equipment strapped close, hairlines razored sharp. They'd crowded in around her, offered names that she couldn't remember, made her repeat over and over what had happened, asked if Leonie had life insurance for her child.

They said they'd found something else where Leonie and Amelia had hiked.

They said they'd found bodies shattered on the glacier like punched teeth.

They said the bodies had necks broken and limbs crushed.

They said the bodies were undressed, missing shoes, shirts, pants.

They said the bodies were once women.

They fed Leonie details one at a time, and she felt them scrutinizing her as she pulled her frayed jacket tighter, as if each word was measured against some guilt they found perceptible in her face, the length of her tears, the authenticity of her bewilderment. She watched them stare at her bare hands.

She was horrified, had dutifully answered questions about her whereabouts years and years ago, had supplied the DNA swabs they'd asked for, and looked at crime scene images so traumatizing she'd screamed her way through nightmares.

She did everything they asked but even then, Amelia had not been found.

And now, she was crippled under the weight of unknowing, unable to live without answers, unable to make sense of the immeasurable dearth of information. She wanted everything in the world to stop until Amelia returned.

But the world did not stop, did not pause. Weeks bled into weeks and people came by less. She had to buy herself groceries and make dinner and pay her bills and avoid people who looked at her with eyes suspicious and accusing and reflective of every way Leonie had failed her daughter.

When her bereavement leave ended, her employer tactfully told her to return to work or they'd need a replacement. And so then she found herself again most days walking into the Market of Choice on Willamette, stocking brightly lit wine racks and answering customer questions about tannins and new Argentinian blends and thinking about her daughter.

And on her lunch breaks Leonie would walk to the little café inside the market and buy a coffee with her employee discount and read the local newspaper and hope there was news about Amelia. But most days *The Register-Guard* ran stories instead focused on the Three Sisters Killer, how the police announced they were reopening cold cases of local women reported missing over the last thirty years, how they cited lack of resources for the large number of previously uninvestigated cases. How they had asked the public for any leads and acknowledged their process was flawed and intended to establish a full public inquiry. How so far they'd identified Brie Anitala, Dee

Mercier, Aiyana Kim, Becky Obidiah, Xochitl Martinez, and Hannah Froyn, and would release more names after the next of kin had been notified.

Each time Leonie read the paper, her stomach clenched and her muscles contracted until she'd gone through all the columns of text. She knew in people's minds her daughter was forever connected to the horror unfolding up in the ice.

But to her, Amelia was completely separate. To her, those women were dead, but her daughter was not. Her daughter was missing, and Leonie knew she could still be found.

Arturo did not agree. He told her that, likely, Amelia had succumbed to the elements, had fallen into a lava crack, had drowned in a river, had died somewhere somehow in the wilderness. He told her it was unfair, a tragedy, but nature was never concerned with wrong or right. He told her he did not blame her, but he could not look for their daughter anymore. That he'd have to instead just remember his daughter in his heart. She refused to listen. She'd quietly hung up the phone, had screamed into her linoleum floor, and on the weekends continued to search.

Her daughter was still out there.

Leonie scanned the deep, velvet lava, noticed how the snow softened the stone margins. She slowed her feet, squinted her eyes east at the undulating landscape. She was grateful there was still snow. She'd be able to spot footprints if Amelia had intersected with the trail recently.

She pictured Amelia's purple shirt, her tiny, army green pants, her smile. Piercing green eyes. She inhaled sharply. She'd been on her daughter's case from day one about looking people in the eyes. Why hadn't she just let Amelia be Amelia? Did eye contact matter all that much?

Tears came to Leonie's eyes and she looked up. The sky felt enormous, like it could fall down at any moment and crush her. She kept moving.

Her feet were on autopilot as she searched, called.

Before she fully realized it, she found herself standing at the base of the Collier Cone. She looked up the gray slope that was patched sloppily with snow and red minerals. Remembered. Her daughter had called her a racist for liking the Oregon Trail computer game. Her mouth twitched. Amelia was so blunt, truthful.

Leonie called again.

No response.

She contemplated going up the crater. But then the wind picked up, carried a soft chiming-humming that pulled at her feet, moved her away from the cinder cone, brought her west instead. The sound was welcoming and joyous and she followed it without thinking.

She moved mechanically up switchbacks—sharp jagged twists in the trail—and then she was hiking parallel to the Collier Glacier. She came to a stop on the flank of Little Brother, in the shadow of the Three Sisters, with the ice gouged out between them.

She stared across at the Collier Cone, looked at the place where she and Amelia had stopped on the trail and marveled at the glacier. Where Amelia told her the glacier wanted a companion. She could see the entirety of the it from her vantage point, even into the side of the ice where the search and rescue team had pulled out all those bodies. Over twelve now, all in appalling states.

She shivered, eased herself down to sit on the rocky ridge, stretched her legs. The wind was strong, insistent. It flowed like a river, wrapped her in a whooshing icy bubble that felt electric, amplified. She listened to the faint thrumming in the background, a pulsing that made her feel as if the mountains were alive.

She stared down, looked blankly at the ice. Sun cups on the surface glistened between snow patches. So many shades of white.

She wondered if more bodies were under the ice.

It felt incomprehensible.

She struggled to understand how right below her, the bodies of so many women had been thrown into the gutter between the glacier and the mountain. How, while the police hadn't said definitely what had happened, they did say they were pursuing the Three Sisters Killer theory. And how they had not identified the killer.

Tears gathered cold in the corners of Leonie's eyes. She pushed them away, looked up at the mountainous spine of North Sister. Gazed around. The surrounding lava flows and high peaks of the

Cascade volcanoes contrasted with the low altitude forests and grass-lands. It was, she could see, beautiful. She bowed her head under the immense weight of her missing daughter, of the countless years that had passed in a single moment.

She lost track of time, sitting on the ridge's edge above the glacier, staring at the mountain, the sky, the clouds. Her eyes were open, but she didn't register. She needed relief, an answer to the untenability of living without Amelia.

Gradually, through her dry, deadened exhaustion, she heard it.

A different type of humming. Not what she'd heard earlier, the cheerful background thrumming. This new sound was peculiar, reedy. High pitched. Growing louder.

It reminded her of the song Amelia had hummed their last day together.

Leonie's throat constricted; joy surged up from her heart. She blinked her eyes, twisted her head, and then, her eyes flared raw as she saw a figure walking up the ridge behind her. Wearing a pink sweater. Holding a stick.

She jerked up onto her feet, ungainly, and, for a single breath, knew it was Amelia. Frenetic exhilaration flashed as her heart leapt into her burning mouth and she choked and her legs liquified.

"Beautiful, isn't it?" the person called.

Her bones shredded.

It wasn't Amelia.

Just an old woman, whistling a reedy tune. Leonie clamped her teeth, tried to hold back a hysterical sob. She fought the wave threatening to overwhelm her, stared at the woman. Took in the silver-white hair, the hands gripping the stick like claws, the huge purple birthmark on her face, the bright steady eyes. Opened her mouth, asked: "What are you singing? I've heard it before."

The woman moved parallel to Leonie, looked out over the gla-cier, the volcanoes, the snow, the stands of burned dead forests. She twisted, looked behind them at the ridges rolling away west.

Something clicked inside Leonie, and she gasped. "I've seen you before."

The woman tilted her head, looked directly at her. "Of course you have."

Wild delirium started to boom somewhere inside Leonie's head. She tried to shake it away, knew she was a hair's breadth from losing control of herself. "You were on the trail the day I lost my daughter," she said, shakily, pulse hammering. The backs of her eyes ached. "What happened to Amelia?"

"Well," the old woman replied conversationally, "The Brother used to be bigger. I know. But he was worn down by the weight of the world. The Sisters, they're worn too. But those women haven't lost as much of themselves." She laughed lightly. It sounded like stones grating.

Leonie gaped at the woman. Took a breath, exhaled, saw waves of desperation encircling her. "I've lost my daughter."

The old woman was silent, her white bob waving in the wind. Then she turned to Leonie. "Loss is not the end," she answered. "We disappear, we return, we disappear again."

Leonie's shoulders collapsed; she let her head droop. Lumps choked her throat, tears blurred her eyes. Every muscle in her body crawled with nerves and exhaustion. "You think I'll find my daughter?" she whispered.

The woman shrugged her shoulders, cavalier. "Does something have to be in front of you to be found?"

Leonie's gut wrenched. "Yes," she whimpered. "I want to hold my daughter again." She looked away, down towards the ice, felt desperation in her stomach and teeth and eyes and hairline. She felt consumed by a piercing, keening impulse to wrap her arms around Amelia, breathe the sweet scent of her daughter. "I'm afraid she's gone."

The woman made a *tsking* sound. "Just because you can't see something doesn't mean it's gone."

Leonie reached out, tried to grab the woman's wrist. Her fingers clawed air, and the woman was suddenly deftly two feet away, unperturbed. Leonie hadn't seen her move. She blinked, worried she was imagining things, felt hot pain pounding in her throat.

She looked down into her hands, her fingernails digging into her own flesh. Beaded up blood flared from her broken skin.

Rocks crunched, and Leonie looked up, saw the old woman walking away.

"Wait," she called.

The woman stopped, turned, seemed to appraise her. Leonie felt stuck in place, balanced precariously. The woman smiled softly, and Leonie felt the rigidity inside herself thaw, loosen. She stood straighter, relaxed her fingers from their tight fists, felt unaccountable adrenaline and pleasure surge over her.

"Don't give up on Amelia." The woman's eyes brightened. "Everyone thinks the future is set. But it's just unknown."

Leonie shook herself, tried to get control. "Are you real?" she whispered.

"Everyone thinks I'm already gone," the woman replied. "But I'm here."

The woman stamped her stick into the ground. Then, quicker than Leonie thought possible, she turned, strode back down along the ridgeline, whistling her reedy melody, a strange song that reached back and wrapped itself around Leonie's core.

Leonie's muscles contracted and she bent at the waist, gasped for air. She stayed bent over for minutes, wheezing. Then, she pushed up with her hands on her knees, straightened, looked around.

She stared at the cliff, down at the ice. The slope cut sharply away. She toed her right foot into the dirt's edge, sent a slab of scree racing over the drop. She felt the wind at her back, the precariousness of her balance.

She closed her eyes, listened.

The humming-thrumming from the landscape had returned, much louder now. It throbbed like running water, danced, wrapped itself around her. Her skin tingled, her blood pounded. Her muscles relaxed, air moved in and out of her lungs with ease.

She listened harder and detected individual lines in the chorus— the grumble of rocks grinding, the squeaks of air releasing from ice, the sighs of compressed moss, the soprano of women singing.

Then, rising out clear as water, she heard it. A melody of laughter. Her heart rose in response. She recognized that laughter.

It wove around her.

She embraced it, leaned into the impossible that glowed within her as the wind whistled fast over the edge of the cliff.

The dark weight dropped from her shoulders, her suffering slipping away and shattering to the ground. Tears flowed from her eyes and she lifted her face, could hear clearly now the elation and ecstasy emanating from the glacier.

She knew that the ice, and Amelia, were singing to her.

She threw her head back and opened her eyes wide, saw blue skies churning, geese soaring above, felt the cool breath of the glacier on her body. She raised her arms, reached with all her might, sang her daughter's name as she fell forward into the ice.

ACKNOWLEDGMENTS

There are so many people and places and warm beverages involved in the making of this book. The writing happened around the edges of most days, on airplanes and along forest trails and sitting in a mildewy town truck on Adak Island and with cats on my feet at home in Eugene, Oregon. A friend once said it looks like I'm always texting. Well, surprise. I'm not. I'm writing.

I'm fortunate and grateful to be surrounded by people who support me and support my writing. People like Tierney Thys, the best National Geographic Society mentor I could hope for—all these years on. People like Sigrún Sveinbjörnsdóttir, Guðný Svavarsdóttir, and Þorvarður Árnason—who ask about my writing every time I set foot on their magical island. And there are those people who stick with you through all the drafts. A lot of drafts. Early drafts that make me cringe and wish these fine friends had never read them. But then—if they hadn't, this book would not be what it is now. Here's to: Christine Carolan, Leslie McClees, Kevin Malgesini, Kjerstin Gurda, and Nassim Assefi. And, there are those other folks, who ply you with coffee and pizza ovens and encouragement and bike rides: Erin Harvey, Jaini Van Scholten, Matt Sprick, and Jordan Vroom.

I take all responsibility for the content within this book—any errors are mine alone. I deeply enjoyed delving into a variety of rabbit holes on topics new to me. I'm grateful to Dylan Farnsworth for his lectures on ham radios, Laurie Monico for all things search and rescue, and members of the Willamette Pass Ski Patrol for sharing countless stories of living and playing in the Cascades.

Writers needs funding and spaces to write. My deep gratitude to Literary Arts Oregon Booth Emergency Fund for Writers and Oregon State University's Andrews Forest Writers Residency. Writers also need support groups. Mine came through the COVID-19 pandemic, when a bunch of science-oriented writers started getting together on Zoom to workshop each other's writing. I am grateful to Alex Johnson, Kelly Koller, Danilo Thomas, Saleem Ali, and, most especially, the Guru of All Things Soil, Emily Toner.

Thank you to Green Writers Press for continuing to believe in me and grow me as a writer. I've learned so much from my intrepid and fierce publisher Dede Cummings, editor Rose Alexandre-Leach, and copyeditor Ferne Johansson. These women should rule our world. Deep gratitude to readers Brenna Casey and Paula Lee whose thoughtful consideration and feedback helped profoundly shape this book. Thanks to Ani Drozdowska, the woman who never gives up on my website. My gratitude to Lyceum Agency, and to one Kate Gannon-Sprinkel in particular.

My absolute awe and gratitude to Laura Marshall, the extraordinary artist who created this book's cover.

My love to Finn and Jon: World.

ABOUT THE AUTHOR

PHOTO © JAKE DYSON, NATGEO

DR. M JACKSON is a geographer, glaciologist, and science communicator exploring the intersections of societal transformation, glaciology, and climate change. Jackson is a National Geographic Society Explorer, TED Fellow, and three-time U.S. Fulbright Scholar, including two U.S. Fulbright-National Science Foundation Arctic Research grants. Jackson holds a doctorate and post-doctorate from the University of Oregon, and a Master of Science degree from the University of Montana. She serves as a U.S. Fulbright Ambassador, an Expert for National Geographic Expeditions, and was a Peace Corps Volunteer in Zambia. Jackson is an active public speaker and author of the award-winning science books *The Secret Lives of Glaciers* (2019) and *While Glaciers Slept: Being Human in a Time of Climate Change* (2015). Jackson is the star of the Netflix hit series, *Pirate Gold of Adak Island,* and the climate and energy host on Crash Course. Jackson has worked for over a decade in the Arctic and Antarctic exploring changing climates and communities.

Visit www.drmjackson.com

Printed in the USA
CPSIA information can be obtained
at www.ICGtesting.com
JSHW082231071223
53097JS00003B/18

9 798987 663127